The God Complex

by

Murray McDonald

First Published by Kennedy Mack publishing

The God Complex

ISBN 978-0-9574871-8-5

Copyright © Murray McDonald 2014

MISSION LOG – EXTRACT 1-1

Deep Space Mission – New Hope
Log entry 1
Mission Commander

It is with great sadness that I look back on the fading speck in the distance that we have called home since birth. We have said goodbye to parents and loved ones that many, or all of us, will never see again. Our only hope of seeing them again would be the failure of our mission, a failure that would condemn our population to a certain death. Our planet is dying, and with it, our future.

Our mission, steeped in secrecy, is known to but the very few, and our future as a race depends on our mission. A weight that bears heavy on us all as we speed towards a solution that we believe lies out there, amongst the vastness of space. A solution that our descendants will deliver for the future, we are destined never to return, but our mission will live on in our children and their children's children, until the time comes when our work will save our people.

The end may not come during our lifetime but in the near future, our work will be our only hope. When the time comes and the end seems nigh, we will have prepared for that day and the end will be but a new beginning.

Chapter 1

His heart nearly stopped beating as the image came into view. *It couldn't be,* he argued with his own eyes. The more he looked, the more he realized it was real.

He grabbed his phone and hit the professor's number on the third attempt. His fingers shook so wildly that he had had to abort two calls to 'Paul', whoever that was, in his contacts list. As the line rang, he pleaded, *Don't go to message, not today, not now.*

"Good God, James! It's half two in the morning," came a groggy voice.

"Professor... you... were... right!" said James excitedly, barely able to get his words out.

Professor Charles Harris sat up, suddenly wide awake. His deputy was not a man prone to excitement. In fact, in the ten years he had known him, he had barely smiled, let alone shown any emotion.

"James, take a deep breath and tell me what you're talking about," suggested the professor calmly.

"I'm calibrating the equipment for tomorrow's inauguration by the President," began James, trying desperately to calm himself down and make sense of what he was seeing. "I wanted to make sure that when you demonstrated its power, you'd make an impression."

The professor nodded on the other end of the phone. He certainly wanted to make an impression. Twenty years and $15 billion dollars of funding later, Hubble 2 was about to go live. Significantly more powerful than its dated predecessor, Hubble 2 could look farther into space and farther than had ever been imagined. However, its capabilities were not limited to space. A large portion of the funding was secured on its ability to look back towards earth, in as great a detail as it could look into space. Hubble 2 was not only the greatest telescope ever built, it was also destined to become the greatest spy satellite ever built - a situation the professor was less comfortable with, but after the inauguration, that would no longer be his problem. The spy functionality would be officially handed over to the National Reconnaissance Office, the US Intelligence agency responsible for spy satellites.

"Its power is amazing, the details of the images are exquisi—"

"You said I was right?" interrupted the professor, frustrated with the padding James was adding to his outburst.

"Yes I did," James replied excitedly. "And you are!"

"I am what?" asked the professor.

"You are right!"

"About what?"

"Everything…" replied James, uttering his last ever words. The bullet passed through his left temple, removing his right temple and destroying his handset, instantly killing the call and the caller.

"James? James?! Are you there?!" shouted the professor into the dead phone line.

The professor dialed James' number but it went straight to voicemail. He tried the observatory's landline number.. No answer. He dialed James' cell again. Voicemail.

"Dad?" a knock on his bedroom door preceded its opening.

"You okay?" asked the professor's son, Copernicus Armstrong Sagan Harris, more commonly known as Cash. In fact, very few knew that 'Cash' was not his given name - a deliberate ploy by a very young Copernicus.

The professor was halfway into his pants when his son entered the room. "I'm fine, son, but something's going on at the observatory."

"Dad, it's 2:30 a.m., I'm sure it can wait."

"James was very excited and James doesn't do excited. He told me I was right."

"Right about what?"

"Everything, apparently, and then the line went dead."

"Okay, but I'll come with you, it's an hour's drive," said Cash. "Just let me throw some clothes on."

Cash, turning to leave, allowed the professor for the first time to see the battle wounds his son had suffered. A large scar surrounded by burn tissue covered the left side of his back. A tear welled in the professor's eye. His actions had driven Cash to enlist and, as a result, suffer numerous injuries during his tours in Iraq, Afghanistan and Syria. It had been almost fifteen years since they had seen each other. Cash's return for the inauguration had been a wonderful surprise. Cash wasn't going to miss one of the professor's proudest moments.

Cash walked back to his childhood room.

"Okay?" asked Rigs, appearing behind Cash.

"Jesus!" said Cash, jumping and pushing his friend out of the room. "Don't do that!"

"What?" asked Rigs.

"Sneak up on me like that!"

"I followed you," protested Rigs. Cash patted his friend on the back as an apology. Rigs couldn't help himself, he was quiet in every sense of the word.

"Copern...?" called out Cash's father as he made his way along the corridor.

"Dad, Jesus, how many times, it's 'Cash', call me 'Cash', okay?!"

"Good morning, Rigs," said the professor, noticing Cash's friend hovering quietly in the corridor. The professor had only met Rigs that day and was still trying to work him out.

"Good morning," replied Rigs quietly, lowering his head as he spoke. He didn't like to make eye contact at the best of times. Rigs was, as Cash described him, complex. Others found him intimidating or odd. Few had ever heard him speak more than a few words at once, Cash was the only person he could talk to and if possible, he relayed conversations through him. 'Dysfunctional', 'loner', 'troubled' were only a few of the words that had followed Rigs through his life.

"You ready?"

The professor nodded.

"Where are you going?" asked Rigs quietly, looking at Cash.

"We need to go to the observatory. Dad's deputy called and Dad can't call him back."

Rigs headed into his room to get ready.

"No, it's fine," smiled Cash. "You grab some sleep, I'll go with my dad!"

"Sure?" asked Rigs.

Cash nodded. "Yeah, nothing to worry about," he said, closing Rigs' door.

"Don't ask," said Cash to the inquisitive look from his father before pulling his sweater over his head and leading the way down the stairs.

"Is he alright?" asked the professor.

"He's not comfortable around strangers but once he gets to know you, he's much better."

"Better, but not fine, not normal?"

"Better," emphasized Cash. "Rigs is…" Cash struggled to find the word. "Special?"

"And you work with him?"

"Wouldn't work with anyone else," said Cash proudly.

"And for the last fifteen years—"

"Let's not go there, Dad. I'm here and I really want us to move on," said Cash.

The professor held up his hands in surrender. "It's all I've dreamt of for the last fifteen years," he said, his voice breaking. "It was such a stupid—"

"Dad," warned Cash.

The professor raised his hands again and nodded in acknowledgment. "So what exactly did your deputy say that's got you up at this hour?" asked Cash, keen to change the subject and not open a wound that after fifteen years was still very painful.

"Just that I was right about everything, supposedly."

"What does that mean?"

"It could mean many things."

"But he was really excited?"

The professor placed one hand on the door handle and paused. He placed his other hand under his shirt and withdrew a chain that hung around his neck with a small flash drive attached to it. "It couldn't be," he mused while turning the door handle.

"Couldn't be *what*?" asked Cash, increasingly frustrated.

"No, it couldn't be that," the professor said confidently, stepping out onto the front porch.

By the time Cash registered the noise, it was already too late. The sound of wet flesh being slapped reverberated in his ears. He tried desperately to pull his father back from the danger, snatching him back into the hallway out of the line of fire, but it was already too late. His father's chest was soaked in blood; the bullet that had hit his heart failed to stop it pumping.

A barrage of spits from the silenced rifle followed, tearing at the door and floor while Cash pulled his father deeper into the house.

His father's eyes pleaded with him to stop. Cash stopped moving and tried desperately to stem the blood but knew it was useless. He knew all too well how utterly useless his actions were. His father reached for his hands to stop him, taking his right hand and placing it over the flash drive on the chain.

The professor mumbled something that Cash couldn't make out. He leaned in closer to his father.

"Sophie..." said the professor with his last breath, pushing the flash drive into Cash's hand, the last action of a dying man.

Cash stumbled back. His father could not have uttered a more devastating blow to his son. It was the one name he never wanted to hear again and certainly not from his father. The fact that he'd said it on his dying breath made it all the more distressing.

Cash was frozen by his father's dying word. He held the flash drive in his hand, not sure what to do. Another barrage of bullets tore into the door. Cash needed to move, he needed to take action, fight back, do something. He needed to avenge his father's murder.

The bullets stopped hitting the door, another change of magazine or an assault on the house. They must realize the house was weaponless.

"Rigs!" Cash whispered urgently.

"Yes!" came the reply from behind the front door.

Cash stood and opened the door to a naked and bloodied Rigs.

"What the...?"

"One sniper, at the end of the drive," said Rigs, looking despondently at the lifeless Professor Harris.

"Can he talk?" asked Cash.

Rigs shook his head and raised a dripping wet pen. "Sorry, I pushed this up under his skull. He's dead."

Cash patted his best friend on the back, it said 'thank-you' in a way that words simply couldn't.

"Do you know why?" asked Rigs.

Cash shook his head and held up the flash drive. "He pushed this into my hand and said…" Cash swallowed hard, his voice breaking, "Sophie."

Rigs had met Cash at basic training fifteen years earlier, and the two had been inseparable ever since. Cash had taken the quiet loner under his wing, while Rigs had accepted a friendship for the first time in his life. There was nothing they didn't tell each other.

"Sophie?" he shrugged.

"My ex fiancée."

"Your what?"

Chapter 2

Santa Cruz, CA

The sound of police sirens killed any explanation.

"Clothes might be a good idea," suggested Cash when the blue strobe lights cut through the darkness.

Rigs, covered in blood and naked as the day he was born, made no attempt to move. He wasn't leaving Cash alone until he knew the danger had passed.

"Police!" came a shout from the front door.

"My father, Professor Harris, has been shot, we're unarmed!" shouted Cash clearly, as he stood next to the body, his hands aloft.

"Copernicus, is that you?" came a reply from the policeman, raising a questioning look from Rigs.

"Cop what?" asked Rigs, it was the second time he'd heard that name being said to Cash.

Cash pointed to his dead father, instantly silencing Rigs, there was a time and a place.

"Yes, it is, Chief," replied Cash clearly.

"I'm coming in, okay?"

The door opened to reveal a far older version of Harry Kramer, the police chief Cash had once known. He was accompanied by three officers who rushed into the entrance, secured Cash, and ordered Rigs to lie down in the hallway with his arms and legs spread.

The Chief knelt down by the professor's body and the side of an old and dear friend. "Copernic—"

"It's Cash, it's been Cash since I was eight," said Cash.

"What happened?"

"He got a call from the observatory and said he needed to go there immediately. We were heading out and a silenced bullet caught him in the chest."

"Someone shot him with a silenced weapon?" he asked, incredulous.

Cash nodded, suddenly realizing the anomaly. "Wait, if it was silenced, how did you know? We're a mile from the nearest house," asked Cash, confused at who had raised the alarm.

"We didn't come about the shooting, it's only when we got here that we saw the bullet holes. It's the observatory, it's been destroyed."

"Destroyed?"

"Up until a minute ago, I'd have said it was a gas explosion, an accident but…"

The president, thought Cash, thinking ahead to the ceremony due to take place later that evening. He was searching for reasons but the president's trip was shrouded in secrecy. Nobody but those deeply involved in the project, itself top secret, were aware of his planned visit.

A handcuffed, bloody, and naked Rigs was lifted from the floor, interrupting the conversation.

"Chief, this is a friend of mine, Captain Jake Miller, US Marines," said Cash, turning to look at Rigs.

The Chief looked at Cash with some discomfort. "Whose blood?" he asked, trying to ignore the nakedness.

"The shooter's," said Rigs nonchalantly, indicating with his head to the pen on the floor, soaked in blood and covered in brain matter. All of Rigs' awkwardness had gone. It was almost as though he had forgotten how awkward he was, how uncomfortable he felt around strangers. "In the bushes, end of the drive," he added.

Rigs was in the zone, one of two zones that Cash knew overrode Rigs' awkwardness. One he knew all too well - killing. When it came to killing, Rigs had little or no conscience. An emotional void, Rigs could kill without the slightest hint of remorse and that had made him one of the US Forces' most accomplished operatives. The other, Cash had to take the word of the many women who, after spending a night with Rigs, were desperate to spend another with him. Fucking and killing were Rigs' two areas of brilliance.

"Check it out," said the Chief to the officer closest to the door. "And somebody get something to cover this guy up!" Rigs was comfortably standing at ease, his hands cuffed behind his back letting the air flow easily over his muscular frame. Cash shook his head in despair. His friend had no body confidence issues, strange for a guy who couldn't look you in the eye or talk to you, but if he hadn't been a soldier, he'd have made a great porn star.

"Chief, I've got the weapon but no sign of a shooter," reported the officer.

"He's at the end of the drive by the rose bush," insisted Rigs.

"Nothing there, Chief," said the officer.

Rigs walked towards the door but was held back by another officer. "I killed him, that guy was going nowhere!"

"You can't have, he's not there," argued the officer. "Perhaps you only wounded him?"

"With a pen through his brain? And a double tap with his own rifle for good measure?" asked Rigs, looking at Cash and not the officer. "Trust me, he couldn't have been any deader!"

"So you fired the rifle?" asked the chief, trying unsuccessfully to catch Rigs' eye.

"Yes."

"The rifle that killed the professor?"

"I assume so."

"So you're covered in blood, your fingerprints are on the weapon that killed the professor, and you'll have gun residue on you from firing that same weapon?"

"Whoa, Chief, rewind a little," said Cash as Rigs shuffled awkwardly to the corner of the hallway.

"You can vouch for him?" asked the Chief.

"Of course, he didn't kill my father," he said, looking at Rigs, whose head was once again dipped, avoiding all eye contact.

"He was with you when your father was shot?"

"Yes. He was upstairs sleeping."

"And then he came running down past you and out into the garden where the shooter was shooting?"

"No, he went out the back and came around from behind the shooter."

"You told him to go?"

"Well no, he must have heard the shots"

"The silenced ones? While sleeping?"

Rigs nodded, sensing the eyes of the policemen on him.

"How well do you know this guy?" asked the Chief.

"I trust him with my life," said Cash.

"Likewise," mumbled Rigs.

"Maybe, but we're not talking about your life, we're talking about your father's life."

***

Pacific Ocean
300 miles due west of Santa Cruz

The barge shuddered as the explosion separated the RIM-161 SM3 missile from its temporary home. The missile rose into the sky as a secondary explosion tore through the barge's hull, sending it to a watery grave deep below the surface.

The missile quickly accelerated to cover a distance of over three miles per second toward its target just over three hundred miles away, programmed and unaware of its imminent demise, in little more than one minute.

***

Santa Cruz

The Chief had heard enough. Rigs was going back with him to the station.

"Officer, take him out to the car," he said pointing to Rigs. "And for God sake put some pants on him."

"Don't be ridiculous, Chief," protested Cash. "Rigs has nothing to do with this!"

"We'll let him do his talking, thanks."

"Chief," Cash pled, "he's not comfortable around strangers."

"Obviously," said the Chief looking down at Cash's father's body.

"He has trouble talking to people he doesn't know."

"And he was a Marine Captain?"

It was Cash's turn to look down at the bloodied pen. "And a very good one. Trust me, you'd have wanted him on your side!"

"We'll let the evidence tell me that. We'll check out the blood at the station. If it's human and not anyone else's here, I'll be inclined to listen but at the moment, I'm liking him for it."

Cash followed the Chief out into the front garden. "Chief, you're making a huge mistake. Rigs is one of the good guys."

"Let's wait and see what the blood on him tells us."

Rigs, clad in ill-fitting jogging pants, was loaded into the squad car.

Cash looked up at the heavens for inspiration. He had just lost his father and the one man on the planet he trusted with his life was being taken away as a chief suspect. A flash drive delivered with the hammer blow of his father's dying word lay uncomfortably in his pocket. In an hour, his world had gone to total and utter shit.

Cash saw the streak of light in the night sky, just before the explosion.

"What the hell…?"

Chapter 3

Santa Cruz, CA

The flash in the night sky signified a hit. The RIM-161 missile had done its job as planned, a perfect hit. Hubble 2 was gone. It was the only part of the plan that had gone without a hitch.

"We have another problem," Gray's radio chirped.

The client had made it clear, they didn't want problems.

"What?" he barked angrily.

"The professor had company."

"And?"

"They took out Blue."

"Took out?"

"Killed, and very professionally."

Gray banged his fist against the steering wheel in frustration. It had been, on paper at least, a simple job - take out the new telescope, Hubble 2. Unfortunately, the reality was somewhat different. He had had to wait two years to complete the assignment. All attempts on the ground had proved futile. The security surrounding the Hubble 2 telescope was unlike anything Gray had ever witnessed. His team took on the jobs that others deemed impossible. For him, that simply meant he could charge more. However, Hubble 2 had looked as though it was going to be his first failure, until he had gotten his hands on a RIM-161 missile. The client hadn't liked it, they hadn't wanted Hubble 2 to see the light of day. There was something they didn't want it to see, something only it could see was to be kept from prying eyes.

Allowing it to be launched had come with caveats. Anyone with any access to Hubble 2's feeds was to be watched and eliminated should they see anything before its destruction. Fortunately, that list had proved short and easily accessible. Professor Charles Harris and his deputy were the only two people who were to have access to the feeds prior to Hubble 2's destruction, twelve hours after its launch.

Gray, thanks in part to his own name, and thanks to *Reservoir Dogs,* had named his operatives by color. Blue had been with Brown at the professor's home, while Red and Green had been watching the deputy who had taken a late night trip to the observatory and not waited until the morning, as had been hoped.

The destruction of Hubble 2 would have been put down to an unfortunate and exceedingly costly space collision. However, owing to the deputy's curiosity, Gray was now in the midst of instigating a major cover-up. Destroying the observatory and killing Professor Harris was going to unleash a massive investigation into the incident, an investigation that he had to ensure did not implicate his client in any way. Not an easy prospect, given he had no idea who his client was.

Dead men didn't talk. He pressed the transmit button. "Make sure there's nobody left who can talk, I'm sending some local help."

Three affirmatives came back to him as he walked across the road to the drug den, home to the Surenos' gang.

Chapter 4

Defense Initiative Services
New York

The DIS offices were at the top of one of New York's most illustrious skyscrapers, with views that stretched across Central Park and the upper half of Manhattan. They were offices designed to impress but were also shrouded in secrecy. Few would ever know what the 'DIS' plaque stood for, and even fewer knew what they did.

It was a question that Mike Yates often asked himself: *What does DIS do?* He had been head of the organization for almost four years and he was still trying to figure out what they did. However, the simple answer given to him on recruitment was 'whatever needs to be done'. As head of the CIA Clandestine Services, tipped for further advancement, it was a job offer he should instantly have walked away from. However, when those recruiting you were two of the more Senior Senators who sat on the Senate Select Committee on Intelligence, you read between the lines. Staffed exclusively by CIA and DIA veterans, it wasn't a giant reach to understand that DIS did the jobs the US Government agencies and their allies wanted to but couldn't.

Although amply remunerated, it had come at a cost. Jobs no longer had meaning or understanding, they were simply to be undertaken without question. The bigger picture was no longer Mike's concern. He was out of that loop. DIS did not worry itself with the *why* something had to be done, it merely delivered, and under Mike Yates' expert leadership, it always did.

Mike had recruited many of the men and women he had worked with over the years as they retired or sought more lucrative work, ensuring his pool of resource was amongst the best and most experienced operatives in the world.

Deniability was the key word. Everything DIS did for its clients had to be deniable by whoever the client was. The simplest way for that to happen was complete and total anonymity. Mike Yates had no idea who ordered each individual DIS operation. He could have tried to guess but over the years, he hadn't even bothered with that. In the beginning, he had struggled to understand how some of their activities could possibly benefit US interests. However, he had to assume that whoever was pulling his strings knew what they were doing. After a while, he became desensitized. The money, travel and perks certainly helped numb any latent intrigue. He had a job to do and the best people in the world with which to deliver.

He looked down at his latest operation, one that had troubled him from the outset and for the first time in years piqued his intrigue. Never before had he been ordered to employ an outside team. Everything had always been handled within their own team. However, the instructions were explicit, even down to the selection of the team to hire. The team was to be headed by a man Mike had known in his CIA days. He was an excellent choice but the update from Gray was extremely disappointing. Gray was a man who was known for his ability to complete difficult and complex missions that few other teams in the mercenary business would even contemplate accepting. Mike read the message again:

> *Deputy at observatory spotted something and had to be terminated but not before he had alerted Professor Harris. We have destroyed observatory and any data that may have been captured and as a precaution, given the transcript below, have eliminated the professor.*
> *"You said I was right?"*
> *"Yes I did. And you are!"*
> *"I am what?"*
> *"You are right!"*
> *"About what?"*
> *"Everything…"*
> *Call terminated at this point. In the process of covering tracks but want to ensure we cover any that lead to client?*

Mike read the brief again. It was certainly explicit. No knowledge or information was to be garnered by Hubble 2 before its destruction. Any suggestion of data having been collected was to be dealt with extreme prejudice to ensure any and all trace of the information collected was destroyed, which included any persons who may have gained that same knowledge. Their simple operation, to destroy an unguarded telescope in space, had just became a nightmare.

Mike had no option but to alert the client. His instructions given the scenario were explicit. He picked up the burner smart phone that had only one number; a new burner was used for each operation and client. Mike copied the text of the message from Gray and waited for a response.

***

It wasn't possible, unless, pondered the client...unless they had known exactly where to look.

He turned to his laptop, and pulled up recent stories for the Professor. There was something he had seen, something that may make sense. He scanned through the results of the search. The first few pages all referred to Hubble 2. Page five was what he was looking for - a front page story, *'Astronomer Turns Archaeologist',* with a picture of the Professor at a dig at Tiwanaku, Bolivia. The article detailed a number of digs the Professor had been involved in over the previous few years. They were all sites of significance from thousands of years earlier. *He couldn't have*, he thought. But the evidence said otherwise, they had known exactly where to look.

He typed a reply to Mike Yates. They had planned for this eventuality and it was going to be messy but necessary.

No tracks lead to me but all of the professor's research must be found and destroyed as a matter of urgency. Additional resources will be made available to you as a last resort. Click here for link to control screen. Plan B should also be implemented. I will arrange for package to be delivered to your operatives for delivery on completion of Plan B.

***

Mike received the reply and forwarded on the relevant portion to Gray. Plan B was most definitely not for Gray's eyes, although he would be fully aware of it in the not too distant future.

"Cancel my breakfast meeting," Mike instructed his P.A. "And get me Steve in Santa Cruz on the phone."

Chapter 5

Santa Cruz, CA

The flash in the night sky blinded them all momentarily.

"…was that?" finished Cash as the brightness above them died and the blackness returned.

"Do you think it's all linked?" asked Cash, reflecting on his father, the observatory and the flash in the night sky directly above them.

"Certainly all very coincidental," pondered the Chief.

The officer escorting Rigs to the police car paused. "You still want him back at the station, Chief?"

"Yes, of course I do!"

"C'mon, Chief. There are things going on here that don't make any sense and they certainly don't involve Rigs," argued Cash.

"And that's exactly why he's going to the station. I have absolutely no idea what's going on and until I do, I'm not taking any chances."

"You're welcome to come with him," offered the Chief, walking back to this car.

Cash looked back at his childhood home and his father's body that lay in the hallway. Fifteen hours was all they had had. After fifteen years of silence, those last fifteen hours would comfort him for the rest of his life. The thought that this could have happened without reconciling at least in some way would have been devastating. However, there was little more he could do there. His friend needed him.

"Chief, hold up!" shouted Cash. "I'm coming!"

Rigs shook his head wildly, as he was being directed into the back seat of the other police car. He didn't want Cash to come. Cash knew he wanted him to stay with his father. After fifteen years, Rigs seldom needed to speak for Cash to understand what he was thinking.

"He's gone and you're all the family I have left," replied Cash abruptly, taking a seat in the Chief's car.

"Keep the scene secure for the Crime Scene Team," the Chief said to the third officer.

"Yes, Chief," replied the officer, turning back to the house with a roll of police tape to secure the scene.

"Are you sure you'd not rather stay here?" asked the Chief as he turned the ignition key.

Cash nodded halfheartedly. He wasn't sure of anything.

"Fair enough," he said, waving for his officer to follow behind in the second car where Rigs was secured as their suspect.

"So when did you get back?" asked the Chief.

"Yesterday about lunch time," replied Cash.

"Staying long?"

"Supposed to be leaving later tonight, right after the opening ceremony. It was meant to be a flying visit."

"Figures," replied the Chief, barely restraining the anger in his voice.

"What figures?" asked Cash, taken aback at the Chief's tone.

"Nothing, I'm not getting involved."

"Involved in what?"

"Your irresponsibility!"

"My what?"

"I suppose I shouldn't expect anything more. Look at you with your own father, what is it, fifteen years since you've been here?!"

Cash was stunned. "A father I've just watched being murdered in front of me!"

"I'm sorry," said the Chief. "It's hard, being a father myself."

"Is there something I'm missing? Has something happened to Sophie?" asked Cash.

The Chief shook his head.

Had things worked out differently, Cash would have been sharing the ride with his father-in-law. Sophie was the Chief's only child and Cash's former fiancée. They had been childhood friends, sweethearts and had been inseparable.

"Sophie's great," said the Chief with a fatherly smile. "She was looking forward to the opening ceremony."

"She's here?" asked Cash. "I thought she lived in England?"

"She does but she's been heavily involved in the new telescope project and was invited to the opening."

"Cool," said Cash, not sure what else to say. The thought of her being a few miles away didn't sit well with him. The thought that he might actually bump into her was not something he had had to consider for the previous fifteen years. What would he even say to her?

"She's got Kyle with her," the Chief said.

Cash nodded. He didn't want to think about her with anyone else. She had been 'it' for him, she had been 'the one'. He'd never find another Sophie and he wasn't sure his heart could take it even if he did.

Silence fell between the two men who had known each other, loved and trusted each other many years earlier.

The Chief fidgeted in his seat, the silence not sitting well with him.

"Jesus Christ, Cash!!!" he exploded. "Fifteen fucking years! Not even so much as a birthday card!"

"I didn't know you cared that much, Chief," smiled Cash, trying to lighten the outburst.

"Not me, you idiot!"

"What happened with Sophie and I is none of your business, Chief. It's best left in the past."

"You are one cold son of a bitch, son," blurted the Chief, shaking his head.

Cash remembered why he had left fifteen years ago, severing all ties with his past. He turned and looked out into the blackness of the woods that surrounding them, his eye catching a sudden movement in the side mirror.

"Chief, floor it!" he said grabbing the radio mic. "What's the name of the officer behind us?" he demanded urgently.

"Fletcher," said the Chief, his eye catching what Cash had already seen.

"Officer Fletcher, take evasive action, bogies on your tail coming in fast!"

"We're on it!"

"Duck!" screamed Cash when the tirade of bullets ate into the two vehicles. The six motorcycles easily outpaced the two police cars and tore past them as their riders unleashed their weapons.

"What the...?" The Chief, threw the wheel into the path of the three motorcycles that had attempted to overtake them, clipping the third bike and taking out its rider in spectacular fashion.

Officer Fletcher had attempted a similar maneuver with the bikes on the outside but with more road to play with, the motorcyclists had easily avoided his swerve. His actions had, however, opened him up to a full onslaught and left Rigs desperately trying to control the vehicle from the back seat with handcuffs and a dead Officer Fletcher blocking the controls. His only option was to try and stop.

"Fletcher's stopping!" shouted the Chief as the motorcyclists turned around and prepared for another pass.

Cash removed the pump action shotgun from its mount and instructed the Chief to stop as well.

"Fletcher?" he said into the mic as they ground to a halt.

No response.

The motorcycles were already heading back. Cash didn't wait any longer. He opened the door and threw himself out and onto the ground, spinning to the far verge. Bullets from the onrushing motorcyclists pinged wildly across the tarmac. Cash stopped rolling and let loose with the shotgun. He caught the front motorcyclist's wheel, sending it careening into a tree; its rider didn't stand a chance. His second shot caught a rider full in the chest and seemed to stop him dead, while his bike continued on riderless.

After two shots, he had no option but to throw himself down the small embankment that straddled the roadside. The other three riders unloaded everything they had at their only threat up until that point. The boom of the Chief's Magnum .44 proved them wrong and another of the riders fell to the ground. *Four down, two to go*, thought Cash, as the last two flew past at speed.

Cash ran for the second car and found Rigs with his head in the driver's foot well covered in blood.

"Get me out of here," mumbled Rigs.

Cash pulled him free. "I thought you were dead!"

"The blood's Fletcher's and all I had to stop the car was my head," he motioned with his hands cuffed behind his back.

"Chief?" shouted Cash, pointing to Rigs' handcuffs.

The Chief tossed keys to him. "They're circling back!" he warned, coughing painfully.

"Are you okay?" asked Cash.

"Fine," nodded the Chief, steadying himself against the car. "I'm not as young as I used to be!"

Cash wasn't convinced. As he uncuffed Rigs, his eyes were drawn to the two bikers who were circling back. "Are they crazy?!" asked Cash. "We've taken out four of them!"

Rigs wrung his wrists before grabbing a handgun from the dead officer's belt.

"They're mine!" he instructed, taking off at a sprint towards the onrushing motorbikes.

"Is he out of his mind?!" shouted the Chief, raising his pistol unsteadily and getting ready to shoot.

"Certifiably," replied Cash. "And he'll be even more so if you shoot one of them, or, by the look of your aim, him!"

"I'm helping him!"

Cash shrugged. Rigs stopped running, kneeled down and let off two shots. The two bikes kept coming, Rigs stood up as they rushed towards him.

"Shoot!" shouted the Chief, his voice rasping.

Rigs turned around, putting his back to the two bikes and their riders. The two bikes screamed past, keeping their course, their riders lifeless, both shot cleanly through the forehead. A hundred yards further down the road, the two bikes crashed off into the undergrowth.

Danger over, Rigs rejoined Cash and the Chief.

The Chief was already trying to radio back to the professor's house. Nobody was answering.

Chapter 6

While the Chief radioed back to the house, Cash walked back along the roadside. The first rider, taken out by the Chief's swerve, lay in a twisted heap. Semi-conscious, the rider had at least two obvious breaks, one of which was not only obvious, but clearly visible as the shard of bone protruded from the lower left leg of his pants.

Cash stepped on the shard. A scream split the night sky but there was nobody to come running to the rider's defense. They had chosen their spot well for the attack. The Empire Grade road cut through deep stretches of forest as it plunged down into the heart of Santa Cruz, cutting alongside the University of California's campus, home to the Astronomy Department, headed by Cash's father. Or, Cash thought, *formerly* headed by his father. As a child, Cash had hated the home deep in the hills above Santa Cruz. However, its isolation was perfect for his father's work. Light pollution was at a minimum but for a young boy, its seclusion was a prison. For a young boy whose mother had died during childbirth, it was hell.

Cash pushed down harder and squinted in the darkness to see the face of their attacker. The young man's neck and face were covered in gang tattoos. 'Sur' and 'X3' were the most visible. Everybody from Santa Cruz knew the Surenos gang.

"Rigs, check some of the other bodies for tattoos, see if any of them have Sur or anything like 13 on them!" shouted Cash over the gang member's screams. Cash had lost friends to the gang in the past and pushed harder with his foot.

"All of them!" he shouted back after a few minutes.

The Chief stumbled towards Cash, wheezing. "Cash, what are you doing?" he struggled.

"Chief, are you okay?" asked Cash turning his attention to the Chief, who was fading quickly.

"I'm fine, got winged during the mayhem," he smiled. A trickle of blood ran down the corner of his mouth and he slumped against a tree.

Cash ran to him, placing him gently against the tree, feeling for the wetness covering the Chief's back. He pulled him forward and searched for the wound. A bullet had entered through his back and, from the Chief's breathing, had definitely punctured a lung.

"Rigs! Radio for an ambulance!" he screamed. He had already lost one father and the Chief had always been like a father to him in the past.

"Cash?"

"Yes, Chief?"

"Promise me…"

"Anything, Chief," he struggled to hold back tears for only the second time in his adult life and within an hour of the last.

"Kyle, please… for me…" his last breath died.

Cash laid the Chief gently against the tree and instantly turned his attention to the whimpering gang member.

"Talk!" instructed Cash.

"Fuck you, bitch!" cried the gang member.

Cash was in no mood for discussion. He placed the end of the shotgun on the gang member's injured leg and fired, removing the damaged lower half cleanly.

"Talk!"

"I only know we were paid to hit the house and anyone who was there," gasped the gang member, scrambling between the waves of pain that were flooding through him.

"Who paid?"

"Someone paid the boss! I don't know who!"

Rigs joined him. "I think he's telling the truth," he said, noting the desperation in the gang member's face.

"So do I," said Cash, allowing Rigs to take the shotgun from him.

Rigs stepped over to the gang member and raised the shotgun, placing the barrel on his forehead.

"Plea…" begged the gang member, cut off by the boom of the shotgun.

"I'll cancel the ambulance then," suggested Cash to a nod of agreement from Rigs.

"So you knew the Chief quite well?" asked Rigs, rubbing the end of the shotgun on the gang member's clothes to clean it.

"He was like a father to me and his wife was like the mom I never had."

"And his daughter?" asked Rigs having pieced most of Cash's secret past together.

"Sophie, the girl I was going to marry."

"But?"

"Exactly. But," replied Cash.

"Not quite what I was hoping for," said Rigs.

"Me neither," said Cash, looking at the Chief. "First, my father's dying word was 'Sophie' and now the Chief's dying word was 'Kyle' – Sophie's new guy. I mean, Jesus, rub salt into the wound, guys," he said more to himself than to Rigs.

"Where to?" asked Rigs, scooping up whatever weapons he could lay his hands on.

"Sophie's place. She needs to know her dad is gone and I'd like to know what's on this," said Cash, holding up the flash drive.

"And then?" asked Rigs, looking at his arsenal.

Cash nodded, reading his friend's mind. "Yes, then we go issue a little payback and see if we can find out what the fuck just happened."

Chapter 7

Santa Cruz, CA

Cash made Rigs circle the area twice before they pulled over. The first time to check the area was clear; the second was nerves. Fifteen years was a long time. For a thirty-five-year-old, it was almost half his life. Sophie had been out of his life for as long as she had been part of it. They had met at the age of five and from the moment he had laid eyes on her, he had planned to spend his life with her. There hadn't been a day in those first fifteen years that they hadn't spoken or been a significant part of each other's life. In the second fifteen years, they hadn't spoken once.

"Can you keep watch?" asked Cash.

Rigs nodded once.

Cash walked slowly down the path. The house was, as expected, in darkness, as it was barely 4:00 a.m. He hesitated as he raised his finger to the doorbell. What would he say? What *could* he say? The Chief was dead, that was what was important about the visit, everything else was irrelevant.

Cash pressed the bell and felt the fifteen years disappear as the all too familiar ding-dong echoed down the corridor.

A few seconds later calls of "who's there?" accompanied a lot of shuffling around.

The door cracked open. Cash's breath caught the back of his throat, his heart pounded and his stomach lurched.

A tall and powerful young man stood before him. "Can I help you?" he asked in a perfect English accent. The man was exactly the same height as Cash, six foot two, with a very similar build. If Sophie had wanted a Cash replacement, she couldn't have picked a more perfect example, only he was younger, much younger.

Cash stepped back and checked the door number. It was the right house, he didn't need to check, it had been his second home, but the young man had thrown him.

"I was looking for the Kramers?" said Cash, stepping forward again.

"Everything okay?" asked Rigs, joining Cash. He had noticed Cash back away from the house. "Holy shit!" he said when he caught a glimpse of the young man at the door.

"What?" asked Cash and the young man at once.

"Kyle, who is it?" came a voice from deep in the house, a voice that Cash recognized all too well.

"You're Kyle?" asked Cash, his mouth dropping.

"How old is he?" asked Rigs, the question aimed at Cash but meant for Kyle.

"I'll be fifteen next month," replied Kyle, not sure who to answer.

"Cash!" came a breathless voice as Sophie reached the door.

"Sophie," replied Cash, gasping for air himself. She was as beautiful as he had remembered, perhaps even more so.

"What are you doing here?"

"Is your mom here?"

She nodded, suddenly wary.

"Best get her. Rigs, meet Sophie and Kyle, you're on coffee duty." Rigs dipped his head, nodded awkwardly and walked quietly into the house and headed for the kitchen.

Sophie and Kyle had to step back as the strange man who wouldn't look them in the eye almost barged them out of the way. He had coffee to make in their kitchen.

"Why is he making coff…" she stopped, the sudden realization of why Cash was there making coffee in the middle of the night. "Dad?" she asked, tears already welling.

Cash nodded and with Kyle's help, they led her into the living room.

"What's going on?" asked the Chief's wife entering the living room, tying the cords on her dressing gown as she did so.

"Mrs. Kramer," said Cash, turning to greet her.

"Cash!" she exclaimed, her voice less than welcoming.

"Mom, it's about Dad!" cried Sophie, cutting off a tirade from her mother that was fifteen years in the making.

Mrs. Kramer's face whitened as she dropped onto the sofa that Cash was sure she was unaware was even there.

"I'm afraid, he's gone," said Cash, nodding at Rigs who was hovering in the doorway to enter with the coffees. He placed them down on a coffee table while the news sank in and left the room to maintain his watch.

Kyle comforted his grandmother, leaving Cash to comfort Sophie, her head sunk into his shoulder, finding the spot she had so readily occupied many years earlier.

"What happened?" asked Mrs. Kramer, breaking the silence.

Cash started at the beginning and informed them of the loss of his own father and the resultant attack by the Surenos gang, where a bullet had caught the Chief and despite it, he had fought on.

"Could he have been saved?" asked Sophie.

Cash shook his head.

"Why would the Surenos kill your father?" asked Mrs. Kramer, trying to make sense of the murders. "I can understand them wanting Harry dead, but your father?"

Cash shrugged his shoulders. "I have no idea, none of it makes any sense."

"Did you say the observatory was destroyed as well?" asked Sophie through her tears.

"Yes, and we were heading there after my dad's deputy had called him and was very excited about something."

"James, excited?"

"Yeah, Dad said that wasn't normal for James. You knew him?"

"Yes, I've been involved in the project. Cambridge University partly funded the program, along with other universities and the US and UK governments," confirmed Sophie. "And as for James, that's an understatement, the man was a miserable son of a bitch on his better days."

Cash looked at Kyle. His eyes were drawn to him; it was hard to believe the young man was only fourteen, soon to be fifteen. He was a powerful looking young man, much like Cash himself had been at that age.

"Just like his father," said Sophie quietly watching Cash's gaze.

"What?" asked Cash, breaking his look.

"Kyle's the star of his team, just like his father was," offered Sophie, resulting in a raised eyebrow from her mother.

"Cash!" shouted Rigs from the front door. "We've got company!"

Cash was up and running in an instant, catching the FN-P90 machine pistol from Rigs as he joined him at the front door.

"So what we got?" asked Cash, cocking the P90.

"I've got some movement in the woods off to the north. I count at least three."

Cash peeked around the doorframe and focused on the wooded area to the north of the house. Like Cash's father, the Chief enjoyed his privacy. The house was a mile from its nearest neighbor and set back a quarter mile from the main road. A lawned area stretched for fifty yards before disappearing into the woods.

"I'll check out the back and try to circle around," said Rigs, leaving Cash to cover the front of the house.

"You three, upstairs and take cover," instructed Cash to Sophie, Kyle and Mrs. Kramer.

Cash watched the targets while his protectees made their way up the stairs. Rigs appeared off to his left. A thumbs-up signaled that the back of the house was clear and he was moving in on the targets. He moved silently and almost effortlessly through the undergrowth. The man was a machine in his element.

Rigs signaled that he was in position. Cash moved out of the house and towards the targets. The three moved, raising their weapons but Cash moved too quickly, already finding cover behind the Chief's car.

The targets' movements had opened them up as planned to Rigs. He raised his P90 and was about to start shooting, when he paused, noticing their clothing for the first time.

"Jesus, don't shoot!" screamed one of the targets. They all dropped their weapons, suddenly realizing they had been outplayed.

Cash stepped out as Rigs whistled the all clear to him.

Three police officers stepped out of the woods, their hands held high above their heads.

"What the hell were you guys doing?" asked Cash.

"We were on our way back from the Observatory when we spotted you in the Chief's car. We tried to sneak up on you but obviously you spotted us."

"I'm afraid the Chief's dead."

Fear turned to anger on all three of the officers' faces and their hands instinctively dropped towards their holsters.

"It wasn't us, they killed my father, Professor Harris, as well," Cash quickly explained, realizing their misunderstanding.

"Cash?" asked one of the officers.

Cash nodded.

"Jesus, I didn't recognize you! It's been so long. Paul Banks," he stepped forward offering his hand.

Cash couldn't place him.

"Banksie!"

"Banksie, as in pot-head Banksie?" asked Cash.

Banksie's face dropped slightly. "All in the past," he said awkwardly.

"Of course. Have you got back up on the way?" asked Cash, scanning the area.

Banksie shook his head. "We've been trying to radio for back up, but nothing. We've tried our cells, none of them are working!"

Cash looked at Rigs, knowingly; it wasn't over.

"Are Sophie and Mrs. K alright?" asked Banksie.

"Obviously upset but yeah, they're fine."

"And that handsome young lad of yours?"

Cash looked at him.

"Seriously," chipped in Rigs quietly to Cash. "You didn't see it?"

Cash shook his head. "No, I didn't." He walked back into the house and straight upstairs.

"Sophie? It's fine, they're police officers," he called out.

Sophie, Kyle and Mrs. Kramer appeared from one of the bedrooms.

"Can I speak to you in private, please?" he said, looking at Sophie, who nodded.

"Kyle?" he began, as they walked into Sophie's old bedroom.

Sophie nodded and began to cry. Cash looked on with contempt.

"Me or my father?" he asked angrily.

Chapter 8

Santa Cruz, CA

Gray grabbed his radio. "Yes?"

"We failed to stop everyone leaving, they even got past the Surenos team that you sent as back up."

"Shit," he said, uncharacteristically. His missions never went anything other than according to plan. "It is imperative you stop them, I've got the mountainside locked down. No cell towers or phone lines are working. Police radios are also blacked out. You have time to clean up the mess. I need to know that every piece of the professor's research is gone."

"His house and all who were inside will be gone, there'll be nothing left."

"Good, I'll deal with his office, did you get the flash drive?"

"What flash drive?" asked Green.

Gray scrolled through his records on his tablet, where every detail of everyone they had watched over the previous two years was noted. Professor Charles Harris wore a necklace with a small flash drive around his neck.

"The one he wore around his neck."

"It wasn't there," said Green.

"Perhaps you missed it?" asked Gray angrily.

"I searched him myself, there was no jewelry on him whatsoever. Hold on," he paused listening to an update from his colleague. "We've found them, they're at Chief Kramer's house."

"Be careful, we can't afford to miss this opportunity or get caught."

"Don't worry, we're on it!"

"Hold on," said Gray thinking through the plan. "I'm going to send up more gang members, use them as cannon fodder. The more you leave behind, the more it'll look like a gang thing and confuse the authorities. Whatever happens, keep us out of it. I have a back-up plan should you fail, so don't get caught there!"

"We won't."

Gray entered the Surenos headquarters, his senses once again assaulted by the stench when he walked into the filth-infested dive. He brushed his tailored suit clean as he walked into the gang boss' domain.

"That bitch got my brother killed!" shouted one of the henchmen, charging at Gray. The man was huge, a hulk of a man, twice Gray's weight. Gray didn't flinch.

As the Hulk was about to strike, Gray moved with a speed that few in the room could even see. His hand lashed out for an instant and he sidestepped the falling hulk, who was dead by the time he hit the floor.

"Anyone else upset?" Gray asked calmly, straightening his tailored jacket.

The boss looked over at the ice-cold killer.

"What do you want? You've already cost me seven men."

"More than that, I'm afraid."

The gang boss was a smart man, that was why he was where he was. Men like Gray were men you appeased, not fought.

"I want more money."

"Fine, name your price," said Gray.

The boss looked again at his henchman. His body hadn't even twitched. He was stone cold dead by the time he'd hit the floor, and the boss had no idea how. He had already gotten $250k for his seven men.

"$1 million."

"I'll wire the funds," replied Gray, handing the boss a note for where to send his men. "But I want forty for that."

The boss nodded at one of his men. Forty loyal gang members would be on their way as requested.

Gray tipped his head as a thank-you and left. A number of gang members eyeballed him as he left the room; word of his killing had spread quickly throughout the rundown house. Gray held the gaze of each of those who dared to stare at him. Wisely, none moved.

On his way out of the house, he didn't look back. He listened intently for the slightest move, but again, none came.

Back in his car, he lifted his tablet. He wanted to know why everything had gone to shit, because *his* plans didn't go to shit.

Gray clicked on the name below the Professor's, Copernicus Armstrong Sagan Harris, the professor's only son. Pages of information scrolled before him, all thanks to the work of Gray's formidable intelligence sources.

'*Copernicus Armstrong Sagan Harris, commonly known as Cash Harris,*' read Gray. A headline below his name reminded Gray of the fact that the investigation was only a cursory one due to Cash being estranged from his father for the previous fifteen years. The reason for the estrangement was listed as unknown.

A bright and very capable student, Cash had had a scholarship lined up at Harvard before inexplicably walking out on his life and enlisting in the US Marines. He was soon redirected to Officer Candidate School, where he sailed through the program with ease. As a fresh faced second lieutenant, he moved onto Quantico and completed Basic Training before being sent on tours to Iraq, Afghanistan and Syria. A recent update noted that he had left the Marines after reaching the rank of Captain and returned to the US to start a new security firm with another Marine, Captain Jake Miller (aka Rigs).

Gray scrolled through Cash's military records. He was an exemplary Marine with fifteen years' service and numerous awards and recommendations. The more he read, the more he smelled a rat. It was too perfect. With a record like that, Cash would have been at least a Colonel. Instead, he had never risen beyond Captain, never gained his own command. Gray made a note; a more thorough check was required. With Cash having been out of the picture, it hadn't made sense to dig deeper. After all, the concern for Gray was Professor Harris, not his estranged son. Gray had a funny feeling that Captain Jake Miller, aka Rigs, was going to have a very similar record to Cash's, if not identical. He made a note; a full background check on Rigs was also needed.

Under Cash's name was listed Sophie Kramer, a significant ex-partner. He pressed her name.

Sophie Kramer, ex-fiancée of Cash and mother to a son, Kyle, had a doctorate in Astronomy and was a lecturer at the University of Cambridge, England, where she had lived for the previous ten years. With an interest in common with the professor, the detail on her was far greater. Gray, however, skipped the early years and moved to the point at which Cash had inexplicably deserted his fiancée and life. Sophie had been working as a research assistant at the observatory at the time. She hadn't started any new relationships. In fact, she had not had another relationship since. Eight months after Cash had left, she had given birth to Kyle. Shortly thereafter, she moved to Yale to complete her studies before moving to Cambridge to take up a teaching post. As far as the report was concerned, there had been little contact between Professor Harris and Sophie. Other than project work for Hubble 2, none had been noted as anything other than professional. There had, however, been absolutely no contact between Sophie and Cash. There had been none between Cash and Kyle, whom Gray could only assume from the timing was Cash's son.

Gray looked back through Cash's records. He was a Marine officer. Honor, courage and commitment were all core to the Marines' code of conduct, within which, responsibility and fulfilling one's responsibilities were essential. What was more important than to ensure you looked after your own children? Something was off. He added another note for it to be investigated further.

He tapped on the link to Kyle Kramer. Very little had been noted, other than his birthday and the few dates on which he had any contact with the professor. It listed his areas of interest, obviously discovered from his internet history, including astronomy sites, as well as his favorite porn sites. He liked brunettes it seemed. He was captain of his school rugby team and, due to his size and ability, he was being closely watched by the US rugby team, who were desperately trying to bolster their pool of players.

He looked down at the notes he had scrawled on his notebook and dialed a number on his cell phone.

"Yes?"

"I need to check a couple of names," asked Gray of his mole inside government.

"It'll cost you twenty."

"Fine," replied Gray easily.

"Shit, you'd have paid more?"

"A lot more," Gray said, smiling. The deal had been struck. "Wired to the usual account?"

"Yes, what are the names?" asked the mole.

"Copernicus Armstrong Sagan Harris…"

"Jesus, that's a mouthful."

"Or Cash Harris for short, and Jake Miller. Both were supposedly US Marine captains."

Gray waited while keys clicked in the background.

"Interesting couple," whistled the mole.

"Why, what does it say?"

"They were Marines, both captains, that bit is right. Hard core too. Force Recon, Det One and MARSOC as Critical Skills Operators. Seriously good operators according to the reports, although there seems to be a lot of psychological reports on Miller. Looks like he's mildly autistic, according to the reports. However, their record ends abruptly about four years ago. Seems Miller couldn't go any further in the Marines given his issues, so they moved elsewhere."

"Elsewhere?"

"Yep, which usually means CIA, DIA, or one of the many US intelligence Agencies."

"You don't think they just left?"

"Definitely not. They're listed as active, but with no unit or detail for the last four years. If you give me an hour, I can probably find out where they are," offered the mole.

"I think I know where they are," replied Gray.

Cash and Rigs were on site and were no doubt the reason the attempt on the two cars failed. Gray radioed Green with an update. Typically, Green, a former SEAL, informed him how he ate Marines for breakfast and he wasn't to worry.

The last resort option was in place.

Chapter 9

Santa Cruz, CA

The slap knocked him sideways. Fifteen years of pent up frustration were released in one swing.

"How fucking dare you!" Sophie screeched.

Cash pulled himself upright, his face still stinging. He'd been punched many times but never slapped. He preferred a punch.

"Shit, that hurts!" he said, rubbing his reddening cheek.

"Try the love of your life pulling a disappearing act for fifteen years and refusing any contact. *That's* hurt!"

"Try the love of your life cheating on you with their father."

"I never slept with your father," she said, lowering her voice almost to a whisper.

"I caught you with him! And let's face it, my father had a bit of a reputation for bedding his research assistants!"

"You caught me very drunk, kissing him; it was a mistake and was over in seconds."

"I can't verify that."

"I thought he was you," she said, halfheartedly punching him in the chest.

"What?" asked Cash.

"I was very drunk, I heard someone come in and thought it was you. I stumbled across and threw my arms around your father and started to kiss him thinking it was you."

"And...and I w-walked in?" stammered Cash.

"And ran out of our lives, yes!" she said and started to cry again.

"Kyle?"

"One hundred percent yours. The reason I was so drunk was because I was pregnant, which I didn't know until after you'd gone. We tried to contact you but you refused every attempt. I sent hundreds of letters, but they all came back unopened. We tried to visit your base but they wouldn't let us in without your consent."

Cash nodded.

"Your dad didn't tell you?"

"He was so pleased to see me. I didn't spend much time with him. He did want to tell me something before the ceremony though."

Cash slumped onto the bed, the bed where he had most likely made a son, a son whose life he had been no part of.

"Does Kyle know?"

Sophie nodded. "But also knows you don't know."

"Your mom?"

Sophie nodded again. "She pretty much despises you and can barely say your name."

"Your dad?"

"You were the son he never had. He always defended you, but was finding it harder and harder as Kyle grew older."

The sound of gunfire pulled Cash out of his despair. He pushed Sophie to the floor, propelling her out onto the landing, ushering Kyle and Mrs. Kramer to join them on the floor.

"Stay down and do exactly as I say!" he commanded as bullets began to tear through the fabric of the house.

"Rigs!" he shouted as he neared the top of the stairs.

"At least ten out front and some out back!" Rigs shouted, rushing into the house, followed by the three police officers. Rigs had moved into action mode, all awkwardness left behind. Cash likened it to stutterers who could sing perfectly without stuttering. Rigs' mind was focused on one thing and one thing alone: neutralizing the enemy.

"Weapons?"

"The P90s, a few pistols, and a couple of shotguns from the police cars."

"Lay down some cover while I get these guys down the stairs," Cash said.

"You heard the man!" shouted Rigs, throwing a P90 to Banks and instructing him and another officer to take the back of the house. "On my count, empty your magazines into the attackers," said Rigs, looking at the third officer who would cover the front with him.

"When he gets to three, I want you to all run as fast as you can down the stairs, keeping your heads low and go straight to the basement door," Cash told Kyle, Sophie and her mother.

"They're getting close!" shouted Banks, panic filling his voice.

"Okay, one, two…" Rigs wanted to see the white of their eyes, "…three!"

Cash watched proudly as Kyle grabbed his mom to help her down the stairs as quickly as possible. He followed with Mrs. Kramer. They barely avoided a collision at the bottom of the stairs when they spun around and into the basement door, which was beneath the staircase.

"In!" prompted Cash.

Kyle stood back to let the ladies in first. *It really isn't the time for English gallantry* thought Cash.

"Rigs!" shouted Cash. "We're down!"

"There are many more than we thought. I've taken six out and they're still coming!"

"Banksie?" called Cash, only to be met with silence.

Rigs and the officer covering the front rushed back to the hallway. The front door buckled when the attackers unleashed a hail of bullets against the solid oak panels.

"Basement," Cash said, pushing the officer and Rigs into the doorway. A Surenos gang member rushed into the hallway from the back of the house, catching Cash cold and unarmed.

The front door gave way under the unrelenting hail of bullets.

Cash dived through the doorway, taking advantage of the startled gang member's lack of experience, and the gang member took the full brunt of the torrent of bullets that passed through the front door.

Cash crashed into the officer and Rigs, sending the three of them tumbling into a heap at the bottom of the stairs.

"Run!" screamed Sophie as the footsteps could be clearly heard racing across the corridor above them.

All three rushed towards her voice and through the small doorway on the far wall.

When the Surenos members filtered back out of the house, Green instructed his two colleagues, Red and Brown, to move forward with him. Green had orders to stay back until the scene was clear. Gray had already lost one operative and didn't want to lose any more. As far as Green was aware, it wasn't that Gray cared for them particularly. Despite their colorful and anonymous names, they were not faceless and untraceable mercenaries. Each of them was a well seasoned ex-Special Forces man with a history that could tie them back to Gray. It was only thanks to Green's quick actions that the police hadn't found Blue's body at the professor's house.

The operatives Green had with him were perfectly capable, particularly against a couple of academics. It was a different matter against trained CIA killers. Gray's men would stay back until all dangers were eliminated.

"We're going in now," advised Green on the radio to Gray.

"We need the flash drive and no witnesses," Gray reminded him.

"Understood."

"Two dead in the kitchen and the rest are in the basement," one gang member said, strutting towards Green.

"All dead?" asked Green.

His shrug was not the solid affirmative he had hoped for.

"Are they dead?" he repeated.

"I don't know," replied the Surenos boss, his face exploding to mush before Green's eyes.

***

The door thudded behind them, quickly followed by a hiss.

"A bomb shelter?" asked the officer, looking around the small room that was stacked floor to ceiling with dry goods and water bottles.

Cash nodded. "The Chief was a bit of a prepper. He liked to know he could protect his family. It's also a great earthquake shelter, which is handy given the San Andreas Fault runs right beneath here."

Cash pushed a bag of rice to the side, revealing a gun cabinet below.

"How did you know that was there?" asked Rigs quietly, keeping his voice almost inaudible to everyone but Cash.

"I helped build this thing. I just hope he didn't change the padlock code." Cash entered the code '0716'.

Sophie watched him, a look of anger flashing across her face. "So you do remember my birthday."

Cash shrugged. No apologies were ever going to make up for what he had done.

A number of rifles lay wrapped in oily rags. "He was sure one day we'd all need to hunt to eat," explained Cash, removing them one by one.

Bullets pinged against the metal door. The officer watched the door intently, as though it were going to burst open any moment.

"It's fine," Cash assured him. "Only a direct missile strike is taking this baby down." He patted the cold walls that encased them.

"Fancy a hunt?" asked Cash with a grin.

Rigs nodded, as did Kyle.

"Not you," said Cash firmly, throwing a scoped M16 to Rigs.

He rubbed down a scoped M4 for himself and directed Rigs towards the far wall of the small shelter, where he pulled aside a pile of provisions to reveal a small hatch at the bottom of the wall.

"Once we're out, close this behind us and only open it if you get the signal," Cash said to Sophie.

Sophie blushed, memories of the "signal" flooding back to her.

"What's the signal?" asked Kyle, having missed his mother's blushes, resulting in even greater embarrassment.

"Let's go," said Cash. He spun the wheel lock and pulled the hatch open.

"Where does it bring us out?" asked Rigs as they crawled along the tunnel. He and Cash were alone now, so his voice found a more normal level.

"Twenty yards behind the treeline, at the front of the house. It took us a whole summer to build it. I always thought he was crazy but here we are, and it just saved our lives."

"We're not saved yet," cautioned Rigs.

Cash reached the end of the tunnel and ascended the small ladder, then spun another wheel to open the hatch to the outside. He peered out carefully, checking that the opening still lay within the woods before motioning to Rigs to follow him out.

All shooting had stopped by the time they exited. Only the loud and mingled voices of men congratulating themselves on a job well done drifted into the darkness of thick woods.

"Too many," Rigs commented. A significant force had attacked them.

Cash reluctantly agreed. He had dearly wanted to avenge the Chief and his father.

"I'm sure we could manage a few pot shots though?" suggested Rigs.

Cash smiled in agreement and signaled for Rigs to head twenty yards one way and he would go twenty yards the other. It would offer them a much wider field and hopefully trick the attackers into thinking there were far more than two shooters. Cash and Rigs would move back towards each other between shots, and then make it back to the tunnel and hopefully disappear safely back to the shelter.

Cash took up his position and surveyed the scene as the first wisps of daylight lit up the Chief's front lawn. The attackers were almost all in gang dress apart from three men in suits, one of whom was addressing the gang members with an authority that few suit wearing men would conceive of. The gang members were the heavies, the suits were the money men and no doubt the men who had paid the gang to attack the Chief's car. Cash lined up a shot. A gang member had his back to Cash and covered most of the suit apart from his head, Cash was more than happy to take him out with a headshot. The suit was going down.

He pulled the trigger right as the gang member's head moved across the sight. The back of the gang member's head split like a watermelon.

The suit was already off and running for cover by the time the body dropped out of the way.

Green was not about to find out what had happened. He didn't care. The scene was dangerous and he had orders. Whatever happened, they could not be linked with the operation. Green ran for cover, signaled to his two men to join him and under the cover of the confusion he caused when he started shooting gang members himself, they jumped in a car and made off at speed.

"Gray, last resort!" he said, hitting the transmit button as they sped out of the driveway and onto the highway.

Gray said nothing. Their last resort plan left doubt where he would rather none existed. However, he was out of options. He clicked the link in Mike's message and his tablet screen showed a black and white view from over 25,000 feet above him, a few miles to the north. A crosshair sat perfectly above the main chimney stack of the Kramers' house. Gray didn't hesitate for a second when he tapped the 'fire' icon on his screen. A counter began to reduce rapidly from 25,000 in the top left hand corner of his tablet screen and as the house became larger and larger, it exploded into a white flash.

MISSION LOG – EXTRACT 1-17

Deep Space Mission – New Hope
Log entry 17 – Mission Commander

After months of monotony, we are finally nearing our destination. The engines have begun the process of gently decelerating the ship as we near our future. An asteroid belt encircles our final destination and requires a careful approach.

The mood on the ship has improved since my previous entry. The realization of how important the mission is has slowly but surely sunk in. The change in rhythm of the engines as we began the slowing process was even met with a cheer.

We have three crew members pregnant, including, I am proud to say, my wife and even prouder to say, with twins. The colony we will begin will already be growing by the time we arrive, a great and hopeful start to a bright future for us all, I hope.

So far, all the readings from our forward scanners are suggesting the atmosphere and environment are about as perfect as we had imagined. The alarms have begun to sound, so we are nearing the final stages of our approach. My next log will be in either low orbit, or even more exciting, from the planet's surface. Our future home beckons.

Chapter 10

Antoine Noble, head of the Atlas Noble empire, swept into the UN building with little fuss, unlike the scores of heads of state who would soon be hanging on his every word. Atlas Noble was a company that owned nothing and everything. With a history dating back to the beginning of records, nobody outside of the Noble family truly knew how old the company was. Although it had been noted, even at the creation of records, some 1,500 years earlier, that Atlas Noble holdings was an old and distinguished company of significant standing, little was recorded of its purpose. With the expert acumen of the Noble family ancestors, nothing had changed. Atlas Noble was still of significant standing and few people had any idea what it did. What it did, however, was simple: it used money to create power and influence.

Atlas Noble was a holding company for a mind numbing and untraceable maze of trusts, charities, banks and businesses that invested in the world's businesses. The first time that a company would become aware of the involvement of the Nobles was the point at which a Noble family member was appointed to their board of directors. Family members spanned the globe and between the various branches of the family, all under the direction of Antoine, they sat on the boards of most of the world's listed companies, and certainly on all of those of note. A company's appointment of a Noble as director of the board was a badge of honor and once public knowledge, always ensured a significant increase in value. Consequently, a Noble removing themselves from a board invariably led to a crash in confidence in a company and was a major warning to investors. Atlas Noble didn't sell for profit, they only ever sold to avoid losses.

The banker, *the* businessman, *the* director, Antoine Noble was known as many things around the world but only by those who mattered. And those who really knew him, knew him as *the* king maker. Antoine Noble's monies, influence, and backing changed the world's democracies as he saw fit. One-term presidents fell at his displeasure, two-term presidents served at his behest.

Publicly, he was little known. Conspiracy theories surrounded the family, their influence and their wealth. Rumors and anecdotes abounded regarding their power and influence, one even suggesting that Air Force One was put on hold to allow Antoine Noble to land first. Not that it was true; it was in fact Antoine's daughter, Amy, who was aboard a Noble jet and who had given up her landing slot to save the President having to wait.

Whatever the case, there was one reason the UN was about to welcome more heads of states than in its entire history. Antoine Noble was addressing the UN and he had asked them to come and listen. One hundred and eighty-eight of the one hundred and ninety-three member states had sent their heads of state. Only five had not, and each of those was excusable due to age or illness, and had sent a significant deputy in their place.

Antoine studied the wall of TV monitors in his dressing room while he waited for the UN Secretary General to announce his entrance. The news stations were having a field-day. The entrance to the UN was more like the entrance to an awards ceremony with a red carpet style analysis of the attendees. Instead of comments regarding what they were wearing, viewers were hearing who they represented. A news banner at the bottom of the screen made reference to the tragic loss of the Hubble 2 telescope and an ongoing development in Santa Cruz but there was only one news story that day that was going to grab the headlines and it wasn't how many heads of state were visiting the UN.

Antoine checked through his speech one more time. He was literally going to blow his audience away.

Chapter 11

Cash felt as though the world had fallen in on him. He opened his eyes. Nothing had changed, the darkness remained. He tried to move. His arms and legs tried but failed to follow his instructions. He listened. Nothing, not even blood pumping through his veins. His last memory was of jumping into the tunnel. The Surenos gang members had spotted them in the treeline and unleashed a torrent of fire towards him and Rigs.

A scrabbling sound caught his attention. Something was rubbing against his leg. His immediate thought was rats. He hated rats. The scrabbling grew wilder. His leg was being tugged.

"Cash." It was muffled, but it reached his ears; it was definitely Rigs.

"I wouldn't give up the day job," said Rigs, clearing the earth around Cash. "You build shitty tunnels."

"Thanks," said Cash, still dazed.

"The tunnel collapsed in front of me and swallowed you up," explained Rigs, catching his breath after his manic burrowing efforts.

"But why?"

"I'd think it was something to do with the explosion," Rigs remarked.

"Explosion?"

"Best guess, a two thousand pounder, direct hit on the house," said Rigs.

Cash pushed past Rigs and made for the exit hatch. The steel hatch and vertical tube that led up to the surface had protected Rigs from the collapse. A few seconds more and both of them would have been buried alive, deep in the tunnel, never to be found. A sobering thought that Cash had no time for.

He pushed the hatch hard. It moved slightly. He pushed harder and as it slowly gave way, a body of a Surenos gang member slid off the lid, no doubt trying to follow them into the tunnel when the explosion struck. Daylight lit the surreal stage. The tree line that had once camouflaged their spot was all but gone. Only the trunks survived, the branches and leaves had been blown away in the blast. Cash turned to face the house. A smoldering pile of rubble remained, leaving only a short chimney stub still intact.

"Oh my God!" His son, a son he hadn't even known he'd had, a son he had barely spoken to, lay beneath the rubble.

Rigs joined him on the surface and exhaled expletives.

Cash ran towards the rubble, dropping his M4 to dig through the rubble in search of the basement.

A cacophony of sirens suggested help was on the way. Rigs didn't wait for the help, he tore into the rubble alongside his partner Cash. Neither spoke a word as they systematically moved through the rubble, clearing it urgently. Within minutes, they were where the doorway to the basement would have stood. A solid pile of rubble lay where the staircase should have been. Neither spoke, they just had to remove the obstruction and get to the basement and the shelter below.

The first fire crew's arrival did not pause their efforts. Calls from the crews that the structure was unsafe were ignored. Only when the first police officer arrived and on seeing the array of tattooed body parts that littered the area were they ordered to stop at gun point. Even then, it took all of Rigs' strength to pull Cash away from his task and avoid the bullet the officer was threatening.

With the arrival of more police officers, the scene became chaotic. Cash and Rigs were placed in handcuffs while the police officers tried desperately to ascertain what had happened to their Chief and his family. Meanwhile, fire crews procrastinated about how safe it was to search through the rubble of the house, almost causing Cash to burst the veins in his temple.

"There are people buried under there!!!" screamed Cash for the tenth time. "Sir," said Cash to the officer nearest him, trying to calm himself. "Call this number, 555-223-4312, and ask for the boss."

The officer looked at him, his interest piqued.

"555-223-4312," repeated Cash.

The officer dialed the number and immediately hung up. He then rushed over to Deputy Chief Sanders who had just arrived and whispered in his ear.

Sanders' head spun to fix on Cash and Rigs. "Okay, that gets you the chance to talk," said Sanders, walking over to the two suspects.

"The Chief's wife, daughter and grandson are buried under that rubble," Cash said urgently.

"We're getting to them, don't worry," said Sanders calmly. "But what in the hell happened here?" he asked, gesturing to the devastation around them.

Cash spoke as calmly and slowly as the situation allowed, given his family was buried beneath them and all he wanted to do was get to them.

"The Chief's dead?!" exclaimed Sanders, when Cash recounted the attack on the cars. "And you think they hit this place with a two thousand pound bomb?" asked Sanders, incredulous.

Cash and Rigs both nodded.

"So who is 'they'?" asked Sanders, looking at Rigs, who in turn looked at Cash, avoiding Sanders' gaze.

The fire crews made progress on the house. The movement calmed him.

"'They'," he answered, "could be any number of people, but I'd start with the Chinese, Russians or North Koreans."

Sanders rocked back as though hit by a right hook. "What?"

"Everything leads back to the observatory and Hubble 2," said Cash.

"Hubble 2?"

"The most powerful telescope ever built."

Sanders was unimpressed, "And?"

"The most powerful spy satellite ever developed."

"Seriously guys, let's get back to reality. Lumps of Surenos gang members are littering this area, not old world Commies."

"A back-up plan for when their initial plan failed," said Cash. "If I'm not mistaken, Hubble 2 was blown up last night by a missile."

Sanders paused. "It was hit by a meteor," he said quietly. "It's only just been reported."

"A meteor that flew upwards?"

"Shit," whistled Sanders. "What do we do?"

"First thing is, we need to cancel the President's visit if it's not already cancelled, and more importantly, we need to rescue my family," said Cash, beckoning for his cuffs to be removed.

"The President was coming here?"

Cash nodded. "Yes, tonight, in secret, to inaugurate the telescope."

"Bullshit. He has a huge entourage, we'd have been informed."

"Only when it's a public visit. This was a very secret visit. It wasn't going to be made public. If nobody knows he's coming, there's far less to worry about."

"And you guys are?"

"Not the guys who should be in cuffs," Cash snapped. "Give me that number again?" asked Sanders with his cell phone at the ready.

"555-223-4312," Cash repeated for the third time.

Sanders dialed the number and, as described by his officer, the phone was answered on the first ring.

"President Mitchell's office."

Sanders took a deep breath. "Could I speak to the President, please?"

The line disconnected.

"No, ask for the boss!" Cash said impatiently. "It's a code that proves you know it's the red line."

"The red line?"

"No matter where he is or what he's doing, you'll be put through to him immediately."

"Bullshit! I bet it's one of your buddies that can do a good impression, it's not…" Sanders spotted a news crew truck that had arrived. He knew the President was at the UN. Everybody knew he was there; it was the only news across every network. He walked over to the truck and ignored every question hurled at him.

"Can you get the news feed from the UN?" he asked the technician in the back of the truck, looking back at Cash and Rigs.

"Umm, yeah," said the techie, looking out at the carnage in front of them. It seemed a bizarre request.

"Any feeds covering President Mitchell?"

The techie flicked through a number of feeds available to the media and found a camera that settled on President Mitchell, leaving it on the screen for Sanders.

"Fantastic, thanks," said Sanders hitting the redial button. He could make out the audio feed from the UN. The Secretary General was introducing the keynote speaker. The President was in no position to accept a call.

He hit redial, keeping his eye on the screen.

"President Mitchell's office."

"The boss, please?" asked Sanders with a sneer.

"Please hold."

After three rings; "Yes?" came the reply of a voice Sanders couldn't fail to recognize but did not match the vision before him. The President was still listening to the Secretary General on the screen.

"That is a fantastic impression of the President's voice."

The techie tried to catch his attention, having listened to Sanders' end of the conversation, but Sanders ignored him.

"Who is this?" demanded an angry President Mitchell.

"The guy who's about to put your buddies Cash and Rigs in jail and throw away the key," he said.

"Was that the President?" asked the techie, stunned, when he hung up.

"Obviously not," said Sanders pointing at the screen.

The president sat motionless listening to the Secretary General.

"One small problem," said the techie, pointing at the screen. A Secret Service Agent rushed into view with a cell phone outstretched. "There's a twenty second delay on this feed!"

Chapter 12

Antoine Noble walked onto the UN stage to rapturous applause after a humbling introduction from the UN Secretary General. The philanthropic endeavors of Atlas Noble through their trust were humbling to even the greatest nations of the world. Immunization for every child, clean water for all, the eradication of malaria, measles and malnutrition were amongst a number of their targets. Unlike many, these were not just wishful targets; Atlas Noble was spending more money than the nations of the world combined in an effort to make it happen. For the previous eleven years, every child on the planet had benefitted from the AN injection, a cocktail of immunizations that had already wiped out malaria and measles for all of its recipients.

Antoine waited for the applause to settle.

"Citizens of the world," he began. "We are truly blessed to live on this wonderful planet, a planet that we have only begun to understand. A planet that merely nine nations, represented here today could, in the blink of an eye, *destroy!*"

Antoine paused, allowing his words to sink in before he changed the direction of his speech to a very different slant than the one he had spun to ensure acceptance of his invitation. The nine member states in possession of nuclear weapons shifted uneasily in their seats.

"Even today, long after the threat of the Cold War and the darkest days of human history, those nine countries between them hold over 17,000 warheads. At Atlas Noble, we strive every day to make the world a better place, yet we all live under the shadow of a past that still haunts us - mutually assured destruction."

Antoine paused once more. Heads were turning towards the nine nuclear states. TV cameras were refocusing their lenses on the individuals, the nine individuals who held the power and ability to destroy the planet.

"Whatever religion you believe in, however you believe the world was created, it wasn't at the hands of those nine men. Those nine men have the power to undo all creation and I, for one, think that is wrong. I believe it is time we asked those nine men whether they agree."

A rapturous applause engulfed the audience. Antoine looked at the UK king, who had recently taken the throne following his aging grandmother's abdication and father's untimely death which, together with his mother's death many years earlier, was considered suspicious. King William looked across at his Prime Minister who stood up and walked towards the stage. The French President followed suit when Antoine's eyes fell on him. Both moves had been carefully orchestrated in advance and both countries would benefit significantly from the support shown to Antoine.

The applause grew louder when the two of the nine neared the stage.

Antoine's eyes fell on the Israeli president, a country that had refused to confirm it even had nuclear weapons. The Israeli President stood, and he too walked slowly to the stage.

The Indian President looked at his Pakistani counterpart, both held each other's gaze, nodded at each other, and they too walked towards the stage.

Antoine motioned to his staff at the side of the stage. Nine desks and chairs appeared alongside him and he motioned for each leader to take one of the chairs.

The applause continued to rise. But the big four didn't move.

Antoine raised his hands to calm the audience.

"Perhaps I can make this decision easier for some of you," he said with a wink to the camera, instantly turning more serious when he addressed the audience. "Any country that fails to sign an agreement here today to eradicate their nuclear arsenal is not a country that Atlas Noble will have any further dealings with. To clarify, what I mean by that, is that all Atlas Noble holdings within that country will either be liquidated or moved to a nuclear weapon free country."

President Mitchell's red line cell erupted as his cabinet members tried desperately to alert him to what he was already fully aware of. Atlas Noble pulling out of America simply wasn't a viable prospect for the ongoing wellbeing of the nation. He rejected all attempts by his Secret Service agents to pass him the cell phone. He looked across at his Russian and Chinese counterparts. He knew that the Russians were in the same boat as him; they would have to sign. The Chinese were trickier. They would spite themselves. As for the North Koreans, Antoine's threat was unlikely to faze them. However, America could not allow the North Koreans to be the world's only nuclear state. The idea was ludicrous and inconceivable. President Mitchell remained seated.

Antoine looked at the young North Korean leader who got up from his seat. Antoine knew they would be the stumbling block. With little outside influence, the North Koreans had little to lose, but as Antoine had promised the North Koreans, they had a huge amount to gain. North Korea was about to see a cash injection that would transform its economy and strengthen the young leader's position within his country, despite giving up his nuclear arsenal.

A roar greeted the young leader as he walked towards the stage, a new experience for the world's most hated nation and one the North Korean leader was certainly enjoying.

President Mitchell appeared as shell-shocked as his Russian and Chinese counterparts that this was really happening. He knew the Russians would eventually go, so he focused on the Chinese President. His face remained impassive. Antoine began to speak rapidly in Chinese. President Mitchell grabbed his headset and heard the same threat repeated again. Obviously, Atlas Noble owned more in China than he had imagined, otherwise the threat was worthless and why repeat it in Mandarin? An almost imperceptible nod from the Chinese President received a far stronger nod from the Russian President and a relieved nod from President Mitchell. All three presidents from the three most powerful nations on the planet walked towards the stage.

A standing ovation followed as the three men shook hands with the six already in place.

News channels broke into broadcasts around the world reporting the auspicious moment. Antoine Noble, the billionaire philanthropist, had changed the face of the world forevermore. In one month, as stipulated by the agreement, signed by the nine premiers and presidents, the world would be free of all nuclear weapons.

***

President Mitchell signed the agreement.

"Are you shitting me?!" shouted the Chairman of the Joint Chiefs of Staff.

"What was he supposed to do?" asked the Commandant of the Marine Corps.

Their regular weekly Joint Chiefs meeting had been interrupted by the breaking news. The seven most powerful uniformed officers in the United States watched on in horror as their most powerful weapon and main deterrent was swept away from under them.

"Nothing he could do," agreed the Army Chief of Staff.

As much as some of them disagreed, deep down, if they were in the President's position, they knew they would all have had to sign the agreement. Atlas Noble was a massive employer.

"That guy is a genius," said the Air Force Chief.

"Genius? He's certifiably crazy!" argued the Navy Chief.

The Air Force Chief said, "Atlas Noble is the world's largest arms manufacturer."

"And?"

"Just wait," said the Chairman bitterly. "We're about to see the largest bump in our budget in years. We're about to see an arms race unseen since the height of the Cold War. Those two aircraft carriers you put on hold, trust me, they'll be dusting off the plans before the end of the day."

Chapter 13

Cash waded into the rubble, keen to assist in any way possible. The fire crews had already cleared the way to the basement and were nearing the shelter.

Rigs, as instructed by Cash, called in their situation. There would be a myriad of agencies fighting over the scene within the next few hours. By the time he had finished the call, a far more relieved Cash was walking towards him, leading the shell-shocked Kramer family.

When Sophie and her mother took in the scene of their devastated home, the home Chief Kramer had built, they wept.

Deputy Chief Sanders walked over and offered his condolences.

"We need a car," said Cash abruptly.

Sanders handed his own car keys to Cash. He was still keen for the President not to discover who his prank caller had been.

"Thanks," said Cash, leading the Kramers away.

"What happened?" asked Sophie, looking at the ruins of her childhood home.

"We're not sure yet but we'll find out," he said, looking at Rigs.

"Cash, don't do anything stupid," said Sophie, reading between the lines.

"Me? Never," he said with a smile.

"Says the guy who disappeared for fifteen years."

"I'll make it up to you."

"It's too late for us, it's Kyle you have to make it up to." Cash looked at the only woman he had ever loved, a woman who, fifteen years later, had only grown in beauty.

"I was a fool."

"You were always headstrong but in your defense, you were seldom wrong."

"I'm never wrong," he smiled again.

"About us?" she asked, climbing into the car.

Once, he thought, *once*.

"So where to?" asked Rigs across the roof of the car.

"Drop them at a hotel," Cash said quietly, "then you and I are going to pay the Surenos a little visit."

"Good call. We'll have to be quick though, to beat the cops."

"Exactly, so stop talking and get in the car."

Cash took the driver's seat. He knew the area, or, a fifteen-year older version of the area. After a few minutes of deafening silence, he felt he had to say something. He had to apologize to the son he didn't know he had but had no idea how.

"So, Kyle, how's school?' he asked awkwardly.

"It's okay," replied the sullen, typical teenager.

"He's his father's son," said Sophie, "top of his class in every subject, driving his teachers crazy with questions they struggle to answer."

"I wasn't top in every class," Cash argued.

"Hmm, yes, physics," Sophie said to Kyle. "Your father pretended to be not so good at physics, so I'd be top of that class."

Cash smirked. "I'm not sure I remember it like that."

"Cash, your father always wished you'd followed him into astronomy," said Sophie. "He reckoned your brain was twice the size of his at the same age."

"So how about sports?" asked Cash, desperate to change the subject. The guilt of the fifteen missed years with his father was beginning to sit heavily on his conscience. At least he had the chance to apologize to Kyle; that opportunity was gone for him and his father.

"Not bad," said Kyle.

"Captain of the rugby team, star of the athletics team," said Sophie.

"Just like my father?" Kyle laughed.

"Swap the rugby for football and yes, just like your father," confirmed Sophie.

"We're here," said Cash. "Wait here while I arrange some rooms."

With Cash gone, Rigs remained silent in the front passenger seat, his eyes looking out for signs of danger.

"You don't say much, do you?" asked Sophie.

Rigs shook his head awkwardly.

"So you've been friends with Cash for a while?"

Rigs nodded slightly. "Fifteen years." He was uncomfortable with the unfamiliar environment and the questioners. "A great friend," he added, keeping his eyes fixed on the hotel entrance, awaiting Cash's return.

"Hmmph," said Mrs. Kramer, stirring irritably in her seat. "He abandoned his son."

"Mom!" Sophie hissed.

"You can't abandon someone you didn't know existed," said Rigs, turning to face his friend's dissenter. Few things riled Rigs, but an attack on Cash he would defend. "Cash Harris risked his life daily to save his fellow Marines. That's not the type of guy who would let his own son down." Rigs turned back to face the front and reenter his own world.

"Well he did," said Mrs. Kramer flatly. "I'm sorry, Kyle, but your father is a…"

"Mom, Rigs is right, Cash didn't know."

Mrs. Kramer stared at her daughter for any hint that she was lying. Sophie didn't blink or look away.

Rigs spotted Cash exiting the hotel and opened the car door to get out.

"Kyle, go with him," Mrs. Kramer ordered. "Mom, Cash didn't run away because I was pregnant," were the last words Rigs heard before he shut the car door behind him.

Rigs placed his hand on Cash's chest to stop him getting to the car. "They've got a couple of things to sort out," said Rigs. "Give them a minute or two."

Cash handed Kyle a key and directed him to the elevators.

He glanced into the car and saw both Sophie and her mother talking heatedly, but couldn't hear what they were saying. All the while, Rigs held him back.

"It's fine," Rigs told him, "let them work it out."

A minute later, Sophie's door flew open and she stormed out of the car, took a key from Cash and disappeared into the hotel without a word. Mrs. Kramer followed, far calmer, and walked over to Cash. He held out a key to her but instead of taking it, she took him in her arms.

"My boy, my dear sweet boy!" she said, before taking the key and, like her daughter, disappearing into the hotel.

Cash looked at Rigs for an explanation.

He shrugged. "Women." And taking a key, he left Cash bewildered as to what had just transpired.

***

Gray watched the drone's feed as long as it was on station, which seemed to be oblivious to the scenes below, staying above the devastation long after the first news choppers had arrived. Gray marveled at how brazen his client was and how well connected he was to have access to an armed drone and a satellite-killing missile. Delivering that capability over a war zone was one thing, delivering it over California was in an entirely different league. A feeling of dread came over him. How could he have been so naïve? These were the missions that required ultimate and total deniability. These were the missions that secretive government agencies used poor patsies to deliver. His head spun around, suddenly everything was a potential enemy.

"Green?" he said into the radio.

"Yes?" came the reply. His team was still okay. "Where are you?"

"ETA, with you, three minutes!"

"Make it two, I've got a strange feeling," he said ominously, hearing a change in engine revs over the radio as a result.

Gray turned his attention to the Surenos' gang house, a hundred yards down the street. They were the ultimate patsies in the mission.

His burner cell buzzed with a text message – the only connection with the client. '*Take out the Surenos house.*' He looked around again; it was as though they knew exactly where he was and what he was thinking. He leaned out of the car window and looked into the morning sky. The drone had left the hillside. He clicked on the link to its feed. It wasn't active but it was still up there. There was no reason the feed would no longer be available, unless…

"Green! Abort! Abort!"

They were watching him.

He looked around. A young mother was pushing a baby in its pram. No one else was on the street. He started his engine. A muzzle flash lit up the Surenos' window. By the time he engaged 'Drive', the flashes had engulfed the house. Not a sound emanated from it. He checked his rear view mirror. Two young men turned the corner behind him. He accelerated, screeching to a halt as the young woman tried desperately to protect her pram from his onrushing car.

The two men were still a hundred yards away. He turned to check on the young mother. She stood looking directly into his car, the barrel of a gun pointed expertly at him.

"Shit!" was all he managed as the bullet tore through the windshield.

"Target down," she said into her mic.

A minivan with blacked out windows sped down the street, pausing to pick up the two men before collecting the woman and her prop pram. The DIS Team Leader, Steve, jumped out and poured a box of files carefully onto the passenger seat next to the still warm corpse of Gray. The box had been couriered to him fifteen minutes earlier, strict instructions made it clear that the files were not to be read nor any fingerprints or DNA deposited onto them.

Another stop at the end of the street retrieved two further DIS operatives from the Surenos house. Within twenty seconds of Gray's death, his body was alone on an empty street with enough incriminating evidence to bring down a government.

MISSION LOG – EXTRACT 5-1

Deep Space Mission – Last Hope
Log entry 1 – Mission Commander

The last window of opportunity has passed. We are the last hope for our people. While they live their lives as though the future was certain, they know nothing of the devastation that faces us. We are the last of five missions that have been sent to save our way of life. We are the last hope. The window of opportunity for any further attempts has closed behind us.

We have studied in detail each of the mission logs from those that ventured before us. All end as they near their entry to the planet's orbit. The belief is that it is simply a communication issue. However, each of the subsequent missions has carried far more advanced communication equipment. None has communicated beyond the atmosphere of the planet we hope will be our future.

Despite that, our mission remains as originally intended. If the previous missions have failed, our mission will already be lost. We can only hope that for all our sakes, it is a communication problem and nothing more sinister.

We, like those before us, mourn our loved ones as we disappear into the night sky but it is for them and our descendants that we must go forward and build a future for us all.

Chapter 14

Cash checked his cell. Twenty-three missed calls, all from the office.

"Twenty missed calls," said Rigs, appearing silently by his side in the hotel lobby, checking his own cell.

Cash led the way out to the car. "Let's go before there are any more." Rigs eyed the patrol car Sanders had loaned them. "Something a bit less conspicuous perhaps?" he suggested.

"I think it's perfect." Cash jumped in and hit the police lights.

Rigs' look of disapproval flickered and disappeared as the strobe lights cried out to his inner child. "Cool!" he said jumping in. While Cash drove, Rigs prepared the weapons. The Surenos were about to wish that real cops were coming to call on them.

Cash's phone buzzed again, followed by Rigs'.

"We need to call in at some point," said Rigs.

"You already did," Cash reminded him.

Rigs looked at him. "You know I'm not very good with those calls," he said without a hint of irony.

Cash nodded. "What did you tell them?"

"'Cancel the President's trip, something's happened'."

"What did you tell them had happened?"

"Just that, 'something'."

"You called in and said six words?" asked Cash, shaking his head. Sometimes he wished Riggs could be a little more talkative.

"I know," said Rigs proudly. "That's good for me."

"Yes it is," agreed Cash, biting his tongue. "After the Surenos, we'll call in."

Office of the National Security Advisor
White House
Washington

"Son of a bitch!" shouted Travis Davies, Director of the CIA, slamming down the NSA's handset for what seemed the hundredth time.

"Not answering?" asked Vince Walters, the National Security Adviser. Travis shook his head. He had been trying to call 'his boys' since the call came in about Hubble 2's demise. Initially, their phones had been uncontactable but they had started ringing out an hour earlier. He knew they were alive. The report in front of him was a transcript of Rigs' call an hour earlier, precise to the point of uselessness. The man barely uttered a word other than to Cash, with whom he seemed to converse normally. Travis had grown tired of the speculation from the psychologists as to what was wrong with Rigs. He didn't care; as long as Cash kept him in line and the two did what they did best, he was happy.

"You gave your boys the red line number?!" screamed the Secret Service Director bursting into the office.

Travis looked around at his Secret Service colleague, Paula Suarez. She was very sexy when she was angry.

"Jesus, you'll make me come in my good suit," he smiled wickedly.

"Are you fucking kidding me?!" Paula screeched.

"Please, don't," he winced, much to Vince's amusement.

"Did you or didn't you?" she shouted, her face reddening.

"I don't recall."

"So it's a coincidence that a local cop in Santa Cruz prank-called the President at the UN?!"

"Is that what that was?" he asked, laughing. They had both seen the feed of the President answering the call during the introduction at the UN.

"It's not funny," she chastised. "*Idiots!*" She left, slamming the door behind her.

"Did you?" asked Vince.

"Did I what?" asked Travis, pointing towards where Paula had stood.

"The number? Did you give them the number?"

"Maybe, in case of an emergency."

"Shit," said Vince. "She'll have you for that."

"Do you think?" Travis asked with a grin.

Vince looked at where Paula had stood. "Have you?" he asked again. Travis smiled, but before he could answer, his phone rang. "Travis Davies," he answered.

"Mr. Director, it's Cash."

"About fucking time!"

"Rigs updated you?"

"You're kidding, right? I've got a six word transcript in front of me!"

"I'm sorry, sir," said Cash looking forlornly at Rigs. Sometimes he wished Rigs was normal; it would save Cash having to do all the explaining. "It's been a tough night."

"Sorry, of course, your father. My condolences."

"Thank you, sir. I'm fine, which is more than can be said for the assassins who attacked us last night. One dead here and another three dead in a car we passed two blocks from here."

"I expect nothing less."

"It wasn't us."

"So who?"

"No idea," said Cash quickly. He was flicking through the files as he spoke. Rigs looked at him with some concern but

Cash shook his head and motioned for Rigs not to interrupt him.

"Anything else?" asked Travis.

"No, sir."

"Keep in touch," said Travis.

"Why didn't you tell him about all this?" asked Rigs, thumbing through the papers.

"Because," Cash flicked back the few pages he had just thumbed through and turned them to face Rigs.

"What?" he asked, glancing at the pages. He let out a low whistle. "Shit!"

"Yep, we'd have implicated ourselves as part of the hit team."

"So the President was the target?"

Cash shook his head. "Publicly maybe but no, I think the target was the telescope. Come on, let's get this stuff out of here before the cops arrive."

"Travis?" asked Rigs.

"He'd have killed us first."

"Good point," said Rigs.

"But he did send us here…" Cash considered. "You drive," he said, throwing Rigs the keys.

"We were an obvious choice, given your father."

"True. Twelve blocks west and then hang a left to get us back to the hotel." He returned his attention to the files.

"Oh my God," he said after a couple of minutes.

"What?"

"The Vice President, it's all linked to the disarmament!"

"He's pro-gun," said Rigs.

Cash shook his head in despair. "It's all bullshit, unless you received a $5 million dollar payment as disclosed here?"

"Don't think so."

"Well I certainly didn't get the $6 million they're saying I got!"

"They paid you more than me?!"

"No," replied Cash. "Nobody paid us anything, Rigs."

"Yes, but they didn't pay you more than me!"

"Six is more than five, so yes they did pay me more than you."

"Yes, that's what I said. They didn't pay you…more than me."

"What?"

"They paid you virtually more than me."

"Virtually, six is quite a lot more than five." Cash grinned.

"You're fucking with me, aren't you?"

Cash nodded.

"Did they even pay you six?"

"No," laughed Cash. "They didn't pay me five, exactly the same as you."

"I'm pleased to see you can see the funny side of this," Rigs said. "We're being set up as fall guys."

"We've got their evidence, plus we didn't get the money, we can prove that."

Rigs pulled to a stop at the hotel lobby. "Let me see the transfers."

Cash handed them over and waited while Rigs used his smart phone to access his bank account. The money wasn't there.

"See," said Cash, we're fine.

Rigs kept scrolling through his account. Several seconds later, he turned the phone around so Cash could see the screen.

"At 5:01 this morning $5,000,000.00 was deposited into my account before being redirected to another account at the same time, which I guess from the code is a numbered private account."

"So if anyone checks, you received *$5 million dollars?*"

"Try yours," advised Rigs.

"I'll have to call them, I don't have online banking."

"So call them."

"I don't know the number or my account details!"

"Seriously?"

Cash shrugged.

***

"They're back," said Steve, the DIS Team Leader into his cell, nodding to his colleague across the lobby.

"Have they got the evidence?" asked his boss, Mike Yates.

"Yes, I recognize the files they're carrying."

A young woman with a pram walked across the lobby of the hotel and pressed the 'Up' button on the elevator as Cash and Rigs approached.

"We can take them out. What do you want us to do?" asked Steve.

"Take them, but only if you can do it quietly," Mike instructed.

***

Cash watched the numbers descend while Rigs cooed at the pram next to them. He'd always been the same around babies, they seemed to be immune to his awkwardness.

"What's your baby's name?" asked Cash.

"Err… Lacey," replied the young mother.

Cash smiled. "You sure?"

"Yes," she said confidently, looking down at the bundle of blankets that covered her baby.

Rigs took out a $50 bill. "A little something for her," he said more to the baby than the mother, his hand moving down towards the bundle.

"No, please don't touch her!" the mother said sharply, surprising both Rigs and Cash. Rigs always did the same thing. He didn't want kids himself but always spoiled them.

"Are you alright?' Cash asked. The mother was becoming increasingly agitated, looking around wildly.

"Perhaps we'll catch another elevator," offered Rigs, his head dipping.

"No, it's fine," said the young mother. "Please, I just don't like anyone touching him."

"Him?" asked Cash.

"My baby," replied the woman, sweat pouring from her brow.

Rigs hadn't missed it either. "Lacey is a him?"

The young mother glanced across the lobby at Steve. He winced at her performance and shook his head imperceptibly. The woman took off at a run, leaving behind her baby. Cash and Rigs had a decision to make. Was she a kidnapper or a bomber? What was really in the pram? Cash went for bomb and pushed the pram into the opening elevator. The steel elevator encased by three concrete walls would contain a significant portion of any blast.

Rigs followed it in, snatching back the blankets to reveal a silenced pistol.

"I think maybe we should find another hotel," said Cash.

"I'd vote another town, state, or country, personally."

Chapter 15

Travis stared at the phone long after Cash had hung up.

"What's wrong?" asked Vince.

"I'm not sure, something they're not saying."

"Your go-to guys are holding out on you?"

"Maybe," said Travis, recalling the conversation. Cash's tone had notably changed from the beginning to the end of the call. "And they're not my go-to guys."

"Yeah. It just so happens that anything you get involved in, your boys turn up?"

Travis ignored him. The breaking news story on the NSA's TV screen had caught his attention.

'Presidential assassination attempt failed' scrolled across the TV screen on the back wall of the office. He hit the volume control.

"...interrupt for breaking news from California. The attacks in Santa Cruz earlier this morning are being confirmed as a failed attempt to assassinate President Mitchell. President Mitchell, who today has signed the historic disarmament treaty, was due to visit the location of the attack later today..."

"Why are we just hearing this bullshit now?" asked Travis.

Vince was already grabbing for his phone, asking himself exactly the same question. He demanded that the press secretary get his ass in gear and into his office in the next five seconds.

"Blindsided us, sir," explained the press secretary. "They haven't even asked us for a comment."

"I take it you've spoken to them now?"

He nodded. "They say they've got enough hard evidence to implicate half the Hill. They've passed on the details to the authorities."

Vince blanched. "Okay, go." The press secretary fled. "What exactly were your boys doing in Santa Cruz?"

"Don't even go there," Travis said. "They were there to protect the President!"

"Because you were worried about a threat to him?"

"There were faint whispers coming through from our sources about a major hit in California and I thought better be safe than sorry."

"So the CIA just *happened* to have two of its most accomplished assassins on site?"

Travis nodded.

"CIA assassins who have no place working in the continental United States?"

"Whatever went down today, it had nothing to do with the President and everything to do with Hubble 2," Travis said. "Let's not forget what we lost today."

"*I* won't, but it's not *me* that's going to be running the investigation, nor me having to explain the presence of two illegal hitmen and a pile of dead bodies."

"You're making it sound way worse than it is."

"Yet nowhere near as bad as it's going to look out there." Vince pointed towards the corridors of the White House.

"I need to speak to the President, this is bullshit."

"I agree," said Vince. "Something smells very bad..."

A knock on the door interrupted him.

Paula Suarez was back, although this time not alone.

"Gentlemen, if you wouldn't mind standing up and stepping away from the desk please."

Both looked at her with some surprise. Travis spoke first. "Sorry?"

"Agents," said Paula, looking at the six burly men who had accompanied her. They moved forward quickly and had both men detained in handcuffs with little effort.

"*What?*" Travis roared. "What's this for? Sexual harassment?"

"No. Treason!" she said with disgust.

"T-Treason?" choked Vince. "I am the National Security Adviser. Are you fucking joking?!"

***

Cash paced outside Sophie's room. He didn't know how he was going to tell her he was leaving. Their five rooms lay at one end of the eighth floor. Rigs was holding the service elevator at the far end, urging him to hurry.

Cash knocked on the door and waited. The door swung open. Sophie wordlessly turned and walked back into the main body of the room and stared at the TV screen.

"I came to say…err…well… to say that, err…" he tried explaining but then stopped dead in his tracks when he glanced at the television.

A photo of his boss, CIA Director Travis Davies, appeared on the screen and underneath the caption read *'Charged With Treason'*. Another photo scrolled onto the screen, that of the Vice President of the United States and the caption remained unchanged. Photo after photo scrolled across the screen and the caption stayed in place. The Secretary of Defense, the Secretary of State, the National Security Adviser, the Chairman of the Joint Chiefs, the photos continued to scroll.

"Rigs!" Cash shouted.

Rigs rushed in, sweeping the room with his P90. Cash pointed at the TV set. Rigs remained speechless until the last two photos scrolled onto the screen.

The caption did change, however only one of the words changed. 'Charged' became 'Wanted' as Cash and Rigs' photos appeared on the screen.

Chapter 16

President Mitchell stared sullenly across the White House lawn. Darkness was setting on a day that should have changed the world for the better. For 99.99% of the population of the world that was true. For Dave Mitchell, the current President of the United States, it couldn't have been darker. Yes, he had signed the historic agreement that would rid the world of its greatest threat, but on the same day he discovered that many men and women he would have entrusted with his life had plotted to kill him.

"It's been a shocking day," said Lynne Bertram, his Attorney General, the chief law enforcement officer in the United States. , taking her seat on the sofa next to Paula Suarez.

President Mitchell turned and faced the room. He was back in the Oval Office after spending the better part of the day locked in his Emergency Operations Center for his own security. The evidence linking the attacks in Santa Cruz to a presidential assassination plot had been delivered during his flight back from New York. His return to Washington had not been with the fanfare he had anticipated. Instead, he was rushed to the bunker under a shroud of bodies and held captive for his own protection.

The White House was still in lockdown. Treble the number of Secret Service Agents were on duty with a small army in reserve at a moment's notice. Nobody was taking any chances.

"Have any of them explained why?" he asked, still perplexed. Many of those implicated with irrefutable evidence were lifelong friends.

"Because of you signing the disarmament treaty," replied Paula who, along with the Attorney General, was leading the investigation. They were in fact two of the very few people allowed to meet with the President. Even those not implicated were being security checked before they were given access to the President.

"I know what the evidence says, but nobody knew it was going to happen," protested the President.

"You knew," said Lynne candidly.

"Yes but—"

"And other world leaders knew," added Paula.

"In fact, was it not just a very well organized and superbly executed plan to force Russia and China to sign an agreement that nobody thought possible?" asked Lynne accusingly.

President Mitchell nodded; it had been an ingenious plan to rid the world of the weapons everyone knew could and probably would, one day, destroy the planet. Whether at the hands of a legitimate government or, more likely, at the hands of terrorists who had managed to steal them, the weapons had no place in the modern world. Antoine Noble was one of the world's most coveted philanthropists and when he had floated the idea, President Mitchell had jumped at it. It was to be his crowning glory. Deep into his second term, President Mitchell had led an unremarkable presidency. The economy was slowly rebuilding after the economic crash, wars were winding down, and the number of unemployed was gradually falling. His epitaph in history was going to be unremarkable until that day, whereupon his signature had changed the face of the world for the better. Now, however, the same day that he would go down in history was the day his own people tried to assassinate him. The British had had Guy Fawkes who, over four hundred years earlier, had plotted against his government and who, over four hundred years later, was still commemorated for having done so. The US now had its own treasonous plot to commemorate. His unremarkable presidency was now about to live on into immortality. What he'd give to have remained unremarkable.

He took another swig of Scotch and offered his guests another as he refilled his glass for a third time. Neither of his companions had touched theirs.

"So none of them are talking?"

"Other than to plead their innocence, no," said Lynne.

"You know what I don't get?" he asked rhetorically while taking another swig. "The people you have in custody…I mean… they're amongst the most powerful men in the world, with access to resources and men to complete any mission. Men and women

I entrust to carry out missions to protect our nation. Missions they successfully complete day in and day out to keep us safe. Missions in which we seldom leave a trace of our involvement…"

Both Lynne and Paula hung on the President's pause; a pause that drifted on and on, past the point of comfort and reason.

"And…?" prompted Lynne, breaking first.

"How could they have so royally fucked it up?" he said, draining his glass again.

Paula looked surprise. "You sound almost disappointed."

"Not at all. It's the one thing that gives me hope that this is all bullshit," he said, pointing drunkenly. "You see, if the men and women you have under lock and key really wanted me dead, we wouldn't be having this conversation."

"The evidence suggests otherwise, sir."

"Your evidence perhaps, but my evidence is a life in the making. I know those people and I know what they're capable of. Killing someone, God yes. Getting caught killing someone? Not a fucking chance!" He waved his index finger for emphasis, swaying gently under the influence of the alcohol.

"The evidence is irrefutable, sir. Bank transfers, emails, photos, surveillance videos…"

"Yes, but where did it come from? Who pulled the evidence together?" he asked. "And… and they attacked on the wrong day! You expect me to believe they would have attacked on the wrong day?!"

"Actually," said Lynne, "that anomaly has been resolved."

President Mitchell turned to her, his enthusiasm fading.

"There was a flight plan filed for Air Force One in error for yesterday and not today. It was quickly fixed but we believe it set the wheels in motion."

The President fell back onto the sofa opposite Lynne and Paula. He stared at them, waiting for them to tell him it was a mistake, some sort of joke.

"But why destroy the telescope?"

"We don't know yet. Best guess is a special interest group with something to hide," said Paula.

"In deepest, darkest space?" President Mitchell scoffed.

"Well, no. But let's not forget it could look *down* as well as *up*, if not better," said Lynne.

"I think I'm going to call it a night," said the President, standing up unsteadily. "Is the First Lady back yet?"

Paula shifted uncomfortably in her seat and looked at Lynne Bertram. She cleared her throat nervously. "Sir, there's no easy way to tell you this, but Mrs. Mitchell…"

"God, is she alright?" He collapsed onto the sofa, this time unintentionally.

"She's fine, sir. She's not come to any harm."

President Mitchell inclined his head as he studied their faces. "NO!" he screamed, reading what neither had the balls to tell him, resulting in a number of Secret Service agents rushing into the room, their guns drawn.

"I'm afraid, she has been implicated, sir," confirmed Lynne Bertram sadly, ordering the agents back out of the room.

Chapter 17

"We need to leave now!" said Cash.

"Are you kidding!" protested Sophie. "You need to hand yourselves in and sort this out!"

"Have you seen who they've arrested? Do you think we'll be able to talk our way out of this?" asked Cash, pointing to the faces scrolling across the television set.

"They've started using my middle name," said Rigs, watching the screen, tuning out everything around him. His name had changed to Jake Joshua Miller. "See? We're screwed! I'd forgotten I even *had* a middle name!"

"What?" asked Sophie in confusion.

"You know, Lee *Harvey* Oswald, John *Wilkes* Booth—they start using your middle name when you kill a president!" said Cash, wincing when his photo appeared with his full name.

Rigs had to do a double take when he saw the screen. "And I thought Joshua was bad!" he gasped. "Copernicus, that's what your dad was saying!"

"We don't have time for this," said Cash walking towards the door. "Sophie, get your mom and Kyle, we're leaving now!"

When Sophie exited the room, Rigs turned to his best friend. "For fifteen years I thought your name was Cash. We *do* have time for this!" he demanded, keeping his attention focused on Cash.

"Nicolaus Copernicus founded modern astronomy," replied Cash.

"Never heard of him," said Rigs. "Armstrong?"

"Neil Armstrong."

"I know him, the guy that went to the moon. Sagan?"

"Carl Sagan, my godfather and another astronomer."

"See, no biggie, Copernicus." Rigs smiled, patting a cringing Cash on the shoulder as he ushered him out of the room.

"What's wrong with him?" asked Sophie, pulling Cash towards her when they met in the hallway, and pointing at Rigs who was rushing towards the service elevator.

"What do you mean?"

"When you're around he talks but when you're not, barely a word!"

"It's complicated," said Cash. "He may be a little autistic." He always found that seemed to satiate the curious.

"Ahh, that makes sense. Although, a Marine officer?"

"Complicated. We made a good team."

"What kind of team?"

Cash shook his head. That wasn't something he wanted to talk about. "Come on, we need to get moving!" He moved back, urging Mrs. Kramer and Kyle to speed up.

Sophie stopped walking and pulled Cash aside. "Wait a minute, why are we coming with you?"

"So we can protect you," he said simply.

"But you're wanted for treason!"

"It's not true," he said.

"And I'm just to believe you?"

"Do you?" asked Cash.

"Of course, but that's not the point," said Sophie. "You'll be making us fugitives."

"And if you stay here, you're targets."

"Targets for who?"

"If I knew that, we wouldn't be having this conversation."

"Why not?"

"Because we wouldn't be running, we'd be hunting," said Cash.

Sophie noted the sincerity in his eyes and didn't doubt him for a second. He had lost as much as her that day, if not even more. She had fifteen more years of memories to treasure with her father.

"Where are we going?" she asked, picking up the few items she had saved.

"A safe house to begin with."

"And then?"

"Rigs and I will sort this out," he said with a confidence she daren't challenge.

"How?"

"With this," he said, showing her the flash drive that his father had given to him.

She reached out for it. "Your father's research!" she said in awe.

"He mentioned your name when he gave it to me," said Cash, looking for a reaction.

"Have you looked at it?" Sophie asked excitedly.

"So you know what it's about?"

"Vaguely. He mentioned a couple of things to me over the years."

"We ready?" interrupted Rigs, with Kyle and Mrs. Kramer at his side. He didn't wait for an answer and led the way into the waiting service elevator.

"Cells," Cash said when they reached the ground floor. Rigs handed over his without question, and the others did the same. Cash unceremoniously tossed all five cells into the trash cans while Rigs guided the group into the back of a stretch limo that awaited their arrival at the service entrance.

"Where are we going?" asked Sophie as they pulled away.

"Airport," replied Rigs.

"You're joking," said Sophie. "You guys are plastered all over the news!"

Mrs. Kramer's ears perked up; it appeared she hadn't been watching the news channel.

"All over the news?"

"It's a mistake," said Cash casually.

"A mistake about what?" asked Kyle. Obviously he hadn't seen the news either.

"Nothing," said Cash. A look from Sophie made it clear the matter wasn't closed as far as she was concerned.

"Does anyone wonder why Rigs is called Rigs?" asked Cash, trying to change the subject.

Nobody bit. "I mean, his name is Jake Miller, so it's not like it comes from his name," he continued to his uninterested audience. No response. "He's from Texas, so cowboy or Tex might be more appropriate, wouldn't you think?"

"Cash, nobody cares," said Sophie, suddenly protective of Rigs now that she was aware of his condition.

"You will when we reach the airport."

"Why, because he's on the no-fly list?" asked Sophie sarcastically.

"Forget it," said Cash and he too, like the rest of the occupants, stared out of the window in silence; a silence that allowed the crushing loss to flood over him.

"So why is he called Rigs?" asked Kyle, suddenly interested. A sign they had driven past directed them towards the executive terminal reserved for private aircraft.

Cash snapped out of his despair. "Well, as I said he's from Texas, so it's not because of that. Or is it?" he teased.

"His family found oil on their ranch?" Kyle guessed.

Rigs laughed and Cash nodded. The car slowed to a stop by the steps of a mid-sized private jet.

"Welcome to Mineta, San Jose Airport's executive terminal," announced the driver. He got out and opened the rear door for the passengers.

"So you're loaded?" asked Kyle, now impressed.

Rigs nodded awkwardly, stepping aside to let the very eager Kyle aboard.

Cash and Sophie brought up the rear while Rigs helped Mrs. Kramer aboard.

"So Rigs' family are oil barons?"

"Their ranch has oil," said Cash. "I don't know how much and I've no idea how big it is. Rigs doesn't really talk about it and has no real interest in it. As far as he's concerned, it destroyed his family and is the main reason he joined the Marines."

"But it doesn't stop him enjoying the benefits."

"First time we've ever flown anything other than coach. Yep, he's got money but he doesn't flaunt it or push it in your face. He's one of the guys."

"With a nickname Rigs, after oil rigs?"

"Only a handful of people know why he's really called that."

"Seriously?"

"Honestly, he doesn't even use it to pick up women."

"And you would?" asked Sophie.

Cash stopped, the twinkle in her eye was a twinkle he remembered all too well.

"I'm sorry," he said.

She looked into his eyes, tearing herself away as the first teardrop began to fall from her own. She dashed onto the plane leaving Cash alone on the runway.

"Come on," said Rigs, popping his head out of the airplane's door. "We need to get out of here!"

Cash looked away from his friend, a tear dropping from his own cheek. He rubbed it away, plastered a smile onto his face, and bounded aboard the flight. There was an empty seat next to Kyle and Cash didn't hesitate to sit next to his son.

"So where to?" asked Kyle.

Cash looked at Rigs, who looked back at Cash. "Nowhere," replied Rigs taking a seat at the back of the plane.

"Next stop, nowhere!" announced Cash, much to the confusion of all aboard.

Chapter 18

Sophie slotted the flash drive from Cash into the laptop she had borrowed from the cabin steward. Professor Harris had mentioned an interest in ancient sites. She had even read the article about him, *'The Astronomer Turned Archaeologist'*. However, Sophie knew the Professor too well; his interest lay in the sky not on the Earth.

The file opened a picture of two interconnecting black circles filled with white dots of varying sizes and intensities that seemed to explode out from the centers of each circle. The further from the center, the more the dots reduced, but not necessarily their intensity, as some even at the extremity of the circles were almost as intense as the dot in the center.

The left hand circle had far less of its area covered with dots, with vast areas of blackness, in contrast to the circle on the right, where only the far extremities of the circle were in blackness. There was something familiar about the image. Its setup was not dissimilar to a star chart, the image of a view of the northern and southern skies, however, Sophie didn't recognize any patterns amongst the dots.

She opened up the file menu for the flash drive. Only the image file showed, no other folders or documents were visible, just one file that was 3.2GB in size. 3.2GB for two black circles with some dots on seemed ridiculously large. She opened the file again, stared at the patterns and drilled into individual clusters. Were they galaxies? Constellations? She didn't recognize any of them. Sophie was one of the world's leading astronomers, and there weren't many galaxies, constellations or stars that she couldn't identify in the sky, even with a fleeting glance. Why had Professor Harris mentioned her name to Cash if the images wouldn't mean anything to her?

The longer she stared, the less sense it made. She had studied vast areas of the galaxy and beyond, with the world's most powerful telescopes. Nothing she was looking at was vaguely recognizable, yet something was familiar.

"Hey, Mom," said Kyle walking past. "How cool is this plane? There's even a shower in the loo!"

"Very cool," she said, looking back to see the restroom was empty. Kyle's mention of it had suddenly brought her need to use it into focus. She stood up and pointed down at the screen. "Look at this and see if it makes any sense to you," she said before making her way to the restroom.

Kyle was already back in his seat next to Cash when she returned. Fat help he was, but it was good to see how comfortable he was with his father. Despite everything that had happened, they were both managing to laugh and joke with each other, ably assisted by Rigs.

Sophie sat back down and stared at the screen. She closed her eyes and the dots remained in her view.

"Hey, Mom?" said Kyle, startling her.

"Hey, you. That loo is very cool," she smiled. "No luck?" she asked, pointing at her screen.

Kyle handed her a magazine that he had gone back to his seat to retrieve.

"A range chart for the Bombardier Global 6000?" she asked looking at the pages he was holding open.

"Look at the map of the world and imagine your circles with dots centered there and there," Kyle said, pointing to Western South America and Northeast Africa.

Sophie laid the map down and did exactly as her soon to be fifteen-year-old son had instructed. The left hand circle was predominantly South America, the dots disappearing where the oceans surrounded the land mass, while the right hand circle was Africa, Europe and a portion of Asia. Once again, the blackness correlated to where the oceans were.

"That's amazing, thanks, son," she said.

"Astronomers," he scoffed with a smile, heading back to his father. "Spend so much time looking out there, they don't see what's right in front of them."

Sophie was instantly reminded of a similar remark from Professor Harris in relation to archaeologists. The answer wasn't always to dig deeper and deeper, sometimes to look back, you had to look up.

Both fields looked to the past for their answers, Sophie considered, although in a very different manner and with very different skills. Ultimately, everyone looked into the past. The time an image takes to travel to your eye is already technically in the past, although due to the small distances, infinitesimally so. However, on the scale of the universe, the distances are so great that the images we see are the images as they appeared in the past. The sun's image is eight minutes old by the time we see it. The image of the closest star beyond the sun is four years old. Others, from the deepest depths of the universe, are billions of years old.

The more you consider the time and scale of the universe, the more mind blowing it becomes. Sophie's lectures always began with a number of mind blowing facts, none more so than the scale of the universe. If one grain of sand represented our sun, the star at the center of our solar system, there are not enough grains of sand on earth to represent every star in the universe. Our sun is a million times the size of Earth, but that is nothing compared to the largest sun discovered, VY Canis Majoris, which is a billion times the size of our sun. To put that into perspective, a passenger plane can circle the Earth in just under two days. It would take over 400,000 days, equivalent to 1,100 years to circle VY Canis Majoris.

Sophie snapped out of her teaching mode and back to the image. She now had a reference point. The map in the magazine wasn't particularly detailed but she knew enough from her basic geography to see that the right hand map centered in Egypt. She could see that in North Egypt, one large dot, larger than any other on the circle was surrounded by smaller dots. The concentration at the center of the dot was far greater than on any other. Had the large central dot signified a star, she'd have been able to identify the name, age of discovery and distance from Earth. Since it was a map of the world, she could only hazard a guess, but given Professor Harris' interest in ancient buildings, she guessed one of the only few sites she knew: the Pyramids at Giza.

The second circle was trickier, with far fewer dots and a center she was struggling to pinpoint. Peru, Chile or Bolivia was as close as she could guess without a more detailed map to use as a reference. Her knowledge of ancient sites in the area wasn't particularly great either. The only one she knew for definite was Machu Picchu in Peru, but without a better map she couldn't be sure and given the number of dots, there were obviously plenty more than she was aware of.

So, all she had was dots in two circles and a huge amount of unaccounted for data. She clicked again on the dots, but nothing happened; there were no hidden links. She moved the small arrow around the page hoping its icon would change to a pointing index finger. She tried the corners of the image and every pixel on the screen. Nothing.

"Ladies and gentlemen, we're making our final approach," the captain announced. "Please fasten your seat belts."

Sophie checked her watch, surprised at how quickly they had reached 'nowhere'. She had been at it for hours. The rest of the cabin had fallen asleep while she had persevered with trying to unlock the mystery of Professor Harris' work.

She hit the keyboard in frustration, and when her palm made contact with the space bar, a small window appeared on the screen requesting a password. A password window unlocked by 'Space'?! She could have kicked herself. She typed 'Sophie', the last word the professor had uttered before dying according to Cash. The window flashed back, asking again for the password; it wasn't Sophie.

Sophie wracked her brain as the plane touched down. What did she know that would unlock the files? It must be something Professor Harris would have known she would know.

"Any luck?" asked Cash, joining her as the plane rolled to a stop.

"Not yet, there's a password protecting his files."

"Sophie?"

"Tried."

"Kyle?"

"He'd have said that to you."

"I didn't know who Kyle was then."

Sophie typed it in and hit 'Return'. The password window reappeared, this time with a warning: , 'One attempt remaining'.

"That's not good," Cash commented.

Sophie closed the lid of the laptop and removed the flash drive.

"Don't we need that?" asked Rigs, directing the question quietly to Cash.

"Yes, but it's borrowed. We'll need to buy one here," Sophie said, handing the laptop over to the steward.

"You've not looked out of the window, have you?" asked Cash.

Sophie bent down and looked at a wall of trees. She looked across to the other side, to another wall of trees.

"Where are we?" she asked.

"Nowhere," said Rigs, turning to Cash. "Ask him how much for his laptop,"

The steward shrugged.

"A thousand dollars?" Cash offered.

The steward immediately handed the laptop over.

"Where are we?" Sophie asked Cash.

"Rigs' family's hunting lodge. You can only get here by plane. It really is nowhere. It's not on any maps or charts."

"It's obviously somewhere…"

"Northern Montana, not far from the Canadian border."

A jeep appeared by the plane's steps as they disembarked. The man that exited the jeep was as mountain as they came, with a rugged and haggard face half covered by a graying beard. His face easily said seventy, while his strong, muscular frame and rigid composure spoke of a man at least twenty years younger. Despite the lines, his face glowed, a welcoming warmth and a sparkle lighting his eyes when he caught sight of Rigs. He rushed forward and threw two meaty, powerful arms around Rigs, bellowing, "Master Jake!"

Rigs took a few seconds to recover from the over familiar and unwelcome contact, although he did his best to hide his discomfort.

"Everyone, this is Uncle Bill, he looks after the lodge," Rigs said, his eyes fixed on the ground.

"Just Bill, please," the big man said, beckoning them towards the jeep and clasping another hand fondly on Rigs' shoulder.

"What about the crew?" asked Cash.

Rigs looked back. "I assume they'll head back to the nearest major airport and pick up another charter."

"Where they will most likely see a news channel or newspaper with our faces on it?"

"Ah, good point, we can't let them do that."

"No, we can't."

Chapter 19

Defense Initiative Services
New York

The relentless onslaught of news continued. The scandal was the largest to have ever rocked the nation. Mike Yates hadn't been able to take his eyes off the screen. The latest revelation was that the first lady was also implicated in the plot to kill the President, which of course was beyond ludicrous, but there it was, being reported as though guilt needn't be proved.

It was all rubbish, every piece of it, fabricated rubbish. Travis Davies, his former boss at the CIA and the man who had made him who he was, a traitor? Never! The man bled red, white, and blue and passed gas to the tune of 'The Star Spangled Banner.' The list implicated almost every member of the National Security Council and a number of the individuals Mike had assumed he had been working with for years. If not them, who was he really working for?

He had spent most of the night with a notepad in front of him, going over the operations that he had undertaken over the years and jotting down what he remembered. There were no other records. To deny knowledge of something meant ensuring there was no proof available that you couldn't deny. DIS up until earlier that afternoon had been proudly paper free, even the toilet roll was a paper substitute, an inside joke to emphasize how paper free they were. The extent of their records was a code number attached to a payment. Invoices were sent to anonymous Hotmail accounts and payments received almost exclusively from small offshore private banks. In short, other than what he remembered in his head, there was nothing that tied DIS to anything.

It was perfect and disastrous. Mike looked again at the news screen to another breaking story. The FBI had been formally put in charge of the operation. Another high-level appointee had passed the treason test, noted Mike, turning back to his pad. He tried to connect the dots, assassinations and industrial sabotage across the globe. High-level officials, large multi-nationals, local reporters and small businesses... there was no discernible pattern, and in many cases, no conceivable reason behind the operations that had been ordered.

He had three current operations that stood out from the crowd: Santa Cruz, California; London, England; and Algeciras, Spain. Santa Cruz had piqued his interest. He could see that someone in the government could have conceivably gained from the initial target— the destruction of the most powerful telescope ever launched into space. However, the subsequent fallout from the incriminating evidence they had subsequently planted on Gray's body, with a copy to the press, had done nothing but weaken the nation. And that was not something Mike Yates had ever signed up to do.

London, England. He considered the target and the operation, but it made no sense. He reached for his phone; it was 11:52 p.m. in New York, 4:52 a.m. in London. The operation was only a few hours away, and his people would be getting ready. In his four years at the helm, Mike had always delivered. He had nagging doubts from time to time, but the money had bought his conscience. *No more,* he thought, *not this time.* He grabbed the handset, and it rang in his hand.

"Hello?" he answered, flustered at the coincidence and timing of the call, instantly on alert.

"Mr. Yates," drawled a voice Mike recognized. It was the chairman of the Senate Select Committee on Intelligence and one of the men who had hired Mike.

"Senator, what can I do for you at this hour?"

"A troubling day, Mike, some truly shocking revelations."

"I caught the news, startling and most unbelievable."

"If only," said the Senator.

"They...they're true?" asked Mike, unable to hide his surprise.

"Mike, as you are aware, we're tasked with a role to protect and defend. Sometimes that role takes unexpected and unchartered turns, turns that none of us think will lead to our destination but ultimately and in time even the route that seemed to take us so off course brings us back to exactly where we wanted to be."

Mike had stopped listening and started looking around. The purpose and time of the call was no coincidence. They were aware of his loss of faith, his loss of trust in DIS. They were watching him.

"Senator, I hear what you're saying," said Mike, checking all of the more obvious spots for pinhole cameras.

"Mike, you realize assignments at DIS don't require an explanation or a justification for why they are to be undertaken?"

"Of course, Senator."

"However, in this instance I may waive that for you. I understand this job may seem to have achieved the exact opposite of what you expect us to do."

Mike sat back down. The call had become far more interesting than concerning. "It certainly does seem strange that almost all those in National Security Council are implicated as traitors."

"What I'm about to tell you is not to be repeated," said the Senator sternly.

"Of course not, sir."

"Twenty people in the US were aware of the disarmament pact prior to today's signing."

"They knew it was happening?" asked Mike, shocked.

"It was very well managed," said the Senator. "Of those twenty, one was the President. Of the other nineteen, we know at least two are planning an attempt to stop the treaty, up to and including assassination. We just don't know which two."

"So they arrested them all and branded them all traitors?"

"What would you rather, that we didn't, and the President was assassinated and the nuclear arms race continues as a result?"

"Of course not."

"So, while we uncover the culpable two, we hold the nineteen."

"And the two assassins?"

"Unfortunate timing for them and opportune for the plan, a good conspiracy needs a couple of government assassins."

"There were plenty among the dead you could have implicated."

"Dead assassins don't pose a threat, they don't create tension for the newshounds."

"I recruited those men into the CIA!" said Mike angrily. "They're good men!"

"Good agents too?"

"Excellent, among the very best."

"In which case they'll prove how good they are. I'm sure they'll survive until the warrant for their arrest is lifted."

"With every citizen and law enforcement officer in the land looking for them, I'm not so sure."

"I've read their files," said the Senator. "Trust me, if they lived up to your expectations after you left the agency, they'll put up a good fight," he surmised. "So are we good?"

Mike considered what the Senator, a man responsible for the oversight and full spectrum of the United States intelligence community, had said. If any man in the country was going to be aware of exactly what was going on, it was him.

"Yes, we're good."

"Excellent, now burn that fucking notepad and go home to your family and that multimillion dollar apartment we pay for," he commanded.

Mike replaced the handset slowly. The confirmation that they were watching him was not pleasant. However, that dulled in comparison to the reference to his 'lovely family and multimillion dollar home'. The threat of what had been left unsaid was even more chilling: *'while you still can!'* Mike was their guy; he did what he was told when he was told. He was bought and paid for, as was his family. Mike struck a match and burned both the notepad and his thoughts.

Chapter 20

Burgess Park, Southwark
London, England

Preparations for the event had been underway for weeks, and it was to be a very special event. Southwark, a suburb to the Southeast of London, was one of the more deprived areas of the capital with an unfortunate title. For the previous few years, Southwark had acquired the title of 'Underage Pregnancy Capital of the United Kingdom', a title that no self-respecting borough wished to acquire, let alone retain for years as the undisputed champion. After many years of hard work, programs and centers, such as the spectacular adventure playground at Burgess Park, Southwark had finally shifted the tide and children were once again enjoying being children. Their underage pregnancy rates had plummeted and they had finally lost their unwanted title.

The results that Southwark had achieved were astounding and an example to all other communities. The Prime Minister and the Mayor of London seldom joined forces for such local achievements, but both were keen to promote Southwark's great work, each trying to claim the credit for the turnaround as a result of their policies. However, neither was responsible for the crowds that had been gathering since early that morning. The crowds were there to see the King, Queen and their young children, the prince and princess, who would also be in attendance.

Giles Tremellan was a professional 'former'. He was a former public school boy, a former Oxford University student, a former officer in the British Special Forces, a former Commander of the Metropolitan Police Force and a former Cabinet Minister. It seemed that everything he had ever done had been 'formerly'. At 57, Giles had become a pundit for the news channels, able to cover innumerable subjects, all highlighting the relevant portion of his experience given the subject matter of the day.

With the overwhelming security task of protecting the royals, the PM and the Mayor in one location, one day after the disarmament treaty, Giles was the hottest pundit in London. His expertise in large police security operations and his insight into the Metropolitan Police Force's Protection Command unit, as its former commander, responsible for all government and royal protection details, were invaluable. His ability to comment on the SAS' Special Projects Team, the UK's hardcore answer to the FBI's Hostage Rescue Team, a team he had intimate knowledge of from his days in the SAS, were unique. His ability to intermingle all of this with his understanding of the impact of the disarmament process as a former Defense Minister in the UK government was priceless.

Today, his phone rang endlessly but remained unanswered. For all the reasons he would have made the best pundit, it also made him the ideal head of the DIS team in London, the one role he was not a 'former' of but for which he was very much in the current, although nobody knew about it, except for his small team and Mike Yates, his boss in the US.

He examined the route again. He knew exactly where the SAS team would be stationed. They were his biggest concern. They were ruthless and their training relentless, as good as his men's.

This was a rush job and would have been far easier had it not been for the time restriction set by the speeches. Whatever happened, the job had to be completed prior to the speeches. Whatever was to be said, it wasn't something the client wanted the world to hear. With a vantage point across the road in a fourth four flat overlooking the conference center in the park, Giles checked his watch. They had fifteen minutes before the speeches were scheduled to start.

"Hard drive and all evidence wiped at source," came a radio update from a DIS operative.

"Copy, out," replied Giles, not taking his eyes away from the entourage that was making its way along Albany Road towards the park.

"All clear here," came a reply from a second DIS operative. "No copies at base location."

"Copy, out," replied Giles. He picked out the DIS agents dressed in Metropolitan Police uniforms stationed at the entrance to the park. The entourage was nearing them; it was going to be close, but they needed to know the base location and other copies had been accounted for.

"Takedown is a go, I repeat, takedown is a go," he said hardly hearing himself speak over the roars that erupted as the young royal family came into view. The Prime Minister in the car behind them was virtually ignored while the crowd concentrated on their new King and Queen.

Chapter 21

Archaeological dig site
Algeciras, Spain

Overlooking the rock of Gibraltar, the Spaniards in Algeciras were reminded constantly of the British occupation of a land they had lost over three hundred years earlier. None of that, however, concerned Dr. Pyotr Vilic. He was interested in a time long before the sovereignty of the land was an issue. After twenty years of detailed research into the history of Neanderthals in the area, he was closing in on what he believed would alter the path of history.

His research had taken him across Europe, tracing the spread of the Neanderthals to the point where he believed the last of the Neanderthals had finally existed, some 30,000 years earlier. The previous evening had been the most exciting of his career. The dig had found an underground cave that his seismic readings had pointed to. With light all but gone, they had had no option but to delay further digging until that morning. However, it hadn't stopped him letting the world know he was on the brink of what he believed to be one of the most important finds in human pre-history. He had not disclosed his location but hinted at a Southern European site. Only he and his five assistants knew exactly where the site was to be found and Pyotr intended to keep it that way until after they had entered the cave. From what they were able to see with their torches through the small hole that had been the final breakthrough, it was mind blowing and history altering.

The slow progress since daylight had broken was both frustrating and exhilarating. The painstaking need to preserve all artifacts meant that their access hole grew only marginally by the hour. After five hours of painstaking work, the hole was finally getting to the point where they could slide down and into the cave. From what they could see, the cave would easily allow them to stand up. They just needed to get in there. The paintings on the walls that they had already been able to catch sight of through the slowly growing hole were groundbreaking and far more detailed than anything ever seen before.

***

The private jet touched down at 10:30 a.m. local time at Gibraltar International Airport. Conrad had never been to the small outcrop before and watched as they sped down the runway which seemed to cross a main road. Cars waited behind a barrier, almost like at a railway crossing. He thought it bizarre, although given his operation brief, it was the least bizarre thing he had seen that day.

It had been a long flight, having departed New York the previous night on very short notice. They would have arrived earlier had it not been for Conrad replacing one of the originally scheduled operatives at the last moment. A new recruit to DIS, it was to be Conrad's first operation and despite his new status, he quickly took charge of the operation, delaying takeoff until the arrival of additional equipment that, as soon as they landed was loaded into the rear of their waiting Land Rover.

Conrad motioned for his colleague, Niklas, to drive, before jumping into the passenger seat. Right as they were about to drive off, an officious looking little man appeared by their side.

"I'm sorry, gentlemen, but you need to clear immigration and customs before you can enter the country."

Conrad remained calm and handed over both his and Niklas's passport. Being both originally German, they had both US and German passports. In this instance, they handed over their German EU passports, which allowed them unrestricted access to the European Union.

"Thank you, and if I could check your trunk? I noticed a lot of luggage was loaded into it."

The UK had some of the strictest gun laws in the world, with little tolerance for anything beyond a hunting shotgun for personal use and even then only after thorough checks were carried out. It was therefore with some trepidation that Conrad led the customs official to the rear of the Land Rover and popped the trunk.

The official took one look and stepped back. "What are those?" he asked nervously.

Conrad followed the official's eye to see what he had spotted. Two helmets sat on top of everything in the trunk.

"Ah, they're for our biohazard suits."

"Biohazard as in diseases?"

"Yes, we're medical specialists," said Conrad.

"Fine, you're good to go," said the official, refusing politely to shake Conrad's hand as they parted.

Conrad climbed into the passenger seat and pulled his tablet from his backpack. Dr. Pyotr Vilic's iPhone was beaming his location to them. Their secret dig, owing to a simple hack of Apple's iPhone finder, wasn't so secret anymore.

Conrad directed Niklas out of the city of Gibraltar, around the Bay of Gibraltar, and up into the hills overlooking Algeciras and the bay below. With less than a mile to the highlighted destination, they stopped and donned their suits.

***

Dr. Pyotr Vilic, pulled himself head first through the hole, wishing he had foregone dinner the previous night. He clawed desperately to squeeze through the hole that would have been more suited to a small child. Despite his premature attempt at a proper view, he was nonetheless afforded a spectacular glimpse of the cave. Paintings adorned the walls, spectacularly vibrant colors covering every space, images of a life long lost played out across the stone surface, drawings of families, dwellings, encampments, animals, of tools and birds, a history of Neanderthals in their own pictures that would rewrite the history books. He pulled himself back through the hole. In another hour, the hole would be big enough to get through.

"I'd fit," said Sara, a petite final year doctorate student.

Pyotr was desperate to know what was around the bend in the cave, ten meters beyond their entrance hole, but he was also desperate to be the first to see it. Twenty years of waiting. However, Sara could be in there beaming pictures back to them on their video camera. He could see what was there.

"Alright," he said. "But you have to take the camera and let us see everything as you see it."

Sarah beamed. "Of course." She rushed towards the small entrance hole, donned a safety helmet complete with light, and shimmied through. Pyotr noted she could probably have been through it an hour earlier such was her slightness of build.

Sara pulled herself up on the other side of the hole and waited for the video camera to be handed to her. A lead led back to a screen that would let her colleagues see what she was seeing and a powerful light above the camera would also help light her way.

Sara worked her way along the wall of the cave that Pyotr had seen, capturing the storyboard as it played out. A tranquil image of a way of life that had been the Neanderthals', before their extinction. Small hunter gatherer communities that seemed to live peacefully. When Sara approached the bend, the images took on a slightly more sinister tone, some basic weapons began to enter into the drawings along with images of battles. Two distinct beings were shown.

Pyotr was astounded, images of battles between what looked like Neanderthal and Homo sapiens— modern man— were played out in the drawings. Nothing like it had ever been seen before.

"What is that?" asked one of his assistants. "Go left, Sara!" he shouted, having caught something in the corner of the screen.

Sara swept the camera around, images flashing past wildly, and shone the light onto the left hand side of the cave.

"What was that?" Pyotr said, catching a glimpse of one of the images during the sweep. "Was that some kind of bird swooping down?"

"With fire spilling out its tail?" said another assistant, having noticed the same image.

"Sara, go back!" they shouted, but then Sara's light fell on the full scale of the cave and the hundreds, if not thousands, of skeletons that filled it.

"Oh my God…" said Pyotr in wonder. All eyes of the group were utterly transfixed to the small screen. So much so, that they had not noticed the arrival of Conrad and his colleague dressed in full biohazard suits.

Sara scanned the camera across the cave, easily two hundred feet wide and twice as deep. Skeletons littered over half of the floor area, while the other half was filled with tools and weapons never before seen. Everything had been pristinely preserved. It was the find of the century, if not millennia Pyotr thought triumphantly which, as a last thought, was not an entirely bad way to go.

Conrad and his colleague wasted no time. By the time the research assistants were aware they were under attack, they were already falling to the ground, with two bullets in each of their heads.

The images on the screen beamed back blissfully unaware of the carnage outside. Sara scanned back and forth, capturing the final drawings, a massacre drawn to tell of a historic battle, the only witness to a catastrophic moment in the extinction of an entire species. If they had had time to analyze the drawings, they would have made the most startling discovery. The Neanderthals had been the victors in nearly every battle, stronger and more intelligent than their homo sapien rivals. It was exactly as evolution had predicted, the survival of the fittest.

"Why are we wearing these stupid suits?" asked Conrad's colleague.

"To protect us from what's down there," said Conrad.

"Skeletons and drawings according to those pictures," he said, moving to remove his helmet. The heat was almost unbearable in the midday sunshine.

"Don't!" shouted Conrad but too late. Niklas removed it and gulped in the fresh air.

Conrad shook his head and instructed him to help deposit the bodies into the cave. They had no concern for artifacts, and enlarged the hole in minutes to ease the depositing of bodies into the cave.

The noise, not unexpectedly, alerted Sara and she scurried towards them, receiving two bullets for her curiosity. Conrad walked along to the main section of the cave and gasped at the scale of what lay before him. The skeletons were neatly stacked, apart from the last few. They had obviously died last. The last images depicted a sick and dying people, imprisoned in a cave.

"What is that?" asked Niklas, dragging Pyotr's body into the main section and seeing the bird with fire tails swooping down.

"That is the moment that Neanderthals were wiped off the face of the planet," replied Conrad.

"Seriously?"

"Yes."

"So what does the bird mean?" asked Niklas.

"Mean?"

"What does it symbolize? It looks like it's breathing down onto the people."

"It doesn't symbolize anything, it's as it is, a disease being delivered to wipe out the Neanderthals."

Niklas looked around at the hundreds of skeletons lined behind them. "So they were all killed by the same disease?"

"Yes, they were the last of their kind. Killed by a disease so deadly it will live on in their bones," said Conrad, raising his pistol to the back of Niklas' head.

"How do you know all this?" asked Niklas suddenly aware of how much Conrad appeared to know that had nothing to do with the images on the wall.

"Because," said Conrad to Niklas' falling corpse, "my ancestors were the ones who wiped them out and left them in this cave."

Conrad gathered up all the communications equipment and set charges at the mouth of the cave to ensure its secret stayed safe for another 30,000 years. He deposited all of the team's communications products across Algeciras on the drive back to the airport in Gibraltar. If anyone tracked their last known location, they would not uncover the dig site. With all of his tracks covered, Conrad boarded the waiting private jet.

"Mr. Noble!" shouted the officious customs officer.

Conrad Noble turned to face him at the top of the steps, etching a strained smile on his face. "Yes?"

"Was everything okay? Have we got anything to worry about?"

"No, everything's fine," he said dismissively.

Conrad Noble was in the air within minutes, jumping the queue of waiting aircraft. He was head of the Atlas Noble

Security division, ultimate owner and only client of the Defense
Initiative Services.

MISSION LOG – EXTRACT 5-14

Deep Space Mission – Last Hope
Log entry 14
Mission Commander

We have slowed and taken up a low orbit around our new home. It is beautiful, with oceans and lands as blue and green as our own. Of the hundreds of billions of galaxies and possibilities our scientists scanned, I truly believe they could not have picked a more perfect new home.

I hope this communication is received, as I am pleased to say that the previous missions have been successful. I repeat, they have been successful. Although we are not able to communicate with our people on the ground, we can see numerous messages laid out across the surface of the planet.

The planet is viable and is, according to the messages we are able to decipher, a perfect solution to our dying home. From what we have been able to understand, the polarity of the planet is responsible for the inability of our communications systems to work once we break through into the atmosphere. It would also suggest the reason no ship has returned, our engines are similarly affected and as a result, the main engines will not have the power to allow us to leave once we land.

We were all aware before we left this was a one way journey, but at least we know it is not in vain. We have a future. Our people will live on.

This may well be the last communication that you receive; we will try once we land as directed by the messages below. If it is, I promise we will be waiting with a warm welcome when you come.

Alain Noble, Mission Commander, Last Hope

Chapter 22

Geneva, Switzerland

Antoine Noble turned away from the mission logs and stared absently across the lake. Whenever he needed the motivation for what needed to be done, no matter how difficult, he found the strength within the logs. Antoine had many houses around the world but after his momentous trip to the UN, there was only one he wanted to visit. Geneva was where he felt most at home. His happiest childhood memories were all forged within the confines of the palatial home, one of the oldest and most magnificent homes to honor the shores of the lake of a city that predated the birth of Christianity.

The secret his family held was known to only a handful of people. The implications on the future direction of the planet, were the truth to be known, would be catastrophic for the plans his family had put in place to save the population. A plan that had been in preparation for more years than even Antoine was aware. His first knowledge of the truth was handed to him on his twenty-first birthday, when his father took him into the confidence of a secret only the Nobles knew about and even then, only a select few at the top echelons of the Atlas Noble empire were fully aware. Antoine would soon be having that same conversation with his own son, although for his son the timescale was all the more pressing. He was destined to live a very different future from Antoine and the Nobles before him who had strived to ensure their children had a future.

Antoine walked across his study to a wall of books that would have been a prized possession of any of the world's great libraries. First editions of some of the most notable works ever to have been published adorned the shelves that stretched the length of the wall and twelve feet to the ceiling. Many visitors to his inner sanctum had noted how priceless the collection was.

Antoine would smile in appreciation, it was nothing compared to what lay behind.

As a child, he had known of the secret doorway. His father had done little to hide it, nor did Antoine. His son likewise was fully aware of the section that would swing open. It was no secret, as the door went nowhere. Behind it stood a wall of metal; no dials or knobs adorned it; it just stood there for no apparent reason. Alex had asked many times what the point of a secret door to nowhere was, as Antoine had asked of his father. Like his father before him, Antoine had simply smiled and promised one day he would know.

Antoine pulled open the not so secret door and pressed the ring his father had bestowed upon him over thirty years before against the metal wall. The wall slid away and allowed Antoine entry to the lift behind. He stepped in and on pressing the panel to his right, closed the metal wall and began the journey to the depths of the Noble family vault, buried deep in the Swiss bedrock, one of the most stable areas in the world. Antoine's mood instantly improved when the elevator arrived at the vault floor. The history of the Noble family's achievements stretched out before him, the vast chamber stretching deep into the distance.

"Antoine?" a voice called out to his left.

"Anya," he smiled, greeting his sister with a kiss.

"Congratulations on the treaty," she said.

"Thanks, at least when the news breaks and we can't hide what's inevitable any longer, nobody can do anything stupid," he said, all the while taking in the view around him.

She shook her head. "You know I disagree with you. I don't think anyone is that stupid." She led the way into the depths of the chamber.

"You've spent your life in a very different world to mine. I deal with these people day in day out, and if there's one thing I can guarantee, when their backs are to the wall and they think they're going to lose control, they'll do anything to show how powerful they are. And don't forget," he added, "it was you that told me that the electromagnetic pulse generated by nuclear weapons, if anyone did use them, would destroy everything you had achieved."

Anya nodded. "Yes, but I didn't say it *would* happen, I was replying to your question if there were any potential risks to our work."

"Even the slightest risks have to be managed. Nothing can interfere with what we're doing, our future and the entire population's future rest on it."

"Hubble 2," Anya said, her tone changing to one of disapproval.

"You yourself warned me of its capabilities and you were correct."

"Not that we'll ever know."

"We do and it did."

"It worked?" she asked in surprise. "But it had only just been launched, how can we know for sure?"

"Because they knew exactly where to look," Antoine crowed.

"They did?"

"Professor Charles Harris, it seems ,worked out where to look."

"Charles did?" she asked, surprised.

"Seems his interest in ancient ruins paid off. An interest, if I remember, he picked up from you."

Anya turned her attention to a computer screen. "Well if he knew exactly where to look, he didn't need Hubble 2."

"He didn't?"

"Not at all," she said starting to walk again, with Antoine hanging on her every word. "Given current technologies, as we near the date of convergence, everything becomes clearer, although it is at the limits of what's currently available but if you know where to look..."

"So if somebody finds his research?"

"Yes, they could uncover the truth before we want them to. It's a shame Charles had to die for the sake of three weeks." Her tone and words were as close to a complaint as she would ever dare make to her older brother and head of the Noble household. His authority was never questioned and never challenged.

Both remained silent as they continued to walk through the chamber filled with antiquities and treasures, each categorized and sub-categorized by date, period and significance. Books, scrolls, tapestries, tablets, the further they walked the older the works became, the first printed book, the first Koran, the first Bible, the first Torah, each step took them back in time. Vases and works of art from the Romans blended into those from the Greeks, the Egyptians and finally the Sumerians. They had reached the end of the chamber, hundreds of thousands of square feet of works that documented and heralded the progression of the human race back to its very beginning, the dawn of civilization.

Anya opened the vault door they had reached at the far end of the chamber and the dawn of civilization. A small sub-chamber appeared with another vault door at the far end. Only once one vault door shut would the other open. The main chamber was strictly controlled from both an atmosphere and security perspective. Constant humidity and temperature were strictly maintained to protect the works. Once the main vault door was closed, Anya opened the second to reveal a corridor that led to a clinical scientific lab, bustling with activity. The Atlas Noble company logo adorned the walls. A wall of glass that stretched the length of the lab, some one hundred feet, had a view of a metal tube approximately three feet in diameter within a tunnel five hundred feet below ground level. The tunnel stretched off into the distance either side of where the glass wall ended, circling for a total of 27km, almost 17 miles. The Large Hadron Collider, the world's most powerful particle accelerator, lay before them, widely heralded as one of the great engineering milestones of mankind.

Its purpose, publicly, was to further investigate theories and principles of physics, advancing the understanding of physics and through it, the make-up and origins of the universe. The scale of the project was massive, with requirements that dwarfed the capabilities of any one country, but thanks to Atlas Noble bringing together over one hundred countries and thousands of companies, the accelerator had been completed. It had been Atlas Noble's single largest ever investment and a personal mission of Antoine.

Antoine looked away from the most advanced piece of human engineering to the other wall, where the schematics and plans for the accelerator were displayed. Not the ones that had been given to the scientists who had subsequently built the accelerator but the originals. Antoine looked at the stone tablets that pre-dated human civilization, ones that his ancestors had rescued from the depths of the great pyramids in Egypt thousands of years earlier, stored for a time when technology could create the device the tablets described in great detail.

"Magnificent," said Antoine, not taking his eyes away from the tablets.

"Truly," agreed Anya, her eyes transfixed on the accelerator. Although to the outside world, her title was Head of Archives, her background was as a physicist, which, given the project underway, could not have been more appropriate.

"How far away are we?" asked Antoine excitedly.

"Hours, days, weeks at most."

"But before the convergence begins?" he asked excitedly.

"Yes."

Chapter 23

Miller Lodge
Montana, USA

Sophie had hardly slept all night. Right now she was staring at the small box that was blocking her access to Professor Harris' research. *'One attempt remaining'* was burned into the back of her retinas. Even closing her eyes was failing to release her from the torment..

"Couldn't sleep?" asked Cash, stretching as he joined her in the kitchen.

"Not well," she said, rubbing at her eyes.

"I'm so sorry about yesterday," he said somberly. He'd slept poorly as well, after a night spent reflecting on their losses.

Sophie nodded and stared out at the lake that appeared to lap at the window's edge. The view down the length of the lake was nothing short of awe inspiring.

"He would have loved it here. God, they both would," she said, smiling. "Look out there, nothing but the wonder of nature."

Cash nodded, he knew exactly where she was going. "Not a single unnatural light source to spoil his view."

"Zero light pollution, the perfect night sky," she smiled.

"Any luck?" asked Cash, turning their attention away from memories and back to business.

"I'm scared I'll lose it forever if I put the wrong password in."

"Will it not go into a timeout and let you try again after a few hours?"

"Maybe, but do you want to take that risk?"

Cash shook his head. "So you've tried 'Sophie' after what my dad said to me, and we tried Kyle."

"Oh my God!" she said. "I can't believe it!"

"What?"

"We never tried you?"

"But my dad said your name when he gave it to me."

"Yes, but what if that's nothing to do with the password and more to do with understanding what's in here?"

"Like, 'you're too stupid son, get Sophie, she'll tell you what this all means'?"

"Well, in a more subtle way, yes."

"So go for it," said Cash.

"You sure?"

"Copernicus. He loved it as much as I hated it!"

Sophie typed the letters in carefully, the "**********" that appeared in the box wasn't overly helpful in letting her know if she had typed the name correctly. She hesitated for a moment, then hit enter.

The password box disappeared and everything else remained the same, the two black circles and their dots remained.

"Oh well," said Cash, pouring coffees for them. "We had to give it a try."

Sophie took the coffee but suddenly noticed there *was* a change. At the very base of the image, some words had appeared. The font was tiny, so she zoomed in.

"The answers you seek, lay around us in our past." Anya.

"What does that mean and who's Anya?" asked Cash.

"No idea, it's not a quote I recognize," said Sophie. "But I'm certain it wasn't there before."

"Anything else changed?"

Sophie zoomed back out and moved the cursor around the screen, the arrow changing from arrow to pointing index finger as it moved across the dots.

"The dots have become links!" she said excitedly, clicking on the central dot on the left hand circle.

Cash rushed over. Sophie clicked the link. The page turned to text, the heading PUMAPUNKA – BOLIVIA popped up with a few bullet points preceding a selection of images and blocks and blocks of text. Cash scanned down the bullets; they simply summarized where and what the site was. The images highlighted a number of the features that made the site so unique. The blocks of text appeared to be detailed notes of what his father had found, although he could only guess. The detail was technical and exactly why his father would have suggested Sophie's assistance.

"How's it going?' asked Rigs yawning as he entered the kitchen, not seeing Sophie buried behind the laptop's screen.

"We just got in," replied Cash.

"Shush!" said Sophie, embroiled in the Professor's notes.

Cash stood and gestured for Rigs to join him on the other side of the kitchen.

"We cracked the password and it's allowed us to click on the dots," whispered Cash. "As expected, they're locations, and from what I could gather, each has very detailed notes about the work my father carried out. Although it's all very technical, he's talking about angles from the horizon, angles between buildings, blocks and how distances and ratios relate to constellations."

Rigs barely whispered, conscious of Sophie's presence across the kitchen, "Where's she looking?"

"Some place called Pumapunka in Bolivia."

"Puma, what?"

"It's ancient, thousands of years old, but according to my father's summary, we'd struggle to build it today. It's incredibly complex and some of the stones used are massive."

Rigs looked over to where Sophie was plowing through the research. "Seriously?"

"Yeah, some over one hundred tons, transported over ten miles, and laid in places that are 13,000 feet up. Some of them are cut so that they'd perfectly interconnect to form walls without any cement or mortar. There are some example images, huge H shaped blocks, that are identical and look like building blocks. It's crazy, the stuff's so precise, you don't even see it today!"

"Thousands of years ago?" Rigs asked in disbelief, glancing at the laptop.

Cash nodded. "Yep, you'll see when Sophie's finished."

"How does any of this help with finding who killed your father?"

"Who knows? It might not even help at all, but my father was keen for me to see it. His dying word was for the sole purpose to help me understand what's on it."

"Guys," interrupted Sophie, "there are very detailed research notes here but there's a problem…"

"What?" asked Cash.

"His findings. He's mapped the site, Pumapunka, along with a place nearby called Tiwanaku and between them, following clues left thousands of years ago, discovered what they were trying to tell us."

"Maybe he didn't finish it."

"He did, only he didn't record the answer in the file."

"So where is it?"

"His head."

"That's not very helpful," Rigs whispered.

"So this is all useless?" said Cash dejectedly.

"Well, no. I understand his notes, which are pretty much unintelligible to anyone else."

"I noticed," said Cash wryly.

"I worked a couple of summers as his research assistant, he taught me his unique shorthand."

"So what? She can work out the answers?" asked Rigs, leaning in towards Cash. "She can, but not from here," replied Sophie pointedly. Noting the look on Cash's face, she backed off. "Sorry, long night," she apologized. "I know what he did there, I can replicate that and find the answers he found."

"You need us to go to Bolivia," said Cash suddenly understanding the implications.

"Yes," said Sophie.

"Just as well we kept that plane and flight crew then."

Chapter 24

The noise carried like a wave, cascading towards the entrance of the park, carrying its royal guests in a public outpouring of love and appreciation. The ring of security awaited their arrival at the park gates where the public crowds gave way to the select few, the invited guests, and the obligatory press pack. The event had amassed a far larger press turnout than the Children's Services Department could ever have dreamed possible. What was to have been a small local event with a national appeal had become an international event. Having said that, the main questions to be thrown at the Prime Minister after his speech were unlikely to relate to teenage pregnancy rates and far more likely to relate to disarmament and the US President.

Yvonne Winston looked at the list of speakers, the King, the Mayor, herself and then the Prime Minister. She hadn't slept all night. She had been born to a young teenage mother, victim of a gang rape in South London. Abandoned at birth by her young mother, she had been raised by her grandparents. Despite this, Yvonne had studied hard and overcome the stigma of being a rape child, had recently graduated from university, and joined Children's Services to help her community. She was to be the spokesperson for the community, telling her personal journey to the world while she promised the young girls in the area a far brighter future, thanks to the fantastic programs being run in Southwark. The statistics she had uncovered the previous day while writing her piece were, she was sure, going to be the talking point of the event and she felt certain, even given the previous day's events, worthy of the front pages. She had wanted to run through the changes with her boss but he had been flapping around like a wild man since she had arrived. He was just going to have to hear them along with everyone else.

The noise of the crowds outside reached a crescendo, indicating that the royals had arrived. Yvonne began to shake. She was only a few minutes away from delivering her speech. A sudden need to visit the restroom rushed over her. She had a couple of minutes before the entourage would enter. A line of dignitaries waited to greet them outside.

Yvonne looked down the greeting line in the conference hall. Everyone looked as nervous as she felt and they weren't even speaking. The back end of the hall was filled with press, while the front few rows sat empty. The dignitaries and other members of the Children's Services team would fill them once the visiting entourage had entered. Police officers lined the walls and covered every exit. The security had been excruciating, taking hours to be allowed into the inner sanctum of the conference hall, even given the fact she was one of the only few speakers.

Her need was pressing. She knew it was nerves but had to give in.

"Bob, I'm nipping to the loo," she said. "I'll be right back."

"Hurry," he said.

Yvonne scurried across the hall to the rest room, a female police officer following her all the way. Almost exactly as she closed the restroom door, the conference hall's main door opened and the King and Queen entered, greeting the hardworking council workers as they worked their way down the hall towards the stage.

Bob looked frantically for Yvonne. As the King edged nearer and nearer, the gaping hole left by Yvonne's absence in the line was evident for all to see. The King came and went along with the Queen, their children, the Prime Minister and the Mayor. Bob took his seat, looking around to the restroom door. The police officer who had followed her had not come out either.

He needed to check on Yvonne. Bob stood up. At the same moment, the King stood up to rapturous applause and stopped Bob in his tracks. He couldn't walk across the front of the stage while the King was speaking.

A short introduction and congratulatory speech was followed by an even more congratulatory speech from the Mayor. Bob looked around frantically and was pleased to see the restroom door open when Yvonne's name was introduced by the Mayor.

"Where is she?" asked the Children's Services' boss, tapping Bob's shoulder and turning his attention away from the restroom door as Yvonne was about to exit.

"A case of nerves, she was in the loo," he said sympathetically. "She's coming." When he turned back around, he saw no one walking towards the stage. He looked back at the restroom, the door was closed.

***

Yvonne had just made it. She checked her watch and could hear the buzz in the hall as the entourage entered. She should have been in the line but there was no way she was going to make it back in time. Sometimes, nature took over.

"Are you Yvonne Winston?" asked the police officer who had followed her in.

"Yes," said Yvonne. She flushed the toilet and heard the officer speaking to someone over the radio.

"I believe you're up soon," said the officer calmly.

"Thanks, a bit of nerves," explained Yvonne.

"I'm not surprised," replied the officer. "I couldn't do it in front of that audience. They're asking if you've got any slides you want to display?"

"No, no slides," said Yvonne nervously, the pressure building.

"They're saying they've got autocue if you want to give them the text."

"It's handwritten I'm afraid," she said opening the door, holding up her notes for the officer to see.

"It's just handwritten notes," radioed the officer, smiling warmly to the nervous Yvonne.

Yvonne made for the door but the officer instructed her to wait, listening to the small speaker in her ear.

"We're going to wait for the Mayor to finish, they don't want you to cut in front of the cameras."

It had been over ten minutes since Giles Tremellan had given the DIS team inside the conference center the 'go'. Still nothing had happened.

"What's happening in there?" he asked. They were getting down to the wire, the speeches had started.

"We're unable to ensure whether all data has been secured on site," replied one of the agents quietly from the conference hall.

"Confirm it and make it happen. You're running out of time, the window is closing," he said urgently.

"It's just handwritten notes," was the next message Giles heard.

Giles didn't hesitate. "Make sure you get them and then we are a go, I repeat go, once notes are in hand."

***

"So that's your speech?" asked the officer, stepping towards Yvonne. "Anything juicy?" she asked, reaching out.

Yvonne reluctantly let them go. When police officers asked for something, people reacted in two ways, trusting or not. Yvonne had been brought up, despite her background and black heritage, to trust the police.

"I have them in hand," said the officer into her mic.

Yvonne hadn't even felt the long stiletto blade enter her left side. It was only as the officer withdrew the thin blade and she felt the wetness that Yvonne realized she was in trouble. Her ability to scream was already disabled, the stiletto had entered her throat almost immediately, killing any sounds from her, other than a wheeze as her body gasped for air.

The officer stepped back, placed the notes inside her stab proof vest and exited the restroom. Yvonne Winston was already dead, her mind just hadn't quite cottoned onto the fact as her eyes searched desperately for help.

"Exiting now," advised the female officer and member of the DIS team. "Mission complete."

Giles Tremellan saw his officer cross the street towards his building as chaos broke out below. The Special Protection teams kicked into action, cars screeched into the grounds and the royals, followed by the Prime Minister, were rushed away at speed from the scene of a murder and major breach of security. The Mayor was last out, his security team looking desperately for a car for him to escape in. None was available. It was at times like that, that you discovered your true worth, thought Giles with a wry smile.

"Piece of cake," said the female DIS agent, handing over the notes and stripping out of the Metropolitan Police Force uniform they had procured for the operation.

Giles scanned down the notes. Something in them had required the young black woman's death. He had read up on her. She was a rising star with a very bright future. Politics and cabinet for sure, if not the first black Prime Minister. Whatever she had uncovered had put an end to all of that.

Giles scanned down the pages. Her history was tragic. Her mother, raped at 13, gave birth to her at 14 and after abandoning her child had died at the age of 18 in a drug den. The programs that had warranted such acclaim and delivered the results for the borough were nothing short of common sense. The statistics of underage births were surprising, particularly as he was unaware that girls as young as ten and eleven were included in them. He was pleased to see that the handful of pregnancies across the UK each year amongst the 12s and under had been eradicated completely in the previous two years. Again, nothing earth shattering, so he read on. The statistics for the under 12s was the same across Europe where the handful had been a few hundred and across the world, where it had been a few thousand each year. Giles stopped reading, withdrew his lighter and set the papers alight. He didn't need to read any further.

No one under the age of 12 had become pregnant anywhere on the planet in the previous two years. Giles wasn't a statistician but he wasn't stupid either, that was not a chance coincidence, that was by design.

Chapter 25

Cash asked whether Sophie minded if he told Kyle that they were going to leave him with his grandmother and Uncle Bill at the lodge while they flew to Bolivia. As with almost every growing teenager, the fight to get them into bed was only beaten by the fight to get them out of it. Kyle grunted a 'yeah fine' and promised to take care of his grandmother. Cash left a note by his bedside to remind Kyle of the conversation he felt sure had gone in one ear and straight out of the other.

"Ready?" asked Cash when he arrived back at the entrance door to meet Rigs, Sophie, and the recently roused flight crew.

Sophie gave him a look. She knew all too well how good her son was in the morning.

"I left a note," said Cash. "And they're far safer here anyway."

"Safer?" queried the captain.

"Figure of speech," Cash said, quickly bending and zipping the satchel of weapons that Rigs had laid out by the door before the crew caught sight of what was inside.

"Pile in," said Uncle Bill, directing them to the jeep for the short drive down to the airfield.

"Are you not worried the authorities will check?" Sophie asked, stopping Cash and Rigs in their tracks, aware of the implications of the fugitive status of her travel partners.

"Off the grid," said Rigs. "My dad's a bit of a prepper too."

Cash smiled. Rigs was becoming comfortable speaking around Sophie. Normally that breakthrough took far longer.

"And the paperwork trail for the aircraft charter?" asked Sophie.

"Through a trust that has no ties to my family; it's clean," said Rigs. He hoisted the weapons bag into the trunk with a metallic clatter. Sophie glanced furtively at the flight crew. "Be careful with my instruments," she said.

"Sorry," said Rigs, under the gaze of the flight crew, closing the lid shut.

"The crew are going to see our faces somewhere," Sophie whispered to Cash, walking around the jeep.

"There's no internet, TV or cell coverage here," Cash replied quietly, "so the most they've done is use the landline to call their families. Next stop is Bolivia. I doubt we'll be top of the news there."

"And after there?"

"One problem at a time," said Cash. He opened the door for Sophie to climb into the front of the jeep.

"Bolivia," said the pilot referring to a small handheld device. "El Alto airport is the nearest airport to El Paz."

"What's that?" asked Cash when he realized the pilot had some type of tablet in his hand and worried he might be connected to something.

"A flight planner," said the pilot, not picking up on Cash's concern.

"Very cool," said Cash, straining to see the screen. The pilot turned it around for him to see. *'Garmin aera 796'*, Cash read from the plastic above the screen that showed the details for El Alto airport.

"So you can't get anything else on it?"

"Don't think so, although perhaps if you pay extra," he pondered.

Cash, Rigs and Sophie relaxed again.

Boarding the aircraft a few minutes later, Bill became refueler as he helped prep the plane for takeoff. Bolivia was within reach to complete the journey non-stop.

"Your trust fund must be taking a hammering," Cash remarked, soaking in the opulence of the Global 6000 again.

Rigs shrugged. "Can't take it with you." He held his champagne glass aloft for a refill, in a diva-esque fashion, very un-Rigs-like, much to Cash and Sophie's amusement.

With a champagne glass by her side, Sophie buried herself in the laptop. She wanted to know exactly what they needed to do when they landed. Rigs, set his seat back for more sleep. Cash also pushed his seat back, with every intention of doing the same, but it stopped halfway. The steward rushed across to assist, pulling out files from beneath the mechanism of Cash's chair.

"Do you need these, sir?" asked the steward, bundling the files together.

Cash was about to say no, then he remembered the files held the evidence that implicated them. Proving that evidence wrong was as key to understanding everything else.

Cash set his chair back to the upright position and joined Sophie in the hunt for clues, only his were slightly more current and didn't require a doctorate in Astrophysics. At least he hoped they didn't.

Chapter 26

Antoine exited the elevator on the sixth floor of the Atlas Noble headquarter building and hugged his cousin, Conrad, who awaited him. The view from the top floor boardroom stretched out across Lake Geneva.

"Our ancestors' secret is safe for another thirty thousand years," joked Conrad, taking the seat across from Antoine.

"I'm delighted you handled it personally," said Antoine. "I believe it could have been rather explosive."

"From what I saw, let's just say it would have raised a lot of questions."

"Questions we're in no position to answer right now. Soon enough, when we can't hide what's coming, we can explain. Until then, it's imperative that the secret remains guarded."

"Of course, although if you don't mind me saying," said Conrad cautiously, offering Antoine the deference to which he was entitled, "the actions in America do seem a little extreme and may well raise more questions than we'd like."

"Extreme but perfectly thought out," said Antoine. He selected the C-SPAN feed on a monitor. The President was on screen entering the Senate Chamber.

"You'll have missed it due to your flight but he's already had Congress ratify the disarmament treaty. He only needs the senate and it's a done deal."

"Without any hassle?" asked Conrad. He'd thought the ratification might have taken weeks.

"No hassle at all. The plan worked perfectly. Nobody dares speak out against the treaty for fear of being labeled a traitor with the conspirators."

Conrad nodded his head in appreciation. "And there's hardly a mention of the Hubble 2's demise."

"The President will receive overwhelming approval. There'll be a few diehards who'll vote against but not enough to cause a problem."

"Genius," said Conrad.

"Not all down to me," said Antoine. "Thank Bertie, it was his quick thinking and effort that put the pack together for your DIS guys to deliver."

Conrad looked up at the screen. Senator Bertie Noble had taken the podium to introduce the President before his speech. As Chairman of the Senate Select Committee on Intelligence, Senator Noble was one of the most powerful members of the Senate and thanks to his family, certainly its wealthiest. The Noble family had infiltrated many of the world's democracies, none more so than the US'. With two senators, seven congressmen and three sitting governors, they were the political elite in the US and the largest political contributor in most elections across the nation. However, they did this under so many different guises that only those who were the ultimate recipients ever really knew who had bought their loyalty.

"He's one shrewd old bastard," said Conrad, admiring their uncle.

"He is that," agreed Antoine. "All the other parliaments and governments are holding special sessions as we speak, to ratify the treaty and make it happen."

"Unbelievable! In less than twenty four hours, signed, sealed and ratified."

"And all thanks to Uncle Bertie," said Antoine. "Although, the pack of evidence he put together quickly was remarkably well prepared."

"Nothing to do with me or DIS," said Conrad.

"Which is somewhat concerning," said Antoine, thinking out loud. "My father always told me be careful of Bertie, his ambition always outstripped his position."

"He's not said anything to me," said Conrad.

"It's probably nothing, ignore me," said Antoine. "He delivered what we needed, let's not forget that."

"But just a tiny speck in the ocean of what's still to be done," said Conrad.

The disarmament treaty was important and would reduce future risk of interference but, as Conrad mentioned, it was only a small part of a very large plan, of which only Antoine was fully aware. The task that had befallen the Noble house was a task entrusted to them and them alone. Their doctrine forbade them from ever sharing their knowledge and ensured that every cent they earned was devoted to the task. The population's future rested in their hands alone. To date, they had kept to the doctrine, as had the countless generations before them. Even though the first transports would be required to begin their journeys shortly, the knowledge of what was to come was too devastating for the masses to ever fully comprehend.

"So how can I be of assistance?" asked Conrad turning the focus back to why Antoine had summoned him.

"We may have an unexpected problem," he said. "Anya has informed me that with the correct information, Hubble 2 is not required. Current technology, given the exact co-ordinates of where to look…"

"But that problem has been resolved!" said Conrad. Security was his responsibility and within that, DIS.

"The son escaped your grasp."

"And is being hunted as public enemy number one."

"That may be but he was there when his father died, a man who had worked out exactly where to look."

"Thanks, Anya," blurted Conrad, knowing of his cousin's friendship during her university years with Charles Harris.

Antoine's look of displeasure at Conrad's criticism of his sister, however warranted, was very clear for Conrad to see.

"I apologize, it was not my place," he said obsequiously.

"However, we are where we are," said Antoine sternly. "And it's your job to rectify it. Let's not forget, the son slipped through your team's hands!"

"I'll get right on it," said Conrad rising to leave, the mood in the room having dropped significantly.

"Obviously, the last thing we need is Cash Harris in the US government's hands. God knows what they'd uncover before we want them to," warned Antoine. "I've also made Bertie aware of the problem, he'll assist you as much as he can."

Conrad nodded and left the room, wondering exactly what he was supposed to do. He had a few hundred operatives scattered across the United States, whilst they had millions of law officers and every citizen in the land looking for him.

"Bea," said Conrad, greeting his cousin as he exited the boardroom. Beatrice Noble headed Atlas Noble's pharmaceutical and medical division.

"Conrad," she said warmly, standing to hug her cousin. "Good mood?" she nodded towards the boardroom and Antoine.

"Sorry, he *was*," he said sheepishly.

"Wonderful," she said, raising her eyebrows before hearing her name being shouted out by Antoine from behind the door.

Antoine's secretary looked over apologetically. "I think he's ready," she said politely.

"Antoine," she said, entering the room.

Antoine waved towards the seat opposite him, not taking his eyes off the report in front of him.

Bea sat and waited patiently. Antoine finally raised his head, his mood having improved. Whatever was in the report had cheered him up.

"It worked," he said pushing the report away.

"Yes," she said proudly.

"Down to that level."

"And beyond if required."

"Beyond? How so?"

"Well, say for example you wanted to exclude a particular eye color from a particular race, or hair color or any number of physical traits, we can do it."

"Fantastic. Can we do above a certain age?"

"I don't see why not. Do you have the final numbers?" she asked.

"Not yet, but obviously seven billion is a number that doesn't work. Even with an eighty year window."

"Don't forget the birth control initiative will significantly hamper the birth rate in future."

"But there are still only about 56 million dying each year. Even with no births that still leaves 2.5 billion and that's too many, even with no births at all."

"So you want to start more radical controls?"

"We should at least conduct trials on them. I'd like to know what we can do if need be."

"Of course. Any thoughts on size of the trial?"

"Nothing too dramatic. We still want to keep things low key," said Antoine.. "Say between a quarter to a half million?"

Bea opened a file on her tablet and scanned down a list. She stopped a third of the way down. "Got it. I'll get the virus coded and we'll start delivering tomorrow."

Chapter 27

FBI Headquarters
Pennsylvania Avenue
Washington D.C.

Despite their police outriders, Secret Service Director Paula Suarez and Attorney General Lynn Bertram could not get near the FBI Headquarters building. Crowds had gathered overnight and swelled during the morning as the news of the treasonous plot spread. The outrage felt by most Americans at the attempt to assassinate the President in order to derail the disarmament process was palpable.

"Do we dare walk through that?" asked Lynne.

Paula Suarez had risen through the ranks of the Secret Service and was more than capable of looking after herself but even she was not sure. The crowd was vying for blood and all but ready to lynch any of the plotters should they have the misfortune to venture within their grasp.

Before they made a decision, another procession of vehicles approached. It was a military entourage with no intention of allowing the protestors to block their way. The vehicles careened towards the crowd, horns blaring. Unsurprisingly, the crowd parted and the vehicles swept through into the underground car park entrance.

"Follow on," Paula said to her driver, who was able to squeeze through before the crowd moved back behind the insistent convoy.

The military vehicles drew to a stop at the elevators, allowing their occupants to disgorge. From the five vehicles— four Humvees and one limousine— only two men exited: a man in full dress uniform and another man who Lynne recognized as the imposing figure of Senator Bertie Noble, Chairman of the Senate Select Committee on Intelligence.

Both she and Paula rushed to catch up with the two men.

"Senator Noble," said Lynne warmly. He was a man you made a point of keeping on your side.

"Ah, Lynne my dear," he boomed, bending down and kissing her on the cheek. "And the delightful Miss Suarez," he added, offering Paula the same courtesy. "This is Colonel Steve Andrews, US Air Force. He's attached to the Special Operations Command."

Both Lynne and Paula nodded in greeting to the uniformed man.

"Are you here for the handover?" asked Senator Noble.

"Thankfully!" said Paula. "This investigation is way beyond our capabilities in the Service."

"To be honest, only 9/11 comes close in scale," agreed Lynne, selecting the executive level button on the elevator.

"Shocking, truly shocking," said the Senator. "You may be interested in why we're here. Who are you scheduled to meet?"

"Deputy Director Howard Kliner. I believe he's going to be personally running the investigation."

"Howie's a good guy. In fact, you'll probably want to come with me. I've called a meeting with the Director and I've a funny feeling Howie will be joining us," he said, patting the laptop safely tucked under the Colonel's arm.

"Why, what's happened?" asked Lynne, noting the sly grin on Senator Noble's face.

"You'll see soon enough," he promised, leading the way to the Director of the FBI's office at the far end of the corridor.

"Jim," he boomed, entering the office without knocking.

FBI Director Jim Walker looked up from his desk, covering the mouthpiece to the phone call he was in the middle of.

Senator Noble took a seat and waved for him to carry on as if he wasn't there. Lynne and Paula waited in the outer office area with the Colonel and the exceptionally perturbed personal assistant to the Director of the FBI. Her boss was exceptionally important and as such, so was she. People didn't barge into her office, let alone the Director's.

"How dare he!" she exclaimed. "Who does he think he is?!"

"A man who does as he pleases," advised Lynne Bertram. Actually, she was the FBI Director's boss.

"Well, I'll be having words when he leaves. I've never seen anything like it!"

"Good luck with that," whispered Paula Suarez to Lynne.

Deputy Director Kliner rushed into the outer office. "I believe he wants me urgently," he said, as he came up against the immovable PA.

"He's on the phone to the—"

"Howie, is that you?" boomed Senator Noble from the inner office, oblivious to everything else around him. "Get in here! Jim's finishing up his call. And bring everyone else with you!"

Howie gave the PA an apologetic look and did as instructed by Senator Noble, ushering Lynne, Paula and the Colonel with him. They entered to find the FBI Director hurriedly ending his call.

"Senator Noble," said Jim, as he replaced his handset. "I believe you wanted to see me?"

"Urgently, yes," replied Senator Noble.

"How can we help?" asked Jim.

"Actually, I'm here to help you," said the Senator, gesturing for the Colonel to bring the laptop to the desk. "Colonel, if you wouldn't mind setting it up here," he said, pointing to the desk facing the guests. "I believe you're in the process of taking over the investigation from the Secret Service?" he asked rhetorically. "Well this may make your job a little simpler. Colonel?"

"Thank you, Senator," said the Colonel. "A short while ago, the NSA alerted us to a communication from a charter jet that included the words 'Cash' and 'Rigs'. Upon further investigation, we discovered we have very good reason to believe that the two main suspects that you are currently hunting, namely the CIA assassins Copernicus Harris and Jake Miller— Cash and Rigs— are aboard that aircraft as we speak."

"Outstanding!" said Jim. "I'll get my teams in place. Where are they?"

"That won't be necessary, we're taking care of it," said the Colonel.

"Like hell you are! I want those boys in my cells downstairs!"

"It's not up for debate," said the Senator, ending any further discussion. "As a courtesy, I've arranged for you to witness the arrest. The Colonel is setting up a link with the feed to the operation. Once the men are in custody, we, of course, will have them transferred to you. Make no mistake," cautioned the Senator, these are two highly trained and exceptionally dangerous individuals. Their files are classified and way beyond the clearance of anyone in this room."

"Even yours," said Jim sarcastically. He had scanned through the files for the investigation earlier in the day with his Deputy, Howie. Solid black lines riddled every document as detail after detail was redacted for security purposes. All Jim Walker knew about Cash and Rigs was their age, height and weight, and even then their weight was as recorded on entry to the Marines fifteen years earlier.

"We are due to intercept them in the next…" the Colonel checked his watch, "…fifteen minutes."

"Intercept?" asked Howie.

"Two F22 Raptors are on course to intercept and direct the aircraft to land at Creech Air Force Base in Nevada where we have a team of Air Force Combat Controllers who are more than capable of taking them into custody."

The laptop screen came to life. The image of an empty sky filled the screen, while the speakers relayed chatter between two pilots and the ground controllers.

"They're around 300 miles from visual sighting of the aircraft," translated the Colonel.

The chatter continued and the sky seemed to zoom closer.

"They've been given the go ahead to intercept. Those were their afterburners kicking in," explained the Colonel.

"Wow," said Paula. "That looked very cool!"

The colonel smiled, "If you want to try—"

"Down boy," warned the Senator, seeing the sparkle in the Colonel's eye.

The Colonel immediately returned his attention to the screen. "The small dot," he pointed to the top right of the screen, "is the target aircraft ,and the chatter you can hear is our attempt to contact the pilot."

"They're not responding?" asked Howie.

"So far no, nothing," said the Colonel, listening intently as the small corporate jet began to fill their screen.

"What's that?' asked Lynne, listening closely.

"Yes, I hear it too, it's like a tapping," said the Colonel, grabbing a pad and pen from the FBI Director's desk and scribbling furiously.

The small plane nosedived on the screen.

The Colonel finished writing. "The pilot was tapping Morse Code to us, using his radio transmitter. He obviously can't speak, and from the dive, I assume either Cash or Rigs realized what he was doing."

"What did he say?" demanded the Senator.

The Colonel checked his translation carefully before speaking. "Shoot us down. He's saying 'shoot us down'."

"Oh my God," breathed Lynne. "That poor brave man."

"But why?" asked the Senator. "Creech was chosen because it's remote. Why would he want us to shoot him down, there's nothing there!"

"It's still within fifty miles of Vegas and let's not forget what these guys were trying to stop," said the Colonel.

"Nuclear disarmament," said Howie.

"You don't think…?" asked Lynne, voicing what the rest of the room was thinking.

"No," replied Senator Noble. "I mean what's to gain from it?"

"Who knows with some of these crazies?"

"Our pilot is asking what he's to do," the Colonel said. "They're not getting anywhere with the other pilots and the course and trajectory they're currently on will take them to the Las Vegas strip."

Senator Noble shrugged and looked at Jim. "They're your suspects," he said. "Your call."

"The pilot is prompting for a decision. He's over open desert with zero chance for collateral damage. That's going to change very shortly," advised the Colonel urgently.

Jim looked at his boss, Attorney General Lynne Bertram, who in turn looked at Senator Noble. He looked away. It was their call. She nodded.

"Take them down," said Jim Walker abruptly, shaking his head in despair for the innocent pilot who had sacrificed himself.

The Colonel relayed the message over the connection and they all watched as the two Raptors fired one missile each into the helpless jet. It exploded before tumbling in a million pieces to the desert floor thirty thousand feet below.

"Well it looks like the US Air Force has saved you the expense and hassle of a major manhunt and resulting trial," announced the Senator, standing up. As far as he was concerned, the meeting was over.

The Colonel closed the laptop.

"We'll obviously want the remains to confirm they were on board," said Jim Walker.

"I'll get the Colonel to come back to you on that. A HAZMAT team will need to okay the site and any remains before anyone gets their hands on anything."

"HAZMAT team? As in, radioactive material?" asked Paula. "Do you really think that?"

"Classified," said the Senator, leaving them all to wonder exactly how much the Senator knew and wasn't telling them.

"I'm not sure I should cancel the manhunt," Jim called to the disappearing Senator's back.

"Trust me, cancel it! They're gone!" he yelled back. The Colonel scurried to catch up with him.

Chapter 28

"Well," huffed the PA, scurrying into Jim Walker's office when the Senator left. "I don't think I've ever met such a rude man!"

"He's not trying to be rude, he just thinks he owns everything," sighed Lynne, taking a seat.

"And probably does," said Jim.

"Coffees?" asked the PA. She had deliberately not offered while the Senator had been present to teach him a lesson.

Taking their coffee orders, she left the deflated atmosphere in the room.

"Do you ever think you're just a pawn in a much bigger game?" asked Howie Kliner, the Deputy Director, taking a seat next to Lynne Bertram. "And you've no idea what the bigger game is?"

"Never more so than today," said Paula. "From the minute this all started, it's smelled rotten."

"I've gone through the evidence against the alleged plotters and it's certainly compelling but where the hell did it come from?" asked Howie.

"Delivered to the news network not long after the attack in Santa Cruz."

"Who compiled it? What agency had the resources to undertake surveillance against some of the most powerful members of the government?"

"Not us," said Jim, answering the question, in case anyone thought he had some shadowy department tucked away within the bowels of the FBI.

"Nor us," said Paula.

"Although you have access…"

"Not to everyone. Remember, the Chairman of the Joint Chiefs and the Secretary of Defense are sitting in your cells below us and their security is handled by the Department of Defense, not us."

"Good point."

"And don't forget I've got eight agents sharing those cells," she snapped.

"Why?" asked Lynne. "There was no mention of Secret Service agents implicated in the evidence, was there?"

"Of course not, but we still have to protect the First Lady and the Vice President."

"Even if they tried to kill the President?"

"If?! When it's definite, I'll get my guys out of there in an instant. Until then, they're still under our protection, in jail or not."

"You've got armed guards within my holding cells?" asked Jim furiously, reaching for his phone.

"No, we've got two unarmed guards with the First Lady and the VP, and another six armed agents stationed outside the cells."

"Santa Cruz…" said Howie thinking out loud. "The attack was supposed to be against the President, who was three thousand miles away."

"We've got over forty bodies at the scene, predominantly Surenos gang members, two professors, a few research assistants and a few police officers. How does any of that equate to a Presidential assassination plan?"

"You're forgetting the use of military grade equipment and the four bodies that we have been unable to identify and whom appear to have never existed. Smacks of conspiracy," reminded Paula, who knew the evidence as well as anyone.

"The forty others were collateral?" suggested Lynne.

"And the telescope, let's not forget the timeline, it was one of the first to go," said Jim, scanning down the report on his desk.

"Do we know why that was targeted?"

"Something to do with the capability for spying. Our 'enemies' were going to be very upset at its capabilities," Lynne said.

"That doesn't even make sense!" exclaimed Howie in frustration.

"Have any of them talked?" asked Paula. "They certainly didn't with us."

"Other than to tell me that I'll be lucky if after this I'm just a down-and-out on the streets," replied Howie, with concern in his voice. "I mean, seriously, the VP, Secretaries of Defense, State, Energy, Homeland Security and Treasury?" He ticked them off on his fingers. "The National Security Advisor, the Chairman of the Joint Chiefs of Staff, the Director of National Intelligence, the Director of the CIA, the White House Chief of Staff and let's not forget the First Lady, all downstairs in our holding cells?"

"Amongst others," added Lynne.

"And your point?"

"Forgetting the First Lady, it's almost the entire National Security Council, the very people responsible for keeping our nation safe!"

"With me here, it's pretty much only the President who's missing," said Lynne.

"You're not thinking...?" asked Jim, then his desk phone buzzed. He lifted it, listened, and replaced it, speechless.

"What?" asked Howie.

"The President's arrived to see the First Lady."

"How secure is this building?" demanded Paula, getting on her cell.

"Nowhere near as secure as the White Hou—"

An explosion reverberated throughout the building.

Chapter 29

Senator Noble's military convoy swept out of the FBI headquarters under a hail of klaxons and horns.

"They'll get out of the way!" shouted the Senator at his driver, urging him to move through the protestors.

The Senator was right and within a few seconds a swath had been cut through the crowds and the convoy was facing a clear road ahead.

"It's amazing what a few tons of armor can achieve," smiled Senator Noble, picking up his cell phone and calling Conrad. "I've taken care of that problem," he said quickly. He spotted something on the other side of the road. "Is that the President's convoy?" he asked the Colonel.

They passed a long line of black Suburbans and a very familiar Cadillac One, the President's armored limousine.

"Looks like it," said the Colonel, following the convoy as it swept past on the other side of the carriageway.

"Drop me here," instructed the Senator urgently.

"We're still a mile from the Capitol building, sir," said the Colonel.

"That's fine, I can walk," said the Senator, clawing at the handle to exit the car.

He stood in the middle of Pennsylvania Avenue, flanked at either end by the symbols of US power, the Capitol and the White House. One he owned, the other he coveted. The same family that had given him the ability to rise to power within the Senate was the same family that had blocked his goal for the presidency. Like his father before him, Antoine had forbidden Bertie from running for the presidency. The Noble family could not afford to be subjected to the level of attention that the presidency would have brought. Senator Bertie Noble had to sit back and watch others take his presidency, just as he had watched his twin's young son become head of the Noble family. But for twelve minutes, he would have been head of Atlas Noble and the Noble empire. Those twelve minutes had robbed him of his throne.

He hit the dial button.

"Yes?" the person answered.

"Go!" said Senator Bertie Noble, Chairman of the Senate Intelligence Committee and the most senior Senator within the majority party.

***

Capitol Building
Washington D.C.

The tentative knock on the door startled him awake.

"I said not to disturb me unless the world was ending!" he shouted angrily at the closed door.

"I'm very sorry, Mr. Speaker, but these gentlemen insisted I interrupt you," replied his secretary. She opened the door cautiously as if something may fly out at her, which, with the Speaker's current mood, was highly likely.

"What gentlemen?" he asked gruffly. He really wasn't in the mood for any lobbyists, particularly from the defense industry. His phone had been going crazy since the UN speech, reminding him of many promises he had made during his campaign. Promises that could only have been kept had he managed to block the ratification of the disarmament treaty and in the process be labeled as a conspirator.

"They've been sent over by the President, sir," she said.

"Well what are you waiting for? Show them in if they're so darned important that I need to be disturbed!" he snapped sarcastically. The secretary ducked back into the outer office, closing the door behind her.

The Speaker shook his head. She was useless, a temp replacing his old warhorse of a protector. Nancy wouldn't have let even the President past her if she'd been at her desk, let alone people sent by him. A short knock was followed by both his office doors being swung open. Whoever it was liked to make an entrance.

"Mr. Speaker, I'm Special Agent Jed Walters of the United States Secret Service," the man announced, confidently striding into the room. "These are my colleagues."

The Speaker sat up. This was unexpected. "How can I help you, gentlemen?"

"Sir, I'm sure you're aware of the situation with a number of individuals—"

"If you're alluding to the conspirators, yes I am."

"Thank you, then you're aware that one of those individuals is the Vice President."

A knock on the door preceded an altercation at the doorway as one of Jed Walters' colleagues stopped somebody from entering the Speaker's office.

"Mr. Speaker!" the new person shouted from behind his door.

"Larry?" the Speaker called.

"Yes, Mr. Speaker, they're not letting me in!"

"Larry's in charge of my security detail within the Capitol Police," explained the Speaker.

"Let him in," said Jed, adding, "unarmed!"

A flustered Larry burst in, brushing down his suit jacket. "Mr. Speaker, is everything alright?" he asked, rushing to the side of the man he had protected for the previous seven years.

"Everything's fine," answered Jed. "The Speaker's been given a security promotion."

"And you are?"

"Jed Walters, United States Secret Service," he replied nonchalantly. He circled his hand above his head to his men. "Mr. Speaker we don't have time for this, we've to take you to meet with President Mitchell ASAP, sir."

"Why?" asked Larry.

Jed ignored him and motioned for two of his men to help the aging Speaker from his desk chair. Another grabbed his suit jacket and before Larry could protest any further, his former protectee was being rushed out of the room.

"You probably shouldn't be in here," said the temp when she saw Larry standing alone in the Speaker's office.

"It's fine," said Larry.

"He, um, he told me to never leave anyone unattended in his office," she said.

"Anyone doesn't include me," he said. "I'm responsible for his security."

She cleared her throat. "Not anymore."

He walked towards her and led her out into the outer office, closing the office doors behind him.

"Are you Larry Puller?" asked a man rushing into the Speaker's outer office.

Larry nodded.

"Good to meet you," he said extending his hand. "I'm Jed Walters, United States Secret Service. The President has asked us to assist you with the Speaker's security."

Chapter 30

"Was it inside or outside?" shouted Jim, grabbing his pistol from his top drawer.

"Inside, I think!" shouted Paula. Her phone began to ring.

A second explosion was followed by another two and then the gunfire started.

"It's definitely inside!" said Howie.

Paula looked at the caller id and rushed towards the door, her own pistol drawn. It was one of her Special Agents from the White House. The President was downstairs and there were shots being fired. She ignored it.

"On me," she instructed Jim Walker and Howie Kliner, the two most senior members of the FBI. This was her specialty.

Her phone rang again and again.

"I'm a bit busy now!" she said, answering the call, about to hang up.

"Madam Director, it's the Speaker…"

She stopped. "What about the Speaker?"

The question stopped both FBI men in their tracks.

"He's been kidnapped!" said Special Agent Jed Walters.

"Jesus! Find him!" she ordered, hanging up.

"The Speaker's been kidnapped," she relayed to her audience.

"And the President and Vice President are currently under attack?" said Jim unnecessarily.

"Which means we are in danger of losing our President and his first two replacements."

"Who's next in line?" asked Howie.

"The President pro tempore, the senior senator within the majority party," said Paula. She knew every one of the members in the line of succession, since it was her job to protect them given just this situation.

"Senator Noble!" exclaimed Jim Walker.

"Yes."

Paula rushed to the end of the corridor with the two FBI men trailing in her wake, her pistol in one hand ready to fire while her cell phone was in the other. "Jed?"

"Yes Madame Director?"

"Get your team to Senator Noble, take him to the PEOC. I repeat, get Senator Noble to the PEOC."

"Understood."

"Lynne," said Paula, "you need to stay here! If we fail to secure the Senator, you'll be next in line, if we discount everyone in the cells below us."

"We need to protect her!" said Howie.

"You stay with her!" said Paula. "I need to try and get to the President."

***

Cell Block A within the bowels of the FBI headquarters had been selected to house the highest profile detainees in FBI history. It was the highest level security wing, essentially a self-contained prison unit built to hold America's most dangerous criminals, specifically high profile terrorists. As such, the unit was the most secure in the building. Unfortunately for the presidential security detail, it also meant the unit had been built with only one way in and one way out.

A long, sloping corridor led down into the unit, creating a kill zone almost thirty yards long. The idea being that any terrorist who had overpowered his guards and escaped would have to venture down the kill zone, guarded 24/7 by FBI SWAT trained team members.

"Someone give us a fucking gun!" screamed Travis Davies, the CIA Director from his cell.

The remaining Secret Service agents within the unit ignored his calls. Their eyes were focused on the door that separated them from the kill zone. Their three colleagues, the last of the Presidential security detail, were on the other side, trying desperately to hold the attackers at bay.

"Mr. President, will you please let us help you!" screamed Travis.

President Mitchell stood by his wife's side with a gun at the ready. He wasn't going to go down without a fight.

"I promise you," she said for the tenth time. "I have done nothing wrong. The evidence is fake and if they faked it for me…?" She left the question hanging.

The Vice President joined Travis from his cell further down the unit. "For the love of God, Dave, let us help!"

President Mitchell turned to the two agents who refused to leave his side and it seemed were going to take as many bullets as they possibly could while they still lived for him. "Give them whatever weapons you can!" he ordered.

***

Atlas Noble Headquarters
Lake Geneva

Conrad barged into the boardroom, breathless.

"I thought you'd left," said Antoine. "What's wrong?" he asked, noting the whiteness of Conrad's face.

"Uncle Bertie!" he said through gasps.

"Has something happened to Bertie?"

"Yes, after what you said, I thought I'd keep an eye on him."

"And?"

"He's been picked up off the street in Washington by a Secret Service team."

"Why?' asked Antoine, his concern growing by the second.

"That was exactly my thought, so I made a few inquiries and it seems the old bastard has engineered taking the presidency."

Antoine exploded. "He's *what?*"

Conrad explained what he had found out so far, namely the kidnapping of the Speaker and the attack on the FBI headquarters where the President and Vice President were present.

Antoine grabbed his phone and hit Bertie's number, but it went straight to voicemail.

"Who's he using for the attack?" he asked desperately.

"They must be mercenaries, definitely not DIS. I can't call off the attack."

"The old bastard's had this planned for some time," said Antoine, banging the table in frustration.

Conrad nodded. "It seems so. The evidence he fabricated moved the key players to where he could get to them."

"Which means he'd have his men in place even before the arrests were made!"

Conrad nodded again.

"He's risking everything for a little bit of power!" fumed Antoine, pacing along the length of the boardroom.

"Try him again!"

"Straight to voicemail," said Conrad.

"Can we send a team in?"

"No, the area is in lockdown, not a chance."

"We have to stop him, this will derail everything!"

"Is there no upside?" asked Conrad. "I mean, having a Noble as President will have its benefits, no?"

"No!!!" shouted Antoine in frustration. "Everyone will think *we* planned this, not Bertie. We'll be ruined! The arms treaty will be ripped up by every other nation. We'll be thrown out of every country in the world. The day Antoine Noble gets the world to disarm, a Noble becomes the President of the nation with the most powerful conventional armed forces in the world?!"

"Ahh," said Conrad seeing the bigger picture.

"Where would they take him?" pondered Antoine.

"Camp David or the bunker?" said Conrad.

"The bunker," said Antoine, grabbing his phone again and hitting the dial button. "They'll assume initially that he's a target as well, they'd get him to the bunker."

"You have the number for the PEOC?" asked Conrad stunned.

"No, of course not, but I need to get it and quick!"

***

Paula Suarez and Jim Walker reached the entrance to Cell Block A and ground to a halt. A fully armed and ready FBI SWAT team blocked their way.

"Why the hell are you not getting in there?!" shouted Jim.

The team parted, revealing a thick metal door with a small porthole, wired with enough explosives to bring the building down.

"That's why!" said the SWAT team leader.

"Bomb squad?"

"On the way, sir"

The shooting continued behind the door. Paula paced anxiously, going as close to the door as she dared in an attempt to see through the small porthole. It was covered on the other side, blocking the view beyond.

"Any idea of numbers or who they are?" she asked. "There was a building crew working at the back of the car park."

"Yes, I saw them this morning, they've been there for days," said Jim Walker. "About twenty of them, resurfacing the car park."

The SWAT team leader nodded. "Yeah them, only we've not been able to find one person in this building who signed off that work, or who even thought it needed doing. Surprise, surprise, the crew have vanished," he said, pointing to the cell entrance.

"Weapons?"

"Whatever they could fit in the trucks, they've been running in and out of here for days."

"Holy shit!" said Paula.

"Coming through!" came a shout from behind. Two men dressed in bombproof gear trudged towards them, a small remote control buggy leading their way.

"Can everyone clear back to a safe distance please?" asked the leader, seeing the door for the first time. "Which would be across the street," he whistled through his teeth.

"I'm staying right here," said Paula. "The second that door opens, I'm through there."

"Me too," said Jim with a little less conviction. The SWAT team looked at their leader, who nodded. There was no way they could leave, but they shuffled back to give the bomb team space to work.

Chapter 31

Everything had gone exactly to plan, every detail up until the point they had been given the go ahead had been as though Allah himself had planned the operation. As far as Imran, the leader of the small group of Taliban fighters, was aware, it was Allah himself who had planned it. The package had arrived some weeks earlier, with travel plans, papers and documents for him and his small band of fighters to take their battle to the heart of the infidel. Every part of their journey was laid out in detail, it was a pilgrimage for them to undertake on behalf of Allah.

Imran and his group had been selected above all others to rid the world of the infidel leaders. The small plane had met them exactly where it was supposed to. As instructed, his men spoke with no one. It delivered them to a city. Imran remembered the word 'Muscat', but he had no idea where it was. There, as promised, they found an apartment. Suitcases filled with clothes awaited them. They bathed and shaved, spending the next few days adding color to their faces, protecting the darker tanned areas with sun cream, while tanning the previously bearded areas.

Imran followed his instructions to the letter. His men spent the evenings in Muscat learning a few basic English words and phrases, perfecting them with DVDs that had been supplied. Photos were taken of the men and posted in the provided envelope. A few days later, passports arrived. Allah had thought of everything.

Over the next few days, they all took separate journeys, followed their instructions to the letter, and a week later, they met once again in Washington D.C. The house was full of all the weapons and equipment they would need— AK47s and suicide vests. This was a pilgrimage that would take them to Allah himself.

For the next few days, they went through the motions of relaying a perfectly good garage floor while building their stockpile of weapons and explosives within the target building. Finally the 'go' had come. His men donned their vests. If all else failed, they would kill anyone within six feet of them and be sent straight to heaven, by Allah's side. The excitement amongst his men was palpable. They were minutes away from Allah.

Imran had the plans to the cell area but over the previous few days had managed to get in for a look. One door led in and out. Behind that door was a small holding area. Beyond that, was a thirty-yard empty corridor that led down to another door, which was the entrance to the cells themselves. Once they shut the main cell entrance and wired it, their jobs were all but done. After that, it was a simple case of his men deciding whether to shoot the prisoners or detonate themselves next to them. Whatever the case, none of them were ever going to see the light of day again, only the beautiful light of heaven, in the glow of Allah.

The President's convoy had swept past them, delivering the President and his security detail to the door at the far end of the garage that led to the cell blocks. The go command came shortly after. Four men guarded the entrance while another two waited by the convoy.

Imran instructed three of his men to take them out. Two walked towards the entrance while the other man walked towards the convoy. The slimline, high tech suicide vests which had been supplied to them were unlike anything he had ever seen before. The fabric itself was the explosive. A small electronic device near the base of the garment was the trigger, which was linked wirelessly to a small button device paired with each vest. The three men looked like innocent unarmed workers as they approached the secret service agents.

Only as they had continued to walk beyond the point the agents felt comfortable with, were they warned to stand back. By that point, it was already too late. The blasts, one after another, decimated the nine human beings, while causing minimal structural damage.

With the entrance clear, Imran and his men grabbed their AK47s and ran towards the cell area. He'd lost another three men to an agent waiting near the entrance to Cell Block A.

With him out of the way, the explosives were laid on top of the main cell block entrance and the door shut behind them. The thirty-foot corridor sat before them.

Two of Imran's men had rushed down immediately to secure the corridor but the agents took them out almost immediately with head shots. His men hadn't stood a chance and their vests were useless at that range. All the additional explosives they carried had been used to secure the door behind them. They were going to have to fight their way to the targets.

Imran had fifteen men, including himself, prepared to die for their cause, thousands of rounds and Allah willing them to succeed. What had surprised him was that the Secret Service agents were themselves prepared to die for their cause. They stood resolute before them in the face of overwhelming power and accurately picked off his men, trading life for life with Imran's men. He was down to eight men. They had lost at least that, if not more.

Imran instructed another two of his men to make the run. All willingly accepted. The sooner their turn came the sooner their trip to heaven and Allah.

Imran opened the door and his two men charged out. He quickly closed the door behind them as two shots rang out. However, this time, his men's screaming and the sound of the AK47 went on for longer. There was also no return fire. Imran opened the door slightly to see the second of his two men still racing towards the bottom of the corridor. The first lay face down a few yards from the door, a smile frozen on his face. The agents at the bottom of the corridor stood with their weapons ready to bludgeon Imran's man.

The Americans were out of ammunition.

His man had spent his thirty rounds and continued rushing towards the agents, closing in to striking distance. Imran closed his eyes. The flash he knew was coming would have otherwise momentarily blinded him.

The corridor was clear. The two agents and Imran's man lay in a bloody mess on the floor.

Imran picked out sheets of paper from his backpack and handed them to his remaining men. The sheets contained photos of the key targets to be killed. Although they were all were to be killed if possible, certain people had been selected to ensure that if, for any reason, they couldn't kill everyone, they made sure they killed the most important ones first. They all recognized the President and he was top of the list. A few recognized the Vice President but beyond that, even Imran didn't know who the people were.

All he knew was that Allah wanted them dead.

**

Presidential Emergency Operations Center (PEOC)
The White house

With the vault door closing behind him, Senator Bertie Noble knew he had succeeded. The presidency would be his. Within the hour, he'd be sworn in and given the seat that should always have been his. The Nobles thought that knowledge alone gave them power, but they had no idea how much power he had at his disposal as President. He would take charge of Atlas Noble and he alone would decide the plans for the new world.

He had never agreed with the grand plan. A far more radical downsizing was required. His military might, once the truth became clear, would give him the power to dictate and shape the world he wanted, a world that he would rule. Once the truth was out, there'd be no more elections, no more governments, just his military might. The Nobles had spent generations upon generations with only one goal: to save the population. Once complete, their role was over. The wealth, the standing, the power, all would disappear in the new world, all would be meaningless in the future that lay ahead. Senator Bertie Noble had a different vision. He had grown accustomed to the power, he lived for it. To keep it, he had to take it, or Antoine would simply give it all away.

A phone began to ring; it was a red one on the corner of the main table that ran down the center of the room. Senator Noble looked at the phone and the senior agent, Jed Walters, who picked it up. *Could this be it?*, he thought. Months in the making, years in planning, decades waiting. He had spotted his opportunity; it was down to the wire but he had spotted it and he had taken it.

Jed Walters nodded a number of times then looked at the Senator and beckoned him forwards. "Senator," the agent said instantly disappointing Bertie. "It's for you, sir."

"Who is it?"

"The Israeli President, sir!"

Bertie's hopes rose again.

"Mr. President," said Bertie taking the phone.

"Senator Noble, I have been unable to reach the President. I wanted to alert him to an issue we had discussed and that we are in the process of resolving."

"All very cryptic," joked Bertie. "Perhaps you can enlighten me."

"It's fine, if you could pass on that message, he'll understand."

"Of course, Mr. President."

"Oh and Senator, your nephew has been trying to reach you."

"I'll call him later," said Bertie nervously.

"No need, he's on the line, goodbye, Senator." The phone clicked but the line stayed open.

"Uncle Bertie," said Antoine. "You're a hard man to get a hold of!"

Bertie desperately wanted to hang up but couldn't, he needed to know what Antoine knew or suspected.

"End it now before it's too late," said Antoine forcefully.

"It's too late, there's nothing I can do."

"In that case, it was nice knowing you."

Bertie laughed. "Are you threatening me?"

"You sad, stupid, old man, you have no idea how far down the chain you really are. You have no idea of our power or reach, or the scale of the operation that our family has built to protect our people."

"I am going to be president of the most powerful nation on earth."

"You won't see the outside of that bunker if you don't stop what you started," promised Antoine.

"Don't be ridiculous, I'm surrounded by agents that will give their lives to save me."

"Perhaps, but look around you, do you recognize anything in that room?"

Bertie humored him and looked around the room, nothing. He couldn't see anything untoward.

"Look closer," said Antoine. "But hurry, if your plan succeeds, you die."

Bertie looked closer. He recognized the small logo on the leg of the table. He looked around some more and noticed it on the phone, the stamp on the hinge of the vault door, the logo on the corner of the computer screens. The very familiar logo of the Atlas Noble empire, an intertwined A and N, buried in an airtight metal tube hundreds of feet below the ground. The AN logo was on the air system.

"You can't! You can't kill me, it's forbidden."

"Conrad!" shouted Antoine over his shoulder.

Conrad hit a button on the laptop in front of him, shaking his head. "We can't," he mouthed. Antoine nodded insistently.

A red light began to blink almost instantly in the bunker above Senator Noble's head.

"What's that?" asked Jed, looking at the red light on the ceiling that had started to flash.

Another agent rushed to the control panel. "The air system's cut out!"

"It's fine, there's enough air for two hours in the bunker," said Jed. "Otherwise we'll open the door."

"You're too late, Antoine," said Senator Noble. "There's nothing I can do!"

"Bullshit, you always have a backup," said Antoine. "Conrad!" he shouted again. The sound of high-powered fans drowned out almost all the noise inside the bunker.

"Your plan has failed, the fans have kicked in," said Bertie jubilantly.

"*Au contraire, mon oncle*," said Antoine. "I think you'll find they're sucking the air out, not pushing it in!"

"Open the door!" shouted Bertie to the agents.

"They can't," said Antoine. "Stop it now or die. Do you not understand? There is nowhere on this planet I cannot get to you. You have no idea how much power I have," said Antoine evenly.

Senator Noble withdrew his phone and switched it back on, the Wi-Fi connection was all he needed. "It's probably too late," he said, hitting the 'Send' button.

"If you're not, I'll turn the air back on. After all, the agents have done nothing wrong," he said, while instructing Conrad to turn it back on in a minute. He couldn't kill Bertie, no matter what he had done.

***

The last agent ran back into the cell block as the terrorist exploded, killing his two colleagues. The agent slammed the door futilely behind him. The lock was on the other side. He joined the last two agents and formed a line. Behind them stood the CIA Director, the Vice President, Secretary of Defense, and the rest of the alleged conspirators. The President stood at the back with his wife. His protests to stand at the front had been rejected by all around him. They would die protecting him, defending the man they had never stopped believing in. He felt ashamed. He had failed them. He had not stood firm when he knew the evidence before him couldn't be true. However well orchestrated the plan and detail, he should have stood by those who would lay their lives down for him.

With no bullets left, they were down to whatever weapons they could pick up. MP-5s and pistols became nothing more than projectiles or bats. They all stood ready to the sound of bullets pinging off the metal door. The terrorists were coming and they knew they had won.

***

"Come on!" screamed Paula as the explosion sounded behind the cell block door. "They need us!"

The bomb experts were working their way through the fourth trigger they had found.

"Jesus, will someone calm her down! These are hair triggers we're dealing with. If she startles us, we're all dead!" said the bomb disposal leader.

Jim took her in his arms and held her firmly. "Paula, they're going as fast as they can."

"How many more, guys?"

"This could be the last one. We'll know in a few seconds…shit!"

A light on the device changed from green to amber and continued to darken towards red.

***

Imran emptied a magazine of bullets into the door as they rushed towards the far end of the corridor. They were on their way to heaven and Allah whilst sending the greatest infidel of all to Hell. He reloaded his AK47 and waited for his men to catch up, ordering them to take up positions while he prepared to open the door. Three men knelt in front of the other three, their weapons at the ready. The moment the door opened, they would unleash a torrent of bullets into whatever lay behind.

Imran held his trigger in his hand and prayed to Allah.

"One, two, Allahu Akhbar!!!!!" he bellowed, opening the door.

His phone vibrated in his pocket.

***

The bomb disposal man snipped the wire when the light turned to red. The explosion rocked him back on his heels and the door flew open.

***

The three agents in front of the most senior members of the United States government threw themselves forwards as the door burst open. They wanted to put as much of their bodies as possible between the terrorists and the people they were protecting.

Their bodies took the full force of the blast, slamming them back towards their protectees. Their bodies flew back like rag dolls, crashing to the ground. The door hung from its hinges, exposing government members and the President to the horrors of terror.

Chapter 32

Jed Walters fought desperately to unlock the mechanisms but the door wasn't budging.

"We've got less than thirty seconds of air left!" said the agent monitoring the system. To their credit and no doubt thanks to their training, every one of them remained as professional as ever, given the situation.

Senator Noble took a seat. He had resigned himself to his death, if not in the bunker, it would happen soon. Antoine would never forgive him. The Nobles were not a family who ordinarily resorted to such extremes but their code was clear. Total and utter loyalty to the leader of the family was expected at all times, although his actions technically hadn't gone against Antoine's direct wishes. Antoine had forbidden Bertie from running for President, not from following the constraints of the US line of succession. However, his intent was clear for all to see. Nobody would doubt that once President, he would have made a move to usurp or remove Antoine as head of the family - a move that would have been unprecedented within the doctrine and code by which the Nobles lived their lives. However, the timing of his coup would have brought the family together under his leadership. The events that faced the population and their way of life were far more important than an uncle deposing a nephew.

Senator Noble began to think more clearly, and the thought of dying wasn't one he relished.

"Thank God!" shouted Jed.

Senator Noble realized then that his thoughts hadn't cleared, the fans had stopped.

"Air reverting back to normal levels," said the relieved agent monitoring the system as the vault door swung open without any attempt to unlock it.

Jed looked at the open door in wonder. "I don't think we'll be using this facility again," he said, running over to the door and wedging it open. *Better safe than sorry*, he thought.

Senator Noble stood up proudly. He had a show to put on, at least until he knew what Antoine had in store for him.

***

Paula Suarez hadn't even checked on the bomb disposal guy who had been blasted backwards towards them before she was on the move. He had just snipped the wire before the explosives had detonated. However, the force from the seven vests exploding in the confines of the corridor had sent a blast wave back down the length of the corridor, blowing the solid metal door from its hinges.

She leap-frogged over the guy, who was flailing wildly in his lead lined suit, and sprinted for the end of the corridor. The mush of flesh that covered every inch of the far end of the corridor was one of the most horrific sights she had ever seen but she slid through it barely slowing down. The sight of her men picking themselves off of the government members with the President and his wife standing safely at the back of the cell block brought tears to her eyes.

***

Antoine caught the breaking news. The President was alive. The terrorist plot had been foiled by the authorities, none having survived to tell their story. It was a fortunate outcome for Uncle Bertie. His backup plan appeared to be fairly robust. There was little chance he was ever going to be linked to the situation and knowing how resourceful the old bastard was, Antoine was certain there would not be a shred of evidence to suggest he ever was.

The Nobles were safe, the plan was safe, the nuclear disarmament treaty would hold. The decommissioning was to start the following day which, thanks to Atlas Noble Defense, who had offered their services for free as part of the sweetener, was more efficient and simpler than ever. The 17,000 warheads would be decommissioned at a rate of over a thousand a day.

A news flash on top of the breaking news interrupted the scenes of relief at the FBI Headquarters. The body of the Speaker of the House had been recovered from the Potomac. Another piece of the Uncle Bertie coup and resultant cover-up fell into place.

Antoine picked up the phone. DIS was not the only service the Noble family had at its disposal to handle difficult situations.

Chapter 33

Astara, Azerbijan

The VW campervan drew to a stop at the back of the small queue of traffic. The Iranian border guards waved through the three cars and two trucks before them, giving them some hope for an easy passage, but a hand signal held high and firmly in front of them made clear that their initial fears for a difficult crossing were well founded. The two couples produced their paperwork, Swiss passports with valid Iranian visas.

"Out," commanded the officer, leading a small team of border guards responsible for protecting the Northeast border of Iran where it met the Caspian Sea.

The four occupants complied. Two men and two women stood alongside the aging VW campervan that had seen better days, decades earlier.

"Purpose visit?" asked the Commander in broken English.

"We're touring around the Caspian sea, mountain climbing, surfing." The driver pointed to the surf boards that overhung either end of the small campervan.

The commander didn't look at the boards, he was too busy analyzing the passports and paperwork of the group - two couples, recently married, all in their thirties.

"We like to visit lesser known areas," said one of the women.

"Empty van," barked the Commander.

The four moved grudgingly and began to empty their copious amounts of equipment. They had packed for every eventuality of the adventure that faced them, climbing gear, cold weather gear, wetsuits, even parasails.

As the gear piled up onto the road, the more frustrated the other guards became. The small queue that had been four or five long was growing. Fifteen vehicles were waiting for the Commander to finish with the tourists. Some of the Iranian licensed trucks, keen to continue their trade, were blasting their horns in irritation.

"Okay, Okay!" snapped the Commander in frustration. He didn't like it, something felt wrong. He'd have liked to have spent a lot longer on the four. From the moment they had pulled to a stop, there was something he couldn't quite put his finger on.

They loaded the equipment back into their campervan and set off. He watched them closely while his colleagues waved the waiting trucks through. The campervan drove off into his beloved country and a feeling of dread washed over him. What was it? Why had they concerned him?

He realized that they hadn't flinched, not an inch. There hadn't been an ounce of concern between them. In the ten years he'd manned the border, no foreigners had ever been that laid back and cool. He'd seen plenty try to act it but deep down there was that nervousness about their brush with the big bad Iranians.

***

"Shit!!" said Ben, keeping an eye in the rear view mirror as the border disappeared behind them.

"What?" asked Gina, who was, according to the paperwork, his wife of two months and his passenger in the front of the campervan.

"The Commander is still staring at us. He's not taken his eyes of us since we drove away."

"We were perfect," said Avi, the leader of the small Sayaret Matkal team.

"Too perfect perhaps," cautioned Hannah who, according to the forged paperwork, was Avi's wife. Avi and Hannah sat together in the back of the campervan.

Sayaret Matkal was the Delta Force and SAS equivalent of the Israeli Defense Forces. Having women amongst their ranks offered them the ability to stage such brazen incursions. No other forces in the western world allowed its female operatives into its elite ranks. The Israelis welcomed them with open arms.

"Hopefully he'll let it go," said Avi, stealing a look at the disappearing view behind them. The border Commander was still watching them. Avi turned back around. He couldn't worry about what was behind them, he had to focus on what was ahead. Their mission was one of the most crucial in the history of their nation.

"Our papers are flawless," said Gina, "we'll be fine."

"Our papers are, but are we?" asked Avi.

"What do you mean?" asked Ben. "We're supposed to be on a trip of a lifetime as newlyweds."

Hannah ran her hand along and up Avi's inner thigh, not stopping when she reached his manhood and rubbed gently at his crotch. He flinched.

She smiled wickedly. "Yep, needs some work."

"Exactly," he said, slightly embarrassed. "We need to be far more tactile with each other."

"I'm up for that." Ben smiled, glancing over at his supposed wife Gina, a beautiful dark haired Israeli beauty.

"Ugh!" she spat in disgust. "Don't make me sick!"

"Just my luck," said Ben, "I get the lesbian."

"You wish," replied Gina, catching Avi's eye in the mirror. Avi was a man blessed with looks that would have graced the cover of any glossy fashion magazine. Unfortunately, Ben was a man who looked to be hitting well above his weight with the beautiful Gina. However, in a tight spot, none would want anyone else by their side. The short, compact Ben was one of Sayaret Matkal's most experienced and feared fighters.

"Everyone calm down, we got across the border. Hannah's right, we need to be a little more tactile, which doesn't necessarily mean rubbing each other off in public," said Avi.

"Shame," said Gina. She kept her eye on Avi, under the watchful eye of Hannah, whose hand had slipped onto Avi's manhood again.

"I'm being serious, guys," said Avi. He pushed Hannah's hand aside gently and a little reluctantly. "We've got a two hour drive to Chalus, I suggest we relax and remember why we're here."

***

Nevatim Air Base, Israel

The satellite feed of the Sayaret Matkal's team progress was being watched with increased interest. The ten-mile to target point increased the excitement even further. The Air Force General looked across at the Mossad chief who picked up his phone and hit the dial button.

"Mr. President," said the Mossad Chief. "We are in position, awaiting your final approval."

"Excellent, you have it" replied the Israeli President.

"Thank you, Mr. President."

The Mossad Chief nodded to the General who gave a thumbs up to his team of controllers. The mission was a go.

Forty of the Israeli Defense Force's newest aircraft were about to be unleashed on the unwitting Iranians. The Lockheed Martin F-35 was the most advanced strike fighter within the Israeli arsenal and thanks to its stealth capability, was immune to the recently upgraded Iranian air defenses. Their new Sayyad 2 missiles would have laid waste to the Israelis' older F15s and F16s that otherwise would have had to have been used.

From the moment Israel had been strong-armed into giving up its nuclear weapons, the planning had commenced to eradicate any potential for the Iranians to achieve their dream of obtaining a nuclear weapon. The other soon-to-be non-nuclear powers were turning a blind eye to the operation, although secretly they were rooting for a total and complete success. No one wanted to see a world where only Iran had a nuclear option. The Americans had even assisted in the development of a very special munition, which was about to tested for the first time, although they would later show public outrage at the aggressive maneuver, as would the other world leaders.

***

Chalus, Iran

Avi strained his neck, struggling to see the top of the mountain from inside the campervan. At almost 16,000 feet, the Alam-Kuh peak was an impressive sight. Its harsh sharpness outlined against the brilliant blue skyline gave the viewer an ominous hint of the power that lay below.

"There it is," said Avi. "Home to the Iranian nuclear arsenal."

Gina leaned across as they disappeared into the darkness of a tunnel. Ben patted her head down towards his lap with a laugh.

"You wish," she said, pulling herself back up.

"Avi said we should get more tactile," said Ben.

"Tactile, not crude," said Avi. "And keep your eyes on the road. Watch where you're going!"

Ben turned just in time to take the sharp bend that had appeared in the tunnel. He steadied the vehicle as the light began to grow at the end of the tunnel. Bursting into bright sunlight, they continued on. Ben had never driven the road before but recognized every yard of the final mile towards Chalus.

"Coming up to our turn," he announced. He took the nondescript road located three quarters of a mile to the north of Chalus. The sign was in Arabic and simply said 'Mountain Road'.

Half a mile down the road, they pulled to a stop at a small, deserted picnic area, shadowed by the mountain looming above them. They unpacked their kit, and within five minutes, they were on their way again. Had anyone spotted them, they looked no different than any group of hikers or climbers, other than the two couples were now hand in hand as they walked. They were two young couples in love, or at least being more tactile, as ordered.

Ben led the way. He had an incredible eye for detail and had studied every inch of the terrain on the satellite images he had spent the last few days devouring.

"It's a quarter of a mile up there," he said, pointing towards a small break in the bushes.

***

The Takavar troops lay prone amongst the bushes when the four hill walkers passed them. The Iranian Special Forces team was amongst the elite of the Iranian forces and answered only to the supreme leader himself.

"Targets have just passed us," the Takavar troop leader whispered into his headset. His seven men awaited his orders.

The alert had been raised at the border a couple of hours earlier by the border guard. On any other day, the alert would have been ignored. However, given the nuclear disarmament treaty, the Iranians were under no illusion that the Israelis would not attempt a strike to disable their capabilities, resulting in the dispatch of the Takavar troops to detain the spies.

"They are now setting up a picnic with a clear line of sight down the access road. Should we take them now?"

The leader's fist remained closed. His men remained still. His orders were to hold until told otherwise.

***

The picnic venue was spectacular, a small hilltop overlooking a green valley that ran towards looming mountains in the distance. A road cut through the valley and disappeared off into the mountainside. The picnic was unpacked as planned with two containers being set off to their side. The front of each of the containers was pointed in opposite directions, one towards the road and the other one hundred and eighty degrees in the other direction.

To anyone looking, they looked exactly like every other Tupperware container they had unpacked.

Small pinholes, almost invisible to the naked eye, were set into the side of each of the two containers, both shining invisible laser beams into the distance, at exact and precise angles.

Hannah donned her sunglasses and thanks to the lenses could see the two laser beams shooting off in opposite directions.

"Okay?" asked Avi.

"Yes," said Hannah.

Avi opened a bottle of champagne and poured a bit for everyone. "To a nuclear free world!" he toasted.

***

Nevatim Air Base, Israel

"Sir, they have deployed the laser guidance system," announced one of the air traffic controllers.

"Are we in position?"

A number of affirmative answers echoed around the room.

"Commence the attack, in three, two, one, go!"

A clock began the countdown; ten minutes to strike.

Eight targets were highlighted on the Iranian map, each one correlating to an Iranian nuclear facility with the potential to further Iran's nuclear capability. All eight targets were to be struck in unison.; four aircraft to each site with eight to Chalus. It was to be a decisive attack with overwhelming force to ensure the Iranians were not about to become the only nuclear armed state in the world, something that Israel could not and would not accept, under any circumstances.

***

Chalus, Iran

The Takavar leader was becoming increasingly nervous. Something was amiss and he was doing nothing.

"What are our orders?" he asked again over his headset.

"Wait until further orders," came the terse reply.

"They're doing something!" he said. His men were as keen as he was to defend their nation against whoever these spies were. And from the look of them, he was guessing they were Israeli or American.

"Wait. Do nothing until ordered," came a voice he recognized and would never question.

***

F-35 Squadron Leader – Chalus

"Base, we have acquired guidance system, on course to drop in one minute."

"Roger, Chalus leader, sixty seconds, you are a go for release."

"Roger."

***

Tehran, Iran

The air defense map showed the location of the forty F-35 strike aircraft. The Iranian equipment was not quite as outdated as their American and Israeli counterparts thought it was. A number of missile launchers were silently tracking each and every one of the Israeli jets and had been since they had crossed Iranian borders. The Sayyad-2 missiles, unlike the specifications leaked, were more than capable of downing the F-35s, particularly given the vast number that were being utilized.

"It looks like they are about to strike," advised the head of the Armed Forces to his small audience, the supreme leader and President of Iran.

He looked agitated. "Should we strike now?"

"No," replied the supreme leader with a nod of agreement from the President. The two men had a plan of which only they were aware.

"They are about to lay waste to our nuclear ambitions," argued the military head. The board lit up with warnings as hundreds of munitions were launched from the forty fighters.

The supreme leader smiled. "Actually, they have just secured them." He stood and led the President out of the room.

"What about retaliation?"

"No," said the President. "Not possible, they have to think we didn't have a chance."

"And the spies?" asked the military chief.

"Capture them, they'll be useful later," said the President. "They'll have witnessed Chalus' destruction."

***

Chalus, Iran

The first bomb swooped over their heads and crashed onto the road surface, almost immediately followed by another seven. It was a bizarre sight. The large bombs cracked against the surface of the road and bounced, skimming off the surface and down the road, each subsequent bounce reducing in height and distance. It was easily a mile to the entrance to the tunnel ahead but the bombs followed each other's path very precisely. The World War II bouncing bomb had its modern equivalent. Only these were designed to a far higher specification and required far less skill to pilot.

The two boxes did all of the targeting work. The first gave the optimal angle for the bomb to follow on its way in, while the second pinpointed the ultimate target - the underground storage facility for the Iranian nuclear arsenal, buried deep inside a 16,000 foot mountain.

The eight bombs struck at different times but all waited for the last to arrive before dispelling its explosive might. Even though protected from the main blast that was contained within the mountain a little over a mile away, Avi and his team were still thrown off their feet by the overwhelming force of the combined explosions.

By the time they were back up, each had two Heckler & Koch G36 sub machine guns pointing at them.

"Shit!" said Avi, looking into the faces of eight very pissed looking Iranians.

Chapter 34

President Mitchell shared a toast in the Oval Office with the Vice President, Senator Noble and the Secretary of Defense.

"Gentlemen," he said, raising his glass, "to the Israelis."

"The Israelis," they all chorused.

The news report playing in the background relayed to the public the United States' outrage at the unwarranted act of aggression by the same people they were toasting.

A knock on the door preceded the entry of CIA Director Travis Davies.

"Mr. President, Mr. Vice President, Mr. Secretary, Senator," he greeted each as he walked across the office.

"Any news?"

"We've recovered another three bodies from the Potomac. They've been positively ID'd as three of the four men who posed as Secret Service agents and kidnapped the Speaker. We presume the fourth man killed them. They've all been identified as foreign guns for hire. Paperwork on them links them to the terrorists, so it is all connected. As for the main terrorist group, the twenty Afghans, we can find no links to any of the major terrorist networks. Nobody's claiming responsibility. It's as if they acted alone."

"Impossible," said the Vice President. "The complexity of what they engineered, the evidence against us?!" He waved around the room. "The connections, the paperwork, the weapons? It goes on and on, this wasn't twenty Afghani fighters working alone."

"What about the two CIA guys?" asked the Secretary of Defense, much to Travis's embarrassment. "Perhaps they masterminded it?"

Travis opened his mouth but was cut off by Senator Noble. "I'd vouch for those men personally, they had nothing to do with this. I've met them many times through our committee's work and there aren't two more loyal men in our service," he said proudly.

"Well thank you, Senator. Unfortunately your words are a little too late and somewhat surprising given your help in tracking them down."

"My words stand. So much so, that I staked my reputation on them," he said, taking another drink. It was the final complication left after his attempted coup.

"You staked your reputation on shooting down my two men?"

"Technically, I never gave the order. Jim Walker gave that order, it was not for me to give."

"Okay, you never technically ordered their plane down but I believe you arranged the situation that allowed it to happen."

"Those men would never have harmed this country. Unlike you guys, they were not in safe custody, they were facing the wrath of every vigilante or trigger happy cop in the land."

"So you shot them out of the sky?" asked the President, incredulous as to what the Senator was trying to say.

"No, I made the world *think* we had shot them out of the sky."

The room silenced as they processed the Senator's words.

"You didn't shoot them out of the sky?"

"A little sleight of hand with our friends down at Creech Air Force Base."

"Creech?" asked the Secretary. "You shot down a drone?"

"Well, it was an aircraft, but a pilotless one."

"So my guys are okay?" asked Travis, smiling for the first time in hours.

"I assume so," said the Senator.

"Assume?"

"Given I have no idea where they are now, it's all I can say, but they're not being hunted so…"

"They'll be fine then," said Travis. He was elated. "They can look after themselves."

"Now you must excuse me," said Senator Noble. "I have a number of calls I need to make."

"Of course," said the Vice President.

"Senator?" said Travis, chasing him out into the corridor.

"Yes, Mr. Davies?" said the Senator, slowing down reluctantly; he was keen to get away.

"We think the malfunction in the PEOC was a deliberate attempt on your life," Travis said.

Another bonus, Antoine's actions to kill Bertie had added to his alibi.

"I assumed it was. They wanted us *all* dead."

"Yes," replied Travis automatically. "And thanks again for my guys, that was quick thinking and clever work!"

Senator Noble nodded with a smile, accepting the thanks but could see the questioning look in Travis' eye. He wasn't fully buying the Senator's bullshit.

"I'm not sure if you knew, but my niece, Anya, was great friends with Professor Harris at university. It's made me keep an extra special eye on young Cash," said the Senator, leaving Travis to ponder that additional nugget of information.

"I never knew that," said Travis, watching the Senator stride away, his cell phone already at his ear.

"Conrad!" said Senator Noble into the phone when his less powerful nephew answered.

"Uncle Bertie!" exclaimed Conrad in surprise. Antoine had not told him what was to be done with him.

"I owe you a heads up, I need to cover up the assassins still being alive."

"I thought you killed them?"

"No, what made you think that?"

"You. You called and told me you had sorted that problem," he said.

"As in the hunt, I stopped the hunt."

"There was a news report they were shot down," said Conrad.

"All a sham. Anyway, I had a lot going on, you obviously didn't get the right end of the stick."

"Yes you did and I didn't have an end to choose from, you only gave me one, the problem was fixed."

"Yes, they weren't being hunted."

"Whatever," said Conrad in frustration. "I need to get my team looking for them."

"Are they not already? Antoine will be—" began the Senator, goading his nephew.

"Don't even try it. This is *your* fault," Conrad cut in, finally losing his patience.

"Well you'd better hurry. The CIA is as keen to find them as you are!" Bertie reached his car, a rueful smile on his face. His driver opened the door for him, revealing a dark haired beauty in her mid-twenties. Her skin glowed, revealing a Mediterranean heritage. Her eyes, dark and gleaming, were intoxicating. Her hair was swept tightly back against her head into a ponytail. She was perhaps the most beautiful woman he had ever seen.

"Hi," he said, breaking into a smile, unable to escape her captivating eyes.

"Antoine sent me," she said coldly.

The Senator's smile disappeared. She was a killer. A member of an elite and very select band of assassins. Very few knew they existed, and even fewer had the ability to contact them. As old as the Noble family, they had been in the business of killing almost as long as the Nobles had been in business.

"Get in," she said.

"You're going to kill me," he said, his voice shaking.

"If that were the case, you'd already be dead. I'm to chaperone you until told otherwise."

Chapter 35

Sophie, for the first time in hours, raised her head from the laptop and the professor's research. A small jolt had disturbed her train of thought.

"Welcome to the top of the world," said the steward, offering her a refill of her coffee.

"Top of the world?" asked Sophie, looking out of the window at what seemed to be a fairly flat area surrounded by mountains.

"We're over 13,000 feet above sea level," said the steward. "We've landed at El Alto Airport in Bolivia."

"Thank you," she said, holding out her coffee cup. "How are my travelling companions?"

"Both sleeping, the quiet, scary one, the whole way; the cute one fell asleep a couple of hours ago."

"Thanks." Sophie grinned tentatively. Hearing the steward refer to Cash as cute reminded her of exactly how much she was attracted to him herself. Those thoughts, however, had to remain locked away. He had destroyed half her life as it was.

He opened his eyes under her gaze. "Hello." He smiled. "Hello," she said, looking away.

"We've arrived." Cash stretched languidly, looking out of the small window.

"Yes," she said. "How did you get on with those?" she said, indicating to the folders strewn across the table in front of him.

"Nothing. No clues whatsoever."

"You?" he asked, motioning to the laptop.

Sophie looked around to see where the steward was. He had disappeared into the cockpit. Her face broke into a huge— and Cash remembered, naughty— smile. A smile that said she knew something she shouldn't or you didn't.

"Unbelievable!" she said the smile remaining fixed.

"You found out why they killed our fathers?" asked Cash.

"No, much bigger."

"You've proved our innocence?"

"What's going on?" whispered Rigs, joining the group. Sophie's smile dropped when she realized her breakthrough with him had been short lived. Rigs was avoiding her gaze again and speaking only to Cash.

"Sophie's found something."

"Clues to why your father was killed?" asked Rigs of Cash, keeping his voice as low as possible.

Sophie shook her head wildly. "No. Well, yes and no, everything, the answer to everything is in here."

"Everything?" asked Cash confused. "So it will prove our innocence?"

"Maybe. Well probably not, but we may be on the cusp of understanding everything, at least about us."

"All you need to know about us is that we're in deep shit," said Cash. "Let's take one problem at a time. Let's clear our names and avenge our fathers before we solve the answer to everything, whatever that means."

'Not 'us' us, I mean us *humans*! Everything means *everything* about humans, the Earth, the universe, *everything*!" she said, her excitement levels increasing.

"Can you explain to me how finding the answers to the universe will help us?" asked Cash.

"Because, your father believes there are people already here who know far more than they're letting on, protecting a knowledge from the past that we've lost."

"Who?"

"He didn't know."

"The government?"

Sophie shook her head. "No, nothing like that, much smaller, guardians… protectors of a knowledge that we are being protected from."

"A secret society, like the Masons?"

Sophie shook her head.

Rigs chuckled quietly. "The Catholic Church, the Knights Templar?"

"Much smaller. He thinks that some of the ancient civilizations were aware of the secret and ultimately paid the price for that knowledge."

"You're saying these guardians are killers?"

"Our fathers are dead."

"And the most powerful telescope ever built was destroyed," added Cash.

"Kind of what you'd do to protect a secret?" nodded Sophie knowingly.

It took just over an hour to reach the site. The sun was hanging onto the last of its daylight. Sophie unpacked her kit and quickly mapped out the measurements that had previously been carried out by Cash's father.

"Amazing!" Cash said, looking out across the landscape. "To think this is thousands of years old."

Rigs looked at the rocks that littered the area, large, perfectly shaped, and carved stones. Some had to weigh nearly a hundred tons.

"Can't be," he said. "Look at that one, it's got drill holes running down that edge."

"Pumapunka, unknown origins," Cash read from the pamphlet he had picked up. "Over there, where Sophie is, that's Tiwanaku, newer but just as amazing." The barren terrain was littered with the most amazing collection of stones he had ever seen. "You can hardly catch your breath. We're so high up and we're supposed to believe they were carving and moving these giant stones around, building these structures?" asked Cash in wonder.

They wandered back to Sophie. Rigs held back, taking great interest in the sun gate as described by the pamphlet.

"How's it going," asked Cash, adding knowingly, "at the Kalasasaya Temple?"

"I'm impressed," she said.

He held up the pamphlet. "Built about two thousand years ago…" he started to read.

Sophie shook her head. "Not according to your father's research, he reckoned nearer ten to twelve thousand years ago."

"No way," said Cash. "That's older than the pyramids!"

"Or about the same age," Sophie said. "Add to that the irrigation system— which is beyond ingenious— and the mathematical intricacy of the site, and you have to seriously question who on Earth was capable of this when we'd struggle with some of it today."

Cash looked around in awe.

"Over there where Rigs is hovering menacingly is—" Sophie started.

"The sun gate." Cash smiled. "And he's not hovering menacingly, he's just awkward."

"You say awkward, it looks menacing. Anyway, yes the sun gate. That's an astronomic calendar. They understood the solar system long before modern astronomers had any idea that we weren't the only planet. "

"It's a stone gate, what nine feet high? How is that a calendar?"

"It's complicated, more so by the fact that your father believes it has been moved. That's why I needed to take the measurements. I'll do the calculations later." The sun had begun to drop behind the mountains and the light was fading fast.

Rigs walked across to them, his shadow stretching off into the distance, alien-like as his body and limbs stretched off across the landscape.

An eerie silence settled when the last of the tour buses departed. It was a barren, desolate location, its thin air adding to the mystery of who had built such an amazing city thousands upon thousands of years earlier, high in the mountains.

Cash shivered involuntarily. The whole place seemed a little... he didn't know what, but closed his eyes and could almost envision how it would have looked millennia before. A bustling city, surrounded by rich, fertile lands, a people who worshipped the skies, understood the solar system long before man forgot the Earth wasn't flat.

A taxi horn tooting brought Cash back to the present. Sophie and Rigs were staring at him.

"You alright?" she asked.

Cash nodded and was led towards their impatiently waiting taxi.

"Amazing," Cash said again after they pulled away.

"First of many," said Sophie, scribbling wildly into a notepad.

***

Travis Davies had made it back to the CIA headquarters in Langley, Virginia to a hero's welcome. A round of applause took him from the entrance almost to his office by the staff lining the corridor to herald their leader.

When he reached his office, he closed his door and took a minute to enjoy the silence after the chaos. His desk was lined with updates and reports by his staff, who had worked diligently to prove his innocence while he was incarcerated. None of it was of any use. Everything led to a dead end, or more precisely, to the twenty dead Afghans who, from seemingly nowhere and with no apparent backing, had almost brought America to her knees.

Travis considered the only piece of good news of the day. Cash and Rigs were alive. Senator Noble's involvement was certainly questionable and worthy of further digging. He made a note to look a little more closely at the all-powerful Senator. An email alert popped onto his screen. 'Cash and Rigs located' was the subject heading. He clicked on the email. Their faces had triggered an image recognition program. He read through the detail. What the hell were they doing in Bolivia?!

***

Conrad Noble received the news shortly after Travis Davies. Thanks to the significant number of ex-CIA personnel, his DIS team was still very well connected within the organization. There was little that went through the agency that DIS was unaware of, particularly in the areas of interest to their clients.

Conrad passed the news to Antoine, who was as in the dark as Conrad as to the significance of Bolivia. However, Antoine knew someone who would know more— his sister Anya.

He travelled down to the depths of the Noble vaults and found his sister next to the Hadron Accelerator with a group of scientists who were all uncharacteristically hugging each other and crying.

"That was quick!" she said, rushing towards him.

"What was quick?"

"I only just left a message for you to come down." She shook her head, clearing her thoughts. "It doesn't matter, we've done it!"

"It-it *worked?*" gasped Antoine, looking at the stone tablets..

"It worked, we have the fuel!"

Antoine sat and soaked in the moment; it had taken thousands of years and a fortune almost beyond comprehension, but they had done it!

"It'll take us a few weeks to make the quantity we need but we've done it!" she cried.

He nodded, enjoying the moment. What they had achieved would save countless millions. What had been a pipe dream and a punt had actually worked.

"I need to speak to Bea, we need to alter our plans," Antoine said, running through the impact of what they had achieved. Up until that point, he had not dared plan for Anya's success; it would simply have been a bonus. He hugged his sister again and stood to leave.

"Wait a minute," said Anya. "If you didn't get my message, why did you come down?"

"Oh, yes," he stopped and turned back. "It was to find out whether you knew of any reason why Professor Harris' son would be in Bolivia?"

Anya's excitement instantly died. She could simply lie and tell him she didn't but she could not lie to Antoine. Total and utter loyalty to the leader of the family was obligatory, no matter what.

"Where in Bolivia?"

"La Paz, I think."

"Pumapunka," she said quietly. "The answers you seek, lay around us in our past," she whispered.

"What?"

"Something I said to Charles many, many years ago. They're following the clues that will lead them to our future."

Antoine grabbed a pen and paper. "Write down every location they could possibly visit. We have to stop them."

"There could be hundreds," Anya said.

"I don't care, list them all! In order of importance!" he commanded, sensing her reticence.

Chapter 36

Sepik River
Papua New Guinea

Doctor Ernesto Rojas awoke to silence. The small village where he had spent the previous few days was rarely, if ever, silent. The young doctor had only recently arrived in the country, as an attempt by the Papua New Guinea government to improve its health offering to its indigenous tribes. They had struggled for years to entice doctors to spend time in the tribal villages. A recent expansion of Cuba's major export had resulted in the young doctor being made available to them. Cuba exported more doctors than the rest of the world's richest and most developed countries combined.

The young Cuban had taken a few weeks to acclimatize to the Iamult people who inhabited the area on the banks of the Sepik River, as had they to him. Thanks to their friendliness and welcome and the outstanding work he had already undertaken, he had won them over, as had they him. Their almost medieval existence, deep in the jungle, separated from any hint of modernity, was frightening and liberating all at once. Phone calls were a three-day trek away. Electricity was restricted to the lightning bolts that lit up the sky during a storm. Food was simply what they caught or grew. Money was irrelevant.

There was always something happening, something being built or carved in the village. Whatever it was, there was never a lack of helpers. Everyone chipped in and did their bit for the village. It was the first real community he had ever experienced and he had grown to love it.

He listened. Still nothing other than the occasional bird call. Not a sound from the village. The ramshackle collection of wood and mud huts had little soundproofing. Snoring, farting, sex, you heard it all, and not only your immediate neighbors. There was little privacy and very few moments when one's thoughts were one's own. He lay still, almost wishing for the silence to break. Minute after minute passed. Still nothing came from the village. The sun was up and while Ernesto was by no means a late riser, by village standards he was positively lazy, rising after the sun.

He listened more intently. The silence was beginning to unnerve him. Something was very wrong.

After ten minutes, no sound had emanated from the village itself. He chastised himself for letting something so ridiculous unnerve him. Perhaps they had a day of silence, a day of rest. Perhaps there was a festival they had all gone to. It could be many hundreds of positive things he told himself, forcing himself from his bed. He threw on a t-shirt and a pair of shorts and stepped out into village. The main square was fifty yards to his right. He looked towards it, nobody was there. Normally, it would be bustling with people. He looked across at the huts on the other side of the small road. The women would normally be chatting in front of their homes, preparing meals for that day. None were there. He looked down the length of the road away from the square, nothing. Not completely nothing; there was something lying in the dirt track they called a road.

He ran towards it. It was a body, that of a young boy he knew as Jay. He had been Ernesto's most ardent helper and supporter. He was always there, always at Ernesto's side, fascinated to learn what the young doctor was doing and why.

Jay was lying face down on the street. It looked as though he had been crawling and had stopped mid-crawl. His skin was loose, wrinkled, unlike how tight and smooth it had been a few hours before.

Ernesto looked around, not wanting to touch the boy without his family's permission. There was no one to ask. Ernesto rolled Jay over. His horrified face stared up at him. His skin was drawn tight against the bones, all muscle and definition had gone, only leathery skin remained. It was as though every ounce of moisture had been drawn out of his body. Ernesto examined the rest of the body; it was the same. It wasn't as though moisture had been drawn out, it was that it *had* been. Jay was desiccated. He had died at some point during the night but had naturally mummified within hours, which wasn't medically possible.

Ernesto ran to Jay's home and, after knocking for a few seconds, he entered. Jay's parents and two younger sisters lay dead in their beds, mummified, just like Jay. An hour later, Ernesto had failed to find a living soul in a village of over ten thousand. The entire village had perished in one night.

Over the next few hours, he travelled to two nearby villages. The story was the same. Ernesto was distraught, terrified and still two days away from a phone. Why had he survived when everyone else had died? The fourth village gave some suggestion of an answer. A young Catholic nun sat forlorn in the village square, a young girl by her side.

"They're all dead, all dried out, like mummies!" she cried when she saw Ernesto walking towards her.

"But she's okay?" he said hopefully, pointing at the young girl.

"She's an orphan I brought with me from another village, she's not Iamult," the nun said through the tears.

"So it's only the Iamult?" gasped Ernesto. He had visited four villages, all roughly the same size, meaning fifty thousand people were dead. But Ernesto knew there were many more villages spread along the river and that the Iamult people numbered nearly 350,000. In one night, they had potentially witnessed the sudden and catastrophic extinction of an entire race of people. He had to get to a phone.

Chapter 37

The trip back to the airport was like a journey through space and time. The clarity of the night sky was enhanced by their elevation and the barrenness of their surroundings was nothing short of awe inspiring.

"You can see why they settled here," said Sophie, straining to look straight up from her back seat vantage point.

"And why they were fascinated by the stars," said Cash. "That's more than I've ever seen before."

"And yet only a tiny fraction of what's out there."

"It is beautiful, no?" said the taxi driver, looking at the sky.

Rigs, who was sitting in the front passenger seat, was nowhere near as impressed. He tapped the taxi driver's steering wheel. The message was clear, he was being paid to drive, not enjoy the scenery.

Cash leaned into Sophie. "He doesn't like not being in control," he whispered. A laugh that was forming dissipated when the smell of her skin, a memory he had forgotten, came flooding back. She smelled exactly as she had all those years earlier. It was a smell that had driven him wild then. He daren't move as he breathed in the beauty of her natural fragrance.

A gentle shove killed the moment and awkwardness returned when Sophie moved subtly but deliberately away.

"I'm sorry," breathed Cash.

"It's fine," said Sophie. He could hear her breath catch as she spoke. She had felt it too.

"Hold on!!!" Rigs screeched, throwing his hands into the dashboard to stop himself going through the window.

Cash threw his arm across Sophie, protecting her from hitting the back of Rigs seat while he clattered into the back of the driver's seat when the taxi skidded to a halt, barely stopping for the steward who had jumped out in front of them.

"Oh my God!!!" screamed the steward hysterically. "Are you okay?!"

Cash got out of the cab in time to grab Rigs as he went for the steward.

"Rigs, it's fine! There must be a good reason why he just risked his life," reasoned Cash. "Sophie, you okay?"

She nodded while the taxi driver hurled abuse at the steward.

"What the hell were you thinking?" asked Cash. The driver quieted, although continued to curse under his breath.

Rigs had gripped the steward by the neck and wasn't ready to let go, and the steward struggled to speak.

"Rigs?"

Rigs relaxed his grip a little, resulting in a gasp from the steward followed by a barrage of single words.

"Police, plane, waiting, wanted, attack, president."

Rigs relaxed his grip completely. People often labeled him stupid because of his difficulties with interactions but he was as quick if not quicker than most. The steward was protecting them.

Rigs stepped away. He knew how intimidating his brooding silence could be, although in truth, his six foot two powerful frame was just as intimidating.

"Please repeat that," Cash said, "but fill in the blanks."

The steward looked warily at Rigs. Cash gestured for Rigs to move away further.

"We saw the news while you were away," the steward said.

"Okay," said Cash.

"We heard all about the failed attempt to kill the President and half the government."

"Failed attempt on half the government?" asked Cash. That was new, the last he knew half the government had tried to kill the President.

"Some elaborate plot," he waved his hands around in the air in an attempt to convey it was all too complicated. "Anyway, your faces came on the screen, saying the reports of your death were incorrect and that you had also been framed and were innocent of all charges."

Cash smiled broadly. "Okay, so what's this all about?" he asked, pointing at the steward standing in front of the taxi.

"I wanted to make sure it was you before I stopped you," he explained. "It was a bit dark and I spotted you a little late."

"Yes, but why stop us?!"

"Because they said you were innocent!" he explained, as though Cash was stupid.

"Yes, but why did you stop us *here*?" interjected Sophie.

"Because of the police."

"What police?"

"Oh," said the steward. "I thought I'd said. The police are waiting for you at the plane."

"But we're innocent?" asked Cash.

"Exactly, so that's why I'm here. They're not friendly looking policemen."

"Did they say what they wanted us for?"

The steward shook his head. "No."

"And they're definitely police?"

"I think so, they had four police cars which they've hidden."

"And they let you go?"

"I unnerved them. Big angry men with guns make me nervous. They told me to go and wait in the lounge area in the terminal."

"How many?"

"Six, well six that I saw."

Cash looked at Rigs who was already moving. The terminal was off to their left, a half mile away down the private approach road.

"Kill the lights!" Cash called to the taxi driver. There was no other traffic on the road. Their taxi's lights were the only ones on the road and they had been stationary on the road for a couple of minutes. Cash could make out their plane in the distance. If he could see it, they could see them.

"Sophie, get back in the taxi," instructed Cash. "You too," he said to the steward.

He climbed into the passenger seat. "We're going to drive slowly towards the plane but take the road to the terminal where we'll stop briefly and drop them off," he said, pointing at Sophie and the steward. "Just at the point we're out of sight of the plane. Then we'll continue slowly towards the plane."

"We're not getting the hell out of here?!" asked Sophie, stunned.

Cash shook his head. "This could be a lead."

"Are you mad?"

Cash shrugged, this was what he did. He urged the taxi driver on.

The taxi driver remained stationary. He was old enough to remember the brutal reputation of the Bolivian secret police, protector of the Nazi war criminal Klaus Barbie for many years.

"No señor." He shook his head.

Cash reached back to Rigs bag and pulled out a pistol, placing it at the taxi driver's head.

"Cash!" shouted Sophie in disgust while the steward screamed in panic.

"Drive," ordered Cash, ignoring them. A couple of minutes later, Cash enjoyed the silence brought on by dropping off the passengers. Sophie had chastised him all the way, not holding back on how little she thought of his abuse of power over the taxi driver, to whom she repeatedly apologized.

In silence, they approached the plane, which sat alone at the far end of the terminal in a special area of the apron reserved for private aircraft.

"Stop here," said Cash.

Cash sat and waited, making no attempt to move. He'd wait all night if need be. The police were going to have to come to him.

Seconds became a minute, a minute became five. Still, Cash sat in the seat not willing to move. Five minutes became ten. Still he waited. He kept his eye on the clock on the dashboard. He sat motionless, not even moving his head. He didn't want it to look as though he was watching the time.

After twelve minutes, the police cracked. They moved. Two exited the plane tentatively, followed by another two. When the first two hit the bottom of the stairs, Cash flicked the door handle and shouted at the taxi driver to accelerate.

As the taxi accelerated towards them, the police dived out of the way, while Cash rolled out from the car to the far side of the plane, his trailing foot kicking the door shut as he braced for impact onto the apron. He rolled over and over into the semi-darkness afforded by the spacing of the floodlights directed onto the plane.

While Cash lay prone, the first bullets pinged at the policemen's feet. Rigs, off in the darkness with a silenced rifle, had four of the policemen at his mercy, caught cold in the openness of the apron. Any attempt to run back to the plane, the only cover they had, was met with a clear warning. Bullets pinged in three burst shots mere feet away from them.

"Throw your weapons down and no one gets hurt!" shouted Cash, his body barely visible as the police struggled against the glare of the floodlights. His pistol was pointed directly at their bodies and he wasn't going to issue warning shots.

The four policemen dropped their weapons.

"And the two in the plane!" Cash snapped. "You've got three seconds!"

"Okay, Okay, don't shoot!" The two policemen's guns flew out of the plane door, quickly followed by their owners.

Cash stood up and walked over slowly, his pistol sweeping across the men.

"Rigs!" shouted Cash needlessly, as Rigs appeared out of the darkness.

"On the ground," Cash demanded.

"Cash Harris?" asked the oldest policeman in the group.

"Grab the concrete!" Cash ordered forcefully.

"Travis Davies sent us," the policeman said, but nonetheless complied with Cash's order.

"How do I know you're not lying?" asked Cash warily.

"He said you'd ask that," said the policeman. "And he told me to say, he'd expect nothing less."

Cash withdrew his pistol and Rigs slung his rifle around his shoulder. Travis always talked of how he expected nothing less of the two. It had become a bit of a catchphrase.

"Apologies," said Cash, offering his hand to help the officer up. Rigs held back. His rifle was on his shoulder but could be back in action with the simplest of movements.

"It'll teach us a lesson," said the elder policemen. "I assume the whiny steward alerted you?"

Cash nodded.

"Amateur error," he said, dusting down his uniform. "Frankly, we couldn't listen to him any longer but I didn't think he'd go running to help you."

Cash shrugged. "So what does Travis want?"

"For you to call him."

"And that takes six men?"

"He thought we'd be safer in numbers, one or two and you might have just shot us."

"Good point," said Cash, watching Rigs nod in agreement.

Chapter 38

The conversation with Travis had started out short, sweet and to the point. He didn't want Cash and Rigs anywhere near the agency. He was cutting them loose. Before Cash could respond in outrage, Travis silenced him with one comment. They were the only two in the whole fucking agency he could trust and for that reason, he didn't want them anywhere near it. The agency was rotten; the whole intelligence network was rotten. It had to be, there was no way twenty Afghans could have pulled off that operation without a network of support. And there was no way that size of operation should have been able to elude the entire US intelligence operation.

"It's worrying," agreed Cash, relaxing into the seat on the plane as they prepared for takeoff.

"The scariest part is I think I'm the only one that's actually worried. Everyone else seems to be relieved," sighed Travis.

"We've got a couple of leads, they're a bit out there though," said Cash, raising an eyebrow from Sophie, who had barely looked at him since the taxi driver incident.

"Anything is one hundred percent more than we've got, but wait, you might be able to clear something up. Senator Albert Noble, or Bertie Noble. How well do you know him?"

"We've gone before him a couple of times in Senate hearings, other than that, not very well."

"He mentioned your father was friends with his niece at university?"

Cash scanned his memory. "Nope, don't remember him ever mentioning it to me, do you know her name?"

"It'll be something Noble. You know their name tells you how senior they are within the family?"

"How does that work?" asked Cash perplexed.

"If their first name begins with an A they're more senior than the one's with a B then the next level down's a C," he nodded.

"Bullshit," said Cash. "That's just some conspiracy theory rubbish surely."

"I don't know but trust me, the higher in the alphabet their name, the more power they have! Atlas Noble, Antoine Noble and his son's called Alex. A bit like different levels of royalty I suppose, King, Prince, Earl, Duke…"

"It'll just be a coincidence," suggested Cash halfheartedly.

"Wait a minute, there's something else. They're all Noble. Come to think of it, they really are all called Noble…"

"Well, they *are* the Noble family," said Cash, not getting what Travis was alluding to.

"Yeah, but you'd normally find other surnames. You know, the daughters marrying someone else? Anyway, sorry I don't know her name but your father never mentioned a connection to the Nobles?"

"My father and I hadn't really spoken much for some time…" said Cash quietly.

"Yes, of course, sorry. Anyway it's no big deal. It all seemed a little off but the Senator was almost killed as well, so it's a bit of waste of time." He stopped himself, bringing the conversation back on track. "You mentioned a lead?"

"It's a bit tenuous," Cash began slowly, as he didn't quite understand it himself. "Hold on, I'm going to put you on speaker." Once he did, he spoke again. "With me is Sophie Kramer, she has a doctorate in…"

"Astronomy," Sophie said, saving Cash the embarrassment.

"She's been going through my dad's research work and…" he motioned for Sophie to take over the conversation.

"Professor Harris had a theory, I think Cash referred to it earlier as being a bit out there and to be honest, he's probably right," she conceded, blowing a silent raspberry to Cash. "But if we start with the principle that Hubble 2 was the target, his theory may hold some credence."

Travis was keen to hear more.

"He believes there is a great secret about our future, one that ancient civilizations were aware of but were wiped out in order to protect it."

"Wiped out?"

"He believed there are guardians who are protecting the secret and who will go to any lengths to protect it."

"Does he know what the secret was?"

"Oh my God!" Cash exclaimed.

"What?" came a chorus from everyone, including Rigs.

"The message from my father's deputy, from the observatory before he was killed. He said my father was right."

"About what?" asked Sophie.

"About everything, but then the line cut out."

"And James, his deputy was working with Hubble 2!" Sophie's level of excitement was reaching fever pitch. "Which was shot out of the sky at the same time the observatory and all of its data was destroyed and James was killed."

"Protecting a secret!" said Travis.

"Exactly."

"We would need Hubble 2 to see it," said Rigs under his breath to Cash.

"Of course," said Sophie. "They destroyed it for a reason. They've not destroyed any other telescopes."

"How long to build another Hubble 2?" asked Cash, trying to rebuild hope.

"Ten to twenty years," Sophie said flatly.

"We don't know if we need Hubble 2. Perhaps the timing was coincidental?" said Rigs.

"Rigs, you're a genius!" exclaimed Sophie. "*Timing*. Professor Harris's research talks about a window of time. It's marked out by the ancient ruins, they map the timing of the event."

"It sounds like you're about to go into details my brain will struggle to comprehend," said Travis. "I also think, given recent events, that we'll keep what you're doing between us."

"Good idea."

"Cash, do you remember that old Hotmail account?" Travis asked.

"Yes," replied Cash.

"Same as previously, we'll correspond through the drafts. If there's anything I can do to help, let me know, otherwise I'll leave you guys to it. How are you guys for transport?"

"Rigs' trust fund is taking a pasting," replied Cash.

"I'll leave a draft email with the details of an untraceable account to use, reimburse Rigs for what he's used so far. Good luck guys!"

Travis hung up.

"So where to?" asked Cash, looking at Sophie. She opened the laptop.

"Machu Picchu, Peru," she said, barely able to believe the Director of the CIA had bought into the idea. She felt a shiver run down her spine. She had a horrible feeling they were about to open a Pandora's box and once opened, there was no way to shut it.

Chapter 39

Alejandro Velasco Astete International Airport
Cusco, Peru

The small corporate jet touched down just after midnight local time. Steve opened the DIS folder. Cusco was home to 350,000 people, elevation 11,152 feet above sea level, a world heritage site and was once the center of the Incan Empire. The detail continued with a full demographic breakdown and history of the city. However, none of it was the least bit helpful. The only relevant piece of information was that it was 47 miles from Machu Picchu.

"We've got a second chance to take these guys." Steve looked across at Charlie, her face flushing red. "Let's make sure we don't fuck it up again," he said, staring into her eyes. He had had to abandon his wife in the middle of an anniversary dinner when the job came through; an anniversary dinner that would have been fine if Charlie had remembered the sex of her fake baby. If she had, these guys would already be dead and no job would have come through.

"Maybe if we stuck to Charlene…"

"I'd remember I'm a girl?" she asked. He had pushed her too far. She had apologized during the entire flight to no avail. His shitty mood wasn't lifting.

"Boss, Charlie gets the point," said Zach.

"Yeah, boss," said Liam, the fourth and final member of the team.

Steve looked at his three young protégés, all plucked directly from the forces, unlike himself, who was former forces and CIA. They may have lacked the investigative and analytical skills he had picked up from the agency, but he wouldn't want anyone else by his side when the shit hit the fan. They were exceptional soldiers.

"I'm sorry, it was a big night. Our twenty-fifth wedding anniversary," he explained. "Anyway, we've got to get there ASAP, this is their most likely destination."

His team didn't need any further orders. They grabbed their kits and headed to the door of the jet, following him down and out, straight to the taxi rank.

"Machu Picchu," said Steve to one of only two taxis waiting outside the airport.

The driver looked at Steve and his three companions eagerly waiting by his side and laughed.

"Machu Picchu? You can't drive there, you need to catch a train," said the driver.

"So take us to the train."

"Next train's at 6:00 a.m."

Steve checked his watch. "12:15 a.m."

"Helicopter?"

"Not allowed, train or trek."

The other taxi driver had wandered over. There was little else going on. He had overheard the conversation. "There's the 5:07 from Sacred Valley. It's the first train of the day and the quickest."

"Fine, take us there!"

"It's a two-hour drive and at this time of night—"

"I don't care how much it costs!"

Charlie was looking up the train times on her smart phone. "He's right, the Sacred Valley train gets in at 6.34, long before the train from Cusco."

"Pile in, we'll take both taxis," said Steve, calculating in his mind how he would have had more than enough time to have his anniversary dinner and still flown down in time to catch the early train. His mood darkened again.

***

Cash woke up when the first hint of sunlight crept through the window. Their flight from Bolivia had taken just under an hour the previous evening and, thanks to his father's research, had highlighted the best place to stay. It had taken some time to get there but it had been worth it. The Machu Picchu

Sanctuary Lodge was a luxury hotel a few hundred yards from the ruins.

Cash jumped in the shower. When he was out and dressed and hearing no signs of life from either of his companions' rooms, he headed out into the fresh morning air. The sun's rays were beginning to peek over the mountain ranges that loomed all around sending shards of light shooting down into the valley below. Cash walked across to the entrance of the ruins. The ticketing office and entrance were unmanned. The first bus from the valley below wasn't due for another forty-five minutes.

He wandered on into the ruins. The terraces cut down the mountainside below him, revealing layers of farming ground, with many structures sitting along the ridge. Similar to the ruins at Pumapunka and Tiwanaku, the stonework was stunning. The lower layers of the buildings featured stones carved so precisely that they sat together without the need for mortar. Their size defied the location. Huge stones, carved to perfection, which would have been transported thousands of feet up a sheer mountainside. Water flowed through perfectly carved channels following Cash as he walked along the length of the ruins.

He closed his eyes, the silence interrupted only by the water running through the channels, as had been planned centuries earlier.

"Cash?" came a shout from up ahead.

He opened his eyes. Sophie was waving at him from the farthest most part of the ruins. She must have been up before him. He walked over to meet her, marveling at the ornately carved stone that protruded from the ground.

"The Intihuantana," she said. "It's part of another astronomical calendar."

Cash looked out across the mountains that surrounded them. "It's an amazing place."

"Lost for five hundred years and only rediscovered in 1911," she said, packing her gear away.

"So it's five hundred years old?" asked Cash.

"Some of it, but not all of it. Your father guessed far older, certainly the earlier structures. You may have noticed a difference in the construction."

"Yeah," nodded Cash. "The lower stones are larger and cut precisely, the higher stones are far smaller and nowhere near as well cut."

"Exactly, it seems the builders got worse as time progressed and tools advanced," she said sarcastically.

"Any idea how old?"

Sophie shook her head and attempted to hoist her bag onto her shoulder. He caught it and put it over his.

"Where next?" he asked.

"I'm done," she said, yawning.

"How can you be done, you said you needed a few hours here!"

She yawned again. "Yep, and like I said, all done."

"You didn't go to bed?"

"I tried but it was such a beautiful clear night and my mind was racing. I'm taking measurements that relate to astronomy, when better than at night?"

Cash looked around, a bit disgruntled. "What if they're watching us?" Sophie pointed along the pathway that led back out of the far side of the ruins, gently sloping towards the peak that overlooked the ruins. A hundred yards away, with a bird's eye view of the entire site, sat Rigs, half hidden amongst the undergrowth.

"One of my protectors is obviously a little more on the ball!"

Cash waved at Rigs to come down and join them.

"How long's he been there?"

"All night. Not said a word, just watched me like a hawk."

"Menacing?" asked Cash apologetically.

"I must be getting used to him. It was quite comforting to know he was there!"

The sound of engines straining reached across to them, quickly followed by a rush of voices. The tourists had arrived. The local buses transported a mass of commercialism up an impossibly steep slope. It was not a journey any of them were looking forward to repeating in daylight; it had been scary enough when they couldn't fully appreciate the drop.

The bird call went unnoticed by Sophie but had Cash on his toes in an instant. He grabbed Sophie and ducked behind the wall that obscured their view back towards the entrance. Rigs followed his call at a low run, tucking his binoculars back into this pack.

"The mother from the hotel elevator!" he said urgently, indicating off towards the entrance, a couple of hundred yards away.

Sophie tried to look but was pulled back by Cash.

"He doesn't mean this hotel or an actual mother! It's one of the killers from Santa Cruz."

"Oh my God!" said Sophie. "It *is* linked!" she almost shouted with excitement.

Cash covered her mouth. He had already concluded the same the second Rigs had issued the warning call. They were being hunted.

"That means she's one of the guardians!" whispered Sophie. "Protectors of the secret!"

"I doubt it," mumbled Rigs to Cash, raising a smile.

"What?" asked Sophie.

"Later," promised Cash.

"We need to speak to her!" Sophie insisted.

"She's here to kill us!"

"She's here to kill *you two*," corrected Sophie. "They've not seen me with you." She was up and moving before they realized what she was going to do, out in the open for all to see. If either Cash or Rigs went near her, they'd expose her as being with them, tantamount to painting a target on her.

"Shit!" said Cash through his teeth when she evaded his diving grasp while Rigs strained to see around the wall without giving away their presence.

"I spot another two with her, they're scoping out the area. They don't think we're here yet."

"They did arrive on the first bus," mused Cash. "They probably don't know we stayed at the local hotel. Or didn't think we could have since they knew we weren't in Peru last night, so they must have known we were in Bolivia."

"A leak?" asked Rigs. "They're not at all interested in Sophie. They've not given her a second look."

Cash looked over the edge of the building that they were hunkered down in, it was a sheer drop down to a terrace twenty feet below. The terraces ran along the length of the ruins.

"If we drop down, we can keep tight against the wall and make our way back to the entrance."

Rigs opened up his small backpack. His Kimber ICQB pistol sat on top, a silencer by its side. He withdrew the silencer and screwed it in place.

"Or we kill them now," suggested Rigs, offering Cash the pistol while withdrawing a 12-inch Mission MPK-T1 knife from the inside of his boot.

Cash stole a look around the wall. The three had spread out. Sophie was wandering as aimlessly as she could, although to Cash, it looked anything but, towards the girl.

"I'll take the guy in the gray t-shirt," Cash said. "You take the olive shirt."

They moved without another word. Cash dropped down to the terrace below, his landing timed and planned not only to minimize the chance of injury but noise. He had the advantage of the pistol, so his route to his kill was far simpler than for Rigs, who needed to get up close and personal.

Rigs rolled across the gap to the adjacent building and worked his way along the extensive ruins, which offered excellent cover for him. Unfortunately, the olive shirt had moved away from the ruins and had opted to walk down the sacred plaza, a large open area, out of striking distance.

***

Charlie caught sight of the woman who appeared from the ruins ahead of them. Initially she had thought nothing of it, but soon realized the woman was keeping an eye on where Charlie was heading and was trying to engineer a route to cross her path.

"The woman off to my right, just under a hundred yards," said Charlie quietly. Each of the team was wearing a tiny state of the art ear piece mic. "She's working her way towards me."

"They're here, guys. Be on alert," Steve responded. "Charlie, good spot."

Zach, wearing an olive colored t-shirt, moved away from the ruins he had been admiring and stuck to open ground. His eyes desperately tracked any movement from where the woman had suddenly appeared.

"Liam, anything?" asked Steve. Liam was off to Charlie's right, skirting the edge of the ruins.

"I can see the woman clearly but neither of the targets," replied Liam.

***

Cash heard the voice above. He edged out from the terrace wall and caught a glimpse of the gray t-shirt. He pulled himself in tight against the face of the wall. Gray T-Shirt would have to lean out over the edge to be able to see him. There were steps off to his right that would take him back to the main level, up and behind the man. He couldn't risk a shot without knowing where Sophie was in relation to the woman.

Cash edged quickly along the wall and crept up the staircase, keeping his head as low as possible. When he reached floor height, he looked along to Gray T-Shirt thirty yards away, hugging the edge of the ruins.

***

"Movement behind you, boss!" said Liam urgently into the earpiece. "Coming up from the terrace below. I don't have a shot! I repeat, I don't have a shot!"

Steve didn't wait to react. He dove into the body of the ruins almost instantaneously. Cash's reactive shot whistled past his ankle.

"I have the shot!" said Liam

***

Cash spotted the move and tried to get a shot off but Gray T-Shirt moved too quickly. It was as though he had eyes in the back of his head.

Rigs spotted the glint off in the distance, a scope. A suppressed flash followed. He looked in panic at Sophie. She was fine. It had to be Cash they were aiming at. Olive T-Shirt was still over thirty feet off to his right in the open. He delved into his bag. It wasn't ideal but he didn't have time, the situation was getting out of control.

He pulled out three shuriken, Japanese throwing stars. It had been a long time since he'd used them in anger. Ideally, he'd have been half the distance away. He aimed the star and threw as hard as he could. One of the four points landed behind his target's ear, it couldn't have been more perfect. The target slumped to the ground.

Rigs spun out of the other side of the ruins and made a run towards Sophie.

***

"Zach's down, I repeat, Zach is down!" said Liam into his mic.

"Is he moving?" asked Charlie, trying to stay calm. She and Zach had been seeing each other secretly for the previous few months.

"No," replied Liam.

Charlie looked for the woman, off to her right still, about forty yards and closing slowly.

"Liam, where's my guy?"

"I think I got him, no movement from the stairwell."

"Keep me covered, I'm going to back up, Steve."

***

Sophie was helpless, the woman abruptly changed course and sped towards her. They did know who she was, or at least that she was with Cash and Rigs. She looked around, neither were anywhere to be seen. She was feeling a little less pleased with her plan. The crowds of visitors were starting to spill into the grounds but they were still way off at the entrance. She diverted her course but the woman matched it. A man in a gray t-shirt was also matching her. There were two of them coming for her. Where the hell was Cash? She turned again, spotted a stairwell down to the next level of ruins and raced down it. The woman leapt down, not bothering to find a stairwell.

The man was right behind her. Sophie turned and ran. She passed through a doorway and turned sharply, her ankle failing to turn as quickly, twisted, sending her crashing to the floor with a scream.

Rigs spun round. He was close. He heard the crash and the scream. He had to stay out of sight and rely on sounds. The sniper had a bird's eye view of the entire site. He changed course and zeroed in on Sophie's whimpers, speeding through the ruins, keeping out of the sniper's view. He darted back behind a wall, but was too late. The woman who had posed as a mother stood over Sophie, her pistol leveled at Sophie's head, her back to Rigs. Fortunately, she hadn't seen him. He pulled out his knife and lunged into the open, in full view of the sniper. Rigs had caught them by surprise and grabbed the woman, spinning her to shield him and Sophie from the sniper.

With the knife slicing into her neck, the woman dropped her pistol without hesitation.

"Don't move," said Rigs needlessly.

"Don't *you* move!" said the man in the gray t-shirt, stepping out from behind the wall with his pistol aimed directly at Rigs' head.

Rigs ignored him and pushed the knife deeper, the blood oozing from beneath its razor sharp edge as it cut deeper into the woman's skin.

"Lower your gun or I take her head off right now!" Rigs stated coldly.

***

Steve had his ace in the hole. His sniper had the target in sight.

"I have the shot!" said Liam into Steve's earpiece.

Steve lowered his pistol and was rewarded by the target lessening his cut. All he needed was to give a slight nod and Liam would pull the trigger. He waited for the knife to relax a little more. The last thing he wanted was a slumping body to slice through Charlie's neck, killing her as a result of a hasty shot.

Steve dropped his pistol to show he meant business. He hoped the guy would reciprocate. He moved the knife further from her neck, fully exposing his face to the sniper when he leaned against the side of Charlie's head.

"I have the shot, give me the signal!" Liam urged.

The guy moved the knife to a safe position. Steve dipped his head slightly.

Sophie's hands covered her face, muffling her scream when the head of the person standing above her exploded into a bloody mush. The body, minus half its head, crashed on top of her as Gray T-Shirt reached down for his pistol.

Her screams continued even after the bloody remains were pulled off of her and she was dragged behind a wall.

"Rigs?" she asked.

He nodded. Sophie calmed down and looked around to see that the woman had been shot while the man with the gray t-shirt had a knife buried deep in his chest, blood trickling from his mouth as he coughed and spluttered his last breaths.

"How did you manage that?"

"I had my ear pressed against hers listening to her earpiece. Their sniper asked for a signal, so when he dipped his head, I moved her head to where mine was and put a knife through his chest," he said, holding up the pistol he had managed to acquire while getting them into cover.

"What about Cash?" she asked.

"He was supposed to have dealt with him," he said, pointing to the dying gray t-shirt clad man.

The sniper fired two shots uselessly against the wall next to them. He couldn't possibly hit them where they were. He followed those with another three, then one then two more.

Sophie broke into a grin. "He took care of the sniper!"

"So that's the secret signal?" smiled Rigs.

"You don't miss much in that world of yours, do you, Rigs?" asked Sophie, impressed he'd remembered the signal from the bunker.

Rigs shook his head and stood up, offering Sophie a helping hand onto her feet. He dug into his bag and with the help of a water bottle and a t-shirt, removed most of the blood on him.

Two tentative steps proved her ankle wasn't too bad and under his guidance, they made their way away from the bodies before the first tourists' screams echoed through the mountains.

Cash met them as they approached the entrance. The crowds were already trying to leave having discovered the bodies. Cash pushed as tight against Sophie as he could. She pulled away.

He pushed back. "Your clothes are covered in blood down this side," he whispered.

"Oh!"

"So where to?"

"A shower please."

"If you insist," Cash had an email to draft to Travis but that could definitely wait.

Chapter 40

Senator Noble had seen the news break from Peru. Four Americans had been killed in broad daylight in Machu Picchu. Four Americans who he knew were linked to DIS. His pulse quickened. This couldn't be happening. He grabbed the phone.

"Who are you calling?" The slight Eastern European twang to her accent added an unnecessarily sinister edge to the beauty who had not left his side. So far, the most he had learned was her name, Katya, not that he believed it was her real one.

"My nephew. We may have a problem," he said. His nerves were not coping well with the new arrangement. She sat in the corner of his office, having spent the night sleeping in his bed, while he slept on the sofa. Even visiting the restroom required the door to be left open, which she was more than happy to do herself. She had no issue undressing or showering in front of him. Although she was the most flawless female he had ever seen, the darkness behind her captivating eyes belied a violence he had no intention of unleashing.

She waved her hand regally as though that were acceptable.

Conrad answered on the second ring. "Uncle Bertie! Enjoying your new companion?" he asked gleefully.

"We have a problem." Bertie would bow and curtsy to Antoine, but not the monkey.

"What?" asked Conrad.

"Have you not seen the news?" he asked, his rage building.

"No, I've just stepped off a plane," explained Conrad, re-engaging once he heard the hint of panic in the anger of his otherwise fearless uncle.

"Your two targets appear to have wiped out a DIS team in Peru, it's all over the news."

"Shit, when?"

"It broke a few minutes ago. Who knows how long since it happened but I wouldn't think long."

"There's nothing on them that will connect them to DIS. They know not to divulge any details about DIS - their families will be amply rewarded," explained Conrad..

"You're forgetting one thing. We're up against actual CIA staff here. We've never used DIS staff in this way before."

"And?"

"I'm exposed!" shouted the Senator, failing to understand why Conrad wasn't seeing it. "I hired the boss, Mike Yates, so there's a direct link to me and Atlas Noble."

Katya sat up in her chair, suddenly taking interest in the situation, especially after hearing the name Mike Yates. Her role was to protect Atlas Noble and Antoine Noble from any fallout as a result of the Senator's 'work'. If, even for a second, it looked like the government were piecing together his involvement in the coup attempt, Senator Bertie Noble would suffer a sudden and fatal heart attack, and Katya would disappear invisibly into the night.

Conrad always considered DIS to be an arm's length organization with no ties whatsoever to Atlas Noble; that was what made it so valuable. The caliber of staff they were able to recruit far exceeded anything on the open market. The ex-CIA, DIA and Special Forces operatives, believing they were joining a highly secretive government agency, were willing to undertake roles that guns for hire wouldn't otherwise touch. It was ingenious, giving Atlas Noble one of the world's premier and most secretive intelligence agencies. None of that came without having to build some credibility and Senator Bertie Noble provided that as Chairman of the Senate Intelligence Committee.

"Perhaps DIS was inappropriate in this instance then."

"You think?" said Bertie sarcastically.

"Our contacts are telling us that the CIA has cut them loose," explained Conrad.

"Cash and Rigs? Not a chance, they're Travis Davies' go to guys. That's why you've got four body bags waiting for a ride home from Peru. If that's what you're hearing, that's what Travis Davies wants you to hear."

"This Mike Yates, is he the only exposure?" asked Katya, interrupting the conversation.

Senator Noble nodded at her. Katya relaxed back into her chair.

"We don't even know if it is a problem," said Conrad. "Dead men can't talk."

"We don't know what they told the CIA guys before they were killed," said the Senator. "They may have already alerted Travis to DIS' involvement. They may already have Mike Yates in custody!"

"They don't," said Conrad confidently.

"You don't know that!"

"I do," he smiled. "You're not the first loose end Katya was sent to deal with," explained Conrad. "Mike Yates, I believe, has a byline on page seven of this morning's *New York Times*," he said flatly, then hung up.

He'd played enough with the old man. DIS had already been pulled from the operation a few hours earlier. Everything the Senator had said was valid, not to mention that Mike Yates was the only link to Atlas Noble in DIS, hence Katya's extra babysitting role. How she had made a man, particularly one as experienced and capable as Mike Yates, jump voluntarily from a skyscraper to his death, leaving behind a genuine handwritten suicide letter, Conrad had no idea. However, that was why Katya and her very special band of colleagues were the best in the world at what they did. And that was why they had replaced the DIS team in the hunt for Cash and Rigs.

Chapter 41

Centers for Disease Control and Prevention (CDC) Atlanta

The first reports of an unknown outbreak in Papua New Guinea trickled in. The first came from the Vatican, alerting the center to a call they had received from a mission based along the Sepik River. A very agitated nun had called them, claiming that everyone was dead. She was unable to give much detail such was her state of distress. Within an hour, another call from a similar area had relayed a similar message.

By the fourth call, less than three hours later, the quality of the message had improved. Medecins Sans Frontières, the leading French humanitarian aid organization, had relayed a message from two of their doctors in the field, using the words 'extinction level event'. Unfortunately, the call was received just as YouTube footage of the mummified remains of an entire village hit the internet.

The CDC's state of the art phone system instantly crashed when the world hit the panic button.

Major General Paul Lockhart MD, recently appointed as the new director of the CDC by President Mitchell, welcomed his crisis management team into his office.

"What do we know?" he asked, pushing a number of packing boxes out of the way to allow his team to sit down.

"Very little so far, and none of which we've been able to verify beyond the YouTube video that's now been taken offline. Reports are of a virus of unknown origin wiping out entire communities in less than twelve hours," said the department head for the Australasian region.

"Twelve hours? That can't be right," he said, walking around the table. He liked to walk and think. "It can't be a virus then!"

If anyone knew it couldn't be virus, it was Lockhart, former head of the USAMRMC unit at Fort Detrick, historically more famous for trying to create the type of virus he was now tasked with defeating.

"I can't agree more," said his head of Virology. There's no virus on earth capable of that level of contagion, fatality and timescale."

"Or certainly none we're aware of. We're probably dealing with one of the least explored corners of the world. There're probably animals, insects and flora in there that we don't even know exist yet."

"Where is the affected area?"

An overlarge map was quartered to allow it to fit on the table; the portion on view stretched from Australia to South China.

"There," said the deputy, pointing to the Northeast sector of Papua New Guinea. The area was a mass of green.

"Do we not have a map with better detail, the towns, roads transport links…?"

"This is detailed," the deputy interrupted, pointing to the coastal towns of Aitape and Vanimo. We're dealing with a region that is almost entirely inhabited by tribal clans, living a subsistence life on the river banks." He put his finger on the Sepik River and traced along its length. "This is their highway, their lifeline, and major food source," he said.

"So we're dealing with an area almost entirely cut off from the outside world."

"I'd go so far as to say that they *are* cut off. If you're not using the river, you'd have to trek through hundreds of miles of mountainous and dense jungle to reach the coastal towns."

"Do we know what the situation is with containment?"

"The river is blocked to traffic and quarantine stations are in place, although I believe they're poorly manned. Papua New Guinea is not known for its military might."

"Potentially, we're facing the deadliest virus known to man and it happens here," he pointed to the map. "Where, with one river being blocked, it's being contained?"

"It would appear so," replied the deputy, as skeptical as Lockhart.

"Great place to test a bio-weapon," he pondered out loud.

"There are approaching 700,000 people potentially affected," added one of the group.

"So it really *is* a great place to test a bio-weapon. We're talking medieval style tribal villagers. Living in close proximity, all drinking the same water and most importantly, buried deep in a jungle that the world knows little about."

"And will remember even less about in a week from now."

"Are we talking genocide here?"

"It still happens— Cambodia, Rwanda, the Balkans, Darfur and Tibet, to name a recent few. Whatever the case, we need boots on the ground and fast!"

***

Bea Noble, head of Atlas Noble's pharmaceutical and medical division, watched carefully as the first results of their experiment were displayed. The unmanned drones hung silently above the area recording every minute of the event via their sensitively balanced infrared cameras. Able to penetrate through the roofs of the simple homes, the infrared could record the impact while the crop duster style aircraft flew the length of the river spraying its deadly load. It didn't take long; the white bodies that glowed in the monitor began to change to a deep red, to over 110 degrees Fahrenheit as their bodies reacted to the spray. The water molecules were grabbing every ounce of energy from the bodies and evaporating. The red glow was the bodies cooking in their own steam. One after another, the images reddened and then slowly returned to their original white and shortly afterwards disappeared from the screen, their temperature having dropped to below that of a living being. The spray had worked.

Bea watched intensely as they tracked the river, like the crop duster had done before. One after another, the villages died in front of them. Tens of thousands, then a hundred thousand, two and then three hundred thousand human beings died in front of their eyes. Bea could hardly take her eyes from the screen. The genetic soup she had mixed, as described in the ancient scrolls supplied by Anya from her archives, had performed perfectly. Even down to the few anomalies that still glowed white. The charity workers and missionaries lay untouched and unaware of the pestilence of a biblical scale that had visited their villages that night.

Bea thanked the three members of her inner team, the only ones aware of what the real purpose of their trip had been. They were all Nobles. Nobody outside of the family could have been trusted, nor would ever be, with the truth of their operation. One other member was required to be congratulated. Her son, the pilot of the aircraft. A thump above told her he had arrived. She exited the operations center and made her way up the tight and confusing galleyways onto the deck. The C-2A Grumman was taxiing to the far end of the aircraft carrier as the sun rose over a perfectly still Southern Pacific Ocean.

To the rest of the crew on board, he was arriving to join the Atlas Noble Trust's vital work in assisting the poverty stricken regions of the world. The former aircraft carrier destined for the British Royal Navy had been sold even before it had been built. The ship was a convenient casualty of the recession and Atlas Noble had purchased it and redesigned it to meet their humanitarian needs, creating the world's most advanced floating hospital with an airwing capable of reaching into almost any part of the world to assist those most in need. Able to sit off the coast, its Grumman C-2As could reach into the heart of countries, far beyond the range of helicopters, delivering medical assistance wherever it was required.

Staffed with almost a thousand doctors and nurses and fitted with the most advanced operating theatres, laboratories and equipment, there was little the floating hospital couldn't tackle.

There was only one thing that could make the operation more of a success. As the news began to break of the tragedy, Bea headed back to the operations center and picked up a phone.

It took her a few tries to eventually get through. The lines were jammed.

"General Lockhart, please," she requested.

"I'm sorry, he's in a meeting at the moment," replied his secretary apologetically. "May I take your name and ask him to call you back?"

"I'm sure he wouldn't mind being interrupted, it is very important."

"I'm very sorry, Madam, but the only person I'm authorized to interrupt him for is the President."

"If you wish me to disturb the President just to get him on the phone so be it, but then I'll be interrupting the President as well," Bea replied more sarcastically than she had intended.

"I'm sorry, I didn't catch your name?"

"Bea Noble, I head up Atlas Noble Pharma—"

"I'm sorry, Mrs. Noble, I'll put you straight through," replied the secretary. "Bea," said Lockhart louder than necessary. He wanted to let his team know who'd interrupted their meeting.

"Paul, how are you my darling?" oozed Bea, who had known him for many years.

"Worried…"

"I can guess why," she said, cutting to the chase. "That's why I'm calling, to offer our assistance."

"Your assistance?"

"Our hospital ship is only a few hundred miles from the affected area."

"You're kidding?"

"Nope, fully manned and as you're aware, with some of the foremost specialists in the field. We're good to go and ready for action."

"I bet they are," he joked. "Considering you secured them almost entirely from Detrick and CDC."

"That's why they're the best," she schmoozed.

"Can you hold?"

Lockhart covered the mouthpiece and turned to his team, relaying the information. "Their ship is as advanced as any facility we have on land, it even has a level four biosafety lab and the staff to man it."

A number of nods rushed around the table. Having that type of facility within such a short range was a godsend and would allow them to work in real time without having to ferry samples back to the US for analysis. BIO safety level four was the highest level of safety and was required for working with the world's most deadly and contagious diseases.

"That would be fantastic," he said. "I'll just need to get you security and presidential clearance for you to act on our behalf before we arrive but I'm sure that'll be nothing more than a formality."

"We have a detachment of security on board that can secure any location in the short term. As for presidential clearance, I'm happy to give Dave a call," said Bea. Her use of the President's first name wasn't missed, along with the casualness with which she delivered it. It had been a long time since Lockhart had heard anyone call the President 'Dave'.

"I'll call him," said Lockhart. "I need to update him anyway. I'm sending a team to your location. They'll fly in via Guam. If you could give Guam your coordinates that would be great."

"Of course. I'll get a team in there and start relaying whatever we find. I'll have my IT boys give your teams back at · CDC access to our systems. You can monitor real time whatever we find."

"You're a lifesaver and in this instance, it couldn't be truer!" Bea smiled when the call ended. It couldn't have worked out better. Atlas Noble was to run the operation of understanding what had caused the genocide of the Iamult people.

Chapter 42

Sophie passed on Cash's offer and after a quick shower was joining him and Rigs in the fight for transport off the Machu Picchu Mountain. The bus service, constrained to the single and winding treacherous path, was buckling under pressure from tourists to flee the deadly scene. Fortunately, the authorities were having as much trouble reaching it as the tourists had leaving it. By the time the scene was sealed, Cash, Sophie and Rigs were already sitting on a train heading back to Cusco. When the carriage began to move, they caught their breath for the first time.

"Are you sure you're okay?" asked Cash.

Sophie nodded. "Amazingly, yes," she said, surprising herself, given what she had just witnessed.

"It would be perfectly understandable if you weren't," said Cash.

"I think my mind is far too preoccupied to compute it rationally," she said turning to him. "It's like my father's death. I'm grieving but I know the real pain will come at some point."

Cash nodded, along with Rigs, it made perfect sense.

"And let's not forget they were going to kill us," said Sophie after a pause, "which gives me even more reason to believe that what we are doing is vital. I won't let my emotions be the reason we fail."

Rigs closed his eyes. Travelling was a chance to sleep and he seldom missed the opportunity to switch off and fully relax, something he wasn't capable of doing while awake.

Cash had been the only one to benefit from a night's sleep. He stared at Sophie as she too closed her eyes, in awe as to how well she was coping. She was one tough and very beautiful woman.

She opened her eyes and stared right at him, aware of his eyes on her. She smiled. "Wake me up just before we get to Cusco. There's somewhere else we need to go!"

"It's not straight through. We need to get a taxi from Sacred Valley."

"The taxi can do a detour on our way to the airport." She closed her eyes and was asleep in seconds, leaving Cash alone with his thoughts of what could have been. He looked at Rigs. Had he not run out fifteen years earlier, they'd never have met. Rigs never would have lasted in the Marines without him. Without that structure, who knew what would have happened to him. Before Cash, Rigs had no one. No one understood him, his family certainly didn't, and had had him institutionalized the second they could.

The day he had arrived at the Officer's Candidate School would have been his last, had it not been for Cash's intervention. They had found each other. Cash was an emotional wreck after his mistaken assumption about Sophie and his father and was keen to find anything to take his mind off of it. Jake Miller (Rigs) had slunk into the class, a tall, powerful young man, similar in size and build to Cash. Whereas Cash stood ramrod straight and proud, Rigs hung loose, his head angled to the floor, his eyes focused intently on a spot four feet in front of him.

When the candidates were told to pair up, Cash made straight for Rigs. He had no idea why. He just did. Perhaps it was a loneliness he felt after losing Sophie that he saw in Rigs. Perhaps it was his upbringing. Cash never liked to see anyone left out. A kid growing up without a mother produced its own complexities. Whatever the case, he had introduced himself and had received a whispered response. From that moment on, they were inseparable. Both were superb athletes and excelled during training, where Rigs came to life. His mind, preoccupied with the job in hand, freed itself sufficiently to allow Rigs to prove how superb a Marine he could be. Written exercises proved no problem either. Rigs was a highly intelligent student and was within touching distance of Cash's almost perfect scores. As a team, they were unstoppable. They shattered previous records and set a benchmark for others to aspire to. As individuals, Cash was as highly regarded as any candidate in the history of the

Corps. Rigs, however, caused great concern. As a Marine in the face of action, he was second to none, fearless, skilled and expert in almost every conceivable method of killing a person. As an officer in charge of a day to day platoon, he was an unmitigated liability. He simply could not communicate with his platoon unless in the heat of battle. Otherwise, he retreated into himself, avoiding eye contact and wherever possible using Cash as his method of communication.

In theory, he should have been failed. His interpersonal skills were not fit for purpose as a Marine officer. In practice, he was one of the most complete fighting Marines they had ever had the pleasure to train.

The decision was Cash's, if he were willing to accept the solution they had envisaged. Where Cash went, Rigs would follow, they were to be an inseparable team.

It was a no brainer for Cash. Rigs had opened up to Cash like he had never with anyone before. His rich family had effectively cast him aside at the age of ten. Boarding schools, camps, the family lodge with Uncle Bill. They did anything to keep their dysfunctional child away from their perfect life. Until he had met Cash, the only person with whom he had any type of normality was Uncle Bill. He and Bill had spent summers hunting and fishing and it was thanks to Uncle Bill that Rigs had destroyed almost every shooting record in the officer candidate school. His parents replaced love with money in an attempt to assuage their guilt, which, from the size of Rigs' trust fund, was significant. However, nothing could replace the love that parents should lavish on a child. Thanks to Cash, Rigs finally felt he had a family. And thanks to Rigs, up until very recently, Cash had felt the same.

He looked at Sophie sleeping peacefully, and realized he was still very much part of a very loving family, one he had walked out on fifteen years earlier. Had he not, though, Rigs, the man he looked on as his brother, would not have been sitting by Sophie's side. The world really did work in mysterious ways.

The train slowed down, jostling his companions awake. Dilemmas would be left for another time. They exited quickly and secured one of the few taxis that awaited the train's arrival. A two-hour drive lay ahead of them. Sophie gave the destination -

the airport via Saksaywaman. Rigs sniggered to himself like a child.

"What?" asked Sophie. Rigs stared out of the taxi window refusing to engage.

"It sounded like you said, airport via sexy women," explained Cash.

"Oh, well it's nothing like that I'm afraid, *boys,*" she replied, a heavy emphasis on boys. She closed her eyes and drifted back off to sleep. On arrival, she barely paused for breath, leading the two men to a site that the professor had highlighted in his research notes.

"Don't you need your equipment?" asked Cash. "No, nothing to measure here, just a wall to see!"

"Why?"

"I'd rather wait until later to explain that. In the meantime, just envisage the work required to build the walls you're about to see and remember we're talking six hundred years ago, or if your father's research is correct, nearer two thousand years ago!"

"Holy shit!" said Cash when he caught sight of the three-tiered zig-zagging wall that formed the walls of an ancient fort.

Rigs looked briefly but continued to remain more interested in the vast numbers of tourists who covered the area. He stayed back, keeping the taxi in sight, while covering both Cash and Sophie.

"Impressive, yes," agreed Sophie.

"How on earth did they manage that? That rock must be thirty feet high and ten feet wide and it's cut perfectly to fit with all of the others around it."

"Not just cut, look, that one has twelve angles and the stones around it have almost as many. These stones were cut and shaped to fuse together perfectly without cement or mortar."

Cash looked at the wall more closely. There wasn't even the tiniest gap. "It's like they've been melted together. But why so large, why not use smaller stones?"

Sophie nodded. "Exactly. Maybe because they didn't need to…" she teased. She glanced back at Rigs, who stood on the brow of the hill, his eyes scanning all around. "Does he ever relax?"

"When he sleeps," Cash replied, "only when he sleeps." So why didn't they use smaller stones?"

"Later. We've got one more stop and then I'd very much like to see my boy," she said.

"Me too," said Cash, sending a flutter through Sophie's chest. "So where next?"

"Somewhere we don't even need to get the plane to stop," she said with a wink.

Chapter 43

To the casual observer, the Route d'Hermance was no different from any other road that led out of Geneva, though it housed some of the more impressive properties bordering Lake Geneva. None of that made it particularly special. It was only once you reached Anieres that the Route d'Hermance became one of the world's more unique roads. There was nothing special about the road itself. What made it special was its level of privacy, even though it was not a private road; it was in fact a public highway that ran through a small village— one that had a diversion in place for those who did not belong. It had managed to be excluded from the intrusiveness of the Google Street View project, a. lone, two-mile stretch of road, unavailable to be viewed online at street level, unlike every other road in the vicinity.

Anieres was home to the Noble family, or as the locals had renamed it, Noble Village. Although security was not overtly visible, it was everywhere. If any driver strayed beyond the diversion, a checkpoint awaited their arrival, staffed entirely by former Swiss soldiers, most recently from the ARD 10 Special Forces detachment. Antoine Noble referred to them as his own Swiss Guard. With motion sensors, cameras and even a lake barrier to prevent unwanted visitors, Anieres was in effect one of the most secure places on the planet.

With over five hundred Nobles living within its confines, they represented half of the world's most powerful family. Anieres was home to the highest concentration of wealth in the world. Although the actual figure was almost incalculable due to the complexity of the family's finances, conservative estimates started at ten trillion dollars, around 5% of the world's wealth, and escalated quickly. The more radical estimates were closer to 75%. The majority hovered between the forty to fifty percent, approaching $100 trillion dollars. Whatever the case, it made for an exceptionally powerful and influential group of people, with whom the Swiss government preferred not to interfere. Anieres was almost a state within a state, not dissimilar to the other area guarded by the Swiss Guard.

Antoine stood out on the sun deck, enjoying the last rays of sunshine, watching the builders erect an impressive marquee on his pristine lawn. They were only days from his son's twenty-first birthday, a very special age for the family and none more so than for Alex, heir to the head of the family. The entire Noble family would gather to celebrate his coming of age and to celebrate his future leadership. For Alex, that leadership would be very different than any before him. The Noble family was in its final throes of power. Its reign on the planet was coming to an end. Their role in history was secure. Alex would be head of the family but the family itself would soon take a back seat, its wealth and influence in the new world would be irrelevant.

The role they had been born into, each and every one of them, was coming to its conclusion and would no doubt be rewarded, but the unknown awaited. He couldn't worry about that yet. First and foremost they had to begin the work that would pave the way for the future. The window of opportunity seemed huge, almost eighty years, but every second and every minute was going to count.

Approaching sixty himself, Antoine would not be around to see the conclusion of his lifelong work, the centuries of preparation by his family. Unlike his father, cruelly taken from them in a boating accident some twenty years earlier, he would see the new world, or at least the beginning of it. Alex and the generations to come would build the new world, a very different world from the one currently inhabiting planet Earth, a world where the Nobles were no richer, no poorer, no more powerful, no more special than any other of their neighbors.

Antoine heard the voices behind him. The doors to his library lay open behind him. His council was arriving, being shown into the inner sanctum. Up until that evening, the meetings had been weekly. Three years earlier, they were monthly. Before then, they were bi-annual. As of that evening, they were about to become daily and as they neared the eve of convergence, more than likely every four hours. There was much to discuss, much to plan, and much to still decide. Although the final decision would be his, his council was made up of family members who he trusted his life with and more importantly, that of a future population.

The noise of gravel crunching on the driveway at the side of the house caught his attention, just as he was about to greet his guests. None would have driven. They all lived in the village. Alex, his son, was the only person due to arrive from outside Anieres. A student at Harvard, it had been months since Alex had been home.

"Good evening," he said to his guests through the doorway. "I'll be with you shortly."

Antoine rushed out to welcome his son as he stepped out of his small sports car.

"Alex, so great to see you, my son!" he said, embracing him almost before he had made it out of the car.

The passenger door opened, catching Antoine by surprise. Alex beamed proudly at his father.

"Dad," he said, waiting for the young woman in the car to get out. "This is Lee, the woman I'm going to marry!"

To his credit, Antoine didn't blink. He walked around and welcomed his son's girlfriend with open arms, not even flinching when the bump stopped him hugging her too closely. She was undoubtedly a beautiful young woman, only heightened by her pregnant glow.

"It would seem double congratulations are in order." He stood back and looked at the young woman.

Alex joined them. "I knew you'd love her," he said.

"Of course, but I'm afraid business calls just now. We'll have dinner together and we can catch up on all your news," he said, looking at the baby bump. "I think your mom has it planned for eight o'clock."

"Sounds good, do you know where she is?"

"Last seen making sure your room was all set for you. I take it she knows?" said Antoine, hiding his anger.

"God no, it's all a big surprise!"

Antoine relaxed a little. Had his wife, Chantal, kept the secret of his son's girlfriend and the pregnancy from him, he'd have been furious.

"Anyway, I'm sorry, I really must go," said Antoine, peeling away. He walked back to his library a far unhappier man than when he had left it. He spotted Conrad through the doorway and waved for him to join him on the terrace.

"I thought your people kept an eye on Alex while he was at university?" he snapped when his cousin joined him.

"They do, he's guarded night and day, although he'd never know it."

"And they never mentioned the little Chinese woman he's been fucking?!" he fumed.

"He's a fit, handsome, young man, he's had his fair share of action," smiled Conrad. "I didn't realize you had a particular issue with the Chinese though."

"I have no particular issue with any of them, as long as he doesn't get them fucking pregnant with Noble seed!"

"Pregnant!"

Antoine nodded, not wanting to repeat the words. Mixing the Noble bloodline outside of the family was forbidden. Mixing the ruling family's bloodline was beyond comprehension. The Nobles married Nobles, preferably second cousins and beyond. However, their genes were so pure, having maintained the tradition throughout their family's history, even closer unions wouldn't cause problems. No Noble had ever contracted cancer that they were aware of, nor had any died of anything other than natural causes or accidentally. The average life expectancy remained in the mid-nineties and excluding pre-Nineteenth Century Nobles, it was now touching three figures. The Nobles protected their bloodline as closely as their wealth, if not more so.

"I'll take care of it," said Conrad.

Antoine shook his head. "No, Bea will have something to sort it a little more subtly. Then you take care of it, a young girl suicidal after loss of her child."

Conrad nodded. "Perfect. I'll talk to Bea after the meeting."

With the family lineage once again protected, they joined the meeting. Antoine took his seat at the head of the table surrounded by his closest family. His sister Anya sat to his left, while Bea's face smiled at the room from a screen at the back of the room. The rest of the seats were filled with Nobles, and only one sat empty, as was the screen behind it.

"Are we waiting for Bertie?" asked Caleb, head of Atlas Noble's gargantuan transport division and Antoine's second cousin.

"Bertie is no longer on the council," said Antoine.

To those who hadn't been aware of Bertie's nefarious plans, his exclusion was the equivalent of the penny dropping.

"He didn't!" exclaimed Blake Noble, the oldest and wisest member of the council. He had been Anya's predecessor within the archives and knew more about Noble family history than any other living Noble. Despite being on the wrong side of a hundred-years-old, his brain was as good as it always had been.

Antoine didn't wish to discuss it, and looked at Conrad who nodded on his behalf.

"Twelve minutes," whispered Blake under his breath.

"Pardon?" said Antoine.

"Hmm, not here, after," Blake mumbled.

Antoine couldn't get through the meeting quickly enough. Anya's success in creating the fuel was applauded, as was Bea's experiment in Papua New Guinea. Population control became a major discussion. The balance between food production and consumption was key. Production over eighty years would not keep up with consumption, even with birth controls that were already in place. The fuel success added even more to the discussion. Whichever way they looked at it, a major reduction in the population was required and although they had proved that race by race control was possible, sometimes entire areas would need to be cleared. Hungry and desperate people were unpredictable and unpredictability led to a loss of control. Control was something that, throughout history, the Nobles were masters of. Another experiment was required, only this one was to leave no survivors.

Chapter 44

Arriving at the airport had been timed precisely. A call ahead to the crew had the plane ready for an instant departure. It also confirmed that the aircraft was, as far as the crew was aware, perfectly safe. Cash instructed the taxi driver to drop them at the door where the plane sat in the VIP section of the airport terminal. Three minutes after they had arrived, they were in the air.

Cash's first task was to check the Hotmail account. His draft to Travis was no longer bold, so he knew Travis had read it. A fresh draft awaited him. Cash opened it. Travis had met with President Mitchell in private, informed him of Cash's update and the 'good' news that they were on to something. The President had told Travis to pass on his thanks and best wishes and insisted that if there was anything they needed, anything, the President was only a phone call away. Both had agreed that they should continue to operate outside official lines. It was a worrying indictment when even the President felt the need to keep the operation a secret, and no small indication of how powerful an enemy they faced.

Cash relayed the first part of the message to both Sophie and Rigs; he left the latter part for Rigs only.

"We're coming up on the location," Sophie said, interrupting Cash's whispered conversation with Rigs. The pilot began to descend to just over a thousand feet above the ground below them.

"I've seen these before," said Cash looking down at the famous Nazca lines, two hundred miles south of Cusco.

"I would have hoped so, but you probably had no idea about the size and scale of them."

Cash looked out across the vast area below them, able to see for miles all around. "Nope, certainly very impressive." He looked beyond the perfectly straight lines and to the shapes. "There's a huge monkey, a bird, a spider…"

"And only visible from up here. We're flying at the perfect height to see them, one thousand feet!"

"When were they made?" asked Cash.

"Over 1,500 years ago and long before then probably…"

"If my father's research is correct," concluded Cash.

Sophie asked the pilot to continue to the next point.

"I thought there was only one detour?"

"It's part of the same detour, twenty miles away," which, by the time she had explained, they had covered the distance.

Cash looked down on another selection of straight line, although these looked more like old runways on top of flattened mountain tops. "Let me guess, same era?"

Sophie nodded. "The Palpa Lines," she said, calling through to the pilot. "Okay, we're done!"

"No measurements?"

"No, I've got all the detail in the research. I just wanted to see the scale and give you an idea what we may be dealing with, or more importantly *who*!"

"Who do you think we're dealing with?" asked Cash.

"Your father believed it, I can only go with what he has uncovered," she said.

"And on what you have seen yourself," added Cash.

"From what we've seen ourselves and your father's work, I'm becoming convinced there was an advanced race of people that once inhabited the Earth. They would have understood astronomy in a far more complex way than we have the ability to even comprehend."

"Aliens?" Cash asked.

"Many people believe they were. Your father was unconvinced but that's where the measurements come in."

"So what do they tell you?"

"Nothing yet, it's going to take a lot of work before they tell me anything and even then we may need more."

"How many more?"

Sophie spun the laptop around, reminding Cash how many dots were on the maps.

"They're not all like where we've been though?" asked Cash.

"Not all, some are even more amazing."

Chapter 45

Antoine had ushered everyone out of the room, leaving Blake and himself alone in the library. Antoine normally loved to spend time with Blake, his mind and memory for every detail within the archives was astonishing. Thousands of years of history instantly available, Blake could recall any event and knew exactly where the detail lay in the vaults below. The mind was an astonishing thing but Blake Noble's mind left others truly wanting.

Antoine poured Blake a glass of water, himself a glass of Scotch.

"Numbs the mind," he said accepting the water and nodding toward Antoine's glass.

"Sometimes it's nice to feel a little numb," said Antoine taking the seat opposite Blake.

Blake nodded. "It is a trying time for us all, our family has worked towards this day for millennia!"

"Yes, I feel the weight of a world on my shoulders."

"You feel the weight of two worlds on your shoulders," Blake said.

"Very true," smiled Antoine. "Two worlds, but only one can survive."

"Only one will survive."

Antoine took a sip. "Twelve minutes?"

"I spoke out of turn, I shouldn't have said anything," said Blake.

"I know you well enough, if you think something is worth saying, it's worth saying."

"Twelve minutes, the difference in age of your father and his brother Bertie."

"Twelve minutes, the difference in time that made him the second son," said Antoine.

"And destined never to head the family," Blake summed up.

"But you meant more than that, I saw the look on your face. This wasn't only about what he did recently."

Blake sat quietly, taking a long sip of water, contemplating whether to speak further. "Twenty years ago, this family suffered a tragic loss. Our leader, your father, had an accident out at sea. His boat capsized and he and his three crewmen died."

"I remember it like it was yesterday," said Antoine. "I was supposed to be with him but Chantal had just told me she was pregnant."

Blake nodded and stayed silent.

Antoine stared at him, waiting for the old man to speak, but he didn't. "No, Bertie was in America," Antoine said, "he was already a powerful Senator."

Blake remained silent.

"If we had both been on the boat, Bertie would have been leader." He let the words hang. "We don't kill our own!"

"No, we don't. And until recent events, I had my doubts but deep down, I didn't believe he could have. Bertie, though, has spent his life outside of the family. His life has been spent with the people who have traits that we have used to shape the world to where we want it to be— aggression, confrontation, contempt, love, loyalty, belief, devotion… all of those traits that make them what they are. The things we used to control them, he has assumed. He has become one of them. He wanted the power and, as the people would have done, he devised a plan to take it."

"And ignored everything that makes us who we are?"

"He stopped being one of us the day he coveted your father's position," said Blake.

"But the investigation was thorough. It was an accident."

"And we don't have any knowledge of a group that can do that?"

Antoine nodded dejectedly. "They're watching him now."

"Bertie Noble is the single biggest threat to our success. He is a loose cannon who believes he should be king and I don't just mean of the Nobles," said Blake.

"I can't order him killed," said Antoine. "His watcher might. Her orders are to protect the family and myself from anything he might try."

"Clever," Blake said thoughtfully. "But I'm afraid you need to make that call. He is a liability that we can ill afford. There are precedents in the past, the grand council has the power to take the decision to take a Noble's life, but it must be unanimous."

Antoine considered Blake's proposal. His ambiguous instructions were already sitting heavily with him. Asking for another Noble's life to be taken, even given what Bertie had done, was against everything they believed. He had been surprised when Bertie had fallen for his bluff in the PEOC, obviously Bertie thought Antoine was capable of breaking their most sacred rule, something he most certainly was not. Nobles did not kill Nobles

"I'll have him brought back to Anieres and placed under house arrest. We'll keep him within our control."

"That is your decision to make but rest assured, his ambition has not been satiated," cautioned Blake, taking a final sip of water and stood up, lifted his cane, and left the room.

Antoine picked up his phone; council or Bertie. He thought of Blake's caution. The wise old man was telling him to deal with it once and for all. But that wise old man wasn't the one who'd be calling the vote or leading the council to a decision.

He hit the speed dial. The cell rang out and went to voicemail. "Leave a message," instructed the female voice in a seductive Eastern European accent.

He dialed the number again. It was his call anytime, instant connection to Katya number. He was the only one with the number and as the client, would always be answered , but it went to voicemail again.

He called Conrad. "Get someone over to Bertie's place now!" he commanded.

Conrad called back within thirty minutes. His people couldn't get in. Bertie's house was surrounded by police. A number of ambulances were in attendance but all his men could see from the road were body bags being loaded into them.

Chapter 46

Travis Davies had just finished his latest draft for Cash when the notification of a new message pinged into the inbox of his secret Hotmail account. No one knew the address, but that didn't mean he wouldn't get offers to enlarge his manhood or earn money from any number of bizarre sources. He saved the draft and clicked on the inbox icon. Bertie Noble was the sender. He had never given Bertie Noble the address. The Senator with too many unanswered questions hanging over him for Travis' liking had just added another question to the list.

Travis clicked on the message. It was empty, save for the subject heading, four letters, capitalized: 'HELP'. Travis clicked the reply symbol and began to type. *Good afternoon, Senator, I believe you may have sent me this message in error.* He stopped. Senator Bertie Noble didn't do errors, certainly not to email addresses he had no business knowing even existed. Everything Senator Noble ever had or did was calculated and deliberate.

He checked the sender email address and not only the displayed name. It wasn't from the Senator's senate account, it was from a Hotmail account. Whatever message he was sending, it wasn't going to show in his system.

Travis reached for his phone and dialed the Senator's office. He was told that the Senator was working from home that afternoon. *Nothing unusual*, thought Travis. He dialed Bertie Noble's home office number and the call was answered instantly.

"Hello?" replied the voice Travis recognized as the Senator.

"Senator—"

"Ah. Mr. Davies," he cut him off. "I was expecting your call. I believe those two young men have been causing us problems again. What a shame we missed shooting them down when we had the chance."

The two men he had vouched for and who he had faked shooting down.

"Although if you ask me, there's only really one of them that's a problem, the other one just listens and does what he's told."

"Well I thought I should keep you in the loop, Senator. We've tracked them down and are about to take them out. You did say you wanted to be kept in the loop, sir."

"Most definitely, I'm very keen to be kept in the loop."

"Leave it with me, I'll see what I can do."

"Excellent, thank you." The Senator hung up.

Travis had quickly caught on. Somebody was listening. The Senator had cut him off before he could say anything that would have exposed the cry for help. If Travis understood the situation correctly, the Senator was telling him that there was one person holding him and that he wanted Travis to come and get him. Of course he could have been completely wrong, it was as clear as mud; but nothing else seemed to make any sense. The call itself didn't, certainly not given their prior conversation about Cash and Rigs.

Cash and Rigs would have been perfect for the job.

He picked up his phone, and stopped. He was about to call his Clandestine Services Director, a man he had known for twenty years, but he was wavering. It was ridiculous. He placed the call and arranged for a team to visit the Senator's house, to check things out.

***

Katya had listened in to the Senator's call with passing interest. It had not been dissimilar to many of the other calls he had received throughout the day, nor any of his subsequent calls. She watched the screen in front of her, it was mirroring his emails, both in and out. He was behaving and taking the threat seriously. She did not know about his burner smart phone, the one he had smuggled into the restroom and with which, over the past few visits, he'd sent his help message to the CIA, entering a couple of letters at a time until at last he hit the send button.

The first sign of a problem to Katya was the birdsong stopping. To most people the random and occasional sound of birds was undetectable. To Katya it was a warning. The Senator's house was unsurprisingly, given his family name, grand. Sitting on top of a small hill, the mini White House style mansion was surrounded by lush and extravagantly furnished gardens securely enclosed by eight-foot walls.

Katya was on her feet and reaching for her MP7 sub machine gun, a compact high powered machine pistol.

"Stay there!" she commanded to the Senator, moving to the window. She looked down into the back garden. No movement. She moved across the hallway and looked out the front. The second floor gave a view out across the walls to the street beyond. No movement, no cars going past, no pedestrians. The street was closed.

Katya looked back at the grounds. No movement. She listened . Not a sound.

"Shit!" she said.

"Senator, with me!"

The Senator was in no position to argue. Her demeanor had changed, her beauty was gone completely, all that was left was a killer.

He was placed in a small restroom at the end of the hallway. Katya closed the door and slid the bolt she had added to lock him in place. With him secure, she grabbed her ammo belt and placed it around her waist before venturing downstairs in a classic stance. Her weapon was up at the ready, and she swept the area in front of her. A pistol and knife were strapped to the ammo belt, along with a number of extra magazines and kit.

The first floor was clear. She hesitated at the top of the stairs that would take her to the ground level. She listened. She heard whispered voices below her. They were in the house. She reached around and withdrew a flash bang from her belt. They hadn't heard her. Their whispers continued. They were making plans.

She edged towards the top of the stairs, keeping out of sight of those below. She carefully removed the flash bang pin, counted to three, and tossed it below, closing her eyes when the initial flash exploded. She rolled down the top few stairs and into a crouched shooting position as the flash dissipated. Four men were caught in its glare. She swept across them, two bullets to each, then rushed back up to the safety of the floor above, avoiding the bullets which began to ping where she had been standing.

A tirade of bullets soon rained down on the staircase as the men below pushed towards her. Katya moved back and waited. Bullets were exploding all around her. The small room she had stepped into was nothing more than a broom cupboard at the top of the staircase. She remained calm when two bullets blasted through the door, one catching her side. She felt the blood flow but ignored the pain. The bullets moved off beyond her. The men assumed she had moved further into the house and had not stayed near the staircase. Katya waited while the footsteps tentatively worked their way up the stairs.

"Check that door?" she heard, and the footsteps neared. She was cornered. Never a good place to be.

Katya crouched, ignoring the pinching of flesh from her side where the bullet had pierced her. The door opened. She paused, the man's view was head height, not two feet from the ground. With no initial reaction from the door opener, his colleagues had moved their attention along the corridor. That infinitesimal pause was all Katya needed. She had them on the back foot. Her silenced pistol put a bullet through the chin of the door opener even before he had looked down to where she was crouched. Before his body had even reacted to the trauma, it was being shoved out of the way and Katya was already shooting. Three head shots, four more down and out of the game. Katya didn't like to be cornered.

She listened for more voices or noises. Nothing from below, but there was plenty from above. *Helicopters.* They had come at them from top and bottom. Stealth choppers. From the number of footsteps rushing across the floor above it was fight or flight. She heard the Senator's voice booming from above.

"It's one woman, what are you waiting for?!!"

They had him. She had failed. *Fight or flight.*

"No, let me stay..." she heard him shouting, his voice disappearing.

He was already gone. *Flight.* Katya disappeared into the night. She would fight another day.

Chapter 47

Kyle rushed to his mother and gave her a hug. "You didn't even said goodbye!" he said irritably. He may have looked like a strapping young man but he was still a boy at heart.

Cash smiled. "Hey, Kyle."

"Hey," he mumbled in return, turning to Rigs. "Hi, Rigs, how's it going?"

Rigs looked briefly and half smiled in response, before being embraced by Uncle Bill.

"I think you're on the shit list!" Sophie whispered.

"Oh," said Cash disappointed.

"That's good," said Sophie. "It means he cares!"

"Where's your grandma?" she called across to Kyle, who was loading bags into the truck with Bill.

"She's making dinner and didn't want to leave it."

"Oh dear God," said Cash in mock horror.

"What?" said Sophie.

"Oh, nothing, I just remember your mom's cooking," he grimaced. "The green thing," he shuddered.

"It's not that bad!" She slapped him on the arm. It was solid and stung her more than him.

The steward stepped up from behind him. "I wanted to say thank you for a few exciting days!" said the steward, admiring Cash's muscles.

"Thank you and the captain." Cash waved up at the captain, who was keen to get going. "You've looked after us fantastically well."

The steward gave Sophie a quick hug and was gone. By the time they were driving away from the runway, the small jet was already leaping into the sky.

"Should we not have kept them here?" asked Sophie, realizing they were effectively stranded.

"It costs thousands of dollars an hour to have them sit here doing nothing," said Cash. "And anyway, they're only going to Seattle tonight, which is less than an hour's flight away."

Cash was pleased to see dinner was not the green thing and he wondered whether Mrs. Kramer's culinary skills had improved in the last fifteen years. Cash smiled at Sophie when he took his first bite and Sophie smiled back.

Cash looked around as everybody dug into their meal. Rigs had paused after his first bite. He was a man who liked MREs and even he was struggling. Uncle Bill smiled painfully and Kyle, who knew what he was doing, kept his head down and ate.

"Mom, Cash was asking if you still made your wonderful chicken and celery dish?"

Chicken and celery. Oh dear God, the full horror of the dish came flooding back. He wanted to tell everyone to enjoy what they were eating, since they had no idea what was in store for them. Cash smiled at Sophie, before turning to Mrs. Kramer. "That's not fair, you've already cooked us a wonderful dinner tonight. We can cook tomorrow."

"Not at all, I insist!" she said. "I'll make it for lunch tomorrow!"

Lunch? Not even twenty-four hours to recover, thought Cash.

Once dinner was finished and cleared away, Sophie got down to work. Charts were spread across every available workspace in the kitchen. Cash hovered for ten minutes and was unceremoniously dismissed for breathing too loudly. He sought out Kyle, who was learning the finer details of fly tying. Uncle Bill was taking him fly fishing in the morning. Cash hung around but seemed to get in the way. Mrs. Kramer had turned in early, as she had most nights, in order to grieve on her own.

Cash went in search of Rigs, who he found lying on a sun lounger on a darkened terrace staring intently at the sky above.

"Amazing?"

Rigs nodded. "It makes you feel very insignificant."

"It's a big place."

"Big enough for more than just us," Rigs remarked.

Cash turned to him. "You think we're hunting things from out there?"

Rigs shook his head. "Nope, I think we're hunting them here; whether they originally came from out there is the question."

Chapter 48

The helicopters had spent the entire day ferrying Atlas Noble staff to and from the hospital ship. Clad in full biohazard suits, the doctors and nurses had worked tirelessly to find and help anyone they could along the Sepik River. When darkness had fallen fully, the living stood at only two hundred thirty one men, women and children. The dead were nearing one thousand times that. It was the single biggest tragedy to have hit the world since the 2004 tsunami in the Indian Ocean and was expected to be even greater. The ten helicopters from the hospital ship had covered most of the river's length but there were still a few villages to visit, though little hope was held out for any more than a handful of survivors.

Doctor Ernesto Rojas, the nun, and the little girl were among the first to be recovered. Ernesto had passed on every detail he could to the staff who had taken care of them. He provided details of the day before the tragedy. It had been a day like any other, nothing, he repeated, nothing was untoward. The doctors had talked to him from behind their masks, asking him countless questions: *The water, was there anything different in its taste? Did he have the same water as everyone else in the village? Did it rain? Was there a flood recently? What was his heritage? His racial background?* The questions went on and on as the doctors and scientists searched for a clue as to what had happened.

Ernesto wracked his brains for anything he thought was significant but he could think of nothing. The little girl with the nun had heard a loud buzzing during the night, which had elicited a significant amount of interest from all around. When she heard the same noise again, everyone looked around. It was the noise of the plane landing on the deck of the ship. The little girl was adamant the noise was the same. The doctors wrote everything down.

The day progressed, and the number of survivors boarding dropped. Fewer and fewer helicopters came back with anything other than news of more dead. Ernesto noted that all the survivors had one thing in common, none of them were Iamult. The vast majority were like him, aid or charity workers. A few were from tribal clans that had been doing business with the Iamults and, in a couple of instances, had married into the tribe. These were the most devastated. Their families had been wiped out, husbands, wives, children. Even although they weren't Iamult, their children were half Iamult and that seemed to be enough. As the day wore on, the number of doctors asking questions reduced, but the questions were the same and just as probing. The same answers came back, nothing out of the ordinary, nothing different, a few people had heard a plane.

With darkness falling, the survivors were sent up onto the deck. A ship lay off to the starboard, a small cruise liner, tiny in comparison to the enormous hospital ship.

"The facilities on board this ship are fairly basic and really only meant for sick patients," said Bea Noble through a megaphone. "We're going to have to quarantine you until we can figure out what has happened here but we feel you deserve a more comfortable environment, given what you've been through."

"Would we not be better in a hospital?" shouted one of the charity workers.

"As far as we can tell, you're all perfectly healthy. However, we will be monitoring you very closely. A team of physicians will stay with you on the cruise ship and you will stay next to us here. Should an outbreak occur, we can have you in an operating theatre within ten minutes."

"I don't mind staying here," said a Médecins Sans Frontières doctor. "I'm an infectious diseases expert."

"That's very kind of you to offer but I'm afraid you are to be quarantined. Not our decision, but the US government's, which has taken over authority of this ship."

"I'm an American citizen," came two shouts that Bea Noble could hear.

"People!" she shouted, her frustration building. "We're going to turn our wards into refrigerators and create the largest morgue in the world. I'm sorry, but this ship is *not* somewhere you want to be!"

The shouts stopped and the survivors queued up for the short hop by helicopter across to the cruise ship. The Seabourn cruise liner had been acquired earlier that day as it had sailed past Papua New Guinea on its way to a south Pacific tour. One of the more exclusive cruise liners, Seabourn offered its passengers one of the highest crew to customer ratios of any cruise liner, along with large and luxurious cabins. The survivors were not going to benefit from the crew to survivor ratio but they were certainly going to enjoy the luxury the ship offered, particularly given the medieval existence they had recently experienced.

As each was shown to their suites, all with ocean views, complaints stopped. If they were going to be quarantined, there wasn't a better place they could think of to have to wait it out.

With the survivors out of the way, the doctors could concentrate on the search for an answer. The virologists had been struggling all day to find anything untoward in any of the samples that had been taken. Even the CDC staff who had arrived late in the day were in the dark. There was nothing that looked out of place, no virus, no disease, no parasite, nothing. It was as though a switch had simply turned off the Iamult race. In effect, that is what Bea had done. The toxin had delivered a genetic code change to the Iamult people, the equivalent to an update for a computer. There was no poison, no disease, no virus. The Iamults' new genetic code had simply switched them off. Their bodies were programmed to expel moisture, thus leaving behind a mummified corpse, saving the world from even having to deal with rotting corpses.

While the team searched for an answer, Bea looked over the survivors' reports. She noted the plane had been mentioned a few times; it was their only oversight. Planes seldom flew over that area at night. It was an anomaly. Thankfully, Bea had the ability to alter the reports before they made it into the database. She left two reports in, one was from the little girl who had never seen a plane, let alone knew what one sounded like. She described it as a buzzing sound. The other was from a man who, according to his report, didn't know where he was and clearly wasn't entirely sane. The seven other reports of hearing a plane were deleted.

Bea moved on to the heritage report. She found it fascinating that the mixed race Iamults also succumbed to the reprogramming. That was an unexpected find and one she would have to consider moving forward. The rest of the list was particularly unremarkable.

A knock on her cabin door was followed by Dr. Paul Lockhart, director of the CDC.

"They said I'd find you here," he said walking in and hugging her.

"It's good to see you," Bea said, moving her papers away. "I didn't think you were coming after the first transport of your people arrived without you!"

"Wouldn't have missed it. No way was I hiding back in the office with this going on here. I had to meet with President Mitchell and caught the later flight. I didn't want to hold my guys up, I'm sure you needed the help."

No, she thought. "Of course," she said aloud. "They've been great but I'm afraid we're struggling to find anything."

"My guys want to concentrate on the water. They think it's definitely something the victims have ingested and as they all have the same source of water…"

"It certainly makes sense."

"I see the survivors are enjoying a little luxury at Atlas Noble's expense, I understand."

"Please, we'd rather keep that quiet. The opportunity arose and we took it."

"It must be costing a fortune, offering to fly two hundred passengers home after compensating them for their loss and hiring a ship for their exclusive use in the meantime?"

Bea smiled. "Atlas Noble can afford it."

"Hell, the US government could afford it, but would they have done that? I don't think so."

"Those people have witnessed a horror beyond our imagination, it's the least we can do," replied Bea, looking down at her sheets and reminding herself again of the wonderful cross-section of the human DNA spectrum offered by the survivors. Combined with their previous exposure, their overnight demise would be chalked up as a delayed reaction to whatever had killed the Iamults.

Chapter 49

It had been a difficult few days for Cash. He had tagged along with Bill and Kyle on their fishing trip but it was clear from the minute they left to the minute they got back that Kyle would have preferred he hadn't. Unperturbed, he joined them the next day for a hunt, dragging Rigs along too, hoping Rigs could keep Bill busy enough for Kyle to have to talk to Cash. Instead, Kyle spent the day talking to an unresponsive and highly uncomfortable Rigs, leaving Cash and Bill both out of the picture.

The third day was to be a hike into the mountains that surrounded the lodge. Cash decided to sit it out. He was trying too hard and getting nowhere. Kyle needed some space and time to come to terms with everything that had happened. It had been less than a week since he had lost his grandfather. Cash suddenly realized that, in fact, he'd lost both his grandfathers! And he was piling on the pressure to get to know him as his father.

"You ready?" called Kyle through the lodge as he and Bill prepared to leave.

Rigs wandered out halfheartedly. Bill had insisted he join the group. Rigs was not looking forward to it. He loved hiking. He loved getting one to one with nature. He simply wasn't keen on the thousand plus questions he was due to be assaulted with over the day.

Sophie and Cash ushered Rigs to the door, ready to wave them all off.

"You not coming?" asked Kyle looking at Cash.

"No," Sophie jumped in. "I need him to help me today."

Cash recovered quickly. "I'd have loved to but…"

"I'm nearly there and I just need a little bit of help."

"Shame… it's a lovely day," said Kyle, turning and joining Bill and Rigs.

Rigs threw Cash a look that could kill and they disappeared.

"What was that for?" asked Sophie, referring to Rigs' angry look.

Cash laughed. "That was for me not going with them."

"Is he jealous?"

Cash laughed even harder. "Only of the peace we'll get from our son!"

Sophie looked hurt.

"He loves Kyle, he just doesn't love his inquisitiveness, particularly of him."

"I don't get it," she said, her arms folding.

"Kyle spent the day firing questions at him, like, which rifle's your favorite? Which one's the best? What's your favorite pistol? Why is it your favorite? And on and on all day!"

"And Rigs answered them all?"

"Not a one, not one answer. Didn't stop Kyle asking though, all day long."

"Poor Rigs. He is a strange one though, sometimes I think I'm getting somewhere and then it's back to the intimidating guy at the back of the room."

"He'll get better, it's a slow process."

"For you too?"

"A little different. The environment was different and we were both coming from places we could relate to."

"Let's not go there," said Sophie, knowing where Cash had come from. He had been with her up until the day he had met Rigs.

"Probably best," said Cash. "So why'd you stop me joining them?"

"He's playing with you, and I wasn't going to let him."

"What do you mean?"

"You'd have rushed, got changed, got all excited about the day and then he'd have ignored you as he has the previous two days."

"No, he's not like that."

"He's a teenager, they're all like that. You've barely known him four days, trust me. And anyway, I do need your help." She led him through to her workspace. The kitchen table had become out of bounds to everyone and it was the first Cash was getting to see what she had spent almost forty-eight solid hours on.

Papers were scattered across the table and the surrounding floor, all covered in calculations. One large sheet lay in the middle of the table, with a few notes and symbols scribbled across it, otherwise it was mainly blank.

"Going well then?"

"It is actually, but as I said, we might need to visit some other locations at some point. I've got enough to keep me busy right now."

"So where do I come in?"

"I need you to listen and tell me how crazy this sounds," she said. "Take a seat."

Cash sat down and waited while Sophie gathered her thoughts.

"Okay, most of this is from your father's research. The measurements I take are to calculate the timeline for the events. The timeline isn't yet complete. I'm struggling with a couple of the calculations, we're talking unbelievably complex calculations here, that even the laptop is struggling with."

Cash edged forward on his seat.

"Your father spent years analyzing every detail across the sites he's highlighted in his research notes, literally thousands of locations where similar structures or artifacts have been uncovered or found. Pumapunka, Tiwanaku, Machu Picchu, Saksaywaman, Nazca and Palpa are particularly special because of how they were built and point to your father's belief that there was a far more advanced race of humans in our past than we're aware of."

"The ones you think are the guardians of the secret?"

"Two secrets, one being that there is a history we're unaware of but secondly, and this is where the research comes in, a secret about our future and more importantly the timeline of when that will be."

"So we might be resolving one of them?"

"No, both of them," she said, pleased with herself. "Well, at least I think so."

Cash said nothing, willing her to continue.

"I believe the second secret foretells the end of the world."

"Oh," said Cash.

"Don't worry, I think it's a long way off," she laughed. "It certainly appears to be from my calculations so far, we're talking hundreds of thousands of years."

"And they're killing people to protect that?"

"I hadn't really put the science and practice together," said Sophie. "It does seem a little extreme."

"Are you sure there's not something else?" asked Cash, looking down at her work.

"Unless I'm missing something really basic…"

She began to wade through her own work, checking and double-checking against Professor Harris' notes.

"Look, see, this place?" she pointed at a printout of an overhead satellite image.

"Impressive," nodded Cash.

"Teotihuacan, built over two thousand years ago, pyramids on a similar scale to those at Giza in Egypt, although nowhere near as grand, but watch."

Sophie took an image that had been printed on tracing paper and laid it on top.

"The buildings match," said Cash, "they sit on top of one another."

"These are the pyramids at Giza, built over six thousand years ago."

Sophie pulled out another sheet, again another printout, and overlaid it onto the two previous ones.

"They match again," said Cash.

"The two sets of buildings are laid out exactly in the way Orion's belt sits in the sky above us. And that's only one tiny example but massive in its own right. I mean, look," she said, pulling out picture after picture, pyramid after pyramid. "They were building them everywhere. But why pyramids? They weren't easy to build, they weren't practical. And we're talking about a time people lived in wood huts, didn't have proper tools, paper to plan things on, an understanding of mechanics, the list goes on. Still, they were somehow able to build these enormous structures and on top of it all, managed to align them to stars in the sky!"

"But why?" asked Cash.

"Nobody fucking knows!" she said exasperated.

"Sophie!" scolded her mother having walked in at exactly that moment. "Sophie," said her mother again, without the 'tone'.

"Mom, not now, we're in the middle—"

"But..."

Sophie ignored her mother and grabbed the images of the Great pyramid. "Let's take this as an example. It's the most perfect pyramid ever built. It's probably one of the most perfect *buildings* ever built. Do you know it was the tallest building in the world for millennia, and if you exclude church spires, probably until the 1800s? And it remains the heaviest!"

"Pyramid?" asked Cash.

"No, the heaviest building in the world. Almost six million tons. The list goes on and on, perfectly aligned to true North, its sides are ever so slightly concave and match the radius of the earth and only visible on the spring and autumn equinoxes from the air. Its cornerstone foundations have been designed to cope with heat and earthquakes. The mortar used has been analyzed but can't be replicated. It was encased in limestone. Its sides would have been perfectly smooth and when the sunlight hit would have been dazzling for miles around. Mathematically, it's pretty much perfect and all this without any plans!"

"It does sound implausible."

"Not as implausible as the Egyptologists' version of how it was built in twenty years."

"That does seem quite a long time."

Sophie shook her head. "There are over 2.3 million blocks, each weighing over two tons and some up to seventy. Let's assume they did it in twenty years. Now bear in mind, the stones were cut and fit together perfectly. Those stones were quarried four hundred miles away. So we need to cut the stones perfectly, transport them across land to the river, sail them four hundred miles, transport them across land before positioning them perfectly up to four hundred and fifty feet high. All of this is over 6,000 years ago, when we don't have any mechanical devices to do any of this."

"Okay," said Cash, not daring to question anything she was saying.

"That they were able to cut these blocks so precisely, move them over four hundred miles and lay them at a rate of one every five minutes, day and night for twenty years, is implausible. If you take it down to only daytime, it would be double that. Every two and a half minutes for twenty years, without any plans."

"So how did they do it?"

"We don't know, and you know why?"

"Because they didn't tell us?"

"Exactly. The Egyptians, who loved their hieroglyphs, just so happened to not leave anything about their single most incredible feat. And you know why?"

Cash nodded, understanding. "They didn't build them!"

"Well, that's what your father believed, and I can't say I disagree."

"But how does that relate to the secret about the end of the world?" asked Cash.

"Yes, sorry, I got off point a bit there…" she said. "Where was I before I got into pyramids?"

"Aligning with the stars I think."

"Yes, that was it. There are examples from around the world of pyramid building by the ancients but why?"

"Are you asking me?"

"No, I'm asking myself. I'm going back to the basics and the basics are that this is worldwide, not just where we've been."

"The guardians travelled the Earth in the past?"

"Yes, but although I agree there was an advanced race, are you talking about flight? Because I'm not sure we're talking that advanced!"

"The Nazca Lines?"

"Visible from a thousand feet up, they may have been able to make a rudimentary balloon of some sort, or perhaps a glider. But travel across the oceans? I don't think so. That's technology way beyond the ancients."

"But not aliens?" said Cash.

"You're going off track even more now, this is potentially about the end of the world," she said.

The kitchen door burst open. "End of the world? What world?" asked Senator Bertie Noble with a smile, as he waltzed into the kitchen, trailing Travis Davies in his wake.

Sophie's mom looked at her. "I tried to tell you I heard a plane but you weren't listening to me."

Sophie didn't say a word. She scurried back to her papers. Something had just triggered another thought.

Chapter 50

Rigs crashed into the kitchen with two CIA bodyguards chasing after him while Mrs. Kramer was pouring coffee for Travis.

"Rigs, it's okay," said Cash calmly, walking over to check on his friend. "It's only Travis."

Travis waved his men out of the room, his disgust at their failure was clear to see.

Rigs could hardly catch his breath. He was covered in undergrowth and had sweat pouring from him.

"I… saw the… plane…" he gasped between breaths. "How did he know where we were?"

"How did you know where we were?' asked Cash relaying the question he should have thought of himself.

"Senator Noble," replied Travis. "He seems to know a lot we don't know he knows."

The Senator shrugged. "It's my business to know things," he mused.

"We should move, if he knows others will know," whispered Rigs, bending down out of sight of the rest of the room behind a large island in the kitchen.

Cash joined him. "Travis wants us to leave here and take the Senator somewhere."

"What about the Kramers?" asked Rigs.

"Travis will look after them."

Rigs shook his head. "We can't trust anyone."

"Then they can come with us."

"Where to?" asked Rigs.

"We were just getting there when you burst in," said Cash. "So I'm not sure yet."

"Go," said Rigs. He stayed where he was, hovering menacingly.

"So you were saying?" said Cash rejoining the group at the table. Sophie had given up and was moving everything into the dining room, away from prying eyes.

"Yes," said Travis looking across at Rigs. "Before we were expertly interrupted. The Senator was rescued by us a few days ago from a female who had taken him hostage. That female managed to kill eight of our highly skilled operatives."

"Do we know who she was?"

"No idea."

"No print matches, DNA, facial recognition, nothing?"

"Ah, you're assuming we caught or killed her. She escaped."

"Do you know why she was holding you hostage?" asked Cash, turning to the Senator.

"No idea. She hardly said a word to me. I can only assume it's all tied into the attempt on the President and perhaps in some way with your father's death."

Cash looked at Travis. He shook his head subtly. He hadn't told the Senator of their suspicions that everything was linked.

"So why us?"

"Because I don't know who else I can trust and I must go to Switzerland, it's my great nephew's 21st and I can't not go."

"How do you know you can trust us?"

"Because Travis does and because you guys were set up just like Travis. You'd hardly set yourselves up if you were involved."

Cash looked across at Rigs. He shook his head, he didn't like it. Neither did Cash.

"I'm sorry, Senator, but we're almost there figuring things out. Travis has lots of really great guys."

"Like the two that missed Rigs bursting into here?" he asked, much to Travis' embarrassment. The Senator wasn't going to take no for an answer. "I heard you say when I came in about the end of the world. Is that where your investigation has gotten you to?"

"It's still very early—"

"I may know a bit about the subject," he offered.

"Sophie!" Cash called. "You might want to come in here."

"And it's got nothing to do with the deaths in Papua New Guinea," the Senator said.

Cash looked blankly at Travis.

"They're off the grid here, they've not heard about the Iamults," explained Travis.

Sophie joined them. "What's wrong?"

"The Senator knows something about the end of the world but he was about to tell us something about the Iamults?"

"It's been all over the news. The Iamults were a race of people in Papua New Guinea, and earlier in the week, they inexplicably died, every last one of them," explained Travis, interrupting to bring them up to speed.

Sophie's interest spiked. "A great death raining down race by race," she said.

"Well not really, they believe it was the river that poisoned them all. There were a few survivors, but they too succumbed a day later. Every man, woman and child. It's caused a huge panic and more than a few declaring the end of the world is nigh!"

"How many?"

"All round the world, I wouldn't even guess," said the Senator.

'No, the Iamults, how many dead, a hundred, a thousand?"

"Over three hundred thousand," said Travis.

"Oh my God!" exclaimed Sophie. "Some of the ancient texts talk about how death will rain down on us, race by race, as the end nears."

"But you said the end was hundreds of thousands of years away, right?" said Cash.

"I've rechecked, I hadn't taken the wobble into account, it's actually more than that. Earth is in no danger for the next million years. With more measurements from other sites, I'll be able to narrow that down."

"If I help you with this, will you take me to Switzerland?"

"Switzerland?" asked Sophie.

"His nephews birthday. He wants me and Cash to keep him safe."

"Safe from whom?"

"Doesn't matter now, I'll tell you later." Cash turned back to the Senator. "Help us how?"

"There's a little known division in the military that deals with this stuff."

"Like Roswell?" joked Sophie.

"Yes," replied the Senator, without a hint of humor, before smiling. "Although I can tell you Roswell never happened, not in 1947."

Cash looked at Sophie who shrugged. He looked at Rigs who shook his head.

The Senator could see it was still close, so he played his trump card. "It would mean a lot to Antoine and Anya, my nephew and niece."

"Anya, the niece that went to university with Cash's father?" asked Sophie instantly.

"You know her?" he asked innocently.

"Pack your things, we're going," announced Sophie.

"You're not invited to Switzerland," whispered Cash.

"Well you'd better get me an invite. I'm coming!"

Chapter 51

The council meetings had started their daily frequency. The previous two evenings had been almost entirely devoted to the hunt for Bertie. His disappearance was causing great anguish, particularly for Antoine. They knew he was alive, their sources knew that much. Beyond that, nothing. Antoine had hardly slept, his mind trying to comprehend what Bertie's game was. As far as Antoine and the rest of the Nobles were concerned, they would do nothing to jeopardize their goal. Bertie had already proven that that wasn't the case for him. If you could kill your own twin, there were no bounds to what you could do.

Antoine stood before his council. "This evening, Bertie is off the agenda. We don't have time for it. Conrad's security teams are doing everything they can. If you do wish to discuss Bertie, I'd ask you to leave it until after the council meeting."

A number of approving nods greeted the news.

"Now, down to business. We are two weeks out from the convergence when the transports can commence. Anya?"

Antoine turned the floor over to his sister. "Fuel production has been better than anticipated and we're close to the point of starting the fuelling process, which, as you're aware, has its own problems. However, I believe Caleb has solved most of those problems and we're in a position to start moving the fuel to the launch site."

Caleb nodded. "Yep, not easy but we've found a way to stabilize it for transport. The actual fueling system itself is still only theoretical, since we've not been able to trial it, but we believe it will deliver. As for the launch site, the spot we've got in the Pacific Ocean is perfect. It's like a black hole, no shipping lanes or flight paths go anywhere near it. The only land nearby are tiny uninhabited islands, on which we've built landing strips for ferrying to and from the area. The stealth capability of the ships should mean that unless actually spotted, no one will ever know we're there. I think Conrad has the situation in hand, should anyone see anything."

"We've got a number of fighters on station to deal with any issues," confirmed Conrad. "Along with a few high speed patrol vessels that will monitor and scare off any shipping that strays off course. Should anyone see anything, we'll shoot first and ask questions later."

The door to the library opened and Bea entered. "Apologies, I'm late!" she said, to an impromptu round of applause, led by Antoine.

"I think, given your achievements, we can forgive you!"

"Thank you," she said, sitting down.

"Using the survivors to test the mixed batch was genius," said Conrad.

"Well, they were an excellent cross-section of the population. But there is one thing you're not aware of," she tapped her nose, resulting in them all leaning forward slightly.

"My son released it on the boat, without any protection."

"A little risky, no?" asked Antoine.

"Not at all," said Blake. "Our genes are as pure as our ancestors who developed the toxin," he said proudly. He was a man who marveled at the family's history.

"And if, down the line, they had been, unbeknownst to us, mixed?" asked Antoine, making his point.

"Irrelevant," said Blake dismissively. "The Noble genes would dominate the inferior genes. As long as there's a Noble in you, you're a Noble."

"But we should never mix!" said Antoine. This was new information, to all of them, he could tell by the looks on the faces of everyone else in the room.

"No we shouldn't, but it doesn't mean we can't."

Antoine was going to have to revisit his decision with regard to his son. He looked at Conrad, who was obviously on the same wavelength, looking right back at him. Antoine would have another late night chat with Blake.

"And the cover story seems to have calmed everyone down. Is the CDC going along with it?"

"We made them think it was their idea but yes, they'll continue trying to find what really killed them. In the meantime, it's being put down to a contamination in the river."

"Do we have a timescale of when we need to start the downsizing?"

The rest of the meeting moved off into the detail of food production, food consumption, and the need for food to be transported, as well as people. Over the next eighty years, food production on the other planet was going to be minimal. Food was going to have to be sent to supplement the population. As the planet died, the food source would dwindle. Everything pointed to a devastating shortage within the first ten years, a shortage that would cause widespread famine across both planets. Famine would cause panic and unrest, which in turn would affect production. Production had to be maintained at all costs.

People had to go about their daily lives as long as possible. Even during the convergence they had to be unaware of what was happening. If they realized there was not space for everyone, chaos would reign and production would be affected. Production was vital.

"We should have started birth control fifty years ago," said Blake. "I warned your grandfather the population was spiraling."

"I know, but things were difficult during the Cold War. We lost control, paranoia ruled, not us."

"The population's doubled since then, you know. And the number of nuclear weapons!"

"We're dealing with both of them now," Antoine said calmly, not wanting to lose his temper with Blake. His points were valid but inappropriate.

"I'm sorry, I'm speaking out of turn. I'm just excited I'll be here for the start when I never thought I would be!"

"So, back to the food. Are we saying we need to start stockpiling now?" asked Antoine.

"Yes."

"I don't think we should start anything until the convergence actually begins though."

A number of nods echoed agreement around the table.

"Do we have a number?"

"Half," said Blake.

"Half a million?" asked Bea.

"No," said Blake, "half the population."

"Three and a half billion in one hit?"

"One big cut is less painful than a thousand small ones."

"It would get us down to a billion in eighty years, given the death rate and reduced birth rate," said Bea.

"It would cause utter chaos!" said Conrad.

"Only once, and we can quickly find a cure that the rest of the world would get, job done. Population under control," concluded Blake.

"It works," nodded Bea. "We just need to work out who goes. Do we do it by race or by area?"

"Race," said Blake. "There are a few I can think of that have done little for anyone."

"Let's leave prejudices at the door, though the principle is sound," cautioned Antoine. "Bea, I'll leave you and your team to work out the detail of who, but let's go with a time just before the first transport is on its way. Or the first ship arrives back, whichever is first."

"Well, that was a far more productive meeting than before, same time tomorrow and remember, the day after that is Alex's 21st, so no meeting that night," he said excitedly. "Blake, would you mind hanging back a few minutes? You too, Conrad."

"If you don't mind, I'll stay too," said Anya, much to Antoine's surprise.

Chapter 52

Cash had insisted they wait for Kyle and Bill's return before leaving. A halfhearted hug from his son was his only reward, but it was enough for him to have justified the delay. Travis was dropping them in Nevada in his Gulfstream G550, where another jet would take them onto their final destination, while Travis would head back to Washington. The four bodyguards were being left at the lodge, the only stipulation Cash had made as part of the deal to accompany Senator Noble to Switzerland.

"I don't like it," whispered Rigs into his ear for the tenth time. He looked across at Senator Noble. "I don't trust him!"

Cash stayed silent. He didn't disagree but didn't want to fuel Rigs' mistrust. Once he went down that road, it was a hard road for him to climb back from.

Sophie was still buried in her laptop, fielding questions from the Senator, who had, Cash noted, a knowing grin. The Senator knew far more than he was letting on and Cash felt sure, far more than he'd ever let on.

The sound of the landing gear dropping signaled their arrival. Cash looked out of the window. Total darkness, no landing strip was visible ahead. Rigs punched him in the shoulder and pointed out the same problem.

"Senator, are you sure we're at the right place?" asked Cash.

"Can you see a runway?" he asked.

"No," replied Cash, "just complete and total darkness!"

"Well, we're in the right place then," he said as the wheels touched down for a perfect landing. "In the daylight it looks like the desert floor, it's painted like a trompe l'oeil."

Rigs looked at Cash. "It's an effect that makes the image look real, like an optical illusion," explained Cash.

"Would hardly be a secret base, if it wasn't hidden," he said as the plane travelled off the runway and into a hangar cut into the mountainside.

Cash looked over at Travis. His face was a picture. He had no idea it existed either and he was head of the CIA!

The Senator looked at them both. "If it makes you feel any better, even the President doesn't know about this place," he said standing. "Welcome to the best kept secret in America, Alien Hunters!" announced the Senator, leading them towards a door at the far end of the hangar. A number of strange craft sat inside the hangar. One looked particularly familiar to Sophie.

"And the work we do at Area 51?" asked Travis, the not-so-secret base he was fully aware of.

"These guys keep an eye on that but they have a far more open remit to explore the possible, or maybe even the impossible. Let's go meet the boss."

"You didn't know about this place?" Cash asked Travis.

"Not a clue. Area 51 is the only area I'm aware of and to be honest, it's really only a testing area for experimental equipment. Nothing like that," he said, pointing at the strange aircraft that sat in the hangar.

"I've seen models and drawings of those aircraft before," said Sophie in a whisper.

"Where?" asked Travis.

"From all across the ancient sites. That one there!" She indicated a small one-seater aircraft with a bulbous front and flat end and an oversized tail. "It's the same shape as a small piece of gold jewelry I've seen. It's been dated over 4,000 years old.

"I'd like to introduce you to the boss here," announced the Senator, gesturing towards a woman who appeared in the doorway, dressed in full uniform and standing to attention.

"This is Colonel Thalia—"

Travis stepped forward. "Valdez," he finished. "We've met before. You were transferred out of Area 51 against our wishes," he said, shaking the Colonel's hand and turned to the Senator. "If I remember correctly, it was because your committee refused to fund Thalia's crazy work. You created this?"

"Not personally, it is legitimate intelligence work," replied the Senator.

"All totally off the books, and with no links to any intelligence division?" asked Travis. "I think we may have an issue with the misappropriation of funds, Senator."

"Before you say another word, why don't we let Colonel Valdez tell us what they do here?"

Thalia stood back and gestured for them to enter the facility. As furious as Travis was, he was as keen as the rest to see what they were doing.

"I'm not sure what the Senator has shared with you about our facility here, but we are tasked with discovering advanced civilizations, whether that be alien or human. Perhaps we should start in the AV room?" She directed them to the second door along an endless corridor.

The AV room turned out to be nothing more than a projector room with around twenty chairs. The Colonel started running through a slide show.

"We've seen most of these," said Cash, as picture after picture of some of the weird and amazing structures from Pumapunka, Tiwanaku and Saksaywaman appeared on the screen. The Colonel's commentary wasn't dissimilar to Sophie's, even down to them having dated the sites older than was officially recognized. The Colonel, noting the unrest, rushed through the slides, culminating in the Great Pyramid of Giza.

"If ever there were a structure on the planet that screamed advanced civilization, it is this one." She ran through the details that Sophie had provided earlier, although there were a few more that even Sophie didn't know.

"You'll notice there is no capstone. We believe that this would have been made of copper and has been stolen at some point. Copper, as you're aware, is an excellent conductor. Consider also the precise location of the pyramid. If you laid the world out flat, the pyramid is the exact center of all the landmass. I'm not a specialist in the area but I'm reliably informed that electromagnetic fields differ around the world, and the great pyramid sits on top of one of the most powerful spots."

"So what are you saying, it channeled energy?" asked Cash. "Like a power station?"

"We're not entirely sure, but potentially yes, either to create power or even more interestingly, to transmit into space. Or even both, the power generated could have been significant."

"So we're talking about airlines?" asked Cash.

"Or just an advanced race who, like us, wished to see if anyone was out there, a bit like the messages we send today for that exact same purpose."

"And the aircraft in your hangar?"

"You recognized some didn't you?' asked Thalia with a smile.

Sophie nodded, a few vaguely but one in particular.

"Working prototypes, using the scale and design from the drawings and artifacts that have been found around the world."

"Working?" asked Sophie.

Thalia nodded. "Fully working, yes!"

"Holy shit!" Sophie said, thinking back to the discussion with Cash. How did the different civilizations all know about pyramids?

"But how can we not know about all this?" Sophie asked Thalia. "How can the world be in the dark about what happened in our past?"

"Are we? If you were to read some passages in ancient texts, the Torah, the bible, many of the oldest documented writings, there are numerous references to gods coming down from the sky in fiery clouds. In many of the ancient artifacts, there are rocket type drawings and symbols. The hieroglyphs have many examples of rocket type drawings. Heaven itself… what is heaven? When we talk of heaven we look to the sky."

"What are you saying, that the gods were aliens?" asked Travis.

"I'm not saying that, I'm saying there's more than one way to read what was written. I mean, if you lived two thousand years ago and saw a spaceship, how would you describe it, if you've not seen anything like it before and no words exist to describe it?"

"But what you're suggesting is that God actually existed as flesh and blood," said Sophie.

Thalia shrugged. "All I can give you is what we can decipher from the clues that have been left to us."

"So the prototypes could be lucky coincidences?"

"They could be. There are many more that didn't work. Although one thing to consider is that nowhere in nature does a flying bird have a vertical tail, something that is a must for us to be able to fly. Many, many examples from across the sites have vertical tails. If they were trying to symbolize birds why turn their tails through ninety degrees?"

Travis got up. "I'm sorry guys but I need to head back to Washington. Keep in touch," he said, looking at Cash in particular, before gesturing for the Senator to follow him into the corridor.

"Travis?"

"Why in the hell is this work not part of Area 51? They're doing work that you and your committee closed down ten years ago!"

"We believed the nature of the work was a little too controversial for mainstream—"

"So you keep it from everyone? They're working on stuff that could be helping Area 51 develop God alone knows what."

"Area 51, about which in 2013 your agency published a paper to explain its purpose? That Area 51?" asked the Senator, raising his voice with each word.

"We're talking about impacts on religion, the perception of our origins, we're talking about real knowledge of potential alien intervention. Do you think the public needs that? Do you think the government wants that? Or the church, the Vatican, the Muslims, the Jews? Can you imagine a world where religions were categorically disproved? The moral code, the ethics which drive people, order, control of the masses, belief in a purpose. As Karl Marx famously said '*religion is the opium of the people.*' Well imagine seven billion people suddenly going cold turkey. A world without any of these would be a world plunged into chaos.

"But you can't just create your own secret agency!"

"And why the hell not! My committee members and I have been elected into our positions by the people of the United States of America to look after their interests. And that's exactly what we're doing."

The Senator turned and reentered the AV room, leaving a speechless Travis Davies behind. Travis had every intention of marching back in to give him hell but it was pointless. The man thought he was beyond reproach, untouchable. Travis rushed back to the hangar. He was already running late.

***

"In your research, have you found any detail about the end of the world?" asked Sophie.

"We've seen a few references to that but to be honest," Thalia replied, "the date we've calculated is so far off that we've left it and moved on to other areas."

"Thanks," said Sophie, although it hadn't helped. They were still in the dark as to why the guardians were so keen to protect a secret that was potentially millions of years in the future.

"If we're finished here, we can grab some food and then you can take a look at some of our prototypes," Thalia suggested.

"Sounds good," said Cash.

"You coming?" asked Cash when everyone started to move away except for Rigs, who sat transfixed on a photo of the pyramid.

Rigs waited until it was only the two of them alone in the room. "We're missing something," he said, his eyes not moving away from the screen. "Something really big!"

Cash looked at the image. A few people were visible like ants at the base of the structure, putting the scale of the pyramid into perspective. It was huge, far bigger than Cash had appreciated.

"We're not dealing with humans," said Rigs standing up.

"So, what? Aliens?" asked Cash.

"I don't know but we didn't build that," said Rigs.

The lights blinked once and the room filled with an ear-bursting pulsating of a klaxon in full flow.

Through it all, Cash heard a scream. *Sophie.* He ran.

Chapter 53

The recorded history of the Sicarii Order was as old as the bible itself. However, their history stretched back into the depths of the Jewish faith. They were trained killers with one goal: to protect the faith at any cost. Through history, their links to the Jewish faith had lessened but their expertise and training in killing had grown. The art of killing had become a lucrative and profitable business. Failure was not an option to the Sicarii. If they took on a job, the honor of each of the twenty-strong order was on the line.

Katya's failure to secure Senator Bertie Noble and keep him safe for the Nobles had resulted in two additional Sicarii being sent to assist her in the hunt to find him. Their Jewish links allowed them access to one of the most extensive and resourceful intelligence agencies in the world. The Mossad and their Sayanim, the Jewish helpers, who, when called upon by the State of Israel, would help where possible. Although not linked to the Mossad or part of the Israeli Government, the Sicarii were at their disposal whenever needed and never at any cost. In return, when the Sicarii requested assistance, the Mossad delivered without question. The only caveat was that they couldn't harm the state of Israel, something they knew the Sicarii would never do anyway.

It had taken two days for the first hit. A Sayanim pilot employed by the CIA had reported that the Senator had boarded his aircraft, but the destination was sketchy, somewhere in upstate Montana.

It had been enough for Katya. She had secured a private jet, the fastest they could get, and headed out west, loading every piece of kit they might possibly need. She wasn't missing an opportunity to secure her target. The New Citation X was being pushed to its limits as Katya raced across the country. The new destination had come in right before they arrived in Montana.

The pilot reprogrammed the new destination for Nevada, where they arrived to find nothing.

They frantically checked the coordinates and their dials. There was nothing below except for dark desert floor surrounded by mountains.

"There's nothing there," insisted the pilot.

A beep on her phone signaled a new message, forwarded from the Sayanim. 'Landed on dark runway disguised as ground. Hangar and facility in mountain, runway only visible through night vision goggles.'

Katya looked at her two colleagues.

"Jump?" she asked.

Both nodded. They were as keen to secure the Senator as Katya. Five minutes later, the three highly trained killers were parachuting from the Citation preparing their weapons on their drift down to the desert floor below. A fast jog after disposing of their parachutes had them standing on the well disguised runway. Their major problem was getting into the actual facility. There wasn't even a hint of seam where they could blow a door to gain entry.

"We could be setting off motion sensors and God knows what out here," said Mika, the younger of the two Sicarii who had joined Katya.

"Katya, I have to agree, we've been a little hasty here," said Levi, one of the older and more experienced Sicarii. He was next in line to lead the order. It was a very simple hierarchy. The most experienced Sicarii led the order, upholding the traditions as they had been followed since the order began.

Katya was about to agree when the groaning sounds began. The mountain was lifting. There were no seams to be seen because there weren't any, the mountain rose from the ground, sliding up into itself. A darkened hangar sat open before them, a full five minutes had passed for the mountain to open. A small jet taxied out of the hangar and out onto the runway. Its engines were already screaming by the time it reached the end of the runway. It shot across the darkened floor in front of them. They lay prone where they had stood, off to the side of the runway. Not a soul was in sight as the aircraft leaped into the sky. The groan sounded again; the mountain was closing.

"I don't like it," said Levi. "We've no idea what we're up against in there."

Katya felt the responsibility of her previous failure mentally and physically. Her wound stung like a bitch. She got up to a crouch and ran towards the hangar. Mika looked at Levi, the senior member of the team.

"Go!" he said.

The Sicarii always stuck together.

Katya had her MP7 up and ready when she entered the hangar, sweeping the area in front of her; Mika and Levi were doing the same on either side of her. Between them they were covering the full arc of the hangar.

Mika had been right. They had triggered a silent alarm. Air Force Security personnel rushed towards them from a small watch room at the back of the hangar. Katya, Levi and Mika opened fire. Their silenced MP7 Heckler and Koch submachine guns sent spit after deadly spit, sending the security forces crashing to the floor. Ten airmen were dead before they even knew it wasn't a drill.

With the hangar secure, they reached the door to the facility; it was a solid steel mass. The alarm klaxon began to wind up, its pulses pounding the ear drums with an aim of disorientating attackers. The Sicarii barely noticed it. Their training covered noise, flashes, tasers. They were desensitized to the normal distractions deployed to debilitate people.

Levi placed a charge and motioned for his colleagues to step back. It blew, the door held. He placed another charge, slightly larger. It blew, the door held.

He placed a larger charge, motioning for his colleagues to step well back. It blew, and the door finally gave way.

***

Sophie screamed when the door at the end of the corridor buckled and then gave way, her ears aching from the klaxons' constant and monotonous pulse. Before she knew why, she was being propelled down the length of the corridor at speed. She whipped her head around to see Cash had her by the arm, her feet were hardly making contact with ground. The Senator was behind her, with Rigs ushering him from behind. Thalia was leading the way, responding to something Cash was shouting at her.

"Armory," she finally understood.

A group of airmen rushed past them towards the door, armed in full riot gear. The sounds of gunfire escaped between pulses.

Sophie found herself being thrown into the armory. The klaxon finally died. Everybody obviously knew they were under attack.

"Grab whatever you need," said Thalia needlessly. Cash and Rigs were already filling their pockets with ammo and every other piece of kit they thought could conceivably help, after having grabbed a couple of HK416s and Berretta 9mms.

"How many security personnel?" asked Cash.

"Twenty and from what I heard from the men rushing past us, ten are already down."

"Layout?"

"One long corridor with rooms off it. It's effectively one long half mile tunnel in the mountain. One way in and one way out."

"Senator, you're looking nervous, any idea who these guys are?"

"There's more than one?!" he gasped.

"I think I heard three," said Cash.

"They're assassins, the one that kidnapped me killed eight men and disappeared."

"The same people from Santa Cruz?"

"God no, those guys were amateurs in comparison. Have you heard of the Sicarii?"

Cash shook his head.

"Very few people live to know their name."

"You know it."

"I wish I didn't."

Cash looked at Rigs, who shrugged, unimpressed.

"I'll take you guys further into the mountain," Cash said. "Rigs will wait here and come at them from behind. Thalia, you lead the way, I'll bring up the rear."

Sophie was ushered to the door by Cash. She looked around to say goodbye to Rigs but he was nowhere to be seen.

Gunfire echoed from up the corridor. The airmen's machine gun fire seemed relentless, until it just stopped.

"Go!" Cash urged Thalia. The silence from behind was not a comforting one. Thalia raced past door after door, the end of the corridor coming into view. A few gunshots rang out behind them, all were quickly silenced.

"What's down here?"

"The last door leads to the plant room, generators, air conditioning equipment…"

"In there," instructed Cash. He had an idea, which he shared quickly with Thalia before closing the door.

"Don't open this unless I knock the signal!" Cash turned. It was time to hunt the hunters.

***

When the door blew, Levi, Mika and Katya were already moving, their weapons up and at the ready, as heads popped though doors. One of them was already on a target and took it out. One shot, clean kill.

While Levi watched the corridor, Mika and Katya cleared the rooms. The first room was nothing more than a small reception room, empty. The second room, an image of a pyramid projected on the wall, empty.

Bullets rained down when Levi ran to join them in the second room.

"Five heavily armed, coming our way," he called, diving into the room for cover.

The deafening noise of the automatic rifles continued as the security team neared the room. Bullet after bullet pounded the door frame, uselessly expending bullets for no reason other than to pin the Sicarii in situ. As long as the bullets rained they knew not to worry.

A brief pause was all Katya and Levi needed. They signaled to Mika. He pulled the door open and he and Levi dived out at foot level into the onrushing security team, their MP7s firing accurately as they rolled across the corridor. By the time they were in the crouch position, the five security men were lying dead.

"Amateurs," exhaled Katya, waving for Mika to join them.

The next few rooms mopped up the last of the security team. Four rooms and another five dead security men.

Katya watched the corridor while Mika and Levi cleared the armory. Mika burst in with Levi at his back. They swept the room, empty.

***

Cash ran back towards the armory. The sound of gunfire had already died. The last of the security team must have been taken out. It was only as he ran back he realized the incline in the floor, a slight upward slope towards the entrance. He stopped. They were above him, their line of sight was above his, they had the advantage.

Cash crouched and fired down the corridor.

The lights went out, plunging the facility into a darkness only possible buried deep in a mountain, with no residual light from any source to give even the tiniest detail of the surroundings.

***

"What was that?" said Katya, using her ears to replace her eyes.

"What?" asked Levi.

"That sucking noise?" she asked

The lights came back on. Mika was on the floor, his throat slit cleanly, silently gasping for air his lungs were never going to get.

"I thought you cleared the armory," Katya said. Her mind had already moved on from her fallen comrade. He was dead. His mind just hadn't accepted it yet.

Levi rushed back with his MP7 at the ready. A ceiling tile was missing.

"He was behind us, he must have gone back towards the entrance," said Katya, her MP7 trying to cover both directions.

"How do you know they've not all played the trick?"

"Did you hear him?"

"No," said Levi.

"Exactly. Trust me, we'd have heard the Senator."

Gunfire rang out again, the same two shots, three, one, then two.

The lights went out, plunging them into darkness again.

Katya spun round. She heard a shuffling and fired a round.

"That's me!" screeched Levi.

Ten seconds turned to twenty, then thirty.

Katya was spinning, tuning in to every tiny noise. Mika's body was still gurgling at their feet.

Levi's breathing was becoming heavier, the darkness was unnerving. Mika's dying body wasn't helping them.

Thirty became thirty five. "We're letting them hunt us," said Levi, infuriated at how easily the tide had turned against them.

Forty seconds. The lights came on. A face appeared in front of him; it was a face he recognized, a face he had been sent to hunt at an ancient site. He raised his MP7 to fire, but it wouldn't move. A vice like grip held its muzzle aimed at his own foot. Rigs smiled and slashed the knife cleanly across Levi's throat, silencing his dying scream.

Katya's vision wasn't dissimilar, only she had no idea who the man was that was less than an inch from her face when the lights came on. Her MP7 also didn't move. She let go of it and moved with lightning speed to her waistband, retrieving a knife and thrusting it into her attacker. Unfortunately, the thrusting motion was what her mind had intended for her body to do, a body that had already been effectively severed from her mind when a 9mm bullet tore through her spinal cord.

"Did you see how fast she was?" marveled Rigs. "She nearly had you and you already had the gun at her neck. Any others?"

"Nope, all gone."

"So they were *Sicarii*, or whatever," Rigs shivered in mock fear. "Two words assholes, night vision!" He removed the Air Force's latest night vision equipment they'd acquired in the armory.

"We're lucky they didn't take it themselves," said Cash. "Can't believe we left the box sitting there."

"They thought they had us," said Rigs. "Too cocky."

He had recognized Cash's first signal. When the lights went out, he knew that was his signal to get out. The first kill had been a bonus, a flick of his knife as he brushed past the man on the way out of the armory. He hadn't had time to pause, he knew the lights would be back on in twenty seconds. His priority was to get clear of his hiding hole and in behind the attackers. At the second signal, he had crept out of his position and been able to communicate with Cash along the corridor as they both moved in for the kill. First signal, position, second signal, kill. They always did it the same way. Cash counted down with one hand three, two and the lights had come on.

"So what now?" asked Rigs.

"Switzerland, I suppose," said Cash.

"Do we have time for a detour?"

"Depends on where."

"Not far from Switzerland, I'd really like to see the pyramids," said Rigs.

"I knew it, you saw something in that photo, didn't you?"

"Maybe," said Rigs. "Maybe."

Chapter 54

Anya hardly recognized the small atoll in the middle of the Pacific Ocean from her plane passing slowly overhead. The former US Air Force base, acquired by Atlas Noble a few years earlier, boasted a massive terminal building that would have rivaled most international airports. The U-shaped atoll, over 1,700 miles from the nearest major landfall, also boasted the world's first spaceport. In less than two weeks, the transports would commence, ferrying the population.

The atoll, which a year earlier had housed a few buildings and was nothing more than an emergency landing strip for aircraft experiencing problems, had been transformed. It was more akin to a major international hub. The terminal buildings covered the island while taxiways ran around its perimeter. Every spare inch had been used to maximize the numbers that could be processed through the center.

Anya was particularly pleased to see how well the platform had come along since her last visit. It stood proudly protruding high above the water level. It was the perfect launch pad for their transports. The colossal metal structure, with its bridges feeding down to the terminals, had become the perfect intergalactic space port, exactly as had been envisioned. All they needed were the aircraft and the spaceships and they were good to go.

All in good time, she thought. The five spacecraft were not going to be brought on site until the convergence. Likewise, the aircraft. None were as opulent as the Atlas Noble corporate jet, however, numbers and efficiency were more important than comfort. All would maximize the number of people they could carry. There would be no classes on board, just as many seats as they could fit in safely. Over fifty Airbus A380s were scattered around the world awaiting the call, each with over eight hundred fifty seats.

The runways were empty, the taxiways clear, four small planes sat on an apron, looking tiny in comparison to everything around them. They were four fighter jets that would clear any inquisitive strays, although the chances of any stray flights in the middle of nowhere were all but impossible. Only commercial jets could reach that far and none would fly that far off course due to the amount of fuel they would need to burn.

Satellites were a concern; Atlas Noble had covered that with some very simple technology.

Anya lifted the handset by her side. "Can they switch it back on?"

Anya waited a couple of seconds for the captain to relay the message. The image below her transformed back to how she remembered it. Thousands upon thousands of panels had been placed on top of every single new building. Anya looked down on the image of how the island had been; it was as though everything they had built had disappeared. The image was remarkable, in perfect synch with the sun's position in the sky, it darkened when the sun set and brightened when the sun rose.

"Wonderful!" She checked her watch. She was on a tight schedule to make it back in time for Alex's birthday. "Can we go to Iwo Jima, please?" she asked. It was the main reason for her trip. She was linking up with Caleb Noble, head of transport, on his first experimental fueling exercise for the spacecraft. A helicopter would meet her at Iwo Jima and fly her out to his deep sea vessel stationed above the Mariana trench, the point of the world's oceans where at its deepest, pressures of 1,000 times atmospheric pressure were known to exist. It was the perfect testing ground for their fueling system.

Chapter 55

The suicide of his boss Mike Yates hit Giles Tremellan hard. The head of the UK DIS team had only agreed to take on the role because of Mike. He had been very comfortable with his occasional TV pundit roles which more than supplemented his enviable pension. Mike's replacement was a capable chap but as far as Giles was concerned, DIS without Mike wasn't for him. He tendered his resignation and walked away to enjoy his retirement with a significant package.

Giles sat in his small country cottage. He had bought it for a steal but had to spend a fortune making it livable. He had gone for a simple country theme for the compact one bedroom, one sitting room retreat. Darkness had fallen as he sat nursing a bottle of gin. The occasional bright flicker from the TV was his only source of light. His mind just couldn't comprehend why Mike Yates would have committed suicide. He had everything to live for. A beautiful family, now devastated, money, security. If there were one man on the planet he'd have said would never have taken his own life, it would be Mike Yates.

The first few words from the news headline caught his attention. For a start, it wasn't about Papua New Guinea or the poisoned river. He had been given an assignment in Egypt the day he resigned.

"An Egyptian aid office was destroyed today in an apparent bombing. Although troubles have continued since the unrest, this is seen as a particularly strange attack due to the target. The three female workers worked with young vulnerable mothers."

Young mothers. He thought back to Yvonne Winston and her report about that exact subject, wondering if it had potentially been the reason for her death. Her death weighed heavily on Giles. He had no issue killing in general but innocents, that was a different matter. Unlike any death he had been involved in before, Giles had dug into her background quietly through a few of his old contacts. They found nothing. The woman was a saint. Her life was all about helping those who couldn't help themselves.

Mike's suicide was shortly after Yvonne Winston's death. Giles knew Mike, and innocents weren't his game either. He rubbed his face. The gin had taken its toll, three quarters of the bottle had gone over the evening. He stumbled to the bathroom and splashed his face with cold water. His mind was racing. Mike Yates hadn't committed suicide, he just wouldn't have.

More awake but just as intoxicated, he opened his laptop and typed a search into google. Three searches later and his hunch was scarily coming together. There had been over forty-two deaths around the world in the previous year of people who had worked with underage mothers. He tried another angle. Statisticians. They hadn't suffered such devastating losses but it was notably higher than any previous year.

He was about to search for teenage pregnancies when he noticed his statistician search had netted a couple of interesting results. A number of government statistical bodies had been outsourced to a private organization. The UK's Office for National Statistics was outsourced in a multibillion dollar deal for the government. He didn't even remember it happening but there it was in black and white, two years earlier. Fed Stats, the US Statistics, the same, a massive windfall for the US government. A more detailed search showed that the same organization controlled the majority of all data gathering companies around the world and had become, as its website proudly boasted, the world's premier data source and analysis company. Even the UN was listed as one of its clients.

Giles grabbed his jacket. A noise from the kitchen stopped him in his tracks. The back door had been locked. He looked around for a weapon, grabbed the gin bottle, upending it, sending the last quarter spilling to the floor.

A face appeared at his living room door. The light from the TV cast an eerie grayness across her face. It was the young DIS woman who had killed Yvonne Winston.

"Giles, are you alright? I've been trying to call you!"

"Why are you here?" he said, raising the gin bottle and ready to use it.

"I'm worried about you. We've not been able to contact you since you left."

"I thought you were in Egypt," he said.

"No, we were turned around even before we landed. DIS was pulled from it. To be honest, we've been pulled from pretty much everything," she said. "You can put the bottle down. Have you got another one? I could do with a drink."

Giles began to relax. His mind was working overtime and the gin wasn't helping.

"Over there," he tilted his head toward the liquor cabinet.

She moved across and opened it, withdrawing a bottle of vodka, pouring herself a good measure. "You?" she asked, looking over at him.

"I think I've had enough," he glanced at his bottle of gin.

As she downed the glass, Giles moved, catching her off guard, swinging the empty gin bottle and crashing it into her temple as hard as he could.

The shock in her eyes was betrayed by the stiletto blade that was in her hand. She slumped to the floor.

"Bitch!" said Giles, taking the blade from her limp hand. "I'm not drunk enough to know you'd have come to the front door! Anyone with you?"

She looked at him blankly, he had hit her harder than he had intended. She was barely conscious.

She was a ruthless killer, emotionless. He slipped the blade through her side in between her ribs and into her heart. "See how you like it," he said.

They had forgotten who they were dealing with. A former SAS commander, Giles knew how to look after himself. It was almost insulting they thought she'd have been able to deal with him, drunk or sober. Giles grabbed his jacket and disappeared into the night.

Chapter 56

"Cash," Sophie nudged Cash trying to wake him up. He rolled over reaching out to her.

"Sophie," he mumbled.

"Cash! Wake up!" She pushed him harder, almost pushing him off his seat.

"Yeah, what?!" he said, coming instantly out of his sleep.

"I need to show you something," she said. "Come with me."

Cash rose, stretched, and Sophie led him back to a large dining table that sat behind the lounge area of the Senator's private Boeing 787 Dreamliner.

"Where is everyone?" he asked, looking around for Rigs and the Senator.

"The Senator went to his bedroom shortly after you feel asleep. Rigs is in one of the guestrooms."

"One of the guestrooms?"

"Yeah there are two, the other's mine when I'm done here."

"And I get a seat?"

"A very comfortable one which you had no difficulty sleeping in. I've been trying to wake you up for five minutes."

"Still, a seat versus a guestroom, seems a bit—"

"Look, I'm working through these numbers again; it still doesn't make any sense. The calculations are taking me around in circles. Can you have a look and tell me if there's something I'm missing?"

Cash pulled up a chair and looked over the work Sophie had spent days poring over.

"This all means nothing to me," he concluded quickly. "Perhaps a quick breakdown of what it all means?"

Sophie stuck her pen behind her ear and stretched across in front of Cash. Her fragrance hit him like a sledgehammer. He reached out. She slapped his hand away. "Not now," she said sternly.

Cash looked at her. She was too busy to notice his smile as she prepared the papers she needed. She had said *'not now'*, thought Cash, not *'never'*.

"It all starts with these drawings and artifacts," Sophie said. "They clearly depict a world exploding. From there, we have a number of calendar references to that same event, but remember the calendar is an astronomical one, so it doesn't give a date as such, it gives us the astronomical event of when that will happen. That's where the measurements come in. A number of structures are placed very precisely and track the movement of the stars, which over time move in the sky; it's all to do with our rotation. The universe itself is constantly moving, but all you need to know is that they move a little over time, so we're talking tiny movements over thousands of years."

"So what is it that's supposed to destroy us?"

Sophie sat back and looked him in the eye. "You see, that's exactly why a fresh pair of eyes can help. I've been entirely focused on the *when* and not the *how*."

"What are all these marks?" he asked looking at one of the drawings.

"Your father found similar ones across many of the sites. They're markers for the precessional cycle. It's a number that's repeated over and over, '25,920'. It's complicated, but it's to do with earth's wobble and is the time taken for the wobble to work through 360 degrees, approximately 25,920 years. It's broken down into the twelve signs of the zodiac, which tells us where we are in the cycle, each sign lasting approximately 2,160 years."

Cash looked at her blankly.

Sophie grabbed a pen and paper. "Okay, imagine March 1st was the first day of spring, and we had the spring equinox on that day. Each year, the equinox— the time when the equator of the Earth is directly in line with the center of the sun— because of the wobble, is a little later. In the span of 2,160 years, it would move by a month. The spring equinox would be April 1st. Over 25,920 years, it would complete a full cycle."

"So summer will become winter and winter summer."

"In theory yes, but not in practice."

"Now you've seriously lost me…"

"Yes, but our calendar takes the precessional cycle into account, so each day the wobble is taken into account. So spring will still be in March. However, the stars aren't, and we can monitor our progress through the cycle with where we are in relation to the stars."

"And they knew about his back then?"

"It appears so. Nobody's certain of when the next cycle is due to start. Some say it's already started, others say it's not for another four hundred years. It's not an exact science and one we're still getting to grips with. Think of it like a spinning top, sometimes the wobble is more pronounced than at other times as it spins. From your father's work, it would seem that the ancients were all in agreement; the new cycle is only eighty years away. All of their markers from your father's work and my calculations say we're on the cusp of the eighty year countdown to the new cycle of Aquarius. I'm not sure why it's an eighty year countdown, but that seems to be the marker they've used across the sites."

"And you're not worried it's the countdown to the end of the world?"

"No, it's the same for each cycle - eighty years before the cycle. None of the other markers for the prediction are in synch, nowhere near. That's why I'm getting numbers from hundreds of thousands to millions of years before the Earth meets the markers for the prediction of its destruction."

"I think I'm getting it, let me have a look," said Cash poring over the papers. He pointed out a couple of miscalculations.

"How do you *do* that?" asked Sophie when he pointed out a decimal point in the wrong place. "I need a calculator to work that out and you simply glance at it and know it's wrong!"

"I'm good with numbers," said Cash.

"I know, and it's why your father was so disappointed you never went into astronomy."

Cash stopped with the papers and looked at her. "Seriously? My father was disappointed I didn't go into astronomy?"

Sophie winced. "He was disappointed about a lot more than that," she admitted. "Though seeing you must have made him very happy," she said, a tear dropping from her eye.

Cash wiped it away. "Please don't.,"

Sophie buried her head into this chest and threw her arms around him, tears streaming from her eyes. Cash lifted her up and took her to the empty guestroom and laid her down gently. She patted the bed next to him, where he lay down and they fell asleep, fully clothed in each other's arms.

***

"We're here," said Rigs, startling Cash awake. Sophie wasn't by his side.

"Where's Sophie?"

"Working on something like a fiend," he said, looking at the fully clothed Cash and undisturbed bedclothes. "Having a good dream were you?"

Cash got up and rushed out to Sophie, who was tearing through her papers.

"What's wrong?" he asked.

"Nothing, nothing at all, just something you said last night. What's going to destroy us... What if the markers aren't for the Earth? What if they're what's going to destroy the Earth?"

"Huh? I don't get it."

"I was working on the basis that the calculations your father was working on were related to the calendar and the precessional cycle. But the calculations were meaningless because, according to the calendars, the Earth is safe for a very long time, which is very different from your father being right about everything. Your father needed Hubble 2. He wasn't working with the calendars as his research suggested. He must have moved on, realizing, like us, that it wasn't about the calendars."

"So what does that mean?"

"It means we're getting closer!"

"Closer to what?" asked the Senator, stretching his arms as he joined them from his slumber.

"To the truth," said Cash. "Of what's really going on."

"Very good," the Senator said without a hint of interest. "You're not going to be long here, I hope. I'd like to be in Geneva before the party starts."

"Thirty minutes is all I need," said Sophie.

"Rigs?" asked Cash.

"That should be fine," he said loading an HK416 and after checking it was ready, tossing it to Cash.

"Expecting trouble?" asked the Senator.

Cash smiled. "We are trouble."

Chapter 57

The Senator had arranged for a helicopter to take them to the pyramids. He had no intention of suffering through Cairo's traffic chaos, especially as he had no intention of staying behind without them.

"You're coming too?" asked Cash in surprise when they exited the plane.

"You're supposed to be keeping me safe, aren't you?"

"We're in the middle of an international airport though."

"We were in the most secret military installation on the planet last night."

"After you," said Cash stepping aside to let him into the waiting chopper.

"Let's go," said Cash, closing the door behind him.

"My God," said Sophie when the pyramids came into view. "They are truly magnificent. Majestic…"

"Big," Cash commented.

Rigs pointed downwards, motioning for Cash to look. The area was closed off. A barrier had been erected restricting access to the pyramids. A throng of tourists were pushing towards the guards at the entrance but they weren't budging. The site was closed.

"Sophie, any ideas?" asked Cash.

"Nope. I checked the website before we left and there was no mention of it being closed."

"Keep circling for now thanks," Cash advised the chopper pilot.

Sophie logged onto the website again. A message had been added in the last hour: 'Closed for structural issues'.

Cash was watching a procession of trucks drive through the gates much to the consternation of the tourists who had probably spent hours in traffic getting to the closed site.

"That looks like scaffolding! Surely not?"

"It says it could be closed for up to three weeks. An overnight tremor has caused damage that requires—"

"I thought you said it was built to withstand earthquakes?" Cash cut in.

"It was but I suppose if it were big enough—"

"Not to knock over a wooden shed that a gust of wind would destroy?" Cash pointed to a number of wooden slums they were circling over, their walls and roofs balancing treacherously.

"Land next to the big one," instructed the Senator, bored of the debating. "I'll keep the guards busy while you get what you need."

***

The Pyramids at Giza had been identified as the number one site by Anya Noble and as such had two Sicarii allocated to it. They had arrived for the opening of the plateau while the final eight foot high solid metal fence was being erected. They both looked for a way in but the fencing had not been erected by the local workforce. A highly professional job had closed off the entire plateau overnight. Only one gate led in and out of the site and the guards stood resolute. Nobody was getting in and no discussion was being entered into.

For days, they had waited, circling the site, the images of the targets burned indelibly into their minds. They felt the trucks before they could see or hear them, the ground vibrating under the mass convoy that was approaching. If the trucks could get in so could they, thought Joel, the elder of the two Sicarii and leader of the order. Whatever the targets wanted, it was on the other side of the fence and hence where they needed to be. He signaled to Ethan, his young protégé, to follow.

Joel jogged back and as predicted, the trucks began to queue too. The guards were far too important to allow the trucks to just pass them. His first plan was to climb into the back and simply hitch a ride but he found it impossible, the rear of the trucks were sealed, their doors padlocked and security tagged.

Joel looked down at the gate some hundred yards ahead. Guards with mirrors were checking underneath, not for people, but for explosives, an aftermath of previous tourist attacks at the site. He watched intently while he and Ethan milled around casually as though not sure what to do with their day. They were checking the undercarriage and the security tags closely.

Joel signaled to Ethan and disappeared in between two trucks, looking up at the helicopter that was circling overhead.

***

The Senator had his most officious face on when the first guard approached the landing chopper.

"Check your paperwork before bothering me," he boomed, leaving the guard who only understood a few words of English clueless as to who or why they were there. The Senator's voice was commanding enough that the guard thought better of challenging him himself. He scurried off to his superior.

"Does anyone know the military chief these days?" Senator Noble asked quietly.

"I know the President is—"

"A patsy. The real power here nowadays is the military. If I throw that name about we'll be fine for a couple of hours."

Sophie looked it up, moving out of the way of the trucks that were beginning to flood the area.

"You can't be here!" a guard barked. It was the original guard, back now with his superior who spoke better English.

"I'd suggest you ditch that tone, son," said the Senator, not waiting for Sophie's search results. He waved them off to do their thing. "My colleagues are here at the request of your military commander in chief, and I suggest you pay them and me the respect we are due."

"Field Marshall Sobhi?"

If the guy were clever, he'd have given a false name, but Senator Noble was a political grandmaster, he knew how to play a person.

"I'll give him a call, you can tell him why you're delaying us."

The two guards scurried away before the Senator could reach for the cell phone he didn't even have.

Sophie moved towards the entrance, looking up at the pyramid. Cash stood beside her, marveling at the scale, while Rigs signaled he was going around the back. The grandeur of the monument passed him by. He had something he wanted to check.

Sophie grabbed the printout of the measurements she needed. They were all precisely detailed by the professor's research. She needed to get to the queen's chamber and with the site closed, she was going to have it to herself. With the schematic in her hand, she worked her way along the robber's entrance, a tunnel dug through the pyramid which linked to the descending passage of the original entrance.

"Up there is where the original entrance was," she pointed behind them as they joined the main passage. "Twenty tons, and swung open with little effort from the inside but undetectable from the outside, such was the precision with which it was made."

"One question?" asked Cash.

"What?"

"Why build something so amazing and then have this tiny little entranceway?" He was bent over, his six feet two inches not ideal for a passageway that was exactly half his height.

"We're here," she said. She couldn't answer him; it really didn't make a lot of sense. "We go up here, this is the ascending passage."

"Genius," said Cash. The passage began to ascend, though its height remained the same.

They took a turn that led them along a level section before entering the Queen's Chamber. "Nearly there," Sophie said. "That wasn't too bad."

"If you're not claustrophobic, it's fine," said Cash, standing to his full height within what was still a fairly small space. "What's this, eighteen by eighteen?"

"About that, yes." Cash spotted the printout she had laid down. "That's full of measurements, right?"

"Not to the preciseness that I need though," Sophie said, setting up a laser that measured angles to six decimal places. "Also, not all the measurements your father suggests are needed."

Cash looked again. He couldn't see an angle that hadn't been measured on the sheet. A noise caught his attention from back down the passageway.

Joel had noted that the guards were not at all interested in the drivers, only whether they had a bomb underneath and that their cargo remained untouched. Approaching from the passenger side, he and Ethan had made short work of two of the drivers, gaining entry to the cabs and knocking them out before stuffing their unconscious bodies in the ample passenger foot wells before covering them. Not that it mattered. When they approached, they handed down the paperwork that the guards would check and waited while they checked the undercarriage and that the tags were secure and matched the paperwork. A wave later and they drove the trucks into the plateau, following the convoy towards the great pyramid.

Joel spotted the helicopter sitting only fifty yards from the entrance, and what looked like a heated discussion. An older man was arguing with the guards. His back was to Joel but he did recognize a man who was walking towards the pyramid entrance with a woman. He also recognized the man who was walking away from them towards the other side of the pyramid.

Their targets! He edged his truck forward and got out. A guard came towards him, shouting at him in Egyptian. Joel waited until he was close enough and obscured from the rest of the site by his and Ethan's truck before pouncing like a cobra. His right hand flashed into the man's neck and sent him crumpling to the ground. A second strike to the back of the neck rendered him unconscious. Joel only killed when he had to, or was paid to. With Ethan's help, he stuffed the guard into the cab, out of sight.

"I'll take the two in the pyramid, you take the one on the outside and see if you can get an ID on the older guy."

Ethan was gone before he was finished speaking, always eager to please. Joel was more deliberate in his actions and made sure his entry to the pyramid went unnoticed.

He travelled through the passage, constantly stopping to hear where his targets were. A couple of conversations gave little away. The tight corridors only allowed you to understand whether people were ahead of you or behind you. When he approached the first turn, there were no sounds from either direction and he guessed wrong, continuing down into the subterranean chamber, an unfinished chamber deep beneath the pyramid.

He turned and headed back up, turning into the ascending passages and was rewarded by voices off in the distance.

***

Rigs had found the area where the overhead image from the previous day had been focused. It was the same area that had been in the professor's notes. Something had caught his eye, a difference in the two images, both of exactly the same section of the East face of the pyramid. Rigs had an ability to recall great detail from any image he had seen. The two images that should have matched didn't quite and he wanted to see why not. Unfortunately, the area that differed was near the top of the pyramid. He worked his way up, pulling himself from level to level. It wasn't easy, especially when the sun began to reach its midday heat.

He heard a grunt and looked back. A man had stumbled behind him. Rigs hadn't even heard him following him. Rigs had kept an eye out for guards for the first hundred feet of the climb and after that he figured he could relax. They wouldn't shoot him and they wouldn't catch him before he got to where he wanted to go. The man behind him had closed to fifty feet without Rigs noticing and if he hadn't slipped in his haste to catch him, Rigs would never have known he was there.

Rigs looked back at the chopper. His HK416 was sitting on the back seat. With the site closed, it seemed surplus to requirements. He patted his belt. His Mission MPK-T1 knife was his only weapon. He looked back at the man who was coming towards him. The man knew he had given his position away and had doubled his speed. Rigs looked ahead. His anomaly sat just thirty feet away, ten levels of blocks. He doubled his speed and raced forward. If he was going to have to fight, he didn't want to have to climb any further.

"Stop!' shouted the man, with a faint Middle Eastern accent.

Rigs carried on, reaching the point in the image that hadn't matched. The stone in question was slightly askew from one image to the other. He pushed at it, it didn't budge. He pushed at the others around it, they didn't move either. He looked at the stone beneath his feet. A scrape was clear where the stone in question had been moved. He withdrew his knife and scraped an X into the stone.

"What are you doing?" asked the man, now within ten feet.

"Marking the spot where you die," said Rigs.

The man laughed, but Rigs continued to carve. There were less than two feet on each of the ledges and an almost four hundred foot fall behind them.

"Why would you want to kill me?" asked the man who was now on the same ledge.

"Why else would you want to follow me?' asked Rigs, finishing his X. "Now if you just come closer."

The man withdrew his own knife. Ethan would have preferred a gun but the terrorist attacks in previous years had meant there was no chance they could get into the area with anything more than a well-concealed knife. He slashed out at Rigs.

Rigs deflected the slash and tried to kick the man's knee but he was too quick. He dropped and tried to swipe Rigs' legs away. Rigs saw it coming and jumped back, his back leg teetering on the ledge's edge. The man lunged forward.

Rigs let his body go with its balance and dropped to the lower ledge, barely avoiding the man's blade.

Rigs slashed out at the man's ankles, the man had seen it coming and was already jumping back and down to Rigs' lower ledge.

"You're very good," said the man.

"Your pals thought so too when I slashed their throats last night," said Rigs.

The man tilted his head, giving away his interest.

"One was Katya. Shame, damn good looking woman as well," smiled Rigs.

The man lunged wildly, fury in his eyes.

Rigs caught his wrist and snapped it back. The man's knife plunged below. Rigs spun him round, and keeping his back to the structure, held the man on the edge of the ledge with his knife pressing against his throat.

"Who are you?"

The man remained silent.

"I'm not going to ask again," he said dragging the razor sharp blade gently across the man's neck.

"I can't tell you," said the man defiantly.

Rigs relaxed his grip and slashed at the man twice, leaving him in a bloody mess on the ledge. He had to get to Cash and Sophie. He bounded down the ledges, trying to keep his speed up while not overdoing it. If he mistimed it and fell, it would be worse than a straight three hundred foot fall, his body would bounce off ledge after ledge leaving a crumpled corpse at the bottom.

***

Cash heard the sound of scraping from the corridor behind them. He waved for Sophie to remain still and quiet. He listened. The sound was getting nearer. Like Rigs, he wished he had had taken his HK416 and had nothing other than his knife. His choice was simple: wait and face them in the chamber with Sophie, where she would only get in the way and be able to be used against him, or go on the offensive. He'd always been a quarterback kind of guy. Offense was his game.

He struggled back into the small tunnel and slid as silently as he could along the level surface. The scuffling noises were getting closer. He reached the ascending passage and could see a man coming up towards him from below. The ascending passage continued upwards, most importantly away from Sophie. Cash entered the passage and pushed on higher, drawing the man away from Sophie, and up towards the Grand Gallery. It was the first place that actually looked like it belonged in the pyramid, thought Cash when he entered. More importantly for that moment, he had space to move in.

"Are you going to let me out of here?"

"Depends. Why are you here?" said Cash. He stood with his knife ready to strike as soon as the man exited the crouched passageway into the gallery.

"I could always turn back and visit the chamber below," he offered.

"You'd never make it."

"You'd bet her life on that?"

Cash stepped back allowing the man to enter the gallery.

"Cash Harris?" asked the man.

"You have me at a disadvantage," said Cash, stepping back and preparing to strike.

"Joel. It's a shame we meet in such circumstances," he said.

"Was it your guys we dealt with in Machu Picchu?" asked Cash.

"Dear God no, they're the reason we're here," he said scornfully. "Amateurs."

Joel flashed his knife at Cash as he had prepared to strike. Joel had sensed his move.

"Any particular reason you want to kill us?"

Joel shook his head. "Money, I'm afraid. I've no idea why they want you dead, they just do."

Cash feigned a move. Joel bought it and flashed his knife as previously. Cash reacted, drawing blood from Joel's forearm.

"Very good," said Joel, rushing towards Cash and catching him with a punch as Cash avoided his blade.

Cash reeled backwards. It was a solid punch that, had his life not been on the line, may otherwise have floored him. He shook it off.

Joel pounced again. Cash was ready for him. Avoiding the blade and the punch, he ducked and swung out his leg catching Joel and sending him crashing back down the gallery towards the entrance. Cash rushed forward but Joel bounced up ready to strike again, stopping Cash in his tracks.

Joel feinted left but struck from the right. Cash had his measure, catching the blade arm, falling to the floor and bringing it down with him. A ledge that ran the full length either side of the gallery was the perfect pivot point to aim for. He pushed Joel's body towards the ledge, while he himself aimed for the three-foot-wide gulley that ran down the middle of the gallery. He caught Joel's elbow on the ledge and fell into the three-foot gulley, powering his full weight and force into bringing the bottom half of Joel's arm with him. Joel's arm bent horribly at the elbow until a loud snap echoed up the thirty foot height of the gallery's ceiling and its full one hundred fifty foot length. Joel tried to stifle his scream but barely managed. His arm dangled helplessly while his body struggled not to go into shock.

He lay on the ledge helpless as Cash stood over him his knife at the ready.

"You okay?" said Rigs, appearing at the end of the gallery.

"Yes, thanks for coming," he said catching his breath.

"There's another one up on the pyramid," said Rigs taking a seat next to Cash. He had raced all the way there, telling the Senator to get into the chopper and shoot anyone that came anywhere near him.

"Dead?"

"Nah, like this one, crippled. I cut both his Achilles tendons; he'll be hobbling for a long while. Not sure how he'll get down though, he's a long way up," said Rigs. "What will we do with him?"

"Are you going to tell us who hired you?" asked Cash, looking at Joel, who was struggling with the debilitating pain.

"No," said Joel resolutely.

Rigs touched the wound, twisting the arm slightly, generating an ear piercing scream from Joel. "Who hired you?"

Joel shook his head, his forehead soaked in sweat.

"Leave him," said Cash. "They're not going anywhere anytime soon. I'll call Travis to arrange for them to be picked up and see what he can get from them. Let's go."

They met Sophie where she was pacing nervously by the entrance. "Thank God!" she whispered when Cash appeared alive and well with Rigs.

She spotted the blood on the corner of his mouth and rushed over, touching the redness on his chin. "Are you alright?" she fussed.

"I'm fine," said Cash, enjoying the attention. The same attention she used to lavish on him after any of his football injuries.

"So, did you find what you were after?" Sophie asked Rigs.

"Yeah, there's something up above us, not sure how we get to it though. The stone didn't budge."

"And you spotted it how?"

"Two photos, taken at different times, there was a stone slightly askew."

'There are over two million stones!" gasped Cash.

"Not all on one side, there can't be more than a few thousand on the side," said Sophie. "Is it about three-quarters of the way up on the East face?" she asked.

"You saw it?"

"Honestly no, but there was an incident a couple of years ago, robbers moved a stone one night, up high where they thought it wouldn't be noticed. All that climb for nothing, sorry. If you had mentioned it…"

"Don't feel sorry for him," Cash said. "Feel sorry for the guy he left up there, crippled."

"A guy that tried to kill him? Not a chance," said Sophie, smiling at the once again silent Rigs. He had retracted into himself. The action was over, his awkwardness returned.

They walked back to a very nervous Senator. He and the pilot were both training the HK416s around the chopper.

"We dealt with them," Cash said.

"Them?"

"Two," said Cash. "Why are you so surprised we're dealing with these guys? We're ex-Special Forces."

"No reason," the Senator said, visibly relaxing.

They took their seats and as they took off, Rigs leaned across to Cash and whispered into his ear. "What if the robbers is just a cover story?"

Chapter 58

Geneva, Switzerland

Cash stepped down from the Senator's jet out onto an empty apron. No welcome awaited the Senator, not even a car.

Cash stepped back into the jet where the Senator was waiting for the all-clear to exit. "Do they know you're coming?"

"I wouldn't think so," Senator Noble said, fastening his coat button. "We may have had a slight disagreement."

"And you didn't call to say you were coming?" asked Sophie.

"My nephew's not the type you call, face-to-face is always better, I find. But give it five minutes, they'll know we're here."

Cash stepped back out onto the steps and noted the cars racing towards them. Three long black sedans tearing down the runway area, stopping aircraft in their wake. The Senator joined him on the steps.

"See, they know I'm here now."

The cars slammed to a halt and eight men dressed immaculately in black designer suits exited the cars. Cash couldn't help but think that's how the Secret Service would look if they had a five thousand dollar clothing budget and a six-two minimum height requirement, even down to the wires that trailed down the back of their necks from their earpieces.

"I'm not sure you need us, if that's your nephew's security?" said Cash, impressed.

"You're coming," commanded the Senator, walking down the steps.

A man dressed in a tuxedo stepped out of the middle car. "Uncle Bertie!" Cash picked up on the lack of sincerity and walked faster to catch up with the Senator. Rigs was close behind with Sophie at his side.

Two security men walked forward and patted down Cash and Rigs, removing their handguns and knives. They protested but the Senator waved for them to accept. Their weapons were placed in a strong box and stored in the trunk of the first car.

Sophie was checked also but hers was accompanied by a number of apologies by the security man who made sure he did not touch any inappropriate areas.

"Conrad!" said the Senator, stepping forward to embrace him. Conrad stepped back, showing the Senator to the back of the car instead.

"My friends will travel with me," said the Senator, waiting for Sophie to climb in before him. Rigs followed, then the Senator. Cash squeezed in, pleased to see two rows of seats. Conrad joined them, squeezing himself between Cash and Rigs.

"I've never seen an Audi this big before," said Cash.

"You wouldn't have," said Conrad, offering little more, his eyes not leaving the Senator.

"Why's that?" asked Sophie.

"They're specially made for us," he said, breaking his stare to smile at her. His manners were impeccable. He was unable to be rude to her.

Sophie took the cue and engaged Conrad in conversation for the rest of the trip. She would do anything to ease the palpable tension. It helped, of course, that Sophie was very pleasing to the eye.

Their convoy swept through Geneva and along the lakeside, cars moving aside as the three Audis carved their way through traffic.

Cash noted the sign for Anieres when they slowed down for a checkpoint which just waved them on. Three minutes later, they were pulling into the drive of one of the grandest chateaux Cash had ever laid his eyes on, helped by the laser and light show that was lighting up the night sky above.

"Wow, this is some hotel," said Cash, stepping out onto the driveway that looped around a spectacular water fountain in front of the chateau.

"It's not a hotel," said Conrad, leading them towards the entranceway. "It's my cousin's home. Welcome," he said grudgingly.

Conrad and the Senator led the way. Cash and Rigs kept the Senator within their reach, although judging by the security they had seen, it was pointless. Armed guards were at the checkpoint and armed guards were patrolling the streets. Cameras were on every lamppost. Cash used the Secret Service comparison again; it was the security they'd have liked to have around the White House if they were allowed to. It seemed nobody was stopping the Nobles.

"Would you mind if I took the Senator from you for a few minutes?" asked Conrad, politely but rhetorically.

The Senator nodded to say it was okay.

"Sure," said Cash. "Will we wait here?"

"You may as well join the party, through that door there and out to the marquee." A security man stepped forward to show them the way..

"Antoine wishes to speak with you privately," said Conrad, guiding Bertie to Antoine's library.

Conrad opened the door and allowed the Senator to enter. Antoine stood up, his hands clasped behind his back, staring out at the lake and the marquee.

"Do you want me to stay?" asked Conrad.

"No," said Antoine firmly.

The door closed, leaving uncle and nephew at either side of the room.

The Senator walked across and poured himself a drink. "Trying to kill me?" he said with fury.

"After what you've done?" said Antoine, turning around and staring him down.

"We don't murder our own!" boomed the Senator in his most commanding voice.

"Tell that to my father. Oh of course, you can't, you had him killed," spat Antoine.

"I *what*?!"

"Don't dare deny it, you just tried again to take power, Bertie."

"Again, what are you talking about?"

"You killed my father in an attempt to gain power, admit it!"

"But *you* gained power from his death. How does that make any sense?"

"I was supposed to be on the boat with him, you'd have killed us both."

"As was I!"

"As were you what?"

"Supposed to be on that boat. There was an emergency session I had to return to the Senate for. Otherwise, I'd have been there too. I loved your father with all my heart, I wouldn't have hurt a hair on his head and I'd kill anyone who did."

"You always wanted the power," challenged Antoine.

"And your father didn't. He knew he was weak as a leader. I offered to sit by his side and help him lead but he knew it would make him look weak to the family. Look what happened during his leadership— a population explosion, the Cold War, nuclear weapons. It was a disaster but he was the leader. It set us back years but he was my brother. What could I do? Twelve minutes earlier and I would have been the leader."

"Yes twelve minutes," said Antoine with disgust. "Twelve minutes that had you kill your own brother for power."

"Are you mad?! We don't kill Nobles! We do not kill one another! I made my move, yes, but it wasn't at the cost of any Noble blood. Do you think I'd have done all that when I could have simply had you and Alex shot, job done?!"

Antoine paused. It was a very good point. "But your lust for power…"

"Yes, I was born for it. Perhaps at the last minute, we turned in our mother's womb and your father came out first, who knows? I was born to lead. But kill my own brother? Never! Kill one of our own, it's against everything we believe in."

"It can be done, the council can—"

"Do no such thing!" shouted the Senator, slamming his hand on the desk.

"It is forbidden! We do not kill our own! It's what separates us from every other being. It makes us who we are. Who said you can?"

"It's written in our history?"

"Anya!" he said, incredulous. She was the keeper of the archives.

Antoine shook his head. "Blake."

The Senator calmed. "Blake, that sneaky old bastard," he said, almost admiringly.

"What?" asked Antoine.

"If we had all been on that boat who would have gained power?"

Antoine thought for a second. "Blake's father,' he said.

"Who would have been in his nineties. Wait a minute, who knows I'm here?"

"Just Conrad and his security men. He got the call to say your plane had landed, told me and we snuck out. Nobody else knows."

"And Blake thinks you have the Sicarii about to kill me, if they haven't already."

"He's over a hundred!"

"And crazy," said the Senator. "He always has been. He thinks he'll live for at least another twenty years."

Antoine suddenly saw it. The old man had played him like a fool. Even forcing his opinion on population control into the plan. He had complained about the mistakes his father had made. The old man with all the wisdom thought he could do it better and knew it all.

"If he kills you both, thinking I may be dead..." thought the Senator.

"He'd be leader," finished Antoine, rushing to the door. "We need to get Alex somewhere safe."

***

"Oh my God!" said Cash. "Have you tried the food?"

"Yes," said Sophie, her mouth full. "It's amazing!" She looked around. "Where's Rigs?"

Cash tilted his head over toward an exit that led to the garden. Rigs stood just inside watching them.

"He's not the party type."

"Do you see who's getting set up on the stage?" she asked.

Cash looked, he didn't recognize anyone.

"They're only like the current number one band, their tickets sell out in seconds, Kyle's a huge fan."

"Who are they?"

"I can't remember what they're called - he's got their posters all over his walls though."

"Well let's go and get him their autographs," said Cash, taking her hand and pushing through the crowd.

Sophie looked around as they walked. "Have you noticed anything strange?"

Cash shook his head, his eyes fixed on the prize, getting his son his favorite band's autographs.

Sophie stopped being pulled and stood in the middle of the marquee, surrounded by men and women.

Cash felt her stop and backed up towards her. "What?"

"Look," she said.

Cash looked around. They were surrounded by women in evening gowns and men in tuxedos.

"You can't see it because you're not out of place," she said. "Look at all the men and then at all the women."

Cash spun around quickly. "We're seriously under dressed to be here?" he asked.

She shook her head. "Look beyond that."

Cash spun around more slowly and began to see it. "Everyone is exactly the same height," he said.

"And build," said Sophie. "Look at the guys, same as you, six feet two, broad shoulders and fit. Not a fat or thin one in sight. The women all five eight, without their heels, and bodies to die for, not a one fat or thin."

"Rich people," said Cash with a smile. "They've got it all."

"There are, what, five hundred people here?" she asked.

Cash stood on his tiptoes and looked around. "Give or take."

"And they're all the same height and build? Seriously, that just doesn't happen!"

"They're all from the same family, it's not like they all look identical."

"Yeah, facially they're a little different but if you look you can see the similarities, even you—"

"Conrad said you were here." A woman approached Cash. Like everyone around her, she stood easily three inches taller than Sophie, who was feeling small at five foot five, despite wearing heels.

Cash looked at her blankly.

"Anya Noble. I was a friend of your father's many years ago. I was so sorry to hear of your loss. He was a great man."

"Anya, 'The answers you seek, lay around us in our past,'" quoted Sophie.

"I'm sure they do," said Anya, holding out her hand.

"Sophie Kramer."

"Ah, Dr. Kramer, I've read a number of your articles, excellent work."

"Thank you," said Sophie. "Do you know the band?"

"Yes, my nephew's favorite."

"My son's too!"

Anya looked at her. "You can't have a son old enough to like them?" she asked, further winning Sophie over.

"We do," said Cash proudly. "Kyle."

Anya looked at him. "I'd love to meet him," she said with a deep sincerity.

Cash didn't have a chance to answer, Rigs was by his side propelling him through the crowd.

"Sorry?!!" said Cash weakly, turning to Rigs. "What the hell are you doing?"

"Trouble," said Rigs, working his way urgently towards the stage, Cash in tow.

***

The Senator and Antoine entered the marquee. Antoine's eyes desperately searching for his son Alex. Over five hundred Nobles filled the tent and he was nowhere to be seen. His wife Chantal caught Antoine's eye and waved him over. "Where have you been? We're waiting for you to make your speech on the stage!"

Antoine looked at the stage. Alex was standing with the band. The two assassins who had been protecting the Senator were fighting their way towards him.

"You liar!" Antoine screeched at his uncle. "Stop those two!" he roared, his voice reaching halfway across the tent, but then drowned out by the music.

The Senator looked around, trying to see what he had made him react the way he had. Cash and Rigs were desperately trying to get to the stage where Alex was. He looked at the stage but knew that Cash and Rigs didn't even know who Alex was, so they weren't going after him.

Antoine ran towards the stage. His son was about to be murdered before his very eyes and he knew he would most likely be next but that didn't even enter his thoughts. He had to save his son. Conrad rushed to his side, three of his security men plowing their way through the crowd to get Antoine to where he wanted to be.

"The two killers! He brought them here to kill Alex and me. He all but told me!" he explained to Conrad.

"But he'd need to kill you as well, we need to get you out of here. Let me save Alex, my men will—"

Antoine pushed past Conrad, he had no intention of going anywhere but to Alex's side. He defied his age and leapt onto the stage, the three security men by his side. Conrad pulled himself up from the ground where he'd landed.

"Shoot them!" ordered Antoine, pointing to Cash and Rigs, who were next to his son.

***

Rigs raced on to the stage, Cash right behind him. He showed Cash two fingers and pointed to the curtain that was obscuring the back stage area. He had spotted something from his vantage point at the exit. A young man wearing a '21' badge stood chatting to the band members by the break in the curtain that Rigs was racing towards. *Alex*, thought Cash. The Senator had mentioned it was a twenty-first birthday party.

"Two stagehands, guns," said Rigs, bringing Cash fully up to speed as they approached the curtain. "Get them out of the way!" he said to Cash, motioning to Alex and the band. Cash moved towards the band and Alex, to keep them safe.

"Shoot them!"

Cash turned around and recognized Antoine Noble easily enough; he just didn't quite understand why he was telling his security men to shoot him and Rigs.

He threw up his hands while Rigs threw himself behind the curtain and straight into the unsuspecting stagehands who had been startled by the shout.

"We're helping you!" Cash bellowed, watching Rigs struggle with the two stagehands through the space in the curtain. Cash couldn't move. Three guns were trained on him. Nobody else could see what Cash could. The curtain obscured their view, except for Alex.

"He's telling the truth!" said Alex.

Cash didn't blink, he raced through the gap and field-kicked one of the stagehands in the head as he scrabbled on the floor with Rigs and was about to reach his gun.

"Took your time," mumbled Rigs, rolling across the floor with the other. Cash grabbed one of the two loose guns from the floor and placed its muzzle on the stagehand's temple. He stopped fighting instantly.

The Senator joined the scene, two of Conrad's security men flanking him on either side. "Good work guys," he said on behalf of the Nobles. "Anyone seen Blake?"

Anya joined the group. "He snuck out of here when he saw you, you'd have thought he'd seen a ghost."

Antoine let go of his son and walked towards them. "I'm sorry…" he said. "You saved my son! I thought…"

"Doesn't matter," said Cash. "It's all good."

Antoine gave him a hug. "Thank you," he said, moving towards Rigs, who took three paces back, ensuring he didn't suffer the same fate.

"Don't mind him, he's special," said Cash, winking at Rigs.

"If there's anything I can do…"

"Well, actually,' said Cash. "There is one thing…"

Chapter 59

The attackers admitted to Conrad and his men everything they knew, which was very little. They had been hired to kill two men, Antoine and Alex Noble. Their passes would get them into the backstage area, where two guns were hidden with the band's equipment. They were to wait until the speeches were underway and then shoot them both, making their escape during the ensuing chaos. It was only after they arrived that they had seen the level of security and realized it wasn't going to be as easy as suggested. They did not know who hired them; it had all been done online. That became irrelevant after Blake, when confronted, admitted it. He said he was what was best for the Nobles. Antoine was an unworthy leader. Everybody, according to Blake, was unworthy. Only Blake really understood what being a Noble truly meant.

"Where are the two attackers?" asked the Senator.

Conrad looked out of the library window to the lake.

"To the Nobles," toasted Antoine, as the three of them shared a drink in the library.

"To the Nobles!" the others chorused.

"Cash and Rigs," said the Senator, "are nowhere near understanding what's going on."

"You want me to call off the Sicarii?"

"To be honest I think you'll find the Sicarii want to be called off. Cash and Rigs have taken out five of them— three dead and two crippled."

"Are you sure they're no danger to our plans?" asked Conrad.

"Call Anya, I'll tell her what I know and let her decide."

"Okay," said Antoine.

After ten minutes of explaining everything they knew, Anya agreed.

"They're nowhere near. If they don't have the professor's results—that he spent years pulling together along with his research— they're months, if not years from putting it together."

"They're looking for what's going to destroy Earth," laughed the Senator.

"You have a soft spot for them?" asked Antoine.

"They just saved my favorite nephew and great nephew's lives, so I guess so."

"Okay," said Antoine. "Done. Now if you don't mind, I have to talk to my son."

The three left the library. Anya pulled the Senator aside while Conrad went to call off the Sicarii. She led him into an adjoining room.

"Thank you," she said, giving him a hug.

He smiled. "What for?"

"How long have you known?"

"The moment he walked in front of my committee. I know a Noble when I see one. I checked his background and lo and behold, his father was Charles Harris, the boy my niece used to gush about at university."

"You brought him here for me?"

"After what happened to Charles…"

"Don't, please. I got to hold him for a few minutes before I had to leave him. I left a note to Charles, telling him I couldn't have anything to do with him or the boy and came home. He tried to contact me through the only details he had for me. I told him to tell Copernicus that his mother had died in childbirth. After that, he never tried to contact me again. What sort of mother…"

"One with no choice," said the Senator, wiping away her tears.

"He-he has a son," she spluttered. "I have a *grandchild!*" she bawled, throwing herself into the Senator's chest.

Chapter 60

"I can't believe all you asked for was the band members' autographs!" said Sophie. "The man has more money than—"

"Everyone," finished Rigs, causing them both to look over. Rigs had taken the seat at the rear of the lounge area on the Senator's plane and they thought he had gone straight to sleep. The Senator had stayed behind to help his family cope with the trauma, insisting they go ahead without him.

"Yes, everyone," she agreed.

"You said Kyle really liked them?"

"He's a teenager, he loves Corvettes as well, you could have asked for one of those!"

"His Uncle Rigs can buy him one of those," smiled Cash, noting a nod from Rigs.

Sophie gave up. The seatbelt sign had lit up.

"We're nearly there," she said.

"Are you sure about this?" asked Cash. "You really need these measurements?"

"Yes," she said.

"Okay, but this time, we're not taking any chances," said Cash. He grabbed his HK416 and checked it was ready for use. Rigs was packing a small rucksack full of ammunition.

"We're landing three miles from the site and it's dark, we'll be fine."

"We will be because we're ready for whatever comes at us," he said, placing the US Air Force's night vision glasses in his top pocket.

The plane touched down at MoD Boscombe Down, a former RAF base and test range for new aircraft. They taxied to the apron where an old Ford sat waiting for them, with 'Alfie's' emblazoned on the side.

The steward apologized; it was the only car service they could find at that hour in the quaint English countryside.

Cash exited first, his HK416 leading the way. Sophie followed with Rigs at the rear. Cash relaxed as he neared the taxi. There was not a soul in sight.

"I'm not sure you're allowed those things in these parts, my lad," offered the taxi driver cheerily as they climbed in.

"It's alright, we have permission," Cash lied. "We're on important business for the government."

"Some people might be stupid enough to fall for that, but important business in Alfie's cab? I'm not so sure. I might sound simple," he turned and faced them, "but it's after midnight and if the tip's big enough, Alfie might just forget what he saw, if there's no trouble, that is."

Rigs handed the driver a wad of dollars.

"No trouble," promised Cash, his fingers crossed just in case.

Less than five minutes later, they had arrived. Sophie eagerly waited for Rigs to give her the all clear. Finally the thumbs up released her. She grabbed her equipment and rushed across to the center of the stone circle. It was dark, with an eeriness that seemed to multiply as you neared its center.

"Stonehenge is a bit creepy," she said, setting up her kit in the pale moonlight.

"So how old's this place?" asked Cash. He scanned the area with his rifle after donning his night vision glasses.

"Ten thousand years, but the majority of the big stonework's nearer half that."

"Five thousand years and they were moving stones like that?"

"Yep." Sophie aimed her laser precisely as described in the professor's notes. "Some of them weigh fifty tons and were transported from one hundred fifty miles away.

"But why here? Why not build it where the big stones were?"

Sophie stopped. "Come here."

Cash looked at Rigs who stood well back, as always, overseeing the whole area. Cash walked forwards. Sophie directed him to the center of the circle.

"Whoa," he said, stepping back.

"What?"

"It's like someone walked over my grave!"

"That's why they built it here, some connection to the Earth's energy."

She hit a button on the laser and a beam shot off into the sky.

"So what is it you're measuring?" he asked, following the beam off into the distance.

"Well, I thought it was simply points that aligned with particular points on the calendar. Which they do at each site, see? The laser just cuts the top of that stone, which relates to a point on the calendar. However, it has been the same at each site, it just nicks a point on the calendar before continuing off into space."

"You think it's pointing to somewhere out there?"

"I think it's pointing to some*thing* out there. Perhaps a comet that is hurtling towards us that we don't know exists?"

"But how would they know ten thousand years ago if we don't know now?"

"You've heard of Halley's Comet?"

"Vaguely," he replied.

"It's visible to the naked eye every seventy-five years as it orbits around the solar system. There are probably many more that we don't know about. Their orbits, maybe every five hundred years, a thousand, perhaps every two thousand years."

"Or every 2,160 years," said Cash.

"Exactly. Maybe they think the next time it comes around, it may hit us."

"Like the movie *Deep Impact*?"

"Precisely," said Sophie.

"So we send up some nukes and blow it into a billion pieces."

"Yes," she said, noting down her findings.

"But we don't have any nukes anymore," said Rigs, who had wandered within earshot.

Chapter 61

Alex Noble played with the new ring on his finger. He couldn't stop staring at it. The talk with his father had changed his entire perception of who he was, what he was, everything. Initially, he had thought his father had gone mad, owing to a near death experience at the hands of their would-be killers. But then he had produced the ring. The ring that opened the door to history. Literally *history*, the history of the world that lay deep beneath where he stood.

They had walked through the archives that chronicled the world as it had been, as his father explained, how the Nobles had shaped it. They had shaped the world into what they wanted it to be, controlling the population in a way that suited them. They walked back through time, his father pointing out the points in history where the Nobles had had to intervene and make changes to how the world thought or behaved, using the humans' base instincts to control them.

They walked back to a time where Muhammad had been born, or as his father had said, was written about. They walked back farther, the birth of Jesus Christ, also written about. They walked back further and further, into the depths of the archives, beyond the time of Noah and the ark, beyond the first civilizations, and came to the end of the archives. A vault door sat in the middle of the wall. An array of glass tubes standing floor to ceiling covered the back wall. A perfectly preserved ape sat in the first tube; the next tube had a slightly more developed ape. Alex walked down the line, tube after tube, with perfectly preserved examples of ancient man. The last two tubes contained a Neanderthal man and a Homo Sapien, modern man.

"Modern man," said Antoine, "nothing more than an overdeveloped ape," he said, waving down the line of tubes.

Alex had stared, not fully comprehending. "I don't understand," he said.

"Neanderthal man," said Antoine with wonder. "He was an amazing creature, stronger and more intelligent than modern man. But too much so, and the look wasn't quite right," said Antoine.

"He can't have been, natural selection, the strongest and fittest always survive."

"You don't get it?" Antoine shook his head.

"Get what?"

"This, all of this, modern man, religions, wars, everything you see in here," he spun around slowly, his arms outstretched, "we created it. Modern man, the missing link from the apes, we're it. We genetically altered them."

"To be like us?"

"To *look* like us, not *be* like us."

"So who are we?" asked Alex, struggling to take in what his father was saying. "Gods?"

Antoine laughed. "To humans perhaps, but no, we're just as mortal as man."

"I don't understand. Why create man when we were already here?"

"We needed workers, we needed to build a world."

"Why not build it ourselves?"

"Why do it ourselves, when we can have the humans do it for us?" asked Antoine, walking back towards the vault door.

"But wait a minute," said Alex, stopping at the vault door next to the start of where history started in the archives, around 6,000 BC and the Sumerians. "The Neanderthals died out about 30,000 years ago and Homo Sapiens were around at the same time. We're talking about a time tens of thousands of years ago, before any of this stuff?" He gestured down to the Sumerian relics. "What were we doing for all those thousands of years?"

Antoine nodded, his son was catching up. "This is only half the story," said Antoine with a smile, opening the vault door.

Chapter 62

Sophie had worked tirelessly on the flight back to the States, collating her work and recalculating it, based on the new theory. They weren't looking for a date on the calendar but a point in space. In theory, if they were thinking along the right lines, the four points that she had from each of the sites they had visited would intersect at some point in space. If they were wrong, they wouldn't.

The professor's research had stopped at the point where he had simply been analyzing his results against the various calendars at the sites. His notes didn't cover the theory that they were now working on. The thought being that he had not updated his notes, which he wouldn't have until he had proved his theory was right, which, unfortunately, was the day he was killed.

"They don't intersect," Sophie had said, as they neared Washington D.C. where they were due to meet briefly with Travis Davies to update him on their efforts.

Cash walked over to the table that was covered with her workings.

"I've tried everything I can think of, nothing works. All of the points are going off at crazy angles, I can get two to intersect but they point to a spot on the moon!"

"Maybe it's a gigantic bomb in disguise," Cash joked, trying to cheer her up.

She smiled at his attempt. "Your father was right, about everything. I'm missing something," she said, her eyes scanning over her work.

"Maybe some rest and try again?" he suggested. "A fresh look at it might change things."

"It can't hurt but I really don't think so. I can't think of what else I could try. I've taken curvature, wobble, everything I can think of into account."

"Sleep," said Cash. "Take some sleep into account. Why not crash here while we check in with Travis?"

Sophie didn't need to be asked twice, she stood up, kissed him on the cheek and disappeared into the guest room.

Rigs raised an eyebrow at the kiss. After Sophie closed the door behind her, he winked. "At this rate, five years and you might just get in there!" he laughed, watching his friend's puppy dog eyes follow her every move.

"Sometimes I wish you did your quiet man shit around me," said Cash. He strapped his seatbelt for landing.

Rigs stared at him quietly.

"Very good," smiled Cash sarcastically. "And they're right, you are intimidating!"

The meeting with Travis had been arranged off site. He didn't want them anywhere near Langley until he knew what and who they were up against and more importantly, who he could trust.

Travis' rookie bodyguards had surrounded the coffee shop. His cryptic message to Cash on the Hotmail account the Senator knew about, simply said he'd be driving out for a coffee. Cash knew exactly where he would be.

No car had been arranged. They slipped into the crowds at Dulles Airport and made their way to the cab rank, both checking for any tails. Happy they were clear, they jumped into the first cab in the line, after watching three move off with other passengers.

"Great Falls, Virginia," said Cash. They were heading for Katie's Coffee House, famous for its Saturday morning car rallies, and equidistant for Dulles and Langley.

They stopped the cab on Walker Street, where Rigs jumped out and walked past the sign for the Village Center, a small shopping complex that housed Katie's. Cash told the driver to drive back to the turnpike while Rigs disappeared between the Wells Fargo and Bank of America buildings.

Giving Rigs a few minutes, Cash then gave the driver the correct address, arriving six minutes after dropping him off. With no signals from Rigs to the contrary, Cash walked into the coffee shop and took his seat next to Travis, who was sitting impatiently waiting.

"I thought you landed an hour ago?"

"Hi, boss," replied Cash.

"Sorry, hi," he said. "A very busy day!"

"I thought you were both coming?"

"Rigs is already here," he said, pointing over Travis' shoulder to a booth near the kitchen.

"Jesus, how the…"

Cash waved him over.

Rigs took the seat next to Cash, leaning in and whispering, "Six, five now. The one out back needs a bit of assistance in the trash store."

"One of your rookies needs a bit of help in the trash store," Cash told Travis.

"I'm going back to my old detail," said Travis. "Even if they do try to kill me, they won't fuck it up!"

"So what have you got?"

"We were kind of hoping you had something for us," said Cash.

"I have nothing. We've been trying to trace the three bodies you left in Nevada. They don't exist."

"The bodies from Machu Picchu?"

"What bodies? They were stolen from the police morgue."

"What did you get from the pyramid guys?" asked Cash

"Nothing."

"They must have said something," argued Cash.

"We didn't get anything because we didn't get them!"

"They couldn't move. The guy Rigs dealt with couldn't walk and he was stuck four hundred feet up a pyramid!" exclaimed Cash, his voice rising.

Travis motioned for him to calm down. "We had a team there thirty minutes after your call. They found nothing. What about the Senator? Did you get anything from him?"

"Nothing as such, but there was an attempt on Antoine Noble's life that we stopped."

"The same guys?"

"God no, amateurs, nothing like the guys we were up against elsewhere."

"But you have to admit the timing is, to say the least, coincidental?"

"I have to agree, but from what we pieced together it was an internal family thing, and a fairly botched one at that. It really was nothing like we've been dealing with."

"I got a call from the Senator before I came here. He told me he doesn't need our protection anymore. He'd handle it himself," said Travis, raising his eyebrow.

"Interesting, but if he's using the family security that met us at the airport in Geneva, he's safer than you."

Rigs nodded agreement.

"They missed an attempted assassination in their own backyard."

"An inside job. Rigs got lucky and caught sight of a gun being unpacked. Otherwise nobody would've stopped it. When the shit went down, they had us cold. They're very good."

"The Senator's been in the mix in a lot of this though," said Travis thoughtfully.

"I've thought the same but every time, I come back to one major flaw, they've been trying to kill him too."

"But not anymore?"

"Or he doesn't trust you or us to keep him safe?"

Travis nodded. "Good point."

"So what do we do now? You guys are being hunted and we're no closer to knowing by whom or—"

Rigs stood up, holding back the waitress who had approached their table with a handset.

"There's a call for you," she said, looking beyond Rigs to the table.

"I didn't tell anyone I was coming here," said Travis looking around for his bodyguards. They were all still in position.

"No, not you, him," she said pointing at Cash.

"I certainly didn't tell anyone," said Cash, reaching out for the handset, intrigued.

"Hello?" said Cash.

"Mr. Harris, you and your friend could have killed us both but didn't. For that I feel I owe you this call."

"Joel?"

"Yes, I wanted to let you know, your bounty has been lifted."

Cash looked around wildly, trying to spot anything, anyone that would hint as to how Joel knew where they were.

"All of us?"

"Yes, goodbye." He hung up.

"Who's Joel?" asked Travis.

"The guy from the pyramids," said Cash.

Travis rose abruptly from his seat, signaling his team to get him out.

"No, no it's okay," said Cash. "He was calling to let me know we're not a target anymore."

"And you trust him?" asked Travis, brushing past Rigs.

"Strangely, yes."

"Well if that's the case, twenty-four hours," he said as his team ushered him out the door. "I need you back in twenty-four hours."

Cash nodded. He had a day to sort out his affairs. With everything else going on, it was as generous as Travis could have been.

Twenty-four hours to sort things out. He had fifteen years to make up for, twenty-four hours wasn't going to cut it.

Chapter 63

CDC
Atlanta

The results from Papua New Guinea and the extinction of the Iamult race was as baffling a week after the events as it had been at the time. The diseased river was nothing more than a cover story to stem the tidal wave of panic that would sweep the world should it be disclosed that they had no idea what had wiped out 350,000 people overnight.

Dr. Paul Lockhart, Director of the CDC had called on every other specialist center he could think of but all had come back with the same conclusion. There was absolutely no reason why the people had died. He had barely slept since the incident. The only sleep he had gotten was due to the fact that, whatever it was, had not affected anyone else.

It was during adversity that you found out who really cared. The work Atlas Noble was undertaking through its trust was astonishing. With no other explanation for such quick transmission, other than drinking water, the Noble Trust had rolled out a project to upgrade and improve every water treatment plant and resource across the Third World. It was a gargantuan effort that, if undertaken by governments, would have taken years to roll out. The Noble Trust had thousands of engineers working the day after the announcement. Filters were replaced and treatment plants fitted with remote devices that would allow the Trust to monitor quality and would enable them to alter the treatment to maintain quality when needed or in the worst case, switch it off entirely if the risk of disease were too great. In any event, the second there was a problem, they'd know about it.

Every day, additional engineers were added to the task. The projections for completion were mind blowing. In two weeks over 70% of the Third World's water supply would be fitted with the new controls. More than four billion people would be protected from future water-borne diseases. The final 30% would take significantly longer, as the more rural and less developed water plants were tackled. With almost a billion not having access to any water to begin with, it was a monumental effort but still, the Noble Trust had promised completion within the year. The costs involved were astronomical, but Atlas Noble had promised the money would be found to ensure the Trust delivered.

"Dr. Lockhart, I have Bea Noble holding for you," announced his secretary.

He picked up the phone instantly.

"Bea, my dear, how are you?"

"Devastated, Paul, we have a major problem."

It was the call he was dreading.

"Our hospital ship, as you know, was on its way back across the Pacific. They found a ship, Paul."

"A ship?" he asked confused.

"All dead, the same…"

"Where?" he asked urgently, grabbing a map of the area.

"Halfway between Pohnpei and Saipan," said Bea, her words breaking.

Paul looked at his map. "That's good, they're in the middle of the ocean, that's what, five hundred miles from either?"

"They had cargo on board from both. We tried to contact both ports and sent planes," she caught her breath.

"God, no," said Paul.

"They've spotted another two ships drifting aimlessly as well and we've got more planes up to see how far it has spread."

"We need to close the area down!" said Paul.

"I agree, we can coordinate the effort within the zone. We're probably the only people equipped to do it," said Bea.

"Yes of course, I'll get you some naval assistance."

"Paul, our ship is built for this, it has the labs and the crew's quarters and wards are biohazard protected. Your sailors would have to wear protection 24/7 and risk spreading whatever this may be."

"You get the area secured so no one gets in and out and we'll do what we can in the controlled zone. Send us whoever you can to our ship to help. But let's keep it from killing anyone else."

"Good call. I'll get the team back out to you ASAP and get the Navy and whatever countries we need to set up an exclusion zone."

"Hold on, Paul, I'm getting an update from our Hawaii office. They've got a drifting ship a few hundred miles to their East but everything is fine there. So I'd say draw a line from Guam. We know they're okay to Japan and from there across to Hawaii and down to Samoa and back. It's a massive area but almost entirely water."

Paul looked at his map. There were few inhabited islands within the zone. It was 99.9% open ocean, so closing it was not going to upset more than a few shipping lines, who for the sake of their crews would stomach a few hundred extra miles onto their trip.

"Paul, I think we're better safe than sorry here. We're only talking a few thousand lives, but if anyone gets out of here and this thing spreads…"

"And you're definitely happy for your guys to cover the area inside?"

"Absolutely. We can reach every island within the zone with our planes. We can check and quarantine the unaffected and investigate the islands that have been. We've got the equipment and the staff…"

"I'll speak to the President right away and get the area closed down, nothing in and nothing out. We'll quarantine all ships in the area until we know it's safe to let them go."

"I'll let our guys know your team's on the way to assist. We'll beat this, Paul."

"Thanks to your help we will," he said, ending the call and immediately interrupting the President's cabinet meeting.

Bea replaced the handset and turned to the council who had listened to every word.

"The area is shut down."

"Excellent," said Antoine, looking at the map. The rough rectangle they had drawn across the Pacific Ocean had Wake Island right at its center.

"I know it's overkill but better safe than sorry."

Nobody gave a second's thought for the tens of thousands of islanders and sailors that had perished only to be better safe than sorry.

Chapter 64

The flight back to Montana was quiet. Sophie didn't stir from her sleep even during takeoff. It was not until they came in to land that she finally woke up, joining Cash and Rigs in the lounge of the aircraft.

"How did it go?"

"Okay," said Cash, telling her about the call from Joel.

"Just okay?" she asked. "Surely that's great news?"

Cash excused himself to use the restroom.

Rigs looked at her and shook his head in despair.

"What?" she asked.

He looked away and down to the land below. "You don't need him to protect you anymore," he said quietly.

By the time Cash returned, they had landed and the door had opened. Kyle rushed on board, trailing Bill behind him.

"Whoa!" said Kyle walking through the Senator's luxurious plane. "This is seriously cool!"

"And seriously late for getting back to its owner," said the captain with a smile. "I'm sorry, but we really need to get going."

"Thank you," said Cash, guiding everyone off the plane.

Cash spent the evening with Kyle. The autographs from the band had rewarded him a few hours of undivided attention. Rigs spent the evening with Bill; it would probably be some time before they had the chance to sit together in silence again. Sophie spent the evening with her mother, the two reminiscing and crying for the Chief. It was a quiet, poignant end to a crazy and traumatic week.

The next morning could not have been more different. Bags and clothes were being thrown around. The CIA jet had arrived early, at 6:00 a.m., to collect them and take Cash and Rigs back to Washington and the Kramers to wherever they wished to be taken, compliments of Travis Davies.

Rigs joined the group as they were boarding the jeep for the short run down to the airfield. Cash was helping Kyle load the bags while Sophie and Mrs. Kramer took a seat.

"A bit cramped?" said Kyle, boarding the CIA's Gulfstream jet.

"How spoiled are you?" said Cash, pushing him onboard and into one of the sixteen business loungers.

Sophie spread her papers across the small table at the rear of the jet and pored over them, she had to be missing something.

"Cash," she called. Rigs looked around. She had been ignoring Cash since Rigs had spoken to her on their arrival the previous night. "There's something I'm missing," she said, laying the papers in order for him.

He looked over them. "Nothing I can see," he said. "You've even got your decimals in the right place."

"But what if we were right?"

"The guardians have called off their attack dogs, maybe we were right and they simply overreacted."

"Do you believe that?"

"No."

"Neither do I. Your father found something and we just need to find what it was."

"Do you have to go back to England?" he asked.

Rigs sat up. *Thank God,* he thought, at last Cash was going to do something.

"Yes, Kyle's missed too much school already. But I'll keep working on it, I'll have some of the brightest young minds in the world to help me at the university."

"And you'll call me if you do?"

"I'll call you first!" she said. "Now come on, one more hour, keep looking, there's something your father did that we're not seeing!"

An hour later, they touched down at Dulles. Rigs allowed them all a quick hug of himself, something Cash made them realize was a great honor. Cash gave them all a huge hug along with a quick kiss on the cheek for both Mrs. Kramer and Sophie, and promised to call them soon.

As they waved the plane off, Rigs couldn't hold his tongue any longer. Something which he had usually not the least bit trouble doing.

"You just let her go? You've been drooling over her for a week, a hug, peck on the cheek, 'I'll call you', that's it?"

"Playing it cool," smiled Cash.

"So cool you'll never see her again?"

"Cool in front of Kyle," he winked.

"You didn't?" he asked. "When?"

"Last night I got a visit in my room and—"

A car squealed to a stop at their feet. "Get in!" ordered Travis from the back seat. "The shit's hit the fan in the Middle East, the Israelis are claiming the Iranians have still got nukes!"

Chapter 65

From the moment he had picked them up, they had hardly had a moment to think. Israel was threatening to bring down the entire disarmament agreement unless they were given a rock solid guarantee that they would not face a world where Iran were the only nuclear power. Iran, who had only recently suffered the humiliation of the devastating Israeli bombings were outraged and in no way ready to offer Israel anything. When the Russian Federation stepped in as an intermediate, Iran agreed to talks, assisted by a significant amount of pressure from Atlas Noble.

The disarmament process was almost complete. The Israeli concern had put a halt to the final batch, which had put all of the nuclear powers on edge. A final batch of less than three hundred warheads awaited destruction. However, Israeli intelligence suggesting that Iran had retained its secret arsenal in Chalus stood in the way.

After a week of negotiations in Moscow failed to achieve agreement, the Israelis threatened to pull out of the disarmament process entirely, going as far as sending a detachment of commandoes to retain possession of its arsenal, which was being held under UN security within the Israeli territory while the decommissioning process took place. A similar situation existed across all of the nuclear states. The UN was ensuring the process went without a hitch. Iran had changed all of that.

After a call from an irate President Mitchell, Travis Davies pulled Cash and Rigs into his office. "Pack a bag, we're going to Beirut."

"Beirut?" asked Cash.

"Back door channels, I'm meeting with my Iranian counterpart."

"You know the boss of the MISIRI?"

"No but, surprise, surprise, some Brit *'went to uni with the chap',*" he said in his best posh English accent. "The Nobles have been throwing some serious weight about and I mean serious weight to make things happen and this is it."

"So what's the plan?"

"I get the okay for you two to take a couple of our weapons experts on a quiet tour of Chalus, check they did bomb the living shit out of it, and placate the Israelis. Easy."

Rigs gave a thumbs up from the back of the office, where he waited near the door. It sounded good to him.

"Well if Rigs agrees, must be good," said Travis. "Let's go!"

Taking the CIA boss into the heart of one of the world's terrorist hubs was no small task. Although great improvements had been made in what used to be known as the Paris of the East, Beirut was still a boiling pot of tensions between many groups, not helped by a significant influx of Syrians following the Syrian civil war. Travis Davies was taking an enormous personal risk and putting a huge amount of faith in the British old-boy network.

Their flight touched down in darkness and a twenty-man CIA team met them, as agreed by the Lebanese authorities, on the runway. From there, it was a circuitous and clever misdirection of numerous identical blacked out SUVs chopping and changing with each other before driving off in three separate directions. Almost ninety minutes after landing, Cash and Rigs snuck out of the CIA aircraft, parked in a secure hangar with Travis Davies and climbed into a beat up Toyota sedan.

"Clear!" said Cash as they exited the airport. Nobody was following them. Thirty minutes later, they were drinking a beer on the terrace of a hillside safe house in Beit Meri, looking down on the lights of Beirut and the Mediterranean beyond.

"Well that was the easy part," said Travis, taking another long pull on his ice cold Bud.

"For him," whispered Rigs. It was he and Cash who had thought up the arrival plan.

"I need to make a call. You two, keep the noise down," said Cash.

Travis raised his drink, Rigs looked out across the city.

"Sophie?" Travis asked when Cash disappeared.

Rigs nodded.

Cash spoke to Kyle for ten minutes, hearing his latest conquests at rugby, a sport he was going to have to get to know a hell of a lot better. Ten minutes was the longest conversation yet, as the two were still in the infancy of getting comfortable with each other. "So, here's Mum," said Kyle.

Cash stopped himself correcting him. *It's Mom,* he thought to himself. The sooner he could talk them back to the States, the better, he thought. Football, that was a game he understood.

"Hey, you," said Cash.

"Hi, Cash," replied Sophie while Kyle was still in earshot. He had spoken to her every day since they had parted over a week earlier but still he could have talked to her for hours.

"It really isn't a great line," she said after a few times having to get him to repeat things.

"I said any luck?"

"No, still nothing. Where are you? The line's getting worse."

"I can't tell you because we're not here."

"Give me a clue," she said.

"Hmm," thought Cash. "I can see a cedar tree."

"Oh dear God, don't give up the day job," she sighed.

"Why not?"

"Seriously, it's only what the country's most famous for after terrorists!"

"Well you're not going to tell anyone, are you?"

"No, but if you get the chance, visit Baalbeck, it's a big part of your father's research and one of the oldest settlements in the world."

"Anything there that can help us?"

"Don't think so, but remember to look out for the foundation stones, there are three of them, that's all I'll say."

After concluding his call, Cash returned to the deafening silence of the terrace. All decided it was time to call it a night.

The call at 6:00 a.m. from the Iranians was not at all what had been expected. Travis hung up having barely uttered a word.

"Well guys, the meeting's off."

What?" said Cash.

"The very fact that I was willing to come to Beirut is good enough for their intelligence Chief. His plane will pick you up in an hour at the airport and take you to Chalus with the weapons' team. I'll head back to London and catch you there when you're done."

Unsurprisingly, given the Iranians' offer to let them tour the site, Chalus was nothing more than a bombed out hole in the mountain. The Israelis had destroyed every inch of the complex with devastating efficiency, even more impressive given how deep inside the mountain the complex had been located.

Ten hours after leaving Beirut for Chalus, they were touching back down again. Their confirmation had already restarted the decommissioning process. Within twenty-four hours, the horror of nuclear annihilation that had threatened the world for over seventy years would be over.

With three hours of daylight left, Cash asked if Rigs minded if they made a short detour before flying to London. Cash headed out to the taxi rank. Rigs pulled him back having caught sight of a map that was on the wall.

"It's miles away, over the mountains," said Rigs, pointing to the private leasing company whose office sat in the terminal building. "I'm sure my trust fund can cover the cost of a chopper."

"Sounds good to me," said Cash, leading the way and starting the negotiations, which were concluded when the cost reached half what they thought it would be.

With two hours of good sunlight left, they landed in the Bekaa Valley, more famous across the world for its ties to drug cultivation and hostage storage during the Civil War than the magnificent Roman ruins.

A tent near the entrance appeared to be a must-stop. Cash and Rigs were ushered in by overly eager locals. It soon became apparent when they entered the tent that their only option was to keep moving through. Lines of glass cabinets displaying the personal mementoes of suicide bombers lined the walls while videos played in the background of attacks on Israeli positions by Hezbollah. As much as they wanted to snap the inanely smiling terrorists' necks, it wasn't going to get them anywhere.

Cash had to keep checking on Rigs. His ability to control his emotions at times was tenuous. Fortunately, he played along. They sped through the tent, remaining silent, not giving away the fact that they were American which, given Rigs' silence was no real issue.

"Let's do something about that before we go," whispered Rigs when they walked into the ruins. Cash nodded eagerly, it had sickened him to the core.

Cash hit the speed dial on his cell.

"Hey, I used to be number one," Rigs protested.

"Hey, you," Cash said when Sophie answered. "Guess where I am?"

"Baalbeck?"

"Shit, will you stop that, how did you know?"

"It was that or outside, but the line's still bad."

"So what are the sites here then?"

"You're looking for tall columns, six of them still standing together."

Cash looked around and saw them instantly, over sixty feet high.

"Got them."

"Go towards them and walk around behind them, .keeping them to your right. You want to get to the back of the temple where you can see the base of the structure."

"We're not far from it. Impressive columns!"

"They were added by the Romans about two thousand years ago. There were fifty-four of them which supported a massive roof. It was one of their most impressive and sacred sanctuaries."

"Okay, we're here," he said, looking at the wall.

"Tell me what you see."

"I see a wall, different sized blocks on the different layers, large then larger then much smaller as they built the walls of the temple. The foundation stones are huge."

"They're bigger than three hundred tons each."

Cash looked at them. "And they lifted them two thousand years ago?"

"The three hundred ton ones are the smaller ones at the base, the larger ones are the three main stones that are at the top of the platform and weigh anything up to a thousand tons each. According to your father's research, they were laid long before the Romans even existed, thousands of years earlier."

"That's not possible. These things are laid perfectly together, twenty feet off the ground, a thousand tons?!"

Rigs looked at him as he repeated 'a thousand tons' and looked up at the wall with greater interest than he had been previously.

"As impossible as you say, it's staring you in the face. Did you know they used to call Baalbeck 'Heliopolis' after the sun god who flew around on his chariot?"

"I've only seen pictures but I imagine without anything other than the three massive stones as a platform, before the Romans built the temple on top, that may have made a good, solid landing site?" Cash mused. "So if the city was Heliopolis, what's the temple called?"

"Temple of Jupiter," Sophie said.

"Temple of Jupiter? Why Jupiter?"

"He was the Roman god of gods, their equivalent of Zeus."

"So nothing to do with the actual planet Jupiter?"

"Well, it *was* named after him."

"Why did they worship another planet?" asked Rigs, only hearing half the conversation.

"They didn't," said Cash. "They worshipped the god not the planet."

"What?" asked Sophie.

"Sorry, I was talking to Rigs."

"What did you say though?"

"I said they worshipped the god, not the planet."

"I need to go," Sophie said and abruptly hung up.

Chapter 66

Geneva, Switzerland

Antoine entered the library to find his council on their feet, applauding him. He was particularly proud to see his son on the right of his seat. Alex had been helping with final preparations at the spaceport, having embraced his newfound place in the family. It was always a danger keeping the true family history a secret until the twenty-first birthday. But given the necessity to integrate with the world, it had been agreed that while in education, it was best for the child that they did not feel different. More importantly, neither were they, as children were prone, in a position to tell the world their fantastical tale.

Antoine walked to the end of the table, accepting the applause with a wave of gratitude. In just two days, it would all commence. Millennia in the preparation, the time had finally arrived. It would be their final council meeting before the first transport would leave while the council members carried out their final preparations before traveling to the spaceport at the remote Pacific island. For the next eighty years, the distance between the two planets would be at a minimum, allowing travel between the two. Their galaxies and orbits in synch for what in celestial times was merely a blink of an eye. The window was finite. After the convergence was over, the distance would increase dramatically as the galaxies shifted in time and space and the route would increase dramatically, along with the risk. They had eighty years to save an entire population. It sounded like a long time but the closer they got to their goal, the more they realized how difficult it would be and the sacrifices that would have to be made.

"On behalf of us all, I thank you," said Antoine, taking his seat. "Any last minute concerns?" he asked, looking around the table and at the two screens on the wall where Bea and Caleb had teleconferenced in.

Nobody raised any.

"Caleb," Antoine looked at the screen. "Everything okay at your end? All tests successful?"

"Everything good at this end. We'll begin the fuelling when darkness falls and aim to have the first transport ready for the 5:57 a.m. launch, in time for the convergence. I assume I'll see you all at the launch site?" A round of 'yeses', circled the table, with only one 'no'.

"Not me, I'm afraid," said Bertie. "I have to be in the Senate, my absence would raise major questions."

"Are you sure?" asked Antoine.

"As important as the first launch is, we have eighty years to cover and although we can't possibly keep this quiet for even a fraction of that, we're not in a position to let it be known yet. That will change very quickly and with time, our strength and power will grow. Very shortly, we will be in a position where we can let the covers down and let everyone know, but not yet. They are already watching me closely. I have a number of bills that I have sponsored hitting the floor at that time. If I'm not there, they'll be looking for me."

"Understood," said Antoine.

"As I will be one of the only Nobles missing the event, may I ask a favor?"

"Of course, what is it?"

"May I trigger the population control?"

Antoine looked at Bea. She had designed the system and the toxin. A simple computer program controlled the water treatment facilities around the Third World, all thanks to the Noble Trust's recent investment.

"I don't see why not. You'll just be clicking a 'yes' icon on the bottom of a computer screen," Bea conceded. "The toxin will be released into the water system and doesn't matter whether it is ingested or just touched, the water will deliver the gene altering toxin, just as we did in Papua New Guinea from the air. Even boiling won't alter the effects. If you want to kill almost four billion people?"

"We have to kill to save," Bertie said. "And to save, I will happily kill!"

"You'd have killed more?" asked Antoine, intrigued.

"I think it's a good start," Bertie offered, ever the politician. His answer really being yes.

"I'll give you the laptop and show you how it works before we leave. We agreed to wait until thirty minutes before the first launch, so that would be 1:30 p.m. D.C. time?"

"That's fine. My bills are up first, so I'll be finished well before lunch."

"Well, if that's all, I think we'll all see each other at the spaceport, if not on the same plane." The council members began filing out of the room. "Alex, Anya, are you flying with me?" he asked.

"Yes," said Alex.

"No, I've got to fly via Cairo," Anya said. "I'll see you out there."

"You're joining us for dinner though?"

"No, sorry, I have quite a few things to see to before I can leave."

Antoine stood up and kissed his sister on the forehead. "I don't know what we'd have done without you," he said proudly.

Anya felt instantly guilty. She was making one other detour she hadn't told him about, an early morning trip to a rugby match in Cambridge, England.

Chapter 67

Cash and Rigs landed in London before ten p.m. Cash checked in with Travis, who didn't need them until the following day. By the time they arrived in Cambridge, only fifty miles north of London, Kyle and Mrs. Kramer were already in bed. Sophie was nowhere near ready to go to bed. She was scribbling furiously and barely raised her head to say hello.

"What's going on?' asked Cash, a little put out by the lack of welcome, particularly as he'd not seen Sophie for nearly two weeks.

She stood up, gave him a hug and kissed him on the lips, repeating the same for Rigs, catching him off guard, but kissing his cheek rather than lips.

"I'm sorry, but it was something you said that got me thinking. What if this wasn't about our planet, what if they were following another one?" She sighed heavily. "It's complicated but trust me, everything's moving up there. I hadn't figured that in either, every second, minute, hour, day, the position's changing. So where you look now, in an hour, it'll be different. I have to do the calculation almost in advance and then look where I calculate at the time I calculated, taking into account where I'm looking from. I've been at it since we got off the phone. I've got two intersecting points and just about to get a third and I've got a time-slot to use the Keck Observatory on Maui booked in," she checked her watch, "an hour from now."

"Maui, Hawaii?"

"Remote access. I can control it from here and instruct it to take images of what it sees. I just need to—"

"Don't mind us, we'll keep out your way," said Cash, taking a seat next to the ever quiet Rigs.

Two hours later, Sophie was looking at a picture that, as far as Cash and Rigs could tell, was meaningless.

"I need a bit of time to analyze it properly but a couple of things stand out. It definitely looks like another planetary system. I'll know more tomorrow when we can analyze the data properly at the university. The interesting thing and the bit that's most surprising is the eighty year countdown, remember that?"

"To the new star signs, every 2,160 years, yeah," said Cash.

"If you go back a month and input the same data, the point in space we'd be looking for would have been much, much further away. I ran the numbers using various dates in and out of the eighty year countdown. In the eighty year window, it's near, but outside of that, it's deep off in space. The precision of the calendars is phenomenal, far beyond anything we could have imagined. To think they made them thousands of years ago, and that it points us to a planet way off in space."

"But that planet's not going to destroy us?"

"God no! It's still a long, long, long, way away."

"So we can sleep well tonight?"

"Rigs might," she smiled coyly.

"Please," said Rigs, leaving the room quickly.

***

When Cash woke up, Sophie was already gone. A note at the side of the bed instructed him what to do with Kyle, namely get him to school by 8:30 a.m. Fortunately, Mrs. Kramer had him up and ready when Cash raced down the stairs, grabbed the rental car keys and rushed him out of the door. Rigs was standing by the car waiting for him.

"You could have woken me up," Cash said grumpily.

Rigs opened the back door and climbed in, letting Kyle sit up front with his dad.

"Are you going to stay and watch?" asked Kyle.

"We're supposed to be in London," said Cash, looking at the time. "But yeah, of course," he said, raising a smile.

Cash and Rigs stood and watched the game unfold, neither entirely understanding why play was stopped, or how players managed not to beat the living crap out of each other.

"Why didn't you punch that son of a—"

"You don't understand, Dad," said Kyle, bringing a tear to Cash's eye, which he quickly swiped away. "Rugby is a game of thugs played by gentlemen."

Kyle ran off for the next play.

Rigs nudged Cash. "He just called you…"

"I know," said Cash. "Don't." He looked away, not wanting to break down in front of Rigs. He noticed a woman standing further down the pitch, one he recognized from Switzerland. He walked towards her. She saw him coming and with a handkerchief wiping her eyes jumped into the back of a waiting limousine.

"Was that Anya Noble?" asked Rigs, catching up with Cash.

"Yeah, there must be a Noble at this school," said Cash.

Cash was tapped on the shoulder, catching both him and Rigs by surprise.

He spun around. A man in a cast stood behind him.

"Joel!" said Cash, his head snapping around to check that Kyle was okay.

Chapter 68

Cash called Travis to bring him up to speed as they raced back to London.

"Remember the guy from the pyramids?" he asked.

"The one who called and said you were no longer a target?"

"Yeah, well he tracked me down."

"I thought you crippled him?"

"Snapped his arm just above, no, just below the elbow," he said to Joel's motions. "Anyway, the Iranians have got another base in Chalus. He wanted to check which one they took us to, before he sent in a team."

"So they're Mossad?"

"No, but they work for them, amongst many others, that's all he'll tell me."

"Go with them," instructed Travis.

"His team are ready to go, they're already in the area."

"I don't give a shit, they're not doing this without you there! Israel can't keep that bomb! Tell him you're going in with their team, whether they like it or not. If not, I'll phone the Iranians myself and tell them they're coming."

Cash relayed the message and with no option but to accept, Joel agreed.

"You're not far from Lakenheath," Travis went on. "It's one of our biggest bases in the area. We'll get you a fast ride to wherever Joel's team is. You'll be able to grab whatever kit you need from there as well."

Forty minutes later, three supersonic F22s were streaking across Europe, topping up their tanks and ignoring every sound restriction in the book. The three pilots had passengers rather than navigators in their back seats.

"We can't land in Damascus. Are you mad?!" said Cash's pilot when Joel learned the location of the team.

"This thing is stealthy, no?"

"Yes, but we just got them and you want me to land it at Damascus Airport?"

"Hold on," Cash spoke to Rigs and then Joel. It was risky but they agreed it was worth a try.

"Okay, here's what we're going to do…" said Cash. He explained the details of the plan to the pilot.

"I can't do what you're asking me to do without approval."

"Whose approval?"

"My commander's."

"How about your commander-in-chief?"

"If President Mitchell asked me to do it, I'd land this baby in the Kremlin if he wanted."

Three minutes later, the President asked the pilot to do as Cash had asked.

As they neared the Lebanese coast, the F22s topped up for the last time and when they neared the Syrian border, they powered right back.

"Joel," said Cash, "give your guys a call."

Three minutes later, Joel gave the thumbs up.

"Sweet mother…!" shouted the pilot, throwing his throttles forward. At full speed the F22 could cover twenty-five miles in a minute. Damascus sat only ten miles from the Lebanese border. It was all about speed and stealth. By the time the F22s were fast approaching Damascus International Airport, Joel's team was in the plane waiting to take off at the end of the runway. When the three jets touched down in formation the visual sighting was the first the Syrians even knew they were there. When they turned next to the waiting jet, their canopies lifted, just enough for Cash, Rigs and Joel to drop unceremoniously to the ground. It was a crushing fall but one they were all trained to suck up. Out of sight of the control tower, they were pulled aboard Joel's team's jet and the three F22s were already shooting back into the sky. The air traffic controller was still holding on the line for the Syrian military to answer.

"Hi," said Cash, greeting the rest of Joel's Sicarii team as the Russian Ilyushin IL-76 cargo plane started its trip down the runway in the wake of the F-22s.

Rigs looked around before he took a seat on the bench that ran down either length of the cargo hold. Fortunately and not unsurprisingly, the man with the slashed Achilles tendons wasn't there.

"So what's the plan?" asked Cash.

"I wasn't supposed to be here," Joel said. "I believe the plan is to pose as Syrian businessmen on a trip to the Caspian Sea Resort of Chalus. The Syrians and Iranians have very good relations, as you know."

"We don't think we'll have a problem at the airport on the way in. Where we'll hit trouble is near the mountains when we take the weapons and the prison to rescue..." Daniel, who Cash guessed was leading the assault, stopped short of finishing his sentence.

"Rescue who?" asked Cash. "This is about the bombs, nobody mentioned anything about a rescue."

"Nobody invited you!" said Daniel.

Rigs leaned into Cash "That's a good point," he whispered.

"What did he say?" asked Daniel, not comfortable with the whispering.

"He was agreeing with you," said Cash.

"He does that," Joel pointed out, having witnessed it throughout the morning.

"And he doesn't mean agree with you, he means whisper," said Cash.

As expected, their arrival was unremarkable. A Syrian group arriving for a trip to Chalus was not out of the ordinary. Joel opted to stay in the aircraft. His arm was a major restriction on his movement and ability.

There were twelve Sicarii, two six-men teams, one was to secure the weapons and the other to rescue a four-man Sayaret Matkal team who had been arrested during the first attack by the Israelis on Chalus. The six-man team to secure the nuclear weapons became eight. Those were Cash and Rigs' only orders.

"So where are they?" asked Cash.

"There's an entrance to a storage area inside a tunnel that runs along the mountainside. We believe they moved the weapons there, prior to our attack, for safekeeping. It's deep inside the mountain and impervious to air attack."

"And you know this how?"

"The team in the prison got a message out through another prisoner when they realized what they had seen in the tunnel."

The truck they hired was not the most comfortable but was the biggest they could get. They just hoped it was going to be big enough.

Daniel listened in to the other team's progress and ordered the driver to slow down. "We want them to hit the prison just before we hit here. They're going to go in as noisily as possible to draw as much attention as they can across Chalus and create our diversion. We go in here quietly, leaving no one to talk or raise the alarm. While the other team and the Sayaret Matkal make a break across the Caspian Sea, we'll fly out unnoticed."

"Sounds easy, wake me up when you're done," joked Cash.

Nobody laughed.

They approached the tunnel and drove through it. Although approaching from the other end, they took the sharp bend as described by the previous team but strained to see in the dark. They couldn't see the entrance they believed was there. Nothing was visible.

Daniel listened to his headset. The other team had just reached the prison and were getting into position.

"Okay, they've gone. We can turn back and go through," said Daniel to his driver.

Cash cocked his H&K MP5SD silenced sub machine gun, checked his holster for his pistol, and got ready to go.

The truck drove back down the tunnel and its lights shone the right way this time. Against the wall on the sharp bend emerged a faint outline of a large door.

"How we getting in?" asked Cash.

The driver accelerated towards the outline.

"I thought you said as silent as possible!" said Cash, bracing himself for impact. "What if it's reinfor—"

They hit the door head on. The truck shuddered on impact and fought against the steel door which soon gave way. The truck continued on, sweeping around to the left, a klaxon blaring.

"This is an old works tunnel, it would have run all the way to the complex you toured but was closed off after it was finished," the driver explained. "They guessed our attack was coming and moved the warheads here as a stop-gap. Well, that was our guess." The first bullets began to tear into the truck. The driver slammed on the brakes and the Sicarii jumped out and went to work. Working as two-man teams, one fired while the other constantly moved forward, pressuring the enemy into making basic errors. Their precision and fearlessness was an impressive sight, and they made short work of the Iranian forces, despite them being their elite Takavar troops. Cash and Rigs stayed back out of their way. They knew what they were doing.

"Clinical," said Rigs, impressed, something he rarely was.

The tunnels spread out into a large cavern where a hastily built structure had been erected. The Sicarii didn't catch their breath, moving in and sweeping through the structure.

"Clear!" was shouted out repeatedly as they cleared room after room.

They heard the occasional soft spit of an MP5, usually followed by a thud as another Iranian fell.

After three minutes, Daniel declared the site clear. "The other team has secured the prisoners," he announced. "The nukes are in the back. Four warheads, one more than it was thought they could have had."

"Will they fit in the truck?"

"Just," said Daniel.

"What are we waiting for?" asked Cash.

Within ten minutes of bursting through the entrance, they were driving back out.

"Impressive work, guys," said Cash.

"From you guys, I'll take that as a compliment," said Daniel.

Rigs leaned over and said quietly so only Cash could head, "They're never going to let us take these off of them."

Cash nodded. Not a chance in Hell.

Chapter 69

Institute of Astronomy
University of Cambridge

Sophie had been at the university since before sunrise. Her mind was racing, although Cash had certainly managed to keep it occupied for most of the night. When sleep came, her mind wandered. At five a.m., she gave in and headed to the university where she could begin to analyze the images properly. She soon realized the images weren't good enough. She recalibrated her calculations for a time slot she had secured at the Keck Observatory for later in the morning.

Although the numbers didn't look significantly different, the result, when it came through, was astonishing. The planetary system was far closer than it had been just twelve hours earlier. It was like the two galaxies were pulling one another ever closer. While she waited for the high resolution images to download, she quickly reworked the calculations. Perhaps the two were going to collide. Perhaps this *was* the end of the world.

The results proved otherwise. Knowing the difference between the two calculations from the previous twelve hours and the decrease in distance that it had made to the planetary system, she could roughly calculate the minimum distance that would be experienced. Of course, that was if the calculations remained correct as per the ancient workings. The distance would narrow slightly until being at its narrowest in forty years. After that, it would very slowly increase again until a great increase in eighty years. The change was dramatic but the universe was a complex and amazing place. Gravitational forces were pushing and pulling it constantly in all directions. It could be that the two galaxies were caught by each other's pull, or a combination of pulls before their orbits pulled them off in another direction. Sophie stopped herself. That was a problem for another day. She checked the system, the enormous files had downloaded.

She opened the first, comparing it to the one the previous day. She checked the next but she didn't need to. She knew exactly what was happening; it was as clear as day. You just had to know exactly where to look. And that was the problem, no one knew where to look. Otherwise, they would have known.

She grabbed her phone and hit the speed dial for Cash, button 2. Her mom had been bumped to 3.

"Cash," she said breathlessly, "I've got it, call me the instant you get this message."

She had to tell someone, but who? She had no idea who to contact, who to tell, what to tell them, or what it even meant. *Travis!* Travis Davies would know what to do. She knew he was staying at the Savoy. Cash had mentioned he was to pick him up from there. She grabbed her laptop and searched for the number. She tried to call but her phone was dead, no signal. Curious. She always got a great signal in the building.

***

Conrad received the images that Sophie had taken that morning. The ones from the previous night hadn't worried him. There was nothing she could see that could tell her anything. The new ones were a different matter entirely. He called her watchers, two Sicarii that had been retained for just such an eventuality.

Antoine had insisted they kept an eye on her and a very close one. Sophie Kramer was a problem. She was the one who had the ability to understand before anyone else what was happening. Cash and Rigs were easy. He knew exactly where they were. Atlas Noble had been instrumental in uncovering the whereabouts of Iran's secret and hidden nukes.

He had two more calls to make, one to Antoine and one to Anya. She had insisted he made her aware of anything pertaining to the issue, anything.

Chapter 70

With six Sicarii and four Sayaret Matkal soldiers causing mayhem in Chalus, all Iranian forces in the area were ordered to proceed there as a matter of urgency. The fact that they were using the same type of truck as the military helped enormously as the sketchy reports of a raid on their secret bunker began to filter in. This allowed the six Sicarii, Cash and Rigs to drive quietly and peaceably to the airport while a small war raged a few miles away on the other side of the city.

They loaded up the Ilyushin and since the Iranians were safe in the knowledge they had their targets surrounded, they took off barely twenty minutes before an Iranian commander had the sense to close it down.

Cash and Rigs looked back on the city below. "We're not waiting for the others?" asked Cash, stunned that they had taken off. They lived by a creed. They never left a man behind, never.

"They have an escape plan, if they can, they will—"

"You're leaving them to die?"

"They knew the mission and accepted it proudly, today we saved our nation."

"I thought you weren't Mossad?"

"We're not, but we will die to protect the Jewish state."

Cash thought back to the cabinets in Baalbeck, the suicide bombers' mementoes. Religion had a huge amount to answer for. Good men, killing themselves in the name of God. If there were one god, why would he let two different groups kill themselves in his name? It didn't make any sense, at least not to him. He closed his eyes as Joel's cell phone rang, thankfully ending the possibility of a debate.

"Cash," whispered Rigs, nudging him. "Cash," he said, his voice louder than normal.

Cash opened his eyes to find Joel standing over him with his gun covering him while the other Sicarii relieved him and Rigs of their weapons.

"I take it that call didn't go well for us?" he asked Rigs and received a nod.

"I'm afraid we've been reengaged to deal with you," said Joel.

***

Conrad called Anya first. She had asked him to. Antoine, on the other hand, had just been asked to be updated should anything happen, knowing Conrad was more than capable of handling the situation.

"Anya, she did it. Sophie Kramer found it. I've sent the Sicarii in to get her. Cash and Rigs are with the Sicarii already," he said.

Anya listened, her heart rate racing, She killed the call, dialing another number as quickly as she could.

"Antoine," said Anya, relieved that he answered on the first ring. She thanked the stars above.

"Anya, what's wrong?"

"You can't kill him, you can't!"

"I've no idea what you're talking about, hold on," he said moving the phone away from his ear. "Alex has Conrad on his phone, he says it's urgent and could impact the operation!"

"No!!!" she screamed too late. He had already muted it.

Antoine came back on the line quickly.

"They found it!" he said. "They've put everything at risk!"

"You can't kill them!"

"They threaten everything we've spent our lives on, our ancestors' lives—"

"No you can't kill them, you can't!" she pleaded and commanded as one.

"Of course I can."

"They're Nobles, you can't order them killed."

"Don't be ridiculous, Anya."

"Cash Harris is my son, Antoine! Kyle Kramer is my grandson!"

"I'll call you back!" he said.

Antoine called back two minutes later. "I can't get a hold of Conrad, I'll keep trying."

"Thank you," she said. "Please! Keep trying!"

"Alex is trying as we speak," said Antoine. "When he gets through he…would you care to explain?"

"What's to explain? I met a man and fell in love. Before I knew what had happened I was already three months pregnant."

"You didn't know?" he asked incredulous.

"Sometimes you don't, and I was taking precautions. This is not really a conversation I want to have with my brother."

"Of course not, but you had the child and what happened?"

"I said goodbye. I had no choice. We don't mix. We never mix our genes. That was what we lived by until…"

"Lee. Alex's fiancée will give birth it would seem not to the first, but the second mixed baby. And if that hadn't happened, if Blake hadn't told us it was okay…"

"We'd still be having this conversation. He may only be half Noble but there's still a hundred percent of me in there! I have regretted leaving him every day of my life."

"Hold on…Alex is through." The call cut off.

Anya waited, her heart pounding in her chest. She checked her watch. She needed to board her plane. She didn't want to lose the signal, but she daren't move until Antoine called back.

Her cell rang, her heart sank, it was Conrad. Antoine wasn't able to break the news himself. He had nearly lost Alex and knew how it felt.

Chapter 71

"Obviously, guns aren't ideal on a plane," said Joel, brandishing a knife. "If you promise to sit still, we will make it painless and some have even in their last breaths described it as pleasant, surprisingly."

"There are two chances that'll happen," said Cash. "And trust me, neither is good."

Daniel stepped forward with a .22 caliber pistol. "That's fine, we have other options we can use on a plane."

Cash was tapping Rigs' knee with his, a tiny movement imperceptible to the eye, just enough pressure for Rigs to know it was a signal. One, two, a cell phone rang. Cash paused.

"Leave it," said Joel.

Cash moved to tap a third time and they would both pounce.

"It says 'CN'," said the other Sicarii.

"Quick, give it here!"

"Leave it, quick give it here," mocked a Sicarii member, tossing the cell to Joel.

Cash waited, he needed to sneeze, he had to control himself. If he sneezed and touched Rigs' knee even slightly, he'd pounce. Cash could feel the tension in Rigs as he waited for Cash's final signal. Cash was using every ounce of his inner strength not to sneeze.

"Everyone relax," said Joel, as Cash released his sneeze and, as expected, his body shook and his knee made contact with Rigs'.

Rigs' body was too tightly wound, he lunged at Joel, taking him off his feet and slamming him into one of the Iranian nukes that sat in the center of the plane. Joel's already damaged arm slammed into the immovable metal bomb and he let out the second loudest ear-piercing shriek Cash had ever heard.

"Stop!" shouted Cash. Fortunately, none of the Sicarii moved. The hit was off and they understood Rigs' reaction. They were men who would have done the same. Rigs whispered an apology to Joel as he climbed off of him. Joel's arm hung loosely, the plaster cast that had held it in place dangling in pieces.

Rigs moved back and took the seat next to Cash. "Why did you do that?" he asked quietly as he sat down.

"I sneezed!" protested Cash.

***

Sophie had given up with her cell and walked back to her office to use the landline. A man stood in her way.

"You need to come with us," he said.

"I will do no such thing," said Sophie, walking between them.

"Your son…"

"My son what?!!!" she screeched in alarm, suddenly thinking the worst. The man could have been a detective. He had that look about him.

"Your son will be coming with us too," said the man.

"Where?" she asked defensively.

"Please don't make a scene, no harm will come to either of you. We have been asked to take you and your son to London."

"By whom?"

"A friend. We have just been asked to get you to London. My colleague is picking up your son as we speak."

"I don't believe you. Let me call him." She moved towards her office, but the man stepped into her path. He was large and powerful. She didn't stand a chance. She did something Cash had taught her many years earlier. She stepped closer to him and then shot her knee into his groin. He stepped back, easily avoiding her clumsy attempt.

"Please, we can do this nicely or…"

"Or what?"

"I tie you up and stick you in the trunk."

"There are too many people around," she said.

He pulled a pistol from his behind his back. "This is a Glock 17, it has seventeen rounds in the magazine and I have another two magazines. One shot, one kill. Fifty-one people between here and my car can die or you can simply come with me and I'll take you and your son to London, where I promise you will come to no harm."

"Well, if you put it like that…" she said with every ounce of strength. She was not going to let him intimidate her. She had to stay strong. "I'll need my bag though," she said defiantly.

"Of course," he said, placing his gun back behind his belt. "I need your cell phone." He stretched out his hand.

"Doesn't work anyway," she said, handing it over before following him to his car with her handbag.

Ten minutes later, she was sitting next to Kyle, who had happily followed the man who had come to collect him to take him to London. She'd be having a very serious chat with her powerfully built son when she had the chance. Did he not remember 'stranger danger' she had taught him as a little boy?

They arrived in London as promised unharmed and were driven onto the apron at Heathrow Airport next to the royal suite, where a special area was reserved for travelling royalty and dignitaries. The car drove to the steps of a waiting Airbus A380, the largest commercial airliner in the world. Its tail bore a monogrammed logo that Sophie had seen many times before, a very classic and elegant intertwined A & N, sparkling gold in the midday sun.

A lady she had met at the Nobles' home, Anya Noble, stood smiling down regally at them from the top of the aircraft steps.

"What's this all about, Mum?' asked Kyle.

"I've no idea, son, but I'm sure your father's somehow involved."

Sophie led the way and they boarded the flying mansion that was Anya Noble's personal jet.

"And I thought the Senator's plane was cool!" whistled Kyle.

"What's this all about, Anya?" asked Sophie. "Those men were—"

"Unfortunately not of my choosing," Anya interrupted, disassociating herself instantly from whatever Sophie had encountered.

"Okay, but what's this all about?" Sophie asked again. "I really need to speak with Cash."

"And that's exactly where we're going, to meet with him now. Please relax and enjoy the flight." She turned to Kyle. "Would you like me to show you around?"

"Please," said Kyle eagerly.

Sophie's mind was racing. Was it just a coincidence that the second she made her discovery, her phone mysteriously stopped working and she was summoned to Anya Noble's flying palace? And it was after Cash saved Alex Noble's life that he got the call saying they were safe. Bertie Noble always seemed to know a lot more than he let on, she thought again. Her mind triggered the thought…the Nobles were the guardians!

Chapter 72

With some help from the Sicarii, Joel was able to talk through the pain of the reignited wound. He explained to Cash that his orders had changed. They were now to deliver Cash and Rigs along with the nuclear weapons. Their death sentences had been lifted again.

"By whom?" demanded Cash.

"We can't tell you who the clients are but you will meet them soon," he said wincing. His eyes flared at Rigs who sat quietly by Cash's side.

"We'll meet them? You're delivering us to the people who want us dead?!"

"You are not to be harmed, not now, not ever. We can never raise our arms against you ever again," said Joel.

"What in the hell does that even mean?" asked Cash. "You can't raise your arms against me…"

"Our order and your bloodline have travelled through many centuries. We're at your service, protecting you when required and it is a sacred oath that our services can never be hired against you. Your bloodline is sacred."

Cash looked at Rigs. "The pain's made him mad," he said, shaking his head.

"If that's the case, give me a weapon to defend ourselves," demanded Cash.

Joel looked up at Daniel and motioned for him to give Cash a weapon. Daniel handed him an MP5 and some magazines.

"And for Rigs?"

Joel shook his head. Cash handed his MP5 to Rigs. Joel instructed Daniel to give another one to Cash.

Cash looked at the two weapons and the seven Sicarii who made no attempt to defend themselves. He placed the MP5 down. "There is some seriously weird shit going on here. Are these nukes leaking?" he asked, getting a laugh from everyone, even Joel.

An hour later, they landed at Cairo Airport. Nobody moved.

"We wait, they're not due for an hour or so," said Joel.

"And you're just going to give them the four nukes?"

"Of course, they are the reason we exist, if not for them there'd be no Jewish state for us to call home."

Cash watched the double decker aircraft land, its livery somehow unsurprising. Deep down, he had known something was off.

"Figures," said Rigs, spotting the logo.

"You guessed?"

"It's always the rich, powerful family. Why do you think they're always shrouded in conspiracy?" he whispered.

"Your family's rich and powerful…"

"And I keep well clear of them."

"But you said I was one of them, Joel?" said Cash. "I'm not a Noble!"

"I simply follow orders. My orders were very specific - you're one of them, you're untouchable to us."

The Sicarii transferred their cargo to the larger jet's hold while Cash and Rigs walked across to the steps that were being placed against the larger plane. Anya Noble appeared in the doorway as it opened. She walked down the steps and kissed Cash on the cheek.

"My son," she said warmly and took him in her arms.

Cash pushed her off. "Your what?"

"My son," she said, staring fondly into his face.

Even Rigs broke out of his reserved shell, mimicking Cash. "Your *what?*"

"We have work to do," she said. "Come, we'll talk as we work."

Cash remained motionless. "I'm going nowhere, until I know what's going on."

"After we're done here, I'm going to take you back to Geneva. We'll meet up with the lovely Sophie and Kyle and we'll talk, but we really must get moving," she said, checking her watch. "We have a lot to cover and little time."

Rigs registered the same hint of a threat that Cash had. She had Sophie and Kyle. He prodded the numbed Cash to follow her, boarding one of the two helicopters that were awaiting her arrival. The Secret Service were back. Two immaculately dressed security men accompanied her, Cash and Rigs. Four Sicarii were told to follow in the other chopper.

"They're amazing buildings, aren't they?" she said.

Cash nodded, hardly looking at the pyramids. He was still trying to compute what was happening.

"Our ancestors built them. They've caused a lot of speculation over the years. Of course, it helps when the rest of the bits are in place."

Cash looked but couldn't see anything. The Great Pyramid was shrouded in scaffolding and sheeting.

Rigs pointed to the very top of the pyramid that could just be seen as they flew in over its top. It had a bright silver capstone.

"I see you noticed the capstone, the largest single piece of silver in the world. It weighs ten tons and, fittingly, is a perfect pyramid to crown the perfect pyramid. The best conductor money can buy."

The helicopter landed and they were shown to the entrance, the real one that hadn't been discovered. A ramp took them up thirty feet on the opposite side to where they had entered previously. A section opened to reveal a grand entrance way more fitting of the pyramid. A gallery similar to the grand gallery led them up and into the King's Chamber, somewhere they had not visited before, and the equipment that filled the room hadn't been there either. Anya walked straight through and along to the Grand Gallery where Cash had fought with Joel. He had noticed the slots at the back of the ledge when he had been there before. Just empty slots. Each now had a perfectly fitting long silver spike that spiraled out of each of the holes to the ceiling high above and looped back down to the corresponding hole in the opposite wall, creating twenty-seven silver archways

Anya continued on and rather than crouching down to the tunnel Cash and Rigs had crawled through, pushed the wall to reveal a staircase down to the Queen's Chamber below.

"It's a bit easier when you know where things are and how to use them." Like above, the Queen's Chamber was transformed. Equipment filled the room, not new but not old, just different looking.

"I'll explain it all later. I need to insert the fuel cell that will power this up for when we need it.

"Anya withdrew a small cylindrical tube from her bag, about the size a large plastic coke bottle and slotted it home into a piece of machinery that sat in the heart of the chamber. She checked it was in correctly and flicked a switch on its side. An amber light shone.

"All done," she said.

Cash couldn't see the tunnel they had entered from before. "Where's the other entrance?"

"Closed. It would affect the power generation," she said, leading them out and closing the door behind them. She placed her ring against the wall next to the doorway which resulted in the sound of a lock sliding into place.

They walked back out of the pyramid and headed over to her helicopter. "I'm afraid Rigs won't be coming to Switzerland with us," she announced as they boarded her chopper. Her two security men blocked his entry.

"I'm not going anywhere without him," Cash insisted.

"What you are about to see and hear is not for anyone but you. After we're done, if you choose to share, that will be your decision. In the meantime, these men will not harm him, I promise you that."

"Sophie and Kyle," said Rigs into Cash's ear. "Go!"

With a heavy heart, Cash boarded the plane. He told himself he had no choice. He told himself that, over and over again.

The four Sicarii were true to Anya's word. They did not harm a hair on Rigs' head as they led him back to the pyramid and with him in it, sealed up the entrance that no one knew was even there. The normal tourist entrance had already been sealed. When the energy in the pyramid built up, it was imperative the building be sealed, such was the power that was generated within it. Why else did it need to weigh six million tons, other than to stop itself from exploding from the pressure that would crush any living thing within it?

Chapter 73

Cash was furious at himself. He had left a man behind. He understood why, as did Rigs. Sophie and Kyle couldn't look after themselves, but Rigs could. Although it didn't mean it was right.

Anya tried to engage with him as they flew back to Geneva, but he refused. She kept promising he would understand when they got there. He really couldn't see how.

"Where are Sophie and Kyle?" he asked when they arrived at what appeared to be the deserted village of Anieres. Other than security guards guarding the actual village, no one was around. They walked into Antoine Noble's chateau and Anya wasted no time in taking him directly to the library.

"Where are Sophie and Kyle?" he asked again, beginning to lose his temper. It was the only way she had gotten him to leave Rigs behind.

"Cash, I'm your mother, will you please trust me?"

"Trust you?" he exploded. "You say you're my mother, which in itself is twisted, and even if you are, you made me believe you died during childbirth, that I had lived and you had died. Even more twisted! Where are Sophie and Kyle? I won't ask again." The threat in his voice brought out the security guards who were waiting in the library. Anya ushered them back out.

She pulled herself together. None of it had gone as she had imagined or dreamed about over the years.

"We should have had this talk fourteen years ago," she said.

"Where are they?!!!" shouted Cash, wanting an answer.

Anya jumped back, shocked at the hatred in his face. "I promise you'll see them very soon, they're perfectly safe. Please, this is hard for me too."

"Are the woman you love and your son being held against their will by a crazy woman?"

"I'm your mother!" she cried.

"Well act like one! Show me Sophie and Kyle and I'll listen to your speech."

Anya had wanted the Alex moment that Antoine had recently had. She wanted the moment she had shared with her father, when she found out the truth. She wanted to share that with Cash. But he wanted his woman and his son. He just wanted to check they were safe, check that his own mother hadn't harmed her grandson.

"Fine," she said. She walked across to the library windows and looked down to the garden below, where the marquee that was there before had been removed without leaving a trace on the pristine lawn.

"There they are," she said pointing to Sophie and Kyle below, standing beside a limousine.

"Thank you," said Cash, calming down. He tried to open the doors but they were as strong as a safe. The glass was thick and bullet proof. He battered it. Sophie heard and looked up. She waved. They were fine. Kyle was fine. She mouthed something to him and then pointed to the sky, something about a planet, another planet. He didn't understand. They were shown very courteously into the car.

"Happy now?" Anya asked, her tone not quite matching her words. "I was hoping you'd trust me. But I do understand."

"Thank you, I've been frantic," said Cash sincerely. He was aware that she still held his family. "With everything else that's been going, you've got to appreciate—"

"I'm sorry. Of course I understand," she said. "It's just that this is a very special moment that we Nobles share."

"Forgive me, I've not been one very long." Cash smiled, straining to make it look as real as possible.

"So where were we? Oh, yes… normally we'd have this chat on your twenty-first birthday and to be honest, until a few days ago, I thought we'd never be having this chat," she said.

Because your family was trying to kill me, thought Cash, forcing another smile.

"Let me take you down to the archives, it's easier there."

Anya opened the library wall, pressed her ring into the steel door, and stood back to allow Cash to enter the elevator.

"We're going down to the history of the world, the world we created," she said proudly.

They stepped into the archives and Anya began to talk, explaining each time period as they walked through the massive vault that stretched off into the distance. They walked back in time, as Antoine had done with his son Alex. However, Cash hadn't had the upbringing the Nobles had had. They felt special, superior, from birth. They looked down on the world. They lived in a world separated by wealth and power, removed from the reality of life, with no comprehension of what real life was all about. Where Alex Noble's journey through the history of the family had been reaffirmed in his superiority, Cash was sickened by it to his core. The Nobles, throughout history, had intervened, incited, controlled, profited.

As they walked back into the birth of the religions, Cash listened while Anya spoke, barely believing what he was hearing. His subconscious constantly reminded him that his family was still under her control, so he kept his thoughts to himself.

His subconscious was struggling to stop him from commenting after what Anya had just said.

"Our ancestors realized the power of belief and faith, the hope it gave the people and how it controlled the masses in a way that governments and rulers could not. It transcended borders, oceans."

"So they took control of religions?"

"Took control?" Anya chuckled. "We *created* them! The Vatican holds one of our largest property portfolios. Its wealth is unimaginable and all thanks to faith - work ethic, moral code, belief. They all helped us sculpt the planet."

"Wars, unrest, millions upon millions of dead as a result of religious conflict?" countered Cash.

"How else could we manage to control the people, seven billion now? Just fifty years ago, it was half that. In 1 AD, it was around one hundred million. We needed a new world and we needed to control those we created to make it."

"But who are you to say they should be controlled?"

"We," corrected Anya, not understanding the despair in Cash's comments.

"Wait a minute, *created?*" asked Cash, realizing what she had said.

"We'll come to that," Anya said.

"No," said Cash. "I think we should skip to that!"

"We can come back to the time the ancestors built the sites you were visiting." Anya walked towards the tubes that Alex had been shown two weeks earlier.

Cash walked down the length of them, barely able to hold his bottom jaw from hitting the floor. *Who are these people?* he asked himself.

Anya led him to the last two tubes. "The final candidates," she said.

Cash looked at her. "What?"

"Neanderthal or Homo Sapiens. They could have played about with the Neanderthals a little more, made them more like us but they were too strong and far more intelligent than had been planned."

"So what…?" asked Cash

"We took action. We culled them in favor of the Homo Sapiens, they were a much better fit. They were like us, but their brain function and traits restricted just enough for us to exert the control we needed."

Cash rubbed at his face, his eyes, trying to understand whether what he was hearing was seriously what Anya was saying. "You *culled* the Neanderthals? What, just wiped them out? How?"

"The same toxin we used in Papua New Guinea a few weeks ago. It alters the genetic code, the code that we designed."

"Who are 'we'?" asked Cash, beginning to lose it when she casually admitted the genocide of almost half a million people.

Anya was unperturbed. She was confident that Cash would soon understand. She opened the vault and led him into a corridor where papers lined the wall.

"In our ancestors' own words," she said.

Cash read the first paper:

> *Deep Space Mission — New Hope*
> *Log entry 1*
> *Mission Commander*

It is with great sadness that I look back on the fading speck in the distance that we have called home since birth. We have said goodbye to parents and loved ones that many, or all of us, will never see again. Our only hope of seeing them again would be the failure of our mission, which would condemn our population to a certain death. Our planet is dying and with it our future.

"So the world is dying…but wait, you said ancestors, not family?" He stopped. "Oh my God," said Cash. "We were able to do things in the past and lost…"

"Yes, but the fuel was the problem. It ran out very quickly once they landed here and there was no way to remake it. The technology didn't exist."

"Wh-what do you mean *landed* here?" asked Cash.

"It's our world that's dying, not this one," Anya said. "Our world, it's our population that we have worked tirelessly to save."

"The planet that's dying isn't Earth?"

"No, it's our home, *our* world that's dying."

"This *is* our home," said Cash.

"It will be very soon. The transports will start soon. Our population will be coming to their new home, their new world. The world that we, the Noble family, were sent out to make for them."

"What about the people here?" asked Cash.

Anya ignored his question. "We were entrusted with a great honor. The King himself chose our family to protect the future of our population. We have eighty years to transfer them here. Our world will be unlivable by the next cycle."

"In 2,160 years," mumbled Cash.

"Yes," she smiled.

"But what about the population here?" he asked again.

"They were only created by us to make this world livable for our people. Without us, they wouldn't even have been here."

"But they are here, living breathing, beautiful people like Sophie and Kyle."

"Kyle is one of us," she said. "He has Noble genes."

"He's only twenty-five percent Noble," said Cash bitterly.

"It doesn't matter," Anya said.

"If it doesn't matter, why didn't you want anything to do with me until now?"

"It was forbidden, but Blake made us aware of how the Noble gene overrides all others."

"Blake, the old man who tried to kill his own family?"

"It's in the archives," she said. "It's irrelevant, a hundred percent of me is in you."

"And the other fifty percent of me is simple Homo Sapien, like my father, who was murdered."

"He was a wonderful man," Anya said.

"But was only here to save the population of a distant world that doesn't need him anymore."

Anya suddenly realized the time. "We need to go," she said. "Wait here."

She rushed to the end of the corridor and opened another vault door, returning shortly afterward with a large wheeled crate with a number of the coke bottle sized tubes.

"But what about the population here?" Cash asked yet again.

"We face a famine if we don't take action," Anya said defensively.

Cash could see he was getting somewhere. Where there had been no doubt, some existed. He didn't want to push it too far, too quickly.

"So when does it start?"

"In approximately twenty hours," she said, rushing towards the door. "We have a long flight ahead of us."

"We?' said Cash.

"All of us, Sophie and Kyle as well. You're going to see the first transports lift off to our old world. And if we're lucky, we may even, depending on the timing, welcome some transports to us."

"So you're sending empty spaceships out there?"

"Yes, we've got five here from when our ancestors first came. They can each carry thousands at a time."

"Where are they?" asked Cash.

"You'll see," said Anya. "We're going to see them rise back into the sky for the first time in a very long time."

"How long?" asked Cash. He didn't want to show interest. What they were doing was despicable. He had just discovered that aliens were real, that he was half alien, and that the world was about to be invaded after being created by those same aliens thousands of years earlier.

Anya stopped rushing. "Let me think...the first mission was 200,000 years ago, then 70,000, 30,000, 10,000, and the last mission, during the last cycle, about two thousand years ago."

"200,000 years and you think it'll still fly?" said Cash.

"Of course, it was probably five times older than that when it left," she said without a hint of sarcasm.

"How old are your people?" asked Cash, taking the crate from her and trying not to look at the archives as they rushed past them. How was he going to stop them? She had his family and they were about to be stuck on a flight for countless hours. He had to hope that Rigs was okay and had reached Travis Davics. He was their only hope. Cash was helpless while she had his family. Life had been far easier when he had only himself to worry about. *And Rigs*, he thought, although he could look after himself.

Chapter 74

Rigs was stuck in a tomb. Ironically, that's exactly what everyone thought it was. However, Rigs had worked out that it was definitely not a tomb, which was obvious since the Nobles had gotten their hands on it. Cabling ran through and up into the ceiling area above him in the King's Chamber. He had tried to get back into the Queen's Chamber but it was locked tight.

Most worryingly, the cabling was shrouded in a metal casing, unlike any he had seen before, which suggested it was being protected from something. He thought back to whatever Anya Noble had put in the Queen's Chamber. The equipment was also of an incredibly sturdy construction. He had a feeling that whenever it was switched on, he was unlikely to survive.

He climbed back up into the spaces above the King's Chamber. Height was what he wanted. He remembered the stone that he had marked. Why would anyone have gone to that height to move a stone? It wasn't just that there was no way it could have been moved, they'd have needed heavy equipment to move it and it would have been tight against the other stones. There had to be a mechanism, as there had been for Anya Noble, only she knew where it was and had the means to use it with her ring.

He reached the top space and was blocked by the pointed roof above him. There was nowhere to go. He lay back and tried to look for even the tiniest hint of a crack in the stonework. There was still almost half the height of the pyramid above the roof to look at. He crawled back down and looked at the cables. They went up into the ceiling above the King's Chamber below, but they weren't in any of the crawl spaces. Where did they go? They were obviously connecting to something else.

He covered every inch of the thirty-by-twenty chamber like his life depended on it, trying not to think that it actually did. He tried the small anti-chamber. Same result. He tried the Grand Gallery, even trying to move the silver hoops in an attempt to stop whatever the pyramid might do. They didn't move. The cabling was impossible to uncouple, and its metal casing preventing any attempt to tamper with it.

Rigs lay down in the gully of the Grand Gallery and waited. He had little else to do.

Chapter 75

Travis Davies had spent the afternoon trying to call Cash and Rigs, although the chance of Rigs ever answering a call seemed remote. They hadn't checked in since he knew their mission in Iran had been a success. The Iranians had been apoplectic ever since, in stark contrast to their restrained fury at the previously unsuccessful Israeli bombing.

After the first hour, he was furious. After the second, he thought they were inconsiderate. When it stretched to beyond three hours, he was worried, very worried. He had called everyone he knew, still nothing. The Israelis he spoke to denied any knowledge of even having been involved, although they were delighted with the result and thanking him if he were involved. Passport checks returned nothing. He was desperate and was going out of his mind with concern. He was about to call the President when he suddenly changed course and called Senator Noble instead.

The Senator promised to make some calls and get back to him.

He made one, to Conrad Noble, and discovered the truth. A truth that Travis Davies could never know. The woman was crazy. They were all crazy. Cash Harris wasn't a Noble. He may have some Noble blood in him, but being a Noble was as much a state of mind as anything else. He had learned long ago that the Homo Sapiens were no better, no worse than those who had created them. Their traits and characteristics were the same. The Nobles lived and worked to a code, just like the overwhelming majority of the population. The Nobles' belief that because two hundred thousand years earlier that they had altered a genetic code in an ape to create Man in their image made them better was a nonsense. Nobles weren't any better, nor any more intelligent. But they all thought they were and they had knowledge and that knowledge was power. The Nobles had used that power to their maximum advantage throughout history, and Senator Albert 'Bertie' Noble had every intention of keeping the knowledge and the power exclusive. He had no qualms about wiping out half the population, or the whole population when the time came. At least he was doing it with a sound understanding, unlike his idiot family. What was she thinking? Telling Cash Harris the truth, was she mad?

He checked the time. If they accepted Cash Harris as a full Noble, they wouldn't lift a finger to harm him. He was furious. The only person who could deal with it was him. No one outside the family could get anywhere near the launch site and the minute Cash Harris had the chance, he'd have Travis Davies, the CIA and the full force of the US military stopping them. What annoyed him even more was that he was genuinely fond of the boy and he was going to have to kill him.

He called his pilot to prep the plane and then called Travis Davies. He told him to stop hunting for the pair. Cash Harris and his sidekick hadn't made it back. He fended off a torrent of questions with 'that's all they would tell me' and 'I'm sorry I can't disclose who they were.'

Travis replaced the handset, almost numb. Cash and Rigs were a constant. When you needed them, they were there. He couldn't believe it. He didn't want to believe it but had to. He looked for Sophie Kramer's number, picked up the phone and thought twice. He was in London, only fifty miles from Cambridge. She deserved more than a call. He called his security team, deciding he'd deliver the news personally.

An hour later he was consoling her mother at Sophie's Cambridge home. Mrs. Kramer was frantic with worry, and had no idea where either her daughter or grandson were. The school had informed her Kyle had been collected earlier that day.

Travis made some calls. Nobody knew anything, he feared the worst.

Chapter 76

Sophie had thrown herself around him when he boarded the plane, whispering in his ear, "It's another planet that's dying. I think the Nobles are the guardians."

"I'm not sure 'guardians' is the right word but yes, they are. But there's more, much more."

Anya left them to chat. She had work to do and disappeared after takeoff to her private office on the upper deck.

The second she disappeared, Cash scoped out the plane, ignoring Sophie's inquisitive look. A security team was stationed outside the cockpit. Four were Secret Service types. They didn't worry him. His biggest problem was the flight door. Even if he did overpower them, the door was the same as those fitted to commercial airliners, made from reinforced solid steel and opening outwards.

Cash found Sophie, made sure Kyle was happily out of earshot, and told her everything, giving her as much detail as had been given to him. She sat shocked, intrigued, disgusted but, as an astronomer, desperate to ask Anya a million questions while strangling her superior body to death.

"They're aliens but they look like us," she said, struggling to get her head around it.

"*We* look like *them*. They created us, well half of me," he corrected.

After an hour, Anya joined them tentatively. "I understand this is a fairly major piece of news," she said. She sat, joining them in a small lounge at the rear of the plane.

Sophie decided to get the practicalities out of the way. "What's the other planet like? What's it called?"

"I've never been there. I've seen videos and images that are in the archives. It's not dissimilar to here, although slightly larger and unsurprisingly, since we named this planet, it's called Earth. We call this one New Earth."

"And your people have been flying around the universe for a long time?"

"Our historical records go back over five million years."

Sophie fired question after question. Anya took them all in stride, detailing as much as she knew about the universe. Much of the detail was lost on Cash as the conversation became more and more detailed about the universe, its size, movements, how it worked, whether they knew of its creation, what they thought and why. Cash could see Anya was enjoying the conversation but he wanted to revisit some far more important topics. He let them talk a while longer eventually, when Sophie never slowed her questions, he asked for a timeout.

"Sophie, would you mind giving me and my mother a few minutes?" he asked.

"Of course," said Sophie. "I'm sorry I've rather taken over. You said you have videos?"

"In the archives, I'll show them to you," promised Anya.

"How are you going to do that?" asked Cash, as Sophie walked away to find Kyle.

"Do what?"

"Show her the videos, if she's dead and you don't need her any longer?"

"People like Sophie will be fine," said Anya.

"Fine because she's with me, fine because she's Kyle's mom or fine because she's intelligent?"

"All of those things," said Anya.

"So how many?"

"How many what?"

"How many need to die for you to bring your people to 'New Earth', the planet the humans prepared for you, unwittingly, and under the illusion that being born here means they belonged here."

"Half," said Anya, looking away.

"Half what?" asked Cash.

"Half the population." Anya swallowed hard.

"How many are you bringing here?" he choked.

"One billion. Our population has been strictly controlled, which should have been the case here."

"Can you not hear what you're saying?" pleaded Cash. "You're talking about billions of Sophies, her father, my father—the world is full of good people, intelligent people who make a difference, do things, help one another. And you're just going to kill them because you have a billion of your own, whose own planet is dying? We'd have welcomed them with open arms, we'd make space for them, help them." He paused. "Don't you see what you've created? Helped create with our hard work?" he said, pointing down to the world below them. "Do you think you're better than us?"

"We created you," she said, her answer wavering.

"You didn't. Antoine didn't. That was tens of thousands of years ago."

"It's not my decision," she said.

Finally, he was getting somewhere.

"Your history goes back five million years, who's to say somebody didn't play around with a few genes and create you guys?"

Anya considered the point. "Who knows?"

"Adolf Hitler," said Cash.

"What about him?"

"He thought because of who he was, he was better than others. He believed that his Aryan race was superior to others. He killed six million Jews. Once you guys get a taste for it, maybe you'll hit six billion," said Cash, standing and leaving Anya alone. He wanted to spend his time with his family.

Chapter 77

The Senator rushed into his library. He only had thirty minutes to get to the airport and make it to the spaceport in time.

The laptop Bea had given him to release the toxin into the world's water supply was sitting where he had left it, along with the post-it note of instructions she had stuck to its lid. He grabbed it and turned back towards the door which was swinging closed. He hadn't closed it behind him. He looked to his left, a man was sitting on his seat by his book-lined wall, in his favorite reading chair. His foot was outstretched having just shut the door.

"Sit down," the man ordered.

"Do you know who I am?" boomed the Senator.

The man pointed a silenced pistol at the Senator. "I won't ask you again."

"This is an outrage," he said defiantly, taking the only seat available, the one behind his desk.

"And please don't think I was stupid enough to leave your gun in the drawer, I'll save you that disappointment."

"What do you want?"

"I want to understand what you're doing."

"Doing?"

"More specifically, I want to know why a subsidiary of a trust that you are a director of has control of most data and statistical analysis bodies and why you are killing innocent aid workers who in particular help young pregnant girls."

"I do no such thing!" boomed the Senator in his most disgusted tone.

Giles Tremellan fired the pistol and caught the Senator on his upper right arm.

The Senator grabbed at his wound.

"That's just to show I'm not playing here."

"Who are you?"

"Giles Tremellan, formerly DIS. Nearly *very* formerly."

The Senator did his best to hide any recognition of the name.

"I was a very good friend of Mike Yates. I noticed you have a very interesting video on your computer there. If you hit the space bar it will play, move the screen around so we can both see."

The screen came alive. Mike Yates was standing up and smiling to greet a very attractive woman. She laid down a phone to allow Mike´ to see. The resolution of the spy camera that the Senator had fitted was good enough to see what had turned Mike Yates' face white. His daughter was on the woman's screen, filmed through the crosshairs of a sniper's rifle that tracked her every movement in the schoolyard. The woman's voice was clearly audible. "In less than five minutes, the bell will sound and the sniper will fire. You'll see it here in front of you, unless you copy this note and then jump off this building. Four minutes thirty seconds," she said. Mike looked at his daughter on the phone for less than a second before he had scribbled the note and ran from the office. His body was seen, a minute later, falling in front of his office window. "And thirty seconds to spare," she said, before picking up the phone and smiling at the spy camera.

Giles had watched it five times already. His anger still swelled when he watched it again. "Why are you killing the aid workers? I won't ask again!" he threatened.

"You wouldn't understand," replied the Senator.

The condescension of the answer infuriated Giles. He squeezed the trigger, sending a bullet thumping into the Senator's chest.

The Senator felt for the wound, his eyes opening wide as the blood pumped onto his desk. He scrabbled for the laptop that Bea had given him. He opened the lid and hit the 'On' switch. Giles stood up and walked around, intrigued at the desperate last motions of the Senator. The screen lit up, a map of the world was displayed, a large area shaded red, predominantly Africa, Asia and South America. The senator was trying to move the cursor to a box that said 'Yes'. Giles watched him struggle for a second before helping him by moving the cursor for him on to the 'Yes'.

"Do you want me to press it for you?' asked Giles.

The Senator nodded, his hand still trying to do it for himself.

Giles pulled the trigger again, moving the cursor off the 'Yes'. "Yeah right," he said. He powered the laptop off and put a bullet through it for good measure. He had uncovered enough over the previous few days about the Senator to realize that whatever he was into was only ever good for the Senator. 'Yes' to him probably meant 'No' to everyone else. Giles would never know it wasn't everyone, only half of everyone. All three point five billion of them.

Chapter 78

Anya had come to find them as they neared what she had hoped would be an exciting part of the flight. Sadly, the conversation with Cash had left her little hope that her son would ever come to terms with who he was. She still wanted to share the moment; it might make them realize they were part of something bigger.

She found them in the front lounge, laughing and joking as a family. She thought back to her days with Cash's father. They had shared scenes not dissimilar. She had even dreamt of moments during the pregnancy when she, Charles and Cash were in the same position.

"Sorry to interrupt," she said. "You may want to look out of the window, we're about to witness something you'll never see again.

***

Caleb directed the submersible expertly well. He had been practicing for a long time and had designed the system himself. The practice runs had been perfect but this was the real thing. He checked the depth meter, almost seven miles below the ocean's surface. It was the deepest part of the ocean floor and one of the most unexplored places in the visible universe, the perfect place to store and hide spaceships, particularly ones that had no fuel or source of power to make them do anything.

That was all about to change. He illuminated the darkness below with spotlights and maneuvered the tube, developed to withstand the thousand times normal pressure, and began to transfer the fuel only recently developed by Anya.

Lights beyond the spotlights illuminated, and the image on Caleb's screen being beamed from seven miles below filled with sediment. The ship was moving. It was pre-programmed to rise to the surface once fuelled. He moved the submersible back and away to its right by a few hundred meters. He had to repeat the same process another four times. He walked out onto the deck of the deep sea vessel that had been stationed over the same spot for weeks and waited. Although darkness had already fallen, the water was lightening. The spaceship was rising. The tip rose first and cut into the surface, opening the way for more of what was a far bigger vessel than he had envisaged. He knew it was big, but didn't realize it was that huge.

***

"Holy f—"

"Kyle!' Sophie screeched when the tip burst through the surface. Their plane was circling overhead.

"I think if there were ever an occasion a boy's allowed to swear in front of his mother that might be it," said Cash, holding in more than a few expletives himself as the full majesty of the spaceship revealed itself.

"It's absolutely enormous!" said Kyle.

Bands of lights reached its full length, each one progressively larger as it worked its way down to the base of the craft. It hovered inches above the water's surface, stretching up almost five hundred feet into the sky.

"They'll put more fuel in it, a pilot will climb aboard and I'm sure they'll switch off the lights before they move off to the spaceport," said Anya. "I'm afraid we need to get a move on. They travel far faster than we do."

Sophie took another long look. "Well, we solved one other mystery," she said.

"What?"

"Why everyone started building pyramids all around the world!"

"Of course, they must have spotted one of these and tried to copy it."

"The only ones we built were the Giza ones, the good ones," Anya said. "They're the only ones that come close to replicating the ships, in size and perfection of design. Just a shame all we had was stone to work with back then."

"Why did you build the Great Pyramid?" asked Cash, thinking back to Rigs, still praying he was on his way to stopping the Nobles.

"To try to contact our home. We've not been able to talk to them since we arrived. The distance outside of the convergence is too great and there are too many systems in the way."

"Convergence is that what you call the eighty-year window,"

"Yes, it's—"

"Please, enough astronomy for the evening," said Cash. "So the pyramid is going to send a signal?"

"Yes it will send a signal when the first transport leaves. It's a hugely powerful bolt of light that will travel faster than the speed of light and deliver the news that we are ready to welcome them to their new home," she said proudly.

"How can light travel faster than the speed of light?" asked Cash.

"You said no more astronomy talk," said Sophie,

"I did," he said. "It needs a lot of power to do that?"

"In any other building, the power left by the bolt would destroy it. The pyramid was built for just this purpose. They didn't have the power source before. They tried tapping into the planet's own but it just needed more oomph."

Anya had work to do and disappeared again.

"I need to make a move. I can't just let them take our planet from us!" said Cash.

Sophie agreed wholeheartedly.

"It means putting you and Kyle in danger."

"I understand," she said hugging him. "If we die, at least we'll die together."

"For the record, I have no intention of you or Kyle dying."

"So what's the plan?" she asked eagerly.

He told her, and she begged him not to.

Chapter 79

Cash walked casually up the stairs towards the upper deck. Kyle was only a few paces behind him. The four-man security team, as they had done every time Cash had ventured upstairs, took note. When Kyle appeared behind him they relaxed. Cash looked round and waved at them, tripping on the last step and falling straight onto the floor.

"Dad!" said Kyle, rushing forward.

"Are you okay?" asked one of the security team walking to check he was unhurt. Cash tried to pick himself up but slumped back down when Anya came to see why Kyle had shouted.

"Help him," she ordered, rushing over herself and trying to lift him despite his being almost twice her weight.

Under orders from Anya, the security men rushed to his aid. Kyle stood back, out of the way, as they rushed to the top of the stairs to help Cash to his feet.

Once in place, Kyle sprang forward, hitting two of the security men with his best rugby tackle. His Noble genes had given the young man a physique and strength beyond his years. Caught completely by surprise, the two guards cascaded down to the bottom of the stairs.

"Kyle!" screamed Anya in horror at her grandson's actions. Cash leapt to his feet, and with only two guards to deal with, he sent a crushing punch into one's neck while crashing the point of his elbow into the other. Both went down. Kyle, despite Cash shouting "no", jumped on top of the one who had been punched in the neck and sent a fantastic right hook across his chin, knocking him out cold.

The one who had been hit with Cash's elbow was going nowhere. Cash bounded down the stairs as the two guards below were still trying to recover. He kicked one out cold and the fourth raised his hands in surrender. Between their ties and other items from around the plane, Cash and Kyle tied and bound them to their seats.

"Okay," said Cash. "Stage one complete!"

Anya stood looking at him with utter contempt.

"If you truly understood being a parent, you'd understand," said Cash, brushing past her.

"You'll never get through the cockpit door," she said.

"I don't need to," Cash said. He reached back, grabbed Anya, and put a knife to her throat. He marched her towards the cockpit door. "I just need them to open it."

"They won't. They're trained not to," she said. "Anyway, I know your plan, you know what we've got on board this plane."

Cash tried not to let her see she had seen through his plan.

Anya heard one of the door locks open. "No!" she shouted. "Jettison the cargo before you open that door!"

Cash threw her out of the way and tried to open the door. He felt the plane shudder and knew the four nukes had been dropped into the ocean below. "Shit!"

The door opened and the captain and co-pilot appeared. He wanted to punch them but managed to hold back.

"I want this plane down at the nearest airstrip you can find!" he said. "Or I swear I will kill somebody."

Anya nodded. She had stopped Cash delivering a nuclear bomb to the island, the last four nuclear bombs in existence. They were out over the ocean in the middle of the Pacific exclusion zone. There wasn't even anyone they could raise on the radio, other than from Wake Island, the spaceport.

The captain landed at an old, disused airbase on the southern area of Enewetak Atoll, pointing out that Cash shouldn't venture to the north of the atoll, as it still hadn't been cleared as safe after numerous nuclear test explosions back in the forties and fifties.

"Everyone out!" Cash had shouted, opening the door and waiting for the internal emergency stairs to unfold.

He helped Sophie and Kyle down and assisted the security men who, with their hands tied, did not find the descent easy. The captain and co-pilot had looked on with disinterest until

Cash had ushered them off also. Anya sat resolute in the front lounge watching Cash throw everyone off of her plane.

"Come on, you next."

"I'm not getting off," she said.

"You may not live to regret that!"

He turned back to the door and began retracting the staircase. Sophie spotted it too late, it was already out of her reach by the time she got to it.

He blew her a kiss and mouthed "I love you!" and closed the door. He walked back to the cockpit, followed by Anya, fascinated at what he was doing.

Cash sat in the captain's seat and began to familiarize himself with the controls.

"You can fly?" she asked.

"I've had a few lessons," said Cash. "The principles are the same. In fact, this is far more automated than the little Piper I've flown."

"Getting up's easy, but you have to land it at the other end."

"No I don't," he said looking down longingly at Sophie and Kyle. Sophie was hugging her son tightly, her body convulsing as he looked up at him.

"You'd sacrifice yourself for them?" she asked incredulously.

"In a heartbeat," replied Cash.

Cash pushed the throttle forward and positioned the aircraft for takeoff. He waved and threw the throttles forward. A buzzer sounded as they hit takeoff speed and he pulled backwards on the joystick that controlled the plane.

"So, Mother, let's you and I have the chat of our lives," said Cash, noting they were due to arrive just ten minutes before the first transport was due to leave.

***

Sophie was inconsolable. When the nuclear bombs were jettisoned, she thought his crazy idea was over. But at least he'd had a chance of coming back. She knew the second he retracted the stairs, he was going to use the plane as his bomb. Cash was never coming back.

Chapter 80

Rigs heard a scrabbling noise. He hadn't heard a thing for hours and rushed back to the King's Chamber. It was coming from the entrance the Sicarii had sealed earlier. He rushed down as the entrance opened. Joel stood in the entranceway, sweat pouring from his brow, his arm once again secured in plaster.

"I just discovered they locked you in here. They really weren't supposed to harm you," he said.

Rigs nodded. "Explosives?" he asked.

"Yes, I brought some in case I couldn't get the door open, why?"

Rigs didn't think there was time to chat. He rushed across to the Jeep that Joel had used and grabbed his bag. He ran back to the pyramid and straight past Joel without slowing down. A faint rumble started. He ran faster. He didn't know what the pyramid was going to do but whatever it was, he thought it best it didn't. He ran back down to the Queen's Chamber door and placed the bag. He ran back up the stairs and into the gallery. The rumble had increased. The floor beneath him was shaking.

"Get out of there!" shouted Joel.

The walls began to shake wildly. Rigs triggered the explosives. He didn't even feel their force, such was the power that was surging through the pyramid. Rigs bounced off the walls as he tried to climb back down the stairs to the Queen's Chamber below. He reached the door, a hole just large enough to squeeze through. The noise was deafening as the power was slowly building. He covered his ears and climbed through the hole, his insides shaking. His teeth rattled wildly in his mouth and his bones vibrated. He fell to the floor, his legs unable to hold his weight. He tried to reach for the switch but his arm shook wildly. He focused all of his efforts and energy on that one point, as though it were the only place in the universe that mattered.

Bea checked the water system again. The Senator still hadn't triggered the mechanism. It wasn't time critical but it was her baby. She wanted to know it had worked. She was going to fly back on the first transport and wanted to know everything was working before she left. She turned to Antoine, but his eyes were transfixed in the distance. She looked around. Five enormous transports were slowing as they approached, dwarfing the space port complex as they positioned themselves on the island's perimeter.

"Magnificent," said Antoine. His moment had come. He had succeeded.

The first ship moved into position, touching down on the platform, which would allow the full force of the ship's power to propel it into space.

Bea spotted the name. *Atlantis*. She hadn't known its name. She thought of the myth of the lost island, and advanced culture lost forever, or more precisely, until Anya had managed to create the fuel their ancestors knew they needed but weren't able to create without modern technology.

Bea looked around. "Where's Anya?" she asked.

"Is she not here?" said Antoine, disappointed. He had insisted that every Noble be present for the momentous occasion. Only the Senator had been unable to attend. He had assumed she had been somewhere in the spaceport complex working on last minute details. She had been more responsible for the success of the event than any other Noble there.

"Her plane's on its final approach," said Conrad.

"Bertie's still not triggered the toxin," said Bea. "I'm about to board, would you mind if I…" She trailed off. Anya's plane; it wasn't heading for the runway, it was heading for the platform.

"What is she doing?"

Conrad radioed the plane. "Anya, what are you doing?" Everyone else started to run from the platform.

Bea's hand hovered on the mousepad, ready to click. The plane was still a few seconds from impact.

"Antoine?" she asked again.

"She still has time to pull up," he said, ignoring Bea. "What is she doing?"

"Anya!" shouted Conrad.

***

Sophie and Kyle kept their eyes fixed on the spot where Cash had last been seen, desperately willing him to fly back. Wake Island was over five hundred miles away to the north. Far too distant to see or hear if Cash had crashed or had changed his mind. All they could do was watch and pray that the plane appeared back.

"Whoa!" said Kyle, closing his eyes at the sun-bright flash of light that filled the northern horizon and most of the sky.

The light died slowly, keeping the brightness on the horizon for some time.

"If that was a takeoff, maybe it means Dad's okay?"

"That was one giant explosion, not anything lifting off," said the captain.

***

Joel tried to move into the pyramid but its vibrations threw him out as he struggled to steady himself with only one good arm. A crack sounded, which he was sure burst his eardrums, and a bolt of light erupted from the top of the pyramid and shot straight up into the sky.

His eyes followed the bolt, his mind realizing everything had stopped. The vibrations had stopped, the rumble and shaking had stopped. He walked towards the entrance, where he found Rigs stumbling uneasily towards him.

"Are you alright?" asked Joel, struggling to help him with one arm.

"Yes, a few chipped teeth but I switched it off," said Rigs.

"Not fast enough, I don't think. Something just shot into the sky."

***

"For my son," replied Anya. "And his family."

"Antoine, the toxin?" asked Bea urgently, realizing Anya's intentions.

They were expecting the plane to crash into the platform and *Atlantis*, but it didn't. Before Bea was able to register Antoine's nod to hit 'yes' and thereby kill half the population, the plane exploded into light, engulfing the entire island and everything within fifty miles in a power so intense that everything simply ceased to exist, incinerated into oblivion. Anya had used her new fuel to devastating effect. The Nobles were gone, along with their transports and plans.

Cash was almost blinded by the explosion as he bobbed in the ocean's swells, safe in the A380's escape pod. The rich really did have it all, they could even escape a plane crash. The pod's sensors had inflated a raft as it touched down on the ocean surface, its mayday beacon pinging after already having pinged his remote location directly to the aircraft manufacturer the second his mother had insisted he eject.

Understanding the sacrifice he would make for his family to stop what they were doing had finally made Anya realize how lost in their own world the Nobles had become. Her act had destroyed everything, far more than he would have achieved simply using the A380 as a guided missile. He would have upset their plans, she had destroyed them. Anya had finally realized, they had not created life, as Cash had pointed out to her, they had merely made a very slight alteration. That did not give them the right to decide life and death, like gods.

Epilogue

Old Earth

The last transporter was ready. The final few hundred had boarded. He stood and looked out on the world that had been their home for over five million years. Five million wonderful years. A civilization beyond equal, the most advanced they had discovered in the universe that they had explored.

He looked at their sun. In the next few hundred years it would explode and destroy their world. It had kept them warm, grown their crops and given them life for five million years. He walked back towards the pyramid-shaped ship and with a final wave to his home, climbed on board.

"Ready," he said to his crew as he boarded. He had always wanted to be the last to leave.

"Sire, we've just received a signal, it says, 'We're ready to welcome you to your new home, the Nobles!'" said his pilot.

The King paused. The Nobles, a name he hadn't heard in a very long time.

"You've never met a Noble, have you?" he asked.

The pilot shook his head.

"Neither have I but my father used to tell me old tales. I swear he made most of them up. They were one of the families sent to find and create a new world. They were given a planet very far away. If I remember correctly, there's only a window every two thousand years that you can even get to it. Our new home is far closer and was always the favored option but nobody told the Nobles. They were the biggest troublemakers we ever had, so power hungry and constantly trying to win favor and influence in the Senate by any means possible. They were always causing upset and unrest amongst our own people. We are a peace loving people, always have been. But the Nobles, never. They were godless warmongers. They were only sent out to find the new world in order to get rid of them; it took some time and

I believe some ingenuity, but their ships had only enough fuel to go one way and their communications systems were nowhere near powerful enough to reach back here. The chosen planet, if I remember, was primitive. If they've created a world to welcome us to, trust me, it's not one we'd ever want to go to, certainly not if they're still there."

"Do you want me to respond?" asked the pilot.

"Good god no, they might track us to our new world, leave them on the one they created for themselves!"

THE END

AUTHOR'S NOTE

I don't often feel the need to give background to my storylines, although I'm sure sometimes it would help with some of my more 'out there' thrillers. However, a short while ago I stumbled across a book I had picked up on what had been a particularly miserable holiday in Portugal. Before the days of Amazon and Kindle, you had to pack your suitcase carefully, always ensuring there was plenty of room (and weight allowance) for the English language novels that would see you through your trip to foreign climes. Unfortunately, on that particular trip the boredom of the resort far outstripped the demand for reading material I had envisaged.

After scouring every newsagent and store in the small and woefully inadequate village (excellent shopping nearby, according to the holiday brochure!) I came across one stand with, if I remember correctly, four English language novels, two flowery romance novels (I wasn't *that* bored), one book I had already read and one other. A tome that was weighty enough to see me through perhaps a couple of days.

It, as emblazoned on the front cover, offered proof of flesh and blood gods that had visited us in the past. I have to thank Portugal for its boredom factor at this point, as I'd have never picked up the book otherwise. *Gods of the New Millennium* (*GOTNM*) by Alan F. Alford was fascinating, certainly more so than the Portuguese resort, and sent my mind racing as fantastical after fantastical wonders of what the ancient civilizations had achieved were revealed. And that's why I felt the need to add this note. The majority of the information I have written about the impossible size weight and intricacy of the stone work across the ancient sites is fact, not fiction.

There are stones at Baalbeck weighing up to a 1,000 tons having been cut, moved and placed with a precision that we would still struggle with today. Unfortunately the tent outside is also there, complete with the glass cabinets, which I had the misfortune of being ushered into with a Jewish friend. That's five minutes of my life I don't want to ever relive. Pumapunka likewise is scattered with amazingly intricate stonework. Saksaywaman, huge stones carved to fit so precisely it's as though the stones are fused together. The Great Pyramid at Giza in itself defies all logic that something built so long ago was so perfectly constructed, to the point we'd find it difficult to replicate even today.

There is some debate as to exactly how we did evolve to where we are today so quickly and why for example would we lose body hair through evolution, only to have to wear clothes to stay warm?

The first half of *GOTNM* was fascinating and has to this day always made me wonder. The second half went off at a bit of a tangent and it's no surprise the author has retracted a large portion of that section since writing it.

As for *The God Complex* and the Nobles, well there are a few families out there with a power and influence that has lasted many centuries. Okay, not millennia, or at least not that we know of! Joking aside, I really do hope you enjoyed the story and if so, please leave a review for others to encourage them to enjoy the ride too.

Many thanks, and thank you, Portugal!

Murray

Other Novels by Murray McDonald

Scion

Critical Error

Divide & Conquer

America's Trust

Traitor

Young Adult - The Billionaire Series

Kidnap

Assassin

Please visit www.murraymcdonald.net to sign up for
updates on new releases and special offers.

Made in the USA
San Bernardino, CA
02 July 2014